just like that

LENA HENDRIX

THE KINGS
BOOK 4

Copyright © 2025 by Lena Hendrix

All rights reserved.

No part of this book may be reproduced in any form or by any electronic or mechanical means, including information storage and retrieval systems, without written permission from the author, except for the use of brief quotations in a book review.

Without in any way limiting the author's exclusive rights under copyright, any use of this publication to "train" generative artificial intelligence (AI) technologies to generate text is expressly prohibited. The author reserves all rights to license uses of this work for generative AI training and development of machine learning language models.

This is a work of fiction, created without the use of AI technology. Any names, characters, places, or incidents are products of the author's imagination and used in a fictitious manner. Any resemblance to actual people, places, or events is purely coincidental or fictional.

Developmental editing: Paula Dawn, Lilypad Lit

Copy editing: James Gallagher, Evident Ink

Proofreading: Julia Griffis, The Romance Bibliophile

Model cover design: Echo Grayce, WildHeart Graphics

Model cover photography: Ren Saliba

Cover Model: Philippe Leblond

Discreet cover design: Sarah Hansen, OkayCreations

For every reader who swore JP King was hiding a secret, filthy mouth ... you were correct.

LET'S CONNECT

When you sign up for my newsletter, you'll stay up to date with new releases, book news, giveaways, and new book recommendations! I promise not to spam you and only email when I have something fun & exciting to share!

Also, When you sign up, you'll also get a FREE copy of Choosing You (a very steamy Chikalu Falls novella)!

Sign up at my website at www.lenahendrix.com

AUTHOR'S NOTE

Just Like That is really going to put the Kings through the wringer. This book contains discussion of ovarian cancer, loss of a sibling, death of a parent, and surprise/ reluctant guardianship. While every state is different, a sensitivity reader was used to ensure the accuracy of Teddy's parental situation was handled with care.

Please be kind to yourself when deciding if these triggers are too much.

JP's book also contains explicit, open door sex scenes with a grumpy, brooding villain with a heart of gold. He also doesn't really care that much for condoms (and when he's fictional, that's a real win in my eyes). Buckle up baby, JP's about to take you for the ride of your life.

ABOUT THIS BOOK

He's my sister's ex, a stubborn jerk, and completely off-limits.

Getting a man to give up custody of a son he didn't know existed should have been easy. Trouble is, nothing with JP King is ever easy.

Suave, grumpy billionaires aren't supposed to have strong hands or filthy mouths, and I never expected our snippy banter to be so much fun.

JP regards me as something he scraped off the bottom of his dress shoe, but when this reluctant single dad looks at my nephew, there's a softness there he struggles to keep hidden.

He may be gruff and uptight, but something simmers beneath his controlled, polished exterior. Sure, I'm wild and reckless, but when we're forced together as guardians, everything changes.

His cold and calculated exterior melts into hushed conversations and lingering stares. The more we fight, the harder we fall.

I'm scatterbrained, unconventional, and ***everything he's been missing.*** The closer we get, the less we understand why we were ever at odds.

. . . until ***just like that*** our lives are turned upside down.

ONE

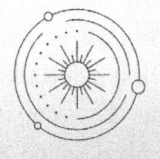

HAZEL

I LOST THE KID.

Four months into being his caretaker and I lost the damn kid.

I swallowed the panic that clawed at my throat as I scanned the bustling sidewalk of a town I had never been to before. Summer was waning, but apparently Western Michigan hadn't gotten the memo. My armpits were sticky, and the thick strands of my hair were clinging to the back of my neck.

Think, think, think, think, think.

If you were a seven-year-old boy in a cutesy little town, where the hell would you go?

The town itself was picturesque. Off in the distance, about a half mile down the road, Lake Michigan sparkled, with the roadway cutting through the quaint little tourist town. Mom-and-pop shops dotted the sides, shoppers filtered in and out of the businesses, and storefronts had signs and sandwich boards enticing people to come inside to shop.

It would have been idyllic had it not been rapidly turning into the third-worst day of my life.

My eyes bounced across the storefronts that dotted the main drag in downtown Outtatowner, Michigan. I quickly dismissed the library, general store, and hardware store as I strode down the sidewalk with the sole purpose of finding my nephew. Crossing the street, I absently waved to a car that honked at me and continued peering through the bodies of people milling around each storefront.

"Teddy?" I called out. My heart rate ticked higher as I looked through each window in search of him.

A neon sign with a grinning skeleton and a beer in its hand gave me pause, but I doubted a lone child would go unnoticed in a local dive bar. I called out anyway and looked around the concrete planters along the sidewalk. "Teddy!"

A bit farther down was a small bakery, and I scanned the large picture window, hoping the sweet smell of cinnamon and sugar had enticed my nephew.

Beyond that, the tattoo parlor was an unlikely choice.

I closed my eyes and took a deep breath.

Universe, please point me in the right direction.

When I opened my eyes, I squinted against the sun and looked down the sidewalk.

Oh, hello.

Outside the tattoo parlor were two men. One was laughing, heavily tattooed and seemingly lost in conversation, but the other . . .

The other was dressed in a bespoke navy suit. His watch glinted in the sunlight, and the dark sunglasses perched on his nose only highlighted his chiseled cheekbones. I swallowed hard and blinked rapidly.

What the hell, Universe? I need to find Teddy, not a midday orgasm.

I huffed and pushed the handsome stranger to the furthest recesses of my mind.

I looked beyond the downtown area toward Lake Michigan. Dread pooled in my stomach when, in the distance of the scenic town, my gaze landed on the lighthouse at the end of a pier.

He doesn't know how to swim.

"TEDDY!" Fear laced with desperation as I screamed his name.

"Whoa, hey." A woman stopped my forward progress. Her light-blond hair fell down her back, and her dark-brown eyes were kind, yet concerned. "Can I help you with something?"

Tears pricked at my eyes. "I lost him. I can't believe I actually lost—"

"Shh. Okay." She held a hand up as she pulled her phone from her pocket and dialed. Looking at me, she continued, "Give me the details. Name and age. Any idea what he was wearing?" Her attention was drawn to the other end of the phone as I struggled to recall the information she needed. "Hey, Amy, it's Sylvie. I have a tourist here who's lost a kid. I'm getting the details."

She looked at me as my brain scrambled. "Um, his name is Teddy. He's seven. About this high." I held out my hand. "Black hair, bluish-green eyes. He was, um, wearing a plaid shirt—blue plaid with a little black bow tie and jean shorts."

The woman's eyebrows raised slightly at my description, but I continued looking over her shoulder and through the bustling crowd for my nephew.

"Did you get that? Yeah. Bow tie should be easy to spot. We'll start looking downtown and I'll alert the Bluebirds.

You got it. Thanks." Sylvie hung up the phone and placed her hands on the outside of my arms. "It's okay. We're going to find him. I called the police and they're on it. He's not the first little guy to wander off in Outtatowner."

From behind us, a huge man with an apron covered in flour walked out of the bakery and looked right at the woman next to me. "Lost kid," she said to him and relayed my description.

"On it," he called out as he put a phone to his ear.

"That's the bakery owner, Huck. Looks like the phone tree's been activated." She smiled at another storefront owner, who gave her a knowing nod.

Beside me, Sylvie called out to someone walking past. "Excuse me. Hi. We're looking for a seven-year-old boy named Teddy. Plaid shirt and a bow tie. Please look out for him." She walked down the sidewalk, then stopped to look at me and gestured for me to follow as she loudly announced to anyone nearby that Teddy was missing. "We're looking for a seven-year-old boy named Teddy. Plaid shirt and a bow tie."

We hurried down the sidewalk, and I watched in awe as more and more people exited their storefronts, temporarily closing their shops and joining us on the sidewalk, walking in all directions and searching for Teddy. Murmurs of the lost boy rippled through the town as we made our way down the sidewalk and toward the lakeshore in the distance.

Sylvie patted my arm as if she understood the intrusive thoughts streaming through my head. "Don't worry. One of the first things we do is call the lifeguards on the beach. They'll be on high alert looking for him too."

I swallowed hard. My throat tightened as I squeaked out an emotion clogged "Thank you."

With confident strides, the pretty blonde beside me

walked down the sidewalk, calling out to anyone who would listen and help. When her phone rang, my heart jumped. "Hey, Whip, what's up?" Her face brightened and she looked at me. "They got him."

My lungs collapsed and I bent over, bracing my hands on my knees and trying to catch my breath.

"Oh, that's great news," Sylvie continued. "I can bring her by. See you soon." The woman looped her arm in mine and helped me up. "Okay, Mama. Looks like Teddy is at the fire station. Let's go get him."

My heart lurched at her calling me Mama. I swallowed hard. "I'm actually his aunt."

"Okay." She simply shrugged and smiled as we continued walking.

"Is he all right?" My lower lip trembled, and I nearly lost it again before swallowing back the emotions.

Sylvie smiled. "Sounds like he's got the fire department wrapped around his little finger already."

We turned a corner, and in the distance an adorable small-town fire station came into view. Bright-red trucks were lined up outside, and one of the large bay doors was open. Mature trees lined the sidewalks, and a slight breeze kicked up from the lake. I sucked in a lungful of coastal air and tried to rein in my frantic emotions.

"He's a slippery little sucker, huh?" Sylvie asked. There was no judgment in her voice, only kindness and a motherly knowing.

I smirked and a wry laugh pushed through my nose. "You have no idea."

I had always been a wanderer. I guess Teddy and I were kindred spirits in that regard. In fact, it had only been since my sister died that I had really gotten to know my nephew. My entire life I had yearned to travel—odd jobs, a new city.

When I outstayed my welcome in one place, I packed up and picked another dot on the map without a single regret.

Well . . . maybe a single regret.

I had missed my sister. My thoughts flicked to the pretty urn that was shoved in the back of a cabinet of the skoolie where I lived. Olive always knew what to do in every situation, and I didn't even know what to do with her ashes.

When Teddy was born, I made a trip back to Chicago to visit her, but then I was gone again. We chatted over video, but life as a single mom was hectic for her. I visited only a handful of times in the seven years since his birth. I was finding my own adventures while Teddy had become Olive's whole world.

My chest pinched. *How was I ever going to be good enough for him?*

"Do you have other kids?" Sylvie asked as we walked.

I laughed at the idea. I liked kids, I just always assumed I'd *be* one. "Just him—but he's actually my nephew. His mom, my sister, died a few months back."

"Oh." She placed a hand over her heart. "I am so sorry to hear that."

I kicked a stone as we marched toward the fire station.

The woman beside me was a stranger, but I found myself opening up to her. She had a calm and welcoming nature that reminded me a bit of my sister.

Strong and resilient.

"We were both kind of free spirits. Olive was always scheming, always one step ahead of everyone. Once she entered our town's baking competition with a store-bought pie because the prize was two thousand dollars. When she won, they put her name and picture on a plaque, and she laughed every time we walked past it."

There was a time when I had found that story funny

and endearing, but hearing myself recount it aloud, it fell a little flat and kind of made Olive sound like a jerk.

I swallowed hard and backtracked. "She could charm anyone and everyone."

Sylvie hummed.

I found myself nervously chattering as we walked. "When Olive found out she was pregnant at twenty-one, she wasn't even scared. She was *thrilled*. She always seemed to know that everything would work out. I envied that."

"My little sister is kind of like that," Sylvie said. "She's always so sure of herself."

I offered a polite smile, and we continued walking in companionable silence as thoughts of my sister flooded my brain.

As her younger sister, I had been terrified for Olive—convinced her life was practically over. She had a string of ex-boyfriends, but none that we had ever met. When my mother demanded to know who the father was, she simply said, *"It doesn't matter. I'm taken care of, and I can do this on my own."*

Olive powered through and started her life as a single mother. My heart ached, knowing I hadn't taken the time to really stop and check in with her . . . to make sure she was okay. I had been too wrapped up in the clout of a blooming social media page full of sponsorships and an exciting paycheck. I called often, but rarely came home for holidays and birthdays. Teddy knew me as a face on a screen and a few bills slipped inside a birthday card.

Why on earth did she think I could take care of him?

As we approached the fire station, I watched Teddy walk out of the open bay door with a firefighter's helmet bobbling on his head. It was too large and heavy for him, so his neck dipped and his little hand came up to steady it.

Behind him were a small group of firefighters, dressed in black boots, navy tactical pants, and T-shirts with OFD embroidered over the left chest pocket.

I ran straight toward Teddy and knelt in front of him. "There you are!" I wrapped him in a hug as his head struggled with the weight of the helmet. "I looked up and you were gone! You scared the shit out of me!"

"You aren't supposed to say that in front of me," Teddy chided. I couldn't help but laugh and pull him in for another quick hug.

"Sorry, kid. I'm working on that." I peered up at his striking blue-green eyes, emotion swimming in mine as relief washed over me. "You really scared me."

His features fell, and he looked away. "Sorry. I just really, really wanted to—"

"This guy belong to you?" a voice called from over Teddy's shoulder.

I looked up to see a firefighter with a wide grin and playful eyes.

I stood and held out my hand. "Yes, thank you so much. I looked away for one second and he was gone."

"I'm Lee Sullivan. It's no problem. Heard the alert over the radio, and we were all keeping our eyes peeled. Turns out this little dude was on a mission." Lee tapped the top of Teddy's helmet, and my nephew's cheeks turned pink as he grinned.

Another firefighter approached Sylvie. I put my arm around Teddy and tucked him into my side. I didn't trust he wouldn't bolt again, and I was still reeling from worry.

Their voices were hushed, but Sylvie and the man were close enough to overhear.

"I think you're gonna want to stick around for this," he whispered. "I had to call JP, and he's on his way over."

Hearing his name aloud sent a chill down my spine.

JP King.

He was the man we had set out to find, but I hadn't been prepared to face him yet—not after everything my sister had revealed in her letter.

My stomach bunched, hoping no one had discovered the real reason Teddy was asking for him.

"JP?" Sylvie scoffed as she looked at the firefighter. "Why in the world did you call *him*?"

The man leaned in, but I could still discern the disbelief and concern laced in his voice. "Get this—the kid said JP's his *dad*."

I blanched.

Oh, fuck.

TWO

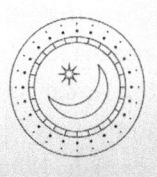

JP

Thirty minutes earlier . . .

My shoes clacked on the sidewalk as I made efficient progress toward my small downtown office. The sidewalks were unusually busy for mid-August, even though it was still considered tourist season in Outtatowner. People were milling around, seemingly searching for something. They all appeared preoccupied by it, but I didn't have time to stop and ask what new drama was unfolding in my small town.

Also, I didn't care.

My life was already too full with carrying the stress of managing a billion-dollar company in the face of a scandal. It was plastered all over the news, and the sharks were out for blood. My father had royally fucked us, and I was charged with making it right.

Outside of his tattoo shop, my brother Royal was scanning the sidewalks when I approached.

He held out his hand in greeting. "JP."

I nodded and took it. "Royal."

I exhaled and squinted against the sun as we watched

the tourists filter in and out of the downtown shops. "This fucking town . . ."

I was never supposed to be stuck here.

King Equities was meant to be the launching pad of my own successful empire, not the family company that had the potential to ruin my entire career—not to mention my reputation. If I wasn't careful, my father's actions would dismantle my entire life brick by brick.

"You could do it, you know," Royal eventually said. I glanced over, unsure of what he meant. "Get out of here," he clarified. "Start over in a big city where you can make a new name for yourself."

I nodded slowly, looking down at my shoes and trying to find the right words to explain the many, many hours I'd spent dreaming of doing exactly that. "I could." A shrug was all I could muster. "I might."

Shock and disbelief at what my father was accused of had made its way through town like wildfire. He'd all but admitted he'd murdered our mother when we were children. She had found out about a second family in Chicago, and she'd had plans to leave him and take us with her. Instead, he took her from us, and we'd spent our entire lives believing she had simply abandoned us.

I was still grappling with the guilt that I'd blamed her for so long. She was trying to take us with her—to leave him behind and keep us safe—when he'd killed her for choosing her children over him.

Many in town went out of their way to express their support for our family. Others stood by the man they had thought my father to be and vehemently denied he was ever capable of murder.

They branded our mother a whore and a flake—claimed my father was a saint for raising six kids when she left him.

They have no idea of the hell we lived through.

I had the money and the power to leave it all behind me. All I had to do was sacrifice any relationship I had with my siblings and I'd be rid of them and the curse of the King name.

I simply didn't have the balls to do it.

"Who am I kidding?" I sighed, hoping Royal didn't detect the slight wistfulness in my voice. "There's too much shit here to take care of. Who's going to help you keep the Sullivans in check, if not me?"

Royal chuckled and clamped a hand on my shoulder. "I appreciate that. You know, I have been thinking Wyatt is due for a little pestering."

Our small town was a ridiculous place where centuries-old family rivalries morphed into grown men pulling pranks on one another and acting like idiots for no good reason. At least, reasons none of us could remember.

Hell, our sister Sylvie had even married a Sullivan and had his kid.

I forced a smile and shook my head. "You are such a child."

Royal pushed my arm. "Nah, I guess they've been all right."

In fact, the family we'd been groomed to hate had been more than all right. Over the past three weeks, the Sullivan family had rallied behind us Kings after we'd uncovered that our father was behind the disappearance of our mother. He had let us all believe she'd left us as children, but we'd uncovered the truth.

He'd taken her from us because she had chosen to love her children more than him.

Together we petitioned the Department of Natural Resources to allow Wabash Lake to be dredged. We didn't know what we might find, but if there was any chance our mother's remains were there, we wanted to know.

I just wanted it behind us, once and for all.

"The Sullivans and Kings working together." I shook my head. "It's weird, though, right?"

Royal laughed. "So fucking weird."

I crossed my arms to cover the tugging sensation at the center of my chest. Part of me was restless, wanting to get back to work and get shit done. The other part—the part that was acutely aware of the gaping hole in my chest that should contain a heart—warned me to at least *try* to connect with my older brother.

I simply wasn't that guy.

"I don't know. Maybe a little change around here is a good thing. Speaking of change . . ." I checked my watch, annoyed that our conversation was taking far too long already. "You planning to keep Veda around for a while?"

Royal unsuccessfully tried to suppress a grin. That man was down bad for his woman. Veda and I had been cordial business contacts in Chicago, and I had brought her into town to help me dig through my father's business dealings.

It hadn't taken long for Royal to charm his way into her heart.

Typical.

"Thinking about it. Why?" he asked.

I laid out the facts. "She's fucking smart. And a hard worker too. I want to bring her onto the team full-time, but I don't need you breaking my new employee's heart and fucking with my plans."

Royal's face split into a wide grin. "If I get my way, she'll be my wife, and then you'll be stuck with her for the foreseeable future."

I smiled back, satisfied. Having Veda on the team would

double our efforts, and I needed someone as cutthroat and efficient as me. "Fantastic." I shook his hand again. "Think she'll want to officially sign on with a company that's completely going to shit?"

Royal laughed. "I'm sure she'll consider it a welcome challenge."

I sighed. Though early, exhaustion was already settling in. I shook my head at Royal. "How you ended up with a woman like her is beyond me, brother."

Before he could come back with a quippy response, my phone rang, flashing my brother Whip's name across the screen.

I held up my hand, cutting off Royal's response.

"JP," Whip said over the line before I could even say hello. "You won't believe this. I've got a kid here who says you're his dad. You know anything about that? I swear, man, he's—"

"Wait, wait. Slow down. What the fuck are you talking about? Where are you?" I pinched the bridge of my nose.

"I'm at the fire station. Are you busy?" he asked.

"Yes." It was ridiculous of him to even ask.

Whip scoffed and kept rattling on, despite my best efforts to brush him off. "You sure you didn't steal from Dad's playbook and have a secret family no one knows about?"

Irritation rolled off me. The constant comparisons between my father and me were plentiful. As if I needed another reminder.

"No," I ground out.

"Cute kid. If he's yours, you can tell me. I won't tell anyone. Just Emily . . . and Sylvie . . . plus Abel. Probably Royal and MJ too." Humor danced across the line, and the ever-present knot between my shoulders tightened.

Of course he'd run his mouth to his fiancée and our siblings just to goad me. I wouldn't expect any less of my ridiculous older brother.

I huffed. "Of course it's not mine."

Whip clicked his tongue in disbelief. "Well, he's pretty convinced—knew your name and everything." His chuckle grated on my already fried nerves. "The kid looks just like you, man. Are you *absolutely* sure?"

I sighed again, my mind spinning. I had a sinking feeling that this wasn't going away until I dealt with it. "I don't know—Jesus, I will be right there."

I quickly ended the call and shoved the phone into the pocket of my slacks.

"Everything all right?" Royal's eyes raked over me.

"I have to go—that was Whip. Apparently some kid at the fire station thinks I'm his dad." The muscles in my jaw flexed, and a hammering throb pounded behind my eyes. Without looking back, I stormed down the sidewalk in the direction of the fire station. "I do not have time for this bullshit."

～

By the time I got to the fire station, my feet were fucking killing me. Twelve hundred dollars for Bontoni Italian designer shoes and I was still losing circulation to my pinkie toes.

I should buy the company and sell it off piece by piece, simply for the inconvenience.

I flicked away the rogue thought and came up short when the small gathering in front of the fire station came into view.

My sister Sylvie was standing next to Whip. Concern

pitched her brows forward as she whispered something to him.

Lee Sullivan was there with his ever-present, shit-eating grin. He was enjoying every second of whatever was unfolding, and I had a feeling it would come back to bite me in the ass if I didn't tread lightly.

Beside him, a little kid was prattling on and keeping his attention.

As I approached, my eyes snagged on a pair of long, smooth legs peeking out of dangerously short denim cutoffs. Legs that seemed to go on forever before flaring out into full hips and a tight, round ass. The woman's hair flowed down her back in wild yet pale strawberry blond waves. The unique color reminded me of an expensive French Rosé Belle champagne as it swung across her back.

Her tank top scooped low over impossibly perky breasts in a way that screamed *distracting*. Her soft brown eyes swept my way, locking onto my face. Every cell in my body sparked and sputtered as they tried to ignite but groaned from neglect. I couldn't even recall the last time I'd had sex, and there was no way in hell I'd forget being with a woman who looked like *her*.

Relief flooded my system.

Clearly there was a misunderstanding and I could be back to the office in a matter of minutes. All I had to do was make yet another problem go away, and I'd be done with it.

I folded my hands in front of me as I stood in front of the mismatched group waiting outside the fire station.

The pretty redhead's eyes widened, and I cleared my throat as a sudden shot of nerves hit me. Clearly I'd been more out of practice than I remembered.

I turned my attention to my brother Whip. "You called?"

His eyes bounced between the mystery woman and me. He must have been expecting some kind of spark of recognition, but the only spark I was feeling currently resided behind my zipper.

The kid stepped between us, his small hand raised in the air for a handshake. "Hello."

I slowly took his hand in mine and shook. "Hello."

"My name is Theodore Adams. You are my father." He was so sure of himself it was almost endearing.

"Uh . . . hi. I'm JP King." A soft chuckle rumbled out of me as we awkwardly shook hands. "I'm afraid you're misinformed. I assure you, I am not your father."

The sheer ridiculousness of it was laughable. No one would ever be so cursed as to have me as a father.

I had always been careful.

A light scoff puffed out of the redhead's nose as she stepped forward, gently placing her hand on the kid's forearm, breaking our handshake. "Teddy . . ."

Her whisper was husky and thick. Instant desire ran through me, and my mind wandered before I could shut it down. I wanted to soak her in and discover if her laugh was as rich and thick as her whisper. I suddenly wanted to know everything about the mystery woman in front of me.

The boy frowned at the woman, and she shook her head. "Bro, come on." She shrugged. "You needed a better opener."

Bro?

The woman guided Teddy beside her as she adjusted the strap of her oversize purse and lifted her warm, brown eyes.

Whip suppressed a smile before jumping in. "I caught Teddy here trying to climb into the Safe Souls baby box."

My gaze flicked to the kid. He had dark hair and sharp

bluish-green eyes, just like me. He was a good dresser—I'd give him that—but there was no way in hell he could be my kid.

He had to be what? Five? Seven? Hell, I couldn't tell.

His nose was in the air as his small shoulder lifted. "Well, isn't that how babies get dropped off?"

I glanced over to where a small box was built into the side of the building next to a red button to alert those inside when a newborn baby was surrendered and left by its caretakers.

My brows cinched down. "You're kind of big. Did you really think you were going to fit inside that thing? Be real."

The woman stepped forward. "You don't have to speak to him like that."

Her temper flared and I hated myself for liking her fire, just a little bit. Still, there was no way on earth I was this kid's father. I sure as hell would have remembered rolling in the hay with a knockout like her. She wasn't the type of woman a man would easily forget.

Her chin rose and fury simmered behind her eyes. "Does the name Olive Adams mean anything to you?"

I avoided her gaze. It was far too distracting, and I could feel the eyes of everyone on me. My brain rifled through the filing cabinet of memories and came up blank.

"Should it?" I asked.

Her nostrils flared, and my eyes roamed to her lush, full lips. A flicker of annoyance pinched my chest. I shouldn't have stared at her mouth.

Whip cleared his throat, cutting through the tension in the air. "Hey, Teddy. Want to see inside the fire station?"

The little boy's eyes lit up like fireworks. "Can I ride down the pole?"

Whip laughed as he guided the kid toward the open bay

door. "Maybe some other time. How about we watch Lee make a fool of himself instead." He tipped his head toward Lee, who followed him toward the station.

Sylvie slunk backward, likely unsure if she should give us a moment of privacy or stay to watch the dumpster fire in front of her.

The gorgeous redhead in front of me was *fuming*.

I looked around, my palms facing upward as I scoffed. "So, what? I'm the asshole here?"

THREE

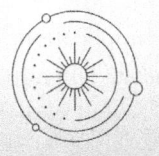

HAZEL

He was definitely the asshole.

I steadied my breathing. The last thing Teddy needed was me coming unglued and ruining his only shot at getting to know his father.

This was not at all how I'd planned for this reunion to go. Not that I was a planner, per se—more of a *wing and a prayer* type of girl—but whatever scenario that had played out in my mind definitely wasn't *this*.

I still couldn't wrap my head around the fact that JP was the same man I'd been ogling on the sidewalk. On the outside, he certainly appeared to be Olive's typical type—rich, handsome, and a total dick.

What I didn't expect was that up close, rugged manliness oozed from beneath that expensive tailored suit. He had tousled dark hair, crystal blue-green eyes beneath dark furrowed brows, broad shoulders, and a permanent scowl.

I lifted my chin, determined to be unfazed by his particular brand of handsome. "My name is Hazel. Olive Adams was my sister."

A flicker of surprise crossed his face—if it was from my

use of past tense or subtle confusion, I couldn't tell. His steely gaze was back before I could decipher it.

"You may not remember her," I continued, "but she certainly remembered you. You were listed as the father on Teddy's birth certificate application."

His intense gaze never left mine. It was as though he was running through every available scenario, but still coming up short.

"Hi. Sorry." We turned to look as Sylvie threw both thumbs over her left shoulder. "I'm going to go. This really feels like a *you-two-don't-need-an-audience* type of conversation." She backed away with a nervous laugh. "Okay, bye."

Without waiting for a response, Sylvie swiveled on her heels and started walking down the sidewalk in swift strides.

"Thank you," I called to her back before sighing and turning toward JP, who had resumed scowling in my direction.

"You said *was*." His voice was quiet and intense.

"What?" I asked.

His brows pinched. "She *was* your sister."

I swallowed past the lump that expanded in my throat. Talking about Olive still stung, regret swimming at the edges of my memory. "She passed away. Four months ago."

JP's lips hardened into a grim line. "I'm sorry."

A flicker of hope sparked in my chest. Perhaps he wasn't a total douche after all and there was an actual human hiding beneath his frosty exterior.

"But the kid isn't mine," he continued before turning his back to me and starting to walk away. "There's nothing I can do for you."

Aaaaand the dick is back.

I followed behind him, my flip-flops slapping against the concrete as I struggled to keep up with his long, efficient strides. "You can at least hear me out. We came a long way, and I have proof."

JP paused and I took the opportunity to dig into the bottom of my purse. I pushed aside a hairbrush, two wallets, empty gum wrappers, and something gross wadded into a tissue as I searched.

When my fingers found the neatly folded papers at the bottom, I held them up in triumph. "Aha!"

JP plucked the papers from my fingers and slowly opened them. My sister's loopy handwriting came into view, and I quickly snatched the top page from him. "That's private."

I didn't need JP reading my sister's heart-wrenching goodbye or the fact that she wrote in circles about her life's choices.

I flipped through the pages, taking out the last one and handing it to him. "You'll see there you're listed on the application." He eyed the pages of my sister's letter, but I shoved them back into the depths of my purse.

"You were also listed as a potential guardian in her will. She asked that I find you after . . ." I fought back tears but was proud my voice was steady after a good throat clearing. "After she passed. She wanted Teddy to have the opportunity to get to know you, though I'm not exactly sure why."

He scoffed as he studied the paper. "Me neither."

I detected a hint of self-deprecating pain hidden in his scoff. Something aching pinched in my chest as I watched him examine the sheet.

He sighed and handed it back to me. "Well, a paternity test will be required. Obviously."

My lip curled. I hated how annoyed, yet efficient, he seemed. *"Obviously,"* I mocked.

I didn't blame him for being skeptical—we had popped out of the woodwork without any notice, after all. But in my heart of hearts, I really thought he'd take one look at Teddy and just *know*.

I patted the outside of my purse, where my sister's last words were safely tucked. "Olive asked that we find you." I clasped my hands in front of me. "So here we are."

He shook his head, and his intense gaze pinned me in place. "Here you are."

The ferocity of his stare set off alarm bells. Heat pooled in my belly, and I shifted to rattle a bit of sense into myself.

The grump just *stared*. His intensity was unnerving. "My attorney will be in touch with you." JP slipped his phone from his pocket and handed it to me. "Enter your contact information and a letter will be mailed when we have more information."

I typed my phone number into his phone before handing it back to him with a scowl. "If you wanted my number, all you had to do was ask."

He blinked twice. "I didn't—I wasn't—"

Pink splotches erupted beneath the collar of his shirt and crept toward his cheeks. It was almost humorous, seeing someone so big and grumpy and used to being in control lose a bit of footing.

My laugh interrupted his obvious, internal meltdown. "Relax. It was a joke. Besides, we're staying in town for a while."

He spun on me, recovering from his sputtering. "In town?"

I looked around and shrugged as Teddy bounded from

behind a fire truck. "Yeah, I mean, why not? Seems like as good a place as any."

His arms folded across his broad chest. "Ah, I see."

My eyes narrowed at him. "What do you see?"

JP's hand flicked my way in a vague gesture. "You're after money, then?" He shook his head as though he had us all figured out.

My temper flared, and I only briefly considered the ramifications of kicking him in the balls in front of Teddy. My finger jabbed in his direction instead. "Watch it."

JP checked his watch as though finding out he had a kid was a mild inconvenience in the middle of his very important day. Anger, hot as a kettle, simmered through my blood.

"Then where are you staying? My attorney will need a way to contact you." His eyes flicked down my front and then back up. When his gaze met mine, it was emotionless, as though he'd locked himself behind whatever cool, dismissive facade he had chosen for the day.

"We live in a bus!" Teddy's enthusiastic shout floated across the parking lot as he walked toward us.

JP only tossed me a terse nod. "Of course you do."

When he glanced down at Teddy, something shifted. The callous jerk who had just accused me of being a money-grubbing drifter evaporated, and in his place was someone with sad, kind eyes.

For a brief moment, my fury subsided.

"Did Whip show you around, big guy?" he asked, crouching in front of Teddy to look him in the eye.

Teddy nodded. "It was interesting, but dirty. I didn't love it."

JP laughed and grinned at my nephew, and the steel around my heart cracked a bit. When he looked at Teddy, there was kindness there.

It was unnerving. I knew what he had done to my sister. Her letter had told me everything I needed to know about JP King, and I wouldn't let him fool me.

"It's time for us to go, Teddy." I shifted my bag and held out one hand for him.

With a pout, he reluctantly slipped his little hand into mine. His soft blue-green eyes lifted to JP's. "Can you come see the bus?"

I stepped forward, hoping to lessen the blow of yet another rejection. "Maybe another day. I'm sure Mr. King is very busy and doesn't have time to interrupt his important day for us." I lifted my eyebrows in challenge.

"You know what?" JP leaned back on his heels. "I'd love to see it."

~

After a short walk back to town, JP guided us to the parking lot near his downtown office, where his car was parked. It was a sleek black number whose rich leather interior still looked brand-new. When he opened the door, I was hit with the scent of new leather mingling with his clean, spicy cologne.

Teddy opened the door to the back seat and peered in with a scowl. "You don't have a booster seat. That's unsafe."

JP's eyes flicked to mine and I shrugged. "I don't make the rules."

"That would be the state of Michigan," Teddy said. "They have 'Buckle Up!' laws. I looked."

Teddy's lips twisted as though he was waging some distraught internal battle over whether to ride in his dad's car or defy the lawmakers of Michigan.

I patted his shoulder. "It's not too far." I gestured

toward the lighthouse. "We parked in the marina parking lot. Plus, it's a beautiful day. We can walk, right, pal?"

Teddy shrugged with a frown. "I guess."

Figuring he was relieved to finally be rid of us, I turned my back to JP and started walking.

"I can take a walk." His voice rumbled behind my back.

I slowly turned, shocked that he wanted to walk with us. When I saw Teddy's face light up and JP returned his smile, I understood that he wasn't doing it for me.

I nodded and we walked toward the lakeshore. Teddy prattled on about boats and sand dunes and changing weather patterns. I simply attempted to breathe without getting tiny, delicious hits of JP's masculine scent.

When we reached the parking lot, I grinned. Teddy bounced as he waited for me to unlock the school bus that I had converted into a fully renovated tiny house on wheels.

"What the hell is that?" JP's dark brows furrowed.

"It's my car . . . and my house." I grinned, suppressing a laugh. "It's my car and my house. You've never seen a skoolie?"

"A what?" He leaned back to take in all thirty-five feet of gloriously renovated steel, painted in a crisp white.

I unlocked and opened the bifold door. Teddy bounded up the stairs. "Hazel turned a junky old school bus into *this* place! Mom said she's super famous." Teddy's grin was proud and innocent.

I swallowed past the gravel in my throat. The way he spoke of Olive was as if she was in the next room, not gone forever. He never seemed burdened with the clawing, aching sadness that consumed my thoughts. Maybe it was just how kids dealt with grief. Maybe I was completely missing the signs. With Teddy, it was hard to tell.

I could feel JP's eyes on me so I shook my head. "I'm not famous."

"Don't lie!" Teddy chided. "Your videos get, like, *billions* of views."

Nerves skittered through me. "Not billions."

"Videos?" JP asked.

I rolled my lips. "I got bored—started renovating an old school bus and posting about it online. At first I sucked, but I taught myself what I could and got help when I needed it. I documented my progress, and I guess people were excited to follow along. It kind of unexpectedly blew up."

JP peered inside my skoolie. "And you live here?"

My forehead creased. The roof had been raised nearly eighteen inches, giving the interior plenty of headspace. With warm wood floors, white walls, gleaming cabinets, a functional sink, and even a wood-burning stove, my skoolie was a work of freaking art.

The benches had mismatched pillows in jade green, deep purple, and burgundy. A beaded curtain separated the driver seat from the main living area. Incense burned in the corner, and my prettiest tarot deck was prominently displayed on a handsewn mat. Woven throw blankets added the perfect cozy touch.

Fuck this guy if he couldn't see how funky and cool it was.

Teddy plopped onto the plush sofa cushion before grabbing a comic book from the end table, and I couldn't help but smile at how he was settling in.

I shrugged. "Home sweet home."

"What is that?" JP pointed to the tarot deck and mat.

"Tarot." I brightened. "Have you ever had a reading?"

His turquoise eyes turned to me with one dark eyebrow lifted. He looked so bitchy I almost laughed out loud, but instead I couldn't stop staring. With his eyes trained on me with such intensity, even a corpse would feel palpitations.

He was intimidating, with a dangerous edge just peeking out from beneath his buttoned-up exterior.

His only response was a dismissive grunt.

The gruff noise vibrated beside me, and I was suddenly all too aware of our closeness. Our shoulders brushed as we both peered into the bus's small entrance. On contact, his head snapped around as if my proximity was personally offensive.

With a step back, he smoothed a hand down his suit jacket. "Will you be here if the attorney needs to contact you?"

I swirled a hand in the air. "Around. I am still looking for a campground nearby that will accommodate the bus for prolonged overnight parking. But it's touristy here, so I'll find something."

His hard stare felt like it lasted forever. When he broke eye contact, I could finally breathe. He pulled a card and pen from his jacket and scribbled something across it before handing the card to me.

I stared at his business card: *JP King, King Equities.* An address was written across it in blocky, precise handwriting.

"You can park there," he offered.

I studied him. He was a walking contradiction of shitty digs and subtly kind gestures. Hard stares and soft smiles. I couldn't quite figure him out, and that worried me.

With a nod, he turned his back without saying goodbye.

FOUR

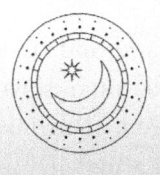

JP

MJ

PLEASE tell me the rumors are true!

> The rumor that Ms. Tiny has a hot new love interest? Couldn't say.

You know what I'm asking. Am I an auntie again?

> No.

. . .

> Maybe.

. . .

> Probably not.

SQUEEEEEEE!

It was late when I finally heard the crunch of tires on gravel and the squeaking brakes of an oversize school bus.

A fucking skoolie, of all things. This woman couldn't get any more impractical.

I had expected Hazel and Teddy to show up at my place right away and be there squatting when I returned home from work. Instead, she'd taken her sweet-ass time, and by the time night descended, I wondered whether she'd be coming at all.

A flicker of hope that this was all a terrible dream died when I saw the ridiculous bus turn in.

By the time her skoolie finally did roll down my driveway, I was fully irritated. All I wanted was for this problem to go away. If that meant she parked her house on wheels in my driveway so I could keep tabs on her and ultimately expedite their departure, then so be it.

Veda had given me the side-eye all afternoon at the office. No doubt my family had a field day with the unexpected development that some kid had claimed I was his father. I had been distracted at the office. I caught myself staring off into space, trying to recount where I'd been, what —and who—I'd been doing seven years ago. I racked my brain but still came up empty.

I had also wasted far too much time reliving every interaction I'd had with Hazel. She was a distraction—I knew it from the beginning.

Beside me, Veda had worked silently, clacking away at the keyboard and adding notes to what I referred to as her *murder board*. The oversize corkboard she'd put up in our cramped office took up the majority of the wall space and was color coded with photos, notes, and timelines.

I had initially hired Veda as a business consultant behind my father's back. I needed someone impartial to look into King Equities and find what my father was hiding. At the time, I had no idea she would be the one to uncover a web of lies and deceit far more unsettling than a few underhanded business deals.

Her tenacity had been the key to unraveling everything my father had done to hide the real reason behind my mother's disappearance. Veda had even bought red string to denote events she suspected were connected. The Post-it Notes were organized by color and highlighted the bits of information we were still looking into in order to ensure, after his arrest, my father never saw the light of day again.

Untangling the web of deceit my father had woven over the course of nearly thirty years was a daunting task. Her board was ridiculous but, admittedly, helpful.

At the very least, Veda knew to keep her mouth shut and work.

She's getting another raise.

I pinched the bridge of my nose and downed the last sip of whiskey in my glass as I peered out the front window. Sighing, I set down my drink and walked out of my house and onto the front porch.

With the setting sun sagging across Lake Michigan, a riot of golden hues illuminated Hazel's strawberry blond hair through the bus's front window, making it sparkle with flecks of gold in the sunlight.

She looked tiny behind the gigantic wheel of the school bus, and the air suspension seat bounced her up and down with every bump. I leaned against the porch column as she parked.

Hazel shot me a grin and two thumbs-up.

I offered a tight smile and raised my hand, letting her know the haphazard way she'd parked at an awkward angle was good enough.

It wasn't like I got any unannounced visitors anyway.

Within seconds, the door swung open and she bounded down the steps of the skoolie. I looked behind her, curious when I didn't see Teddy hot on her heels.

"He's asleep," she said as though she could read my mind.

Hazel walked across the grass in her flip-flops, and I focused on the trees behind her rather than the way the breeze lifted her soft red hair.

When she got close enough, there was a ripple of uncertainty that fluttered across her perfect features. For a split second, she almost looked scared.

It was gone in a second, though, and in its place Hazel stepped up and rolled her shoulders back.

"Honey, I'm home!" Hazel's soft brown eyes crinkled at the corners from her wide grin.

My breath expelled in an impatient huff.

Hazel mirrored my sigh and looked around with wide eyes. "Woof. Tough crowd . . ."

Her humor almost pulled a wry smile from me.

She swallowed hard and met my unyielding eyes. "Did you change your mind about me parking here?"

I gritted my teeth. It was the most practical solution I could come up with on the fly. "It's fine. Did you have a better option?"

Hazel laced her fingers together, pushing her shoulders back and straightening her spine. "I'm a go-with-the-flow kind of girl. This isn't much different."

The way her lips quirked to one side was cute and endearing. I caught myself staring at her mouth. It was plump and lush and looked like a hell of a good time.

I tore my gaze from her mouth when Hazel looked over

my shoulder to the house at my back. "You live here?" she asked.

My house was custom built and far too large for any one man. The black siding nearly vanished under the towering trees. A trail of flat cobblestones wound a path from the driveway to the steps of the porch, and I'd made sure the landscaping melded seamlessly with the surrounding trees. At the back of the house, floor-to-ceiling windows provided spectacular views of Lake Michigan. The house stood proudly on top of a towering sand dune that led to a private beach.

Sure, it was a beach I never had time to enjoy, but it was mine.

My home was a few miles out of town, which offered me the seclusion and privacy I craved. Why on earth I thought it was a good idea for her and Teddy to camp out on my property was beyond me.

It had to be the stress. That was the only excuse for giving up my privacy to a woman and child with a ridiculous claim that I was the kid's father.

I tried my best to appear unaffected by her poking. "Are you surprised that a bachelor has taste?" I shot back.

Her eyes narrowed but didn't waver as she stopped at the base of the stairs. "Surprised to see you live in an overpriced, secluded hideaway where no one would hear it if I screamed? No. No, that tracks."

I stepped down to stand beside her and leaned forward, pulled by an invisible tether that drew me to her sass and inconvenience. I was close enough to hear the hitch of her inhale as I soaked in the warmth of her skin. My gruff whisper floated across her ear. "If the neighbors can't hear my woman scream, then I'm not doing my job right."

As soon as the words were out, I bit back a curse. My

eyes sliced to the side, immediately checking to see if Teddy had heard my slip of the tongue, but the inside of the bus was dark and still.

Fucking idiot.

Something about being near Hazel Adams made me lose my composure. Like there was a feral animal locked inside a cage in my chest and she stood on the outside, waving the key.

Taunting me.

I turned to go inside.

"Do you want to have breakfast or something tomorrow?" Hazel asked as I climbed the stairs. I slowly faced her, unsure of how to gently tell her that sharing a meal with her was the absolute *last* thing I needed to be doing.

Against the setting sun, she looked sad and tired.

And young.

"How old are you?" I asked, ignoring her question about breakfast.

Her chin lifted. "Twenty-five."

Just as I thought—young. Too young.

"So . . . breakfast?" Her teeth toyed with her lip.

I shook my head. "No."

Her soft brown eyes widened with hope and a little sadness. "Don't you even want to get to know him?"

"Not really." My chest filled with a sense of haughty superiority, regret hot on its heels when I saw her pretty face fall.

Without waiting for her response, I strode through the kitchen and up the stairs at the back of my house. I didn't stop until I was cocooned inside the sanctity of my bedroom. I picked up the discarded novel on my bedside, simply because it was the closest one I could find, and settled into the high-back chair in the corner.

From the window, I could see her skoolie, but I ignored it.

I flipped the book open, but my eyes refused to focus on the words.

Everything is going to be fine. This is just another problem that needs taking care of.

Just like everything else, I would bear the brunt of the setback and make it go away. The claim that Teddy was my child was utterly ridiculous. Impossible. Lots of kids had dark features and light eyes and a good sense of fashion. That didn't make me their dad.

I considered when all this was over, I could take some time off. Relax. Disappear where no one knew my name and one bad business deal didn't mean losing *millions*. Somewhere I didn't have the burden of expectation. Somewhere my father's horrific actions didn't follow me.

I loved the coastal air, but I'd never seen the mountains. There was an appeal to standing at the base of something grand, forged millions of years ago by nature, staring up and feeling your insignificance.

I flipped a page in the book, my eyes glossing over words that weren't even registering as I let my mind wander. Maybe on my sabbatical I'd meet a cute girl in some quaint mountain town, someone with thick thighs, blondish-red hair, caramel eyes, and a mouth made to pout. This mystery woman would have an easy laugh that cracked me open in new and unexpected ways. She'd make it easy to open up, to laugh. During the day, she'd show me around her town and we'd get lost on random hiking trails. At night we'd be nothing but tangled limbs and heavy breaths.

My eyes glazed over as I realized I hadn't read a fucking word. I leaned my head back, closing my eyes and relishing the feeling of my dick twitching to life. I could almost feel her hot breath on my skin, her whispers in my ear, her taste on my tongue.

My eyes flew open when I realized it was Hazel starring in my unhinged production of *JP's Mountainside Mental Breakdown*.

I pinched the bridge of my nose and forced the ridiculous fantasy aside. It was utterly inappropriate to be having the thoughts I had about Hazel. She was convinced that her nephew was my son—that her sister and I had been together and gotten pregnant.

The fact that *anyone* would claim me as a father was the most absurd part of it all. I had never wanted kids and had *always* been careful. Besides, I would have been, what? Twenty-four, twenty-five when she claimed to have gotten pregnant?

Dread pooled in my stomach when the pieces started to click together. It would have been around that time I was spending the summer and fall interning for one of my father's clients in Chicago. Dad had claimed the position would give me the big-city experience I needed to truly level up. I'd worked hard by networking and making solid connections that still served me today.

But out from under my father's thumb, I'd also spent a few reckless months partying hard and fucking my way through Chicago.

I slammed my book closed. Nausea swirled in my gut, and I felt sick. I swallowed back the bile and tried to focus on breathing.

Jesus, I was an asshole.

A grade A prick.

The son of a killer.

Teddy was a cute kid, but he certainly didn't deserve to have me as his father.

FIVE

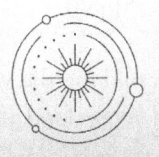

HAZEL

I WANTED TO HATE HIM. I *should* hate him.

At first glance, JP was a dick, but I couldn't ignore the gnawing feeling that behind his cool, blue eyes was a lost little boy who was scared to death. It was almost as if he was working hard to gloss over any semblance of a human being with his grunts and dismissive remarks.

Sure, he could treat me like a stranger, but I wasn't going to let him toss Teddy to the side without a fight. My sister's letter was clear—JP was his father, and despite how everything had gone down between the two of them, her dying wish was for Teddy to have the chance to know him.

But I could tell—JP was guarded. It was like he was desperately hiding *something*.

I didn't know what it was, but I knew one thing—in a small town, people *loved* to gossip, and I considered getting people to open up to me as one of my gifts.

With a sigh, I stretched my neck and took a deep, cleansing breath. While Teddy was getting dressed for the day, I soaked in the moment of quiet. When I closed my eyes, I chuckled a little to myself—it felt like yesterday when I'd set out with a newly renovated skoolie and a wild dream. All I wanted was excitement and adventure. Everything about my life up to that point had been *too* quiet. Then everything was flipped upside down when Olive died.

She had never even told me she was sick.

I shoved down the regret and unshed tears. I grabbed my favorite tarot deck to do a quick reading before Teddy was ready to go. I closed my eyes, shuffling the deck and repeating the same question over and over in my mind.

Okay, Universe. What do I need to know today?

I pulled three cards: Ace of Wands, the Fool, and Death.

Well, okay then.

I swallowed and arranged the cards in front of me, filtering my knowledge of the cards through my intuition.

"Oh! Do mine next." Teddy came out from his bunk at the back of the skoolie, wearing a pair of blue shorts and a red-and-white-striped shirt with a collar.

A little professor.

I smiled. "Just a quick reading before I start my day."

Teddy sat across from me. His soft blue eyes landed on the Death card. He pulled his lower lip into his mouth, but stayed quiet, his eyes not leaving the drawing of a skeleton in a black cloak.

"Hey." I reached across the table to pat his arm. "This card isn't scary. Do you want to know what they mean?"

He nodded, his eyes not moving from the set of three cards in front of me.

"Well . . ." I exhaled, sinking into my heart chakra. "It looks like I'm starting a new adventure." I spun the Ace of Wands card so he could see it. "See this one? This one means creativity or new beginnings. Right there is a hand coming from the cloud. It means new opportunities. And this one . . ." I moved the Fool closer to him. "The Fool—"

I waggled my eyebrows and Teddy giggled at the name.

"The Fool," I continued, "usually means excitement for new things that are coming. Jumping feetfirst, even if you don't know the outcome. Daring to make the first leap!"

"Like coming here?" he asked.

The kid was so smart. I smiled and nodded. "I think so. It's been a good adventure so far, don't you think?"

He nodded again but didn't answer. Teddy's little finger gestured toward the Death card, but didn't touch it—as though Death itself could reach out and snatch him. "But that one's bad."

I shook my head, keeping my voice calm and confident. "No, it really isn't. This isn't death like *death*." I patted his arm in quiet reassurance. "Usually the Death card is like rebirth or beginnings—a new life that can come from the end of something else."

His brow furrowed as he studied the card. "Kind of like you and me?"

My chest pinched. I gently squeezed his arm. "*Exactly* like you and me. We're starting the next chapter of our lives, and I just know it's going to be a great adventure."

I scooped the cards into a pile and began shuffling. "Want me to pull some cards for you?"

Teddy's gaze moved to the skoolie's windows as he looked across the yard to JP's house. By the time we'd woken up, JP's car was gone and the house was dark and quiet. I wanted so badly to look inside Teddy's head to see what he was thinking.

Am I totally screwing this up? What do you need from me, kiddo?

Instead, I swallowed past my own guilt and uncertainty and waited for him to reply.

"No," he finally said. "I'll just find out when it happens."

∼

DESPITE THE PINT-SIZE curmudgeon at my side, I was determined to have a good day in Outtatowner. No doubt JP was working hard to disprove my sister's claim that Teddy was his child, but until we could go in front of the court, what else could we do?

A day at the beach would be better than sitting around feeling sorry for ourselves.

"I'm ready," Teddy announced from the back of the skoolie.

I looked over and suppressed a laugh. He was dressed in blue swim trunks and a matching long-sleeved rash guard. His swim goggles were already on, along with a noseclip. His feet were shoved into black water shoes, and his hands were on his hips.

"Wow," I choked out, using a cough to cover the humor in my voice. "You seem well prepared."

"The sun's rays contain UV light that damages DNA. One in five will develop skin cancer in their lifetime." Teddy looked down at his covered arms. "But not me."

My heart squeezed. "Not you, bud. Come here."

He waddled forward in his water shoes and allowed me to wrap him in a hug. I climbed behind the wheel and buckled myself in while Teddy found a seat on the couch behind me. "Ready for the beach, Skipper?"

"Aye, aye, Captain." Teddy saluted me as the engine roared to life. I turned the bus in a wide circle, narrowly missing the manicured plants at the edges of JP's property.

In Outtatowner, it felt as though everything was *three doors down* or *just a block over*, but JP had chosen to live on the outskirts of town like the sourpuss he appeared to be. As a result, I'd be hauling my entire house around if I wanted us to go anywhere.

I cranked up the radio and sang along as we made our way back toward town and followed the signs for North Beach. Despite it being only 10:00 a.m., the parking lot was nearly packed. She could be bulky, so instead of cramming into one of the tight spaces in the lot, I parked the skoolie up the road.

Once we were settled, I grabbed an oversize bag and stuffed it with a blanket, my wallet, a few snacks, and sunscreen. "Should we stop somewhere to buy some beach toys?"

Teddy shook his head. "I have my book."

I scoffed as we exited the bus. "If you say so."

From the outside of the bus, I set up my phone to take a few pictures. The beach was just visible behind the skoolie. I grinned, giving a thumbs-up. My caption read *Bus life, beach life!*

I posted it to my social media profile and slipped my phone into the beach bag. We received a few odd glances and smiles as I locked up the skoolie. A couple of people took pictures and asked about my house on wheels. Teddy and I walked down the long hill that led toward the sandy beach.

In the distance, the pier jutted into the Lake Michigan waters, and an adorable lighthouse stood proudly at the end. The pier was busy with people fishing, couples walking hand in hand, and families taking photos near the lighthouse. The air was crisp and clean. Though summer was waning, the sun was warm and I hoped a day at the beach would be what Teddy and I needed to feel centered again.

I gripped his hand—he was too easy to lose in a crowd, and I had learned my mistake the first time. We made our way across the soft, pale sand toward the water's edge. Teddy kicked up bits of sand with every step, and I adjusted my bag, searching for a small opening for us to set down a blanket and relax.

After weaving through families setting up extravagant tents with coolers, tables, and umbrellas, I plopped my bag down a few feet away from a pregnant woman and her daughter. Grabbing a blanket from the bag, Teddy helped me smooth it across the sand, and we each kicked off our shoes before sitting cross-legged on the ratty quilt.

"Want to jump in the water?" I asked, lowering my sun hat across my eyes.

Teddy's mouth twisted as he gripped a book in his lap. I followed his gaze to the young girl kicking the waves and laughing. "Maybe."

I rubbed his back. "You're allowed to have fun sometimes."

He shot me a plain look. "Reading *is* fun."

"I agree. But so is swimming in the ocean and finding seashells." I bumped my shoulder into his.

"It's not an ocean," he retorted.

I grinned. "Even better! No salt water to sting your eyeballs or give you a parasite or whatever other weird shit you look up on the internet."

When he scowled at me, I grinned and playfully stuck out my tongue, which earned me the tiniest smirk. Teddy only harrumphed, but didn't chastise me for cursing in front of him again.

I lay back, stretching across the blanket and soaking in the DNA-damaging rays while Teddy fidgeted beside me and contemplated his choice.

I let the beach sounds fade away, and it was grounding to feel the soft sand beneath the quilt and the sun's rays warm my skin. There was no denying that slowing down and feeling a connection to the earth made everything else—losing my sister, becoming Teddy's guardian, tracking down his dad, trying to find myself in the midst of all of it—seem slightly bearable.

I needed that strength if I was going to help Teddy absorb the crushing blow of JP's inevitable dismissal.

I turned my head and peeked at Teddy through my eyelashes. My heart filled with love for my little nephew. It would be JP's loss in the end. Teddy was an incredible human, and if he couldn't see that Teddy was worth getting to know, then he didn't deserve him in his life.

Teddy was still staring at the lake and the children playing in it as if they were a personal affront to his sensible nature. He picked at the threadbare blanket beside him.

"Fine. I'll go." Without any further explanation, Teddy stood and stomped toward the water.

A laugh burst from my chest and I sighed as I sat up to keep a closer eye on him. He was cautious, but I knew he wasn't a strong swimmer, and I didn't want him getting too far without me.

A soft laugh floated next to me, and I looked over to see the pregnant woman smiling at Teddy's back. "For what it's worth, I think you did the right thing"—her head gestured toward Teddy dipping a toe into the lake—"letting him make the choice on his own."

The woman was gorgeous, with brown hair piled on her head and large black sunglasses shielding her eyes. Her two-piece swimsuit was bright yellow with little ruffles at the hip. Her exposed belly was very pregnant as her left hand stroked across it.

I smiled at her. "I'm still kind of figuring it all out."

The brunette nodded. "We all are." She leaned toward me and held out her hand. "I'm Lark Sullivan. That's Penny." She pointed to the little girl I'd seen kicking the waves earlier. Lark rubbed her belly. "This is Ethan."

I shook her hand and smiled. "Pleasure. I'm Hazel and that's Teddy." The woman's name sparked a memory as I thought about the kind, silly firefighter from yesterday. "Sullivan? Any relation to Lee? Firefighter . . . mischievous smile . . . ?"

Lark nodded. "That would be Lee. He's my brother-in-law. You know him?"

I smiled again. "We met yesterday. Teddy took off on a little adventure of his own and wound up at the fire station. He and a few of the crew there kept an eye on him until I could get him."

"Oh . . . so you're JP's mystery woman." Lark sat at attention and scooted forward.

Heat traveled up my neck, and I was certain my cheeks were stained red. I swallowed hard as JP's words from the night before rattled in my brain.

If the neighbors can't hear my woman scream, then I'm not doing my job right.

My uncomfortable laugh passed between us. "Definitely not his woman, but wow—news travels fast around here."

She looked at me over the rim of her sunglasses. "You have no idea."

Lark continued to look at me, though I didn't get a sense

of judgment. Only pure, unbridled curiosity. It was practically oozing from her perfect, poreless face.

"So you know JP King?" I asked.

Lark watched her daughter play in the waves, and we shared a smile when Penny invited Teddy to play with her sand toys.

"Everyone knows everyone in this town—at least, if you're a townie. But the Sullivans and the Kings have a unique, generations-long history. The families are old-time rivals, but we're also kind of family now. The men still pull petty pranks on each other from time to time, but it's mostly harmless." She swatted a dismissive hand between us as she continued, "Since Russell King was arrested for the murder of his wife Maryann, things have been quiet. Deep down I think we're all working together to find a happy ending to such a heartbreaking story. It's a trauma bond, I'm sure. Ha!"

The uncomfortable laugh burst from her chest at the end of the ramble, and I simply blinked at her as my brain ping-ponged with all the information she had thrown at me.

It was . . . *a lot* to take in.

I had seen the reports in the news about prominent businessman Russell King. His fall from grace had made headlines after he was accused of harming his wife, who had disappeared over two decades earlier. In fact, it was one news station that had made a passing mention of his son, John "JP" King, taking over their business, that was the final piece to finally finding Teddy's dad. Olive's letter had mentioned the Michigan town and the name JP King.

Clearly it was a sign.

Had it not been for that café with the news turned up too loud, I might never have had the guts to set out and find him.

The universe had been looking out for us, that I knew for sure.

I squinted at the sun, wondering whether Lark might reveal more information about the elusive grump. "Well, would you like to hear my side of it?"

Lark squealed and scooted closer. "Would I ever!"

I liked Lark. She seemed like the kind of woman you could confide in. Olive had always been my best friend, and the pain of knowing that, despite our bond, we never really knew each other stung.

I could be a better friend next time.

Maybe I could start with Lark.

SIX

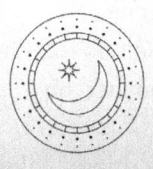

JP

Nine days.

Nine days of feeling like my home was a prison and watching from a distance as Hazel and Teddy slowly acclimated to life in Outtatowner. I kept my distance, not wanting to insert myself, unsure of *how* to even do that—not that I wanted to.

Every morning I drank my coffee black and watched them through a slit in the curtains. They played on my private beach, lay in the grass and pointed at the clouds, giggled, and came home with bags of produce from the farmers' market—all while I stood on the outskirts trying to figure out what Hazel's true intentions were.

Maybe it really is as simple as wanting money in the midst of the King Equities chaos.

While she was staying on my property, I pulled every string I could find to get Hazel and me in front of a judge and get them out of my hair for good. Small-town courts were notoriously slow, and we needed a resolution as quickly as possible.

I stared at the clock on the wall in my office as seconds

crawled forward. I needed to leave if I was going to make it to the Remington County courthouse on time.

"I thought you said the meeting was at four?" Veda asked without looking at me.

I glanced at her. She was standing with her back to me, barefoot with hands on her hips in front of her *murder board*.

"Can I ask you something?" I didn't want to think about anything but work. I needed to keep my head down.

Focus.

Veda turned to me with a raised eyebrow.

I plopped the newspaper in my hand onto my desk, ignoring the grainy black-and-white photo of my father splashed across the front page. "What happens if we fold?"

Her eyes narrowed on me before she exhaled. "The sharks are circling, there's no denying that. Selling the company now would get you fractions of pennies on the dollar—which, given the fact King Equities and its assets are worth close to a *billion*, would still be more money than any of you would ever need."

My jaw flexed. "And if we tough it out?"

Veda crossed her arms. "We weather the storm, hope that our current investors don't pull their funds. We stand by our firm. We prove that King Equities is more than the black mark your father created. We do that, and King Equities will no longer simply be a mergers-and-acquisitions boutique—we could be serious contenders on a global scale."

The corner of my mouth ticced up. I liked the sound of that. "World domination?"

Veda scoffed before turning back to her board. "You're damn right."

I smiled at her back. I wouldn't let it show, but I needed

Veda's pep talk. More and more I'd been questioning what the hell I had worked my whole life for. Since childhood I'd been groomed to take over my father's business, and for what? To find out that he'd used the company as an elaborate shell game to hide what he'd done to my mother?

But, damn it, I was tired.

I swiped my keys from the desk. "I'm out of here. Try making yourself useful and working on that global domination while I'm gone."

She offered a salute over her shoulder as I walked toward the door. "On it."

~

Attorney Joss Keller looked almost as good in a suit as I did.

Almost.

I walked down the quiet corridor at the Remington County courthouse and sized him up as he stood across from Hazel and Teddy. She was dressed in ripped jeans and a faded Rolling Stones T-shirt tied in a knot at her belly button. Over it was a long gold jacket that seemed to be velvet and fell to her knees. Her hair was haphazardly tied up with a scarf.

Her choice of clothing should have appeared disheveled and out of place, but for her it somehow worked despite the sterile, buttoned-up atmosphere of the courthouse. Teddy fit right in with another short-sleeved checkered shirt. This time he was wearing a slim blue necktie. His sneakers were the only reminder that he was a little kid and not a tiny CEO.

Hazel was laughing softly at something Joss had said, but when I approached, her soft laugh faded.

Without a smile to greet him, I walked up to Joss, placed my hand in his, and shook. "Keller."

"King." Joss squeezed back.

"Hey, kid," I said to Teddy with a nod.

His chin dipped to mirror my greeting. "Hi, Dad."

Hazel sputtered as my throat went dry and the room around me narrowed.

She herded him in the direction of the bathroom. "Teddy, why don't you use the bathroom before we head in."

Unfazed, he went in, and I turned to Joss and Hazel, still reeling from Teddy's flippant use of *Dad*.

Joss's head shook as he sized me up. It was no secret that the pretty-boy attorney was friends with the Sullivans, and given our muddy history, his obvious skepticism made sense.

My eyes roamed over Hazel, unable to stop staring at how the loose tendrils of hair perfectly framed her pretty face.

I wrenched my gaze free to look at Joss. "Are you here providing legal representation?"

Joss's winning smile grated on my already fried nerves. His eyes moved back to Hazel, and his grin widened. "This was simply a lucky chance meeting. Ms. Adams was looking a little lost."

Joss slipped his card from the inside pocket of his jacket and handed it to Hazel. "But if you ever need anything, please, don't hesitate to reach out."

A disgusted noise rattled in the back of my throat before I could stop it. Hazel's long lashes swooped down as she looked at his business card and accepted it with a soft smile. I rolled my eyes as he turned and his loafers clacked down the hallway.

"Problem?" she asked as she turned toward me.

I stared down at her. "Several, actually."

Once Teddy returned, I gestured to the door to Judge Burns's office, and the pair entered before me.

Hazel's face twisted. "Do you like *anyone*?" Hazel asked as she passed in front of me, but she didn't wait for my response.

No, not really.

I checked us in with the receptionist and waited to be called back to the judge's chambers.

Teddy looked up at me. "Have you considered the loss of consumer trust?"

I looked down, confused. "What?"

A serious line creased Teddy's eyebrows. "I've been thinking about it. The news reports say things are *bad* for King Equities. You should start by acknowledging and apologizing."

A laugh sounded from my chest. I had never been a kid person, but Teddy seemed different—like a sixty-year-old man trapped in a child's body. "How do you know about that?"

He shrugged. "Google."

I nodded. *Fucking Google.* "Thanks, I'll keep it in mind."

I then focused my attention on my watch and tapped my foot as the minutes ticked by.

4:07—*the judge is late.*

"Got somewhere better to be?" Hazel asked, annoyance dripping from her silky voice.

I didn't need to look at her to perfectly picture the crease between her eyebrows. My arms crossed. "Some of us have jobs to get back to." I glanced down at her. "What is it you do again? Social media . . . something or other?"

Her nostrils flared as she stared ahead at the large wooden door of the judge's chambers. "Influencer," she gritted between clenched teeth.

I huffed. *Figures.*

Before Hazel could fire back, the door to the judge's chambers opened. I stood, smoothing a hand down my suit, and stepped forward. "Judge Burns, pleasure to see you again, sir."

We shook hands as Hazel looked on. She turned to Teddy. "You're going to sit out here and read for a little bit. No wandering off."

Teddy nodded and propped himself up in a chair in the waiting area.

"Promise?" Hazel asked.

Teddy simply drew an X over his checkered shirt and opened his book.

With a kind smile, Judge Burns gestured for us to enter, and I stepped inside while Hazel shook his hand and followed. Two chairs were positioned in front of his large oak desk.

"Please, sit." He gestured to the seats as he rounded the desk.

I waited for Hazel to sit before unbuttoning my jacket and sitting in the chair beside her.

Nerves rolled off her in waves. She clutched a piece of paper in her lap, and her foot bounced.

"Well," Judge Burns began, "sounds like we've got a bit of family drama. Well, *more* of it, I should say." The judge winked at me, and I stifled another eye roll.

"Sir, if I may." I leaned forward. "Ms. Adams believes that her sister Olivia and I—"

"It's Olive," Hazel interrupted.

I turned to her. "What?"

"Her name was *Olive*, not Olivia. You don't even remember her *name*?" Emotion was thick in her voice, and I immediately felt like the world's biggest asshole.

I cleared my throat. "My apologies. Olive." I looked at the judge. "Clearly I don't know this woman, or her child. He's a cute kid, don't get me wrong, but he's not mine."

Judge Burns turned his attention to Hazel. "Why don't we start with you, miss. Who are you and how can I help?"

Hazel gathered her strength and straightened in the plush, white chair. "My name is Hazel Adams. My sister was *Olive*—" Her eyes sliced toward me. "That's Teddy's mom. She passed away in April."

The judge's pale-green eyes were soft and kind. "I'm sorry to hear that. Losing a sibling is a special kind of pain. Your sister left custody of her son with you?"

Hazel's lower lip pulled between her teeth. "Um . . . kind of. As next of kin, I was granted custody, but her wishes did also include possible shared custody with Teddy's father." Her gaze flicked to me, then back to the judge.

Custody? What the fuck?

My heart pounded as my back stayed glued to the seat.

The judge's features pinched as he focused on Hazel. "But he's grown up with you, correct?"

She blinked rapidly and fumbled with the papers. "To be honest, I wasn't living near them—a large part of my career is—*was* traveling. But things change." Hazel raised her chin. "It has become clear that he wants nothing to do with his son, which is fine. I've spent the last several months with him, and now I want to have full custody."

I slapped a hand on my thigh. "Fine. I can sign away custody right now. Done."

As soon as the words were out, I was caught off guard by

a sharp stab beneath my ribs. I pushed past it and focused on steadying my breathing and ignoring the image of Teddy's sweet face that popped into my mind.

Judge Burns held up a hand and shook his head. "I'm afraid it's not that simple, Mr. King. You cannot give up custody of a child that isn't proven to be yours. You yourself stated Teddy was not your son. Clearly there is a question of paternity. Unfortunately, in the best interest of the child, I am not able to make a recommendation until the issue of paternity is resolved."

"How long does that take?" I asked, pinching the bridge of my nose.

"Weeks? Months?" Judge Burns sighed. "It's difficult to say how quickly these things get pushed through. Once the issue of paternity is established, the court can make a ruling on custody. If you're proven to be his father, you can sign your rights over to Ms. Adams at that time."

The room tilted as I attempted to gain my bearings.

Months?

Hazel slipped a piece of paper from her purse. "This is Olive's application for Teddy's birth certificate." The coral nail polish on her index finger was chipped, and I briefly wondered whether nerves had caused her to pick it off. "She put his name right there."

I leaned forward to see my name, *JP King*, written in the space for the father's full name.

Judge Burns hummed. "Mr. King's name is on the application, but if he never signed anything, in the state of Michigan, his name wouldn't appear on the actual birth certificate. However, her last will and testament did nominate both you, Ms. Adams, and you, Mr. King, as guardians." The judge frowned and turned to me. "I take it having a child with the late Ms. Adams was not in the plan?"

My gaze was unfocused as I stared at the wood grain of his desk. "No, sir."

"Did Olive ever contact you in any way to inform you of—"

"Absolutely not." I dipped my chin in a steely, confident nod.

"I object!" Hazel held a folded piece of paper over her head.

Judge Burns shook his head and chuckled. "Ms. Adams, there's no need for that. This is not a formal hearing."

"She did try, and I have proof." Hazel leaned forward, smoothing a handwritten letter open, splaying it across the judge's desk. Tucked inside the folded letter was an old photograph.

Shock radiated through me as I stared at a younger version of myself. In the picture I was wearing some kind of crimped, blond, eighties-style wig. My eyes were half closed and I looked drunk as fuck. Tucked into my side was a pretty woman I didn't recognize. She was grinning at the camera as it captured a moment in time I simply could not recall.

I scraped a hand over my jaw and sat back.

Judge Burns whistled softly. "Sure does look a lot like you, Mr. King."

I swallowed as I stared at my stupid, love-drunk happy face. "Yeah."

"While we wait for paternity results," Judge Burns continued, "it can be presumed JP is the father and would have the right to visitation with Teddy, if you choose to honor your sister's wishes."

Beside me, Hazel swallowed hard. It was clear she loved

her sister deeply and, despite her disdain for me, wanted to abide by her sister's dying words.

We both sat in stunned silence.

Judge Burns sat back in his chair, lacing his fingers over his abdomen. "Or . . . given the information presented today, I believe there is another logical way to move forward . . ."

He should have been dressed in a black executioner's cloak. I clenched my teeth and waited for the judge to swing the ax and seal my fate.

SEVEN

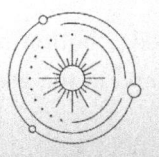

HAZEL

My entire body shook with nerves.

Confusion, fury, anger, sadness—it all soaked through me and was directed at one person.

Him.

First he got my sister's name wrong, and his continual dismissal of Teddy was enough to make a girl want to haul off and slap the handsome right off his face.

JP was still staring at the photograph on the judge's desk. His brows creased as though he was performing mental gymnastics, trying to figure out where the photograph had come from.

The judge's voice stole my attention. "Given the information presented today, I believe there is another logical way to move forward." His kind smile was the only comfort I could find. "Perhaps young Teddy could weigh in and have a voice in whether or not he would be comfortable spending time with Mr. King?"

My mouth opened and closed like a fish gasping for air.

Sure, I'd set out to Outtatowner to honor my sister's final wish to allow Teddy to get to know his dad, but as soon as I'd realized what an epic jerk he was, I had been left with no choice. Teddy would never feel unwanted as long as I was there to care for him, and if that meant seeking full custody, then so be it.

Judge Burns pushed a button near his phone. "Margerie? Can you please send in the young man in the waiting room?"

Moments later Teddy's face peeked out from behind the door.

"Come on in, son," Judge Burns greeted. "We don't bite."

Teddy's eyes turned to mine, and I found the courage to smile. A sense of ease washed over me. The relationship Teddy and I had formed over the past four months was stronger than ever. He didn't even *know* JP, and I was confident Teddy's logical brain would make the right choice.

If JP wanted to deny the fact he was Teddy's dad, then he didn't deserve to have such a cool kid in his life anyway.

My nephew stood between the chairs and looked at the judge.

The judge's voice was soft and confident. "You've been through a lot, young man. I was saddened to hear about the loss of your mother."

Teddy showed no emotion and my heart rolled.

The judge gestured between JP and me. "I've been having a conversation with your aunt Hazel and Mr. King—"

"He's my dad," Teddy said proudly. I placed a hand on Teddy's back and rubbed.

JP looked like he was about to throw up all over the judge's desk, and there was a low ringing in my ears that wouldn't go away.

The judge smiled. "We're going to have some scientists

run a test to make sure that's the case. It helps us dot the i's and cross the t's. Does that make sense?"

Teddy nodded.

"Good." Judge Burns chuckled. "While we wait for that, how would you feel about spending some time getting to know Mr. King?"

JP ran his palms down the thighs of his slacks.

Teddy shrugged. "It's why we're here, isn't it?"

The adults laughed, easing the uncomfortable tension that had filled the room.

I looked up at my nephew. It didn't matter what I wanted, this was about Teddy, and I needed to remember that. I gently squeezed his shoulder. "Yeah, I guess it is, isn't it?"

"Besides," Teddy continued with a confident smile. "Being public-facing with a kid like me could help demonstrate empathy to the public." He looked directly at JP. "This could help you and your business."

My mouth dropped open.

JP shook his head and smiled. "I appreciate you thinking about the business, but I can manage. What do *you* want?"

Teddy looked at JP with seriousness. "I want to get to know you. My mom told me once that you had a good soul."

My eyes sliced to JP, daring him to crush Teddy's sweet little heart in front of me. Instead of the dismissal I expected to come from him, JP laughed and looked at Teddy with something akin to awe.

My heart fluttered, but I pushed it down.

JP stood and held his hand out for Teddy to shake. "If you want to get to know me, I'm good with that." He leaned in conspiratorially. "But I'm afraid you'll find my life around here is pretty boring. Lots of meetings."

He and Teddy shared a smile and my heart clunked. He wasn't supposed to look at my nephew with softness. He wasn't supposed to make self-deprecating jokes.

He was the enemy.

With a satisfied chuckle, Judge Burns dismissed us and walked us out of his office. Stunned, I followed JP and Teddy down the corridor of the courthouse and out into the late-summer sun.

JP walked us toward the parking lot, and as soon as the skoolie came into view, Teddy took off like a shot. "Last one home is a rotten egg!"

JP shouted. "Be care—"

"Slow down!" My voice overlapped with JP's and we looked at each other.

Silence grew legs and filled the space between us.

I shielded my eyes from the sun as I watched Teddy reach the bus. I stopped and turned to JP. "Why did you do it? Agree to get to know him?"

He kept his focus on Teddy, who was doing a pretty impressive impersonation of JP, with a hand on his hip and his foot tapping. "It's not the kid's fault his mom got his dad wrong."

Annoyance flitted through me. "She's not wrong. You saw the picture."

My attitude must have struck a chord because JP's jaw flexed as he turned toward me. "You've barely seen your nephew in seven years and I'm the asshole?"

An indignant noise shot out of my nose. "Less than two weeks in and suddenly you think you're the father of the year?"

His icy eyes pinned me in place. "You weren't even here for two days before you lost track of him. I don't think it'll be difficult to raise that bar."

"Dick," I spat as I stomped away.

"Hex," he called to my back.

"Hex?" I turned and scoffed.

His eyes raked over me. "A hex. A witch."

I strode away from him, a wicked grin spreading as a laugh shot out of me.

Buddy, you have no idea.

EIGHT

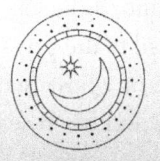

JP

I couldn't sleep.

Living in seclusion was supposed to be peaceful, but I'd always been a light sleeper. With the weather cooling, I'd opened the house, hoping the distant crashing of waves would lull me to sleep.

No such luck.

Instead, my brain became acutely aware of every single noise inside *and* outside the house. My brain looped on a thousand questions: *Did Hazel remember to lock the bus? How secure was that thing? Does Teddy wear a seat belt inside of it when she's driving? Why did she have to smell so good?*

When I heard the metal groan of the school bus door, I immediately thought Teddy was sneaking out again. Already wide awake, I padded to my window and looked out of the second-floor window. The yard was cast in eerie, shifting shadows.

Below me, Hazel was walking away from her skoolie in a thin yellow nightgown that barely covered her ass. She moved silently across the lawn until she disappeared around the corner. Curious, I threw on a pair of sweatpants and made my way downstairs. I peeked behind the curtain at the kitchen window and saw her standing across the lawn on the edge of the sand dune cliff. Beside her was the wooden staircase that led to the private beach.

Hazel looked like a ghost with her short pajamas billowing in the breeze and her rose gold hair floating away from her shoulders. She spread her arms wide. For a moment fear kicked in and I thought she might jump, but instead she crouched and curled into a tiny ball on the ground. I stared until I realized her shoulders had begun to shake, and soft sobs floated through the window.

I dragged a hand across my face. "Fuck."

There were a thousand reasons why I shouldn't have gone out there. Hazel had upended my life. She was a pain in my ass. A stranger. She was a distraction that I absolutely did not need to entertain.

Despite my logical reasons, I sighed and made my way to the front door. As quietly as I could, I unlocked and opened the door to walk out onto the front porch. Two steps down the stairs and the wood creaked under my weight.

Hazel startled and immediately began wiping away her tears. She stood, clearing her throat and making a beeline back across the grass toward the bus. "Sorry, I didn't mean to wake you."

I held up a hand to stop her. "You didn't."

I lowered myself to the stairs and gestured beside me. "Want a seat?"

She eyed the space next to me before her eyes roamed over my bare chest. A tiny breath escaped between the small gap in her velvety lips. Tension crackled in the night air as she didn't make a move to sit.

After an eternity, she folded herself onto the step beside

me. Her bare knee brushed mine, and I was all too aware of the heat that traveled up my thigh and settled between my legs.

Hazel was quiet beside me as we looked out onto the lawn and toward the beach in the distance. I tried not to stare at her long, bare legs as the wind rustled the leaves in the trees.

"Heavy day," I finally said.

"Yeah." Her humorless laugh made me smile. It was better than more tears.

"Look, I know today didn't go how you had planned. Believe me—me neither—but in a few months it'll all get worked out."

She nodded. "I know. I just can't help but feel like I'm failing her."

I tilted my head toward her. "Your sister?"

Hazel's elbows rested on her knees, and she twined her fingers out in front of her. "Yeah, Olive was always the strong one. So centered and sure of herself. She would do anything to get ahead, no matter what life threw at her. I didn't even know she was sick."

Jesus, that's rough.

I hummed, hoping my vague acknowledgment kept her talking. I liked the sound of her voice in the darkness.

"We were close, even though I was traveling a lot. It was just the two of us growing up. Our mom was a single mom and she died several years ago . . . the same ovarian cancer that took Olive, ironically."

"Fuck." I wiped my hand over my mouth.

"Yeah . . . yay genetics!" Her joke landed flat in the darkness, and a heavy sadness rolled over her shoulders as she slumped. Hazel picked at her coral nail polish. "I found out that I have the same genetic mutation, which means I have to decide to risk the same fate or—" Hazel made a squelching sound and made a removal gesture from her belly outward. "No babies for me. Having kids wasn't even on my radar, and now I feel like I have to make major, life-altering decisions."

I fought the uncontrollable urge to wrap my arms around her and hold her. In the pale light, her vulnerability flickered, and I was a moth to the flame. My hand flexed to keep from giving in.

Between the two of us, there was no doubt in my mind who was better equipped to be a parent.

I had never had kids, but I saw the joy my sister Sylvie got from being a mother. I also deeply understood how the loss of choice was a tough pill to swallow. In the moonlight Hazel looked so young—too young to have to worry about things like cancer and infertility issues.

"That . . ." I fumbled to find the right words.

"Sucks," she said.

We shared a sad laugh. "Yeah, it does. I'm sorry." It was hard not to feel her sadness at having lost her mother and sister. When my mother was taken from me, I was only five, and I had very few actual memories of her. My entire childhood was tainted by my father insisting that she had abandoned us. That she didn't love us enough to stay. I hadn't mourned the loss of my mother—I'd hated her for it.

It hit me that Teddy wasn't that much older when he lost his own mother, only he had Hazel to remind him how loved he was and who the person his mother was. Because of Hazel, he wouldn't have to suffer like I had.

My voice was gravelly and thick. "He's lucky to have you."

Hazel sniffed. She pulled her hands under her chin,

resting her face in them, and looked at me. "Even though I'm a witch?"

A sharp arrow pierced my heart. *Me and my damn mouth.*

A tiny smile tugged at the corner of my mouth. "Even if you are a witch."

She harrumphed, but smiled. For a beat we stared at each other. Temptation scratched my thoughts and a hit of possibilities looped in my brain.

Maybe.
Maybe.
Maybe.

With a stifled yawn, Hazel stood, giving me a clear view of just how thin her pale-yellow nightgown was, and my jaw tightened.

The breeze shifted, molding the thin fabric to her body, clinging to the V between her legs. Beneath the fabric, I could just barely make out the outline of what looked like nipple piercings. My cock instantly sprang to life, perking up at that new, tempting detail. Every inch of me stiffened. The outline of her full breasts taunted me. My hands begged to feel their fullness.

Her exhale thrummed in her throat. "You know, when you're not trying to be an uptight asshole, you're really not so bad."

I stood next to her. The front of her billowing pajamas tickled my bare chest, and I became acutely aware of the inches that separated us. Our mouths were close—*too close.* It had been an eternity since I'd kissed a woman, and I hated myself for even imagining what Hazel's mouth would feel like on mine.

My eyes dipped to her lips, and I heard her quick inhale.

Fuck, she smells good.

It would be wrong—and so fucking complicated. Hazel had just poured her heart out to me and was likely feeling really vulnerable. Not to mention she was under the impression I'd gotten her sister pregnant. Her nephew called me *Dad*, for Christ's sake.

My molars ground together as we stood for what felt like an eternity. As much as I wished I could be the type of man to lean in and take exactly what he wanted, I couldn't. I needed to remain in control.

With clenched fists, I stepped back.

"Look, I—" When my eyes lifted to hers, she stepped forward and slammed her mouth to mine.

I stood in stunned silence for a fraction of a second before instinct took over. One hand fisted in her soft hair, tilting her head to deepen the kiss. She opened for me, and a growl tore through my chest. I fisted her nightgown in my other hand as I pulled her body against mine. Her mouth was lush and soft.

My tongue swept over hers before she stepped back.

The abrupt end to our kiss had me blinking down at her. The back of her hand was pressed against her mouth and her eyes were wide and round with shock.

"Oh my god." Hazel took two stumbling steps down the stairs and turned back to look up at me. "Oh my god."

Her toes sank into the soft grass. Her fingertips pressed into her eye sockets. "I can't believe I did that. I mean—sure, typical, impulsive Hazel, but—oh my god."

"It's fine." My voice was rough and cracked on the last syllable. I cleared my throat and dragged a hand across the back of my neck.

Her cheeks were flaming pink, and I hated myself for loving how it looked on her. I wondered if her skin would flush the same pretty shade as I drove into her with my cock. Her nipples poked through the thin cotton of her nightgown, and I wanted more than anything to know if she was naked beneath it.

The muscles in her legs worked as she nearly sprinted back to the skoolie.

Rooted to the spot, I stared at her in the pale moonlight. "Don't worry, Hazel," I called to her. "You can go back to hating me tomorrow."

At the base of the skoolie, she turned to look at me. Her eyes were dazed, but she hit me with a megawatt smile that was a punch to the chest. She lifted her hand in a wave and nodded. "Deal."

I stayed on the porch steps and watched her climb into the bus. Her shadow moved across the large windows and disappeared toward the back of the vehicle. I scraped the bottom of my foot along the edge of the stair.

What the hell was that about?

I had no business kissing her. I wasn't even attracted to her . . . right?

My dick twitched and I laughed at just how *wrong* I was.

I closed myself within the sanctuary of my house and climbed the stairs to the second floor. Inside my bedroom, I flopped onto the bed and stared at the ceiling. My cock was not getting the memo that Hazel Adams was strictly *off-limits*.

She was too young, too complicated, and altogether too tempting.

With a groan, I slid my hand down my bare stomach, dipping below the waistband of my sweats. My dick was so hard it practically begged me for a quick release. I eased my sweats down below my hips. My eyes shut as I wrapped my fist around my cock.

With a sharp exhale, I thought of her.

I relived the moment she shot forward, pressing her body and mouth against mine. Her kiss was still fresh on my tongue. Her soft hair floated around us, wafting sweet smells of citrus and spice. Her tight body had melded to mine, and for the briefest moment, she'd given in to whatever tension had been fraught between us.

As I worked my fist up and down, I imagined how it would feel to lay her down, spread her open, and drive into her. Sex had always been a means to an end for me, but something about Hazel told me it wouldn't be the same. Like she would find a way to consume me as I devoured her.

I grunted and panted as I stroked myself. It jerked and pulsed in my hand, and I imagined shoving my cock into her and making her scream my name. My dick surged painfully against my hand, and I worked it, ping-ponging between images of stretching her open and slipping the shaft down her throat. I moaned and doubled my efforts, squeezing harder as I stroked.

If Hazel had just been some tourist on vacation, things would be different. We wouldn't have remnants of the past hanging between us. No questions about paternity or guardianship or fake smiles covering old hurts.

No, if it were different, it would simply be her and me.

Maybe she wouldn't mind when I took control or used filthy words to tell her exactly how I'd make her come. Maybe she'd beg for it. Maybe she'd match me stroke for stroke as she rode my cock and cried out for more. I jerked myself to the image of her perfect, pierced tits bouncing as we fucked. I came in quick, hot pulses at the thought of her riding me, slack-jawed and lost in the moment.

With my head against the bed, I exhaled. The quiet around me closed in and self-hatred was hot on its heels.

I cleaned up in the en suite bathroom without bothering to turn on the light. I didn't need to see the prick in the mirror staring back at me. In my bedroom, I paused at the window and gently pushed the curtain aside to look down at the bus.

This was complicated.

A real problem.

I stared hard at the bus parked in my driveway. I wasn't used to a problem I couldn't find my way out of. I was about to turn when a small light at the back of the bus flicked on, then off again.

Shit. Could she see me?

I eased back into the shadows of my room when the light flicked on, then off again. Curious, I reached over to the lamp by my side. With a quick flick, I flashed it on, then off again.

Maybe it was ridiculous, but somehow it felt like it meant something. Like a silent reassurance that things might just work themselves out.

But who was I kidding? Things didn't just magically work themselves out for men like me.

No, men like me were handed problems and expected to put in the work to figure shit out.

And I would.

But damn was I exhausted.

~

THE NEXT MORNING I remained a prisoner in my own house. Weekends for some meant days off work to rest or for weekend warriors to chip away at random house projects.

Not me.

For me, Saturdays were just another day, and oftentimes that meant working at the office while my siblings ran off and lived their lives.

They were starting families and falling in love.

I was stuck.

Noises from the front yard seeped into my awareness, and I slammed back the bitter remnants of my morning cup of coffee.

Forgoing a full suit, I'd dressed in dark slacks and a short-sleeved knit shirt. Despite jerking myself off to the image of Hazel—*twice*—I slept like shit and was still keyed up. The musical notes of her laughter floated through the open window, and I slammed it closed.

I'll just turn the air conditioner back on.

With a frustrated growl, I grabbed my keys and sailed out the door. My steps came up short when I spotted another car in the drive. Teddy zipped past me with a squeal, a trail of bubbles floating behind him. Hot on his heels was Penny Sullivan. She was chasing him, but clearly giving the kid the advantage of slowing her run so he could escape.

I frowned, trying to work out why the hell she was in my yard.

"Morning!" a woman's voice called to me, and I squinted in the sun.

Across the yard, Lark Sullivan was standing next to Hazel and waving.

I guess that explains Penny.

I offered a terse smile but didn't return her greeting.

Next to the skoolie, Hazel was arranging two rectangular foam mats. A bottle of water was next to one.

Rhythmic, undulating beats flowed from a wireless speaker next to the other mat.

I walked toward my car, refusing to make eye contact with Hazel for fear she'd somehow know the depraved thoughts I'd had about her since last night. When she walked into the skoolie without looking my way, I could breathe again.

"Hi, JP," Lark called once more. "Hazel and I became friends at the beach."

I nodded. "I see that."

Lark smiled and smoothed a hand over her pregnant belly. "She's going to show me some prenatal yoga moves. I hope it's okay that Penny pals around the yard with Teddy while we stretch."

I paused and leaned my forearm on the open door to my BMW. "Would you leave if I said it wasn't?"

"No." Her smile widened as her playful eyes twinkled. I had turned to get into my car when she stopped me. "I was telling Hazel that we're having a party at the speakeasy. Sylvie will be there. You should come."

I eyed Lark. She was always kind and impartial to the King–Sullivan feud despite being married to Wyatt. It was still a mind-fuck to remember that after years of disdain, our families were bonded by Duke and Sylvie's marriage.

"I'll think about it," I lied.

No, the only thing I'd be thinking about is Hazel's ass and how her tight black top was cropped too short. It was a sick hell knowing those matching bike shorts revealed that my imagination was nothing compared to the real thing.

NINE

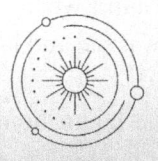

HAZEL

"Now remember"—I crouched to straighten Teddy's already perfectly straight tie, a bolo tie this time—"just be polite, and if the food sucks, I'll get you something later . . . you don't have to *tell* someone their cooking is trash."

Teddy's lips twisted. "That was *one* time."

I squeezed his shoulder and stood tall. Some deep yet untapped maternal instinct inside me wanted to ruffle his hair and pull him in for a hug, but I held back. My relationship with Teddy was still finding its footing, and I didn't want to push him too hard or make him think that I was trying to replace his mother in any way.

Like when you kissed the father of her child.

Guilt racked me. I still hadn't figured out what came over me. Maybe it was the way he quietly listened to me talk about Olive. Maybe it was remembering the sweet interaction he'd had with Teddy. Hell, maybe it was as simple as how ridiculously hot he looked without a shirt on.

Whatever it was, I'd officially lost my damn mind. I could hardly think about anything other than how, instead of pushing me away, *he'd leaned in* and fisted my nightgown as he deepened the kiss. He'd taken control in a way that was wholly unexpected and brutally hot.

I squeezed my thighs together and shoved the memory into a little box in my mind where I could take it out and use it to get off when I was sad and lonely.

Again.

I squinted up at the house numbers that matched the address Lark had given me for her aunt Tootie's place. My knuckles rapped at the front door of the large farmhouse. The massive wraparound porch was stylishly decorated with plush seating and cozy nooks for enjoying iced tea on hot summer days. The large windows with tall shutters gleamed, and I sighed at how gorgeous the home was.

As a fellow influencer, I'd watched Kate Miller renovate her aunt's farmhouse with her now-husband. It truly was a work of art. During the renovation, Kate's Instagram had blown up, and she and her husband, Beckett, even had their own television show now. A flutter of nervous butterflies tickled my belly.

Keep it cool. Casual.

The front door to the farmhouse opened, and Sylvie answered with a smile and an adorable little boy on her hip.

"Hi! Come on in." She shifted, allowing space for us to enter. "Lark mentioned you might stop by. We're glad you could make it!"

Inside, the farmhouse was an open concept with the living room to the left and a gorgeous kitchen with a huge island to the right. From the back of the kitchen, a man walked through a doorway. He was tall and imposing with dark brows and a scowl. The little boy on Sylvie's hip lit up as soon as he walked in, and the man's face softened.

"I can take him," the man said, already reaching for the little boy.

Sylvie smiled, handing the young boy over. "Thank you. Duke, this is Hazel. Hazel, my husband, Duke, and our son, Gus."

I offered a polite wave and smile. "It's a pleasure to meet you. This is my nephew Teddy."

Duke nodded. "Nice to meet you. I'm going to head down unless you need anything?"

Sylvie beamed at her husband. "All good here." She turned to Teddy. "Duke is going down to the speakeasy. Would you like to go with and see the secret entrance? Penny is already down there."

Teddy looked up at me.

I nodded and smiled. "Go on if you want to."

With a shy smile, Teddy followed Duke to the back of the house. As they disappeared around a corner, I heard Duke say, "I like that tie, man." I bit back a smile.

"I should formally introduce myself." She stuck out her hand. "I'm Sylvie Sullivan, formally King. I'm JP's sister."

I shook her hand and smiled. "Nice to officially meet you. I never had the chance to thank you for your help when Teddy wandered off."

She swatted the air between us. "Oh, it's nothing." She turned to follow Duke. "Come on. We're having drinks in the speakeasy, and then we'll enjoy dinner out on the back patio if the weather cooperates."

Through the gloriously renovated home, I soaked in every detail. The doorway opened to a large mudroom at the back of the house. The floors were made of a weathered brick, and there was a bench just inside the door. There were hooks for hanging jackets and beautifully painted cabinets. It amazed me that no amount of television or pictures could truly show the craftsmanship of the house.

In the floor, a trapdoor was propped open. We walked

to the edge and I peered in. Voices and jazzy music floated up the stairs.

"Pretty cool, right?" Sylvie could practically read my mind. "When Kate and Beckett were renovating this place for Tootie, they found it. We don't know how long it had been forgotten, but it's strange to think it had been there all the time."

In awe, I followed Sylvie down. Sconces illuminated the path downstairs, and though the stairwell was narrow, it opened to a large space beneath the house. A huge oak bar was along one wall. An ornate mirror was behind the bar, and several framed photographs were beside it.

Teddy and Penny were sipping fizzy drinks with maraschino cherries while Duke propped Gus higher on his hip. At one of the stools, Lark smiled at the man mixing drinks behind the bar.

She turned to me. "Glad you could make it!" She gestured to the man who had held her attention. "Wyatt is mixing up bourbon lemonades if you want one. Regular lemonade for us lightweights." She ran a hand over her belly with a laugh.

I stepped forward. "I guess I'll try the bourbon one."

"Coming up." Wyatt smiled and started mixing. I turned in a circle to take in the speakeasy. Beneath the earth, it should have felt cramped and dingy, but instead it was rustic and spacious. In my bones, I could feel the presence of everyone who'd come before me. It was a place steeped in history, where secrets were whispered and plans were conspired.

I leaned in to look at the framed photographs on the wall. One in particular caught my eye. It was a picture of two men and a woman. All three were smiling and dressed to the nines in clothes that reminded me of the 1920s. The two men wore dark pants and dress shoes. One had on a dark tie, loosened at the neck, while the other wore a light, collared knit shirt with the top two buttons undone. The woman was in a dainty floral print dress and heels. Her hands were on her hips, and she was captured mid-laugh.

Lark sighed next to me. "I love that photograph."

"Who were they?" I asked. My eyes were pinned to the man on the right. If you squinted hard enough, he'd be a dead ringer for JP.

"That's Philo Sullivan, Helen Sinclair, and James King." When I glanced at her, Lark's eyebrows waggled. "They were all bootleggers together. Philo and Helen married and left the business. James took it hard, and he teamed up with Helen's brother to stir up trouble."

"More than trouble," Wyatt scoffed as he slid a drink in front of me.

I picked it up and saluted him in thanks before taking a tiny sip. It was sweet and tart with just the right amount of kick from the bourbon.

Wyatt wiped down the bar top. "A long-standing feud. Years and *years* of Sullivans and Kings being rivals."

"And it started with these three?" I asked, utterly intrigued.

"It's where it started," Sylvie said as she climbed onto a stool next to Lark. She lifted a shoulder. "But, unfortunately, my dad made it infinitely worse."

Duke clamped a hand at the base of her neck in a show of affection and solemn support. He gazed down at his wife. "But it ended with us."

Pride and love were evident in his voice. Poets could write epic tomes based on how Duke looked at his wife, and they still wouldn't measure up. A lump formed in my throat.

"And now look at us." Lark raised her lemonade. "Sullivans and Kings celebrating the end of summer with a barbecue and babies. Speaking of Kings"—Lark looked at me—"did JP decide not to show?"

My mouth opened and closed.

Was I supposed to know? Did parking in his driveway and accidentally kissing him mean I was supposed to keep tabs on him?

Sylvie snorted. "Oh, I doubt he'll come. JP doesn't really do family."

My brows scrunched. "What do you mean he doesn't *do* family?"

Sylvie's smile slowly melted. She swallowed and tried to smooth things over. "Well"—she gestured toward Teddy, who was giggling with Penny—"maybe things have changed."

My molars pressed together, and I swallowed past the burn in my throat.

Even his siblings didn't think very highly of him.
Fantastic.

An awkward silence yawned and filled the room.

A nervous laugh tittered from my throat as I suddenly felt like a fool for accepting Lark's invitation. "The speakeasy really is very cool. You'd never know something with so much character was down here."

Thankfully Lark understood my sudden turn in conversation. Her hands tapped a rhythm on the smooth oak bar top. "Kate and Beckett spruced it up. We have no idea how long it had been hidden away, but it was forgotten for a long time."

Sylvie's brown eyes locked with mine in a soft, knowing look. "It's amazing what you can uncover if you look beneath the surface." She turned to the kids. "Okay, who's hungry?"

~

BY THE TIME dinner was served, voices overlapped and my head was spinning. On the back patio of the farmhouse, two long tables were nestled under a wood pergola. More of JP's siblings showed up. I was introduced to his oldest brother Abel, his wife, and their twins. Royal and his girlfriend, Veda, had arrived just in time to eat. Burgers and hot dogs were cooked on the grill, and after everyone had eaten, the kids took to chasing Tootie's chickens in the yard.

Despite the feud everyone loved to talk about, Kings and Sullivans were intermixed at the tables, reaching over one another and generally having a relaxed and pleasant time.

I stood in awe on the outskirts, a quiet onlooker soaking it all in. I'd never been a part of a large family, let alone one as big as that one. From the corner of my eye, a huge rooster pecked at the grass.

"Watch out for that one," Beckett called to me. He pointed a long skewer with a marshmallow at the tip in the rooster's direction. "That one's a son of a bitch."

Kate's laugh rang out, and they were folded into the conversation about the perfect marshmallow toastiness. Movement at the corner of the yard, near the driveway, caught my attention.

My heart pounded as I saw JP standing at the edge of the lawn. He was frowning, because of course he was, but he also looked a little lost. He was dressed in jeans and a fitted navy T-shirt. The fabric strained against his muscular chest and hung closely to his trim hips. My jaw went slack at the way he effortlessly pulled off the casual look.

In his hands was a pie box. His eyes scanned the crowd, but JP didn't attempt to join the group. Instead, he clung to the outskirts, quietly observing and seemingly unsure of himself. It was jarring to see his cocky facade falter.

It dawned on me that he was an outsider amid his own family, and my heart ached for him.

Our eyes locked, and when the corner of his mouth lifted, my heart flopped over. His subtle shrug was enough to melt my insides to goo. I shook my head and hid my smile behind a sip of lemonade before starting off in his direction.

I stood in front of him and looked up. "Hi."

His eyes flicked to my mouth and back up again. "Hi."

"What are you doing here?" I asked.

His eyes narrowed. "I could ask you the same thing. It's *my* family after all."

I playfully shrugged and took an exaggerated sip of my drink. "I was invited. Were you?"

He chuckled. "Ouch."

I leaned over to look through the clear plastic top of the box in his hands. "Cherry? Classic choice."

He tsked. "Strawberry rhubarb. It's MJ's favorite." He flicked his finger through the bottom strands of my long hair. "It also kind of looks like a certain strawberry blonde I know too."

A flutter danced across my chest. It was surprising to hear that JP might be considerate after all.

Had he lost as much sleep as I had last night?

"Is Teddy having fun?" he asked as he watched the kids squeal across the far end of the lawn.

I laughed. "A ball. More kids showed up too. Apparently Penny was telling them about how a chicken named

Henrietta and something called a Beakface had a little romance. There are new chicks in the henhouse. I think he's half in love with Penny already."

JP chuckled. "He needs to be careful with the wild ones. They'll put you under a spell."

His eyes glittered, and I wondered if his *spell* reference was intentional after he'd called me a witch.

Unsure of what to say, I cleared my throat. Behind me, I heard Royal call out: "Look who decided to grace us with his presence!"

JP scoffed and shook his head. As he walked past me, he lowered his voice. "Wish me luck."

I watched in awe as he sauntered up to the group. Gone was the unsure boy on the outskirts, and in his place stood a man full of swagger and confidence. He greeted his siblings and their spouses along with the rest of the Sullivans.

JP offered a polite nod to the Sullivans' aunt Tootie, then bent down and placed a soft kiss on his aunt Bug's cheek.

"Don't wait around for us to start playing trumpets, sit down already." Bug fussed with her napkin, but when he pulled back a chair to sit next to her, she smiled.

It comforted me to know I wasn't the only one there who felt like a bit of an interloper. There was something fascinating about the Sullivans and the Kings, and the mystery only deepened when Duke leaned forward.

He looked over his shoulder, seemingly content that the kids were out of earshot. "We've got news about the lake."

TEN

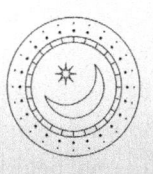

JP

My ears pricked up when Duke mentioned Wabash Lake. When my father was arrested, it was presumed that the lake was likely the area he'd hidden evidence . . . maybe even our mother's body. My eyes moved over the distant blueberry fields to where Wabash Lake was nestled within the forest at the heart of the state-funded hiking trail.

My blood pooled just thinking about it.

Duke was all business. "The Department of Natural Resources gave us the green light. I signed off on permission for them to use my land as a bypass. They'll access the lake through my land so as to not disturb the hiking trail."

Sylvie's hand held her husband's. "They might not find anything, but at least we can stop wondering."

Eyes were cast downward as a somber hush floated over the tables. The tension was palpable, and a knot formed behind my shoulder blade. I wanted to run. To break something. To make this all go away so I could stop seeing the sad looks on everyone's faces.

To my left, a soft throat clearing caught my attention. "If I may?" Hazel was digging through her oversize purse when our attention was drawn to her. She pulled a small candle from her bag and set it at the center of the table.

Just then, Teddy and Penny walked up to the table. "Oh!" Teddy exclaimed. "Setting intentions is my *favorite*."

Curious glances sliced his way, but I did my best to offer him an encouraging smile.

What the fuck was happening right now?

Hazel lit the candle and held out her hands. We all stared.

Jesus, maybe she really was a witch ...

"It's all right," she said. "Hold hands, please."

She pinned me with a *come the fuck on* look, and I held my hands to my left and right. One by one, Sullivans and Kings all joined hands around the table, the lit candle flickering in the center.

Hazel smiled and closed her eyes. "We honor Maryann King. We lift you up with our hearts. May you find peace and grant peace to those who loved you."

Everyone's eyes were closed in silent prayer, but the entire time she spoke, I stared at her. With her face turned up to the setting sun, she was stunning, completely unaware and unfazed by the curious peeks of those around her. When her eyes opened, she let out a deep, cleansing exhale and grinned.

"That was lovely," Sylvie said softly. "Thank you."

"May she find the rest her soul craves." Hazel's throat cleared. "And may the person responsible for her disappearance suffer the wrath of the universe by any means necessary, including, but not limited to, a tragic fall down a flight of stairs."

Kate sputtered as a cackle cracked out of Royal. Tootie whispered a soft *oh my* that was the group's undoing. A ripple of much-needed laughter passed through the circle.

Hazel extinguished the candle with a quick puff. "Who wants pie?" she asked with a sparkle in her eye.

We dropped our hands and started passing plates for dessert.

Royal leaned down to whisper in my ear. "Did she just cast a hex on Dad?"

"Let's hope it works . . ." My brother Abel grumbled beside me, pulling his wife closer to him.

I stifled a laugh. Apparently Hazel was the breath of fresh air we needed to lighten the mood.

Conversations flowed around me, and I was surprised when Teddy sat beside me.

"Did you get a s'more?" I asked.

His lips twisted and he shook his head. "Too messy."

"You like pie?" I slid a small paper plate with a slice of pie in front of him.

Teddy poked it with a fork and tried to dissect it.

"Here." I took a large forkful of pie from my plate and shoved it in my mouth. "See? It's good."

Satisfied, Teddy took a scoop and shoved it into his mouth. He smiled and nodded, and something shifted in my chest. I bumped my shoulder into his and took another bite. When I looked up, Hazel was staring.

"What?" I asked around a mouthful of pie.

My sister MJ leaned toward Hazel. "Did your heart just melt? Because mine did." MJ sighed and rested her chin on her hand. "You're so cute."

"I am not cute," I grumbled, shoving the last bite of pie into my mouth. "And stop talking about your melting heart. We're Kings."

The women laughed, and I suppressed the smile that threatened to spread across my face. I needed to keep my attention on Teddy. I was supposed to be getting to know him, not obsessing over his far-too-tempting aunt.

MJ and Hazel had started talking about her skoolie when their conversation piqued my interest.

"What about taking a hot bath? Or even a shower?" MJ asked.

Hazel smiled, seemingly used to the question. "No baths, unfortunately. There is a shower in the skoolie, but it's not great. A lot of times I find it easier to visit a campsite with showers rather than having to constantly empty the gray water tanks."

I frowned. That was inconvenient . . . and also kind of gross.

"But even with the rooms there's hardly any privacy, right? You're practically on top of one another, I'd guess." MJ was curious, but I still noticed the subtle shift in Hazel's energy.

There wasn't a malicious bone in MJ's body, but I could detect that Hazel wasn't used to the nosy, direct questioning of my curious little sister.

To make matters worse, my ever-wary brother Abel decided to step in. "You should be mindful of predators. A woman and child traveling solo is a risk." He'd spent time in prison and couldn't help his mind from wandering to the worst-case scenario in many situations.

"If you want," he continued, "the brewery has twenty-four-seven security cameras. It wouldn't be a problem if you parked there."

"Or if you need a break from the bus," his wife Sloane interjected, "there's a cute little bed-and-breakfast we love—the Wild Iris."

It was clear we weren't all in on some inside joke as

Abel's cheeks flamed red and Sloane playfully leaned into him with a giggle.

Lee Sullivan leaned far back in his chair. His eyes sparkled with mischief. "There's a couple of guys down at the fire station who wouldn't mind a little security detail. They're used to overnight hours and would be happy to make sure no one bothered a pretty woman like yourself... maybe even show you around town on their days off."

His eyebrows waggled.

When my eyes narrowed to slits in his direction, he tipped his chin toward me. "Besides, that's not really your kind of thing, right, boss?"

Royal cackled from his seat at the end of the table. "You're not wrong. JP was born with a ledger in his hand and a stick up his ass."

The collective laughter grated on my nerves.

"There's a reason they called him *Johnny Protocol* in high school," Wyatt offered with a chuckle.

"I thought it was *Just Perfect*?" Lark asked her husband with a frown.

Apparently busting my balls had become a cross-family affair.

"Are we done?" I asked, doing my best to appear unaffected by their playful ribbing. In fact, none of the childish nicknames from high school carried any weight.

I followed protocol because I *had to*. I tried to be perfect because if I wasn't, I was met with my father's disdain.

It became clear early on that the weight of King Equities was mine to bear, and every decision I made was so that they didn't have to.

I did it to protect my siblings, whether they knew that or not.

I gently slapped my napkin onto the table. "While I'm

sure she appreciates your concern, it's unnecessary. Hazel and Teddy are moving into my house."

I don't know why I fucking said it.

Maybe it was the way MJ's questions were borderline judgy or the subtly resigned tone of Hazel's answers. Maybe it was the genuine concern in Abel's voice. Maybe it was the fact that Lee thought horny firefighters camping outside her bus was a good idea.

Whatever it was, I made a decision.

It was done.

"Oh . . . well, that makes sense," MJ said with a slow, widening grin.

My eyes flicked up to see Hazel pinning me with a death stare from across the table.

Clearly we hadn't discussed her moving in *at all*.

Beside me, Teddy perked up. "Move in? Do I get my own room? Can I pick it out? Will there be a bookshelf in it? Can I have a desk to do science projects on?"

My eyes stayed trained on the pie crumbs in front of me. "Yeah, um . . ." I circled my fork as I searched for a plausible answer. "We'll figure it out."

Like a shot, Teddy was up from the table and racing across the yard toward Penny and her cousins. "Penny! I'm getting a bigger room!"

I finally grew the balls to glance up at Hazel, who was staring at me with one eyebrow perched higher on her forehead.

She was not pleased.

With a low chuckle, MJ eased herself away from the table, giving us space as the conversation continued without us.

A sheepish smile was all I could muster. "So," I chuckled. "Want to move in?"

ELEVEN

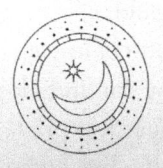

JP

I had really stepped in it.

After the family barbecue at the Sullivan place, Teddy begged to ride with me while Hazel drove the skoolie back to my house. I glanced up at him in the mirror, satisfied that he was safely strapped into the new booster seat I'd gotten for him. He rambled the entire drive home, asking about me, the town, why the farmers planted wildflowers near the blueberry bushes, and about a thousand other questions I didn't have the answers to.

Why couldn't he be curious about mergers and acquisitions again?

When we pulled into my drive, he was passed out cold, slumped against the door. Soft snores floated out of his open mouth.

I was grateful for the moment of absolute silence.

While I waited for Hazel to park the skoolie, I looked at him in the mirror. His bolo tie was askew, and his dark hair was poking up in all directions.

It sucked that the kid hadn't gotten a fair shake—his

mom was dead, he thought *I* was his dad, of all people, and he was clearly years ahead of his peers in terms of style.

At least he had a badass aunt who was more than likely a witch with a heart of gold.

Better shake than most of us got.

I climbed out of the car and closed the door as quietly as I could. I may be a heartless prick, but I didn't want to be another adult in his life who made things *more* complicated.

Hazel locked up the skoolie and walked up to me with a huge yawn. In her hand was a small duffel bag of what I assumed were overnight essentials.

I gestured toward the back seat. "He fell asleep."

Hazel hiked the bag onto her shoulder and pulled open the car door. "Can you grab him? He's getting really heavy."

I frowned and hesitated. I was out of my depth with no idea how not to wake a sleeping child. Being unprepared was not a feeling I enjoyed.

"Trust me, he sleeps like a log. Just unbuckle him and throw him over your shoulder." Hazel didn't wait for me and instead started walking toward my house.

Unsure of exactly how to manage it, I leaned in to unbuckle Teddy. His breath whooshed out in a soft, sleepy rhythm. He smelled like dirt and too much sugar.

As carefully as I could, I slid an arm around his back. Teddy slumped forward, and I caught him with my shoulder. True to Hazel's word, he shifted and moaned but didn't wake.

I stood, jostling him gently to get him adjusted. His limp arms hung over my shoulder, and his head rested against my chest.

My heart hammered beneath my shirt.

The sun was just starting to set over the lake, and the

sky was splashed with inky blues and a riot of pinks. At the top of the stairs, Hazel leaned against the post with a soft smile as she watched me.

"You're a natural," she said as I approached.

I grunted in acknowledgment, ignoring the tightening in my chest as I carried him up the stairs. I carefully shifted Teddy to the other shoulder.

"Keys are in my pocket," I announced.

Her eyebrows shot up. "You want me to fish them out for you?" she teased.

I exhaled, despite my traitorous dick perking up at her offer. "I got it."

Her soft laugh floated on the cool breeze. With not much grace and an awkward shove, I managed to unlock and open the door, stepping aside to let Hazel enter first.

She quietly slipped inside, and I closed the door with my foot. I headed through the open living space toward the stairs in the back. Without waiting for her, I climbed the stairs and walked Teddy to the end of the hallway and into a spare bedroom. Originally intended to be an office, it was a corner room with built-in bookshelves and a reading nook I thought he might like. The bed was staged with a no-nonsense gray comforter and several pillows.

With one hand, I pulled the comforter back and gently deposited Teddy into the bed. He immediately rolled over and curled into a ball. The world dissolved as I stared down at him.

Could he really be my kid?

I hadn't let myself even entertain the thought, but for a brief moment, with his black lashes swooped low over his cheeks, it was hard to not see the similarities. From his dark features to his serious personality, every interaction I had with him made me question it more.

Who had Olive Adams been? Where had we met? How could I have not known for so long that I'd fathered a child?

Frustration ate at me and I turned on my heels. My fist clenched as I thought of all the unanswered questions that swirled in my mind.

I was the man with the answers. This wasn't at all how I'd built my life to be.

As I walked past, I peeked into another unused bedroom, surprised to see Hazel hadn't followed me upstairs to claim a room for herself and turn in for the evening.

Of course she didn't.

With a sigh, I walked back downstairs in search of her.

The house was quiet as I surveyed the living room and kitchen. I quickly peeked out a window and didn't see her at the skoolie either.

I braced my hands against the counter and let my head hang. Stress had been building for weeks, and I felt at my breaking point. I had constantly been juggling it all —work, my dad, Hazel and Teddy's arrival, my fucked-up family.

I could feel my chest cracking open, and I didn't have time for a breakdown. I needed to keep my shit together and power through—like I had always done.

With a sigh, I looked up.

The breath was stolen from my lungs.

Far in the distance, she was walking along the beach. Much like the night I'd seen her in her nightgown, Hazel looked like a ghost. This time she walked along the water's edge with her sandals in her hand, gently kicking her feet as the waves lapped over them.

Something deep and feral coiled in my gut. For the briefest moment I enjoyed watching her—imagining what it would be like if she were mine, if we hadn't stopped that kiss.

But it was impossible.

Her nephew was very likely my kid, which meant, at some point, I'd been intimate with her sister. Shooting my shot with her would affirm I really was the asshole I'd worked so hard not to become.

The breeze that floated through the kitchen window was cool. I watched as Hazel wrapped her arms around her middle and I shook my head.

Rifling through my liquor cabinet, I pulled out a bottle of Blanton's single-barrel bourbon and two glasses. On my way out the door, I draped a long-sleeved flannel jacket over my forearm.

With only the light of the setting sun, I walked across the lawn to the bluff. Using the wooden staircase, I climbed down the dune and made my way toward the beach. Hazel had turned and was walking up the beach toward me.

She kicked a small wave and smiled as I closed the distance between us.

I lifted my arm to gesture toward the flannel jacket. "It got chilly."

Hazel's smile widened as she grabbed the jacket from my arm. "Thanks. I was under the impression it was still summer, but man . . . sure feels like fall tonight."

I nodded and herded her toward a large piece of driftwood. "Around this time, evenings get chilly. It's that slow transition into fall that lets us know summer is pretty much done with."

Hazel leaned against the tree trunk that had fallen and been stripped of its bark by the tide. "Mmm," she hummed and looked out onto the indigo waters of Lake Michigan. "That's okay. Autumn's my favorite anyway."

"Me too." I balanced the two cups on the tree trunk. "Bourbon?"

"Sure." She smiled and I poured two fingers in each glass.

Hazel lifted one glass. "To roommates?"

I lifted my glass. "Uh." I shook my head. "Sure. To roommates."

Hazel took a deep sip, and I watched the muscles in her neck work as the alcohol coated her throat. "Didn't want to run that one by me first?"

I sheepishly smiled like a kid who'd just gotten into deep shit. "About that . . . I just didn't like people thinking I was okay with your current, possibly unsafe, living conditions. But if you want to stay in the skoolie, that's fine with me."

"And break Teddy's heart? I couldn't possibly." She took another sip. "It's okay. In all honesty, it will be nice to have a dishwasher again." Her eyes moved to me. "You do have a dishwasher, right?"

I chuckled. "Yes, I do. Two, in fact."

Her eyes rolled playfully. "Of course you do. You're so extra."

I scoffed. "What? There's a scullery kitchen for prep behind the main one. It just makes sense. Is my home not up to your standards?"

Hazel scrunched her nose. "I mean, it is ridiculously fancy, but . . ."

"But what?" I prodded.

"It's very . . . sterile." She looked at me, daring me to disagree.

Trouble was, she was right. I conceded with a shrug and sipped my bourbon. "You know, it also has a hot shower and a toilet that flushes."

A gentle laugh crackled out of her as her hand came to her collarbone. "*Oh . . . you spoil me.*"

I leaned against the driftwood, both of us facing the water.

I could see it—what it would be like to spoil her. Like it would be the easiest thing in the world.

If only it weren't so complicated.

We both stayed quiet, watching the rolling tide lapping at the beach. It was calm and peaceful as night descended and tiny sparks of starlight overtook the vast sky.

"Thank you for trying to get to know him," she finally said.

I nodded. "He's a neat kid, but *man*, does he not stop asking questions."

Hazel giggled. "You have no idea. On the way here, I swear I was doing everything in my power to avoid the question game. It doesn't help that I think he might actually be smarter than me."

I smirked, a chuckle pushing through my nose. "I think maybe you've got more going for you than you give yourself credit for."

She shifted, dramatically blinking in my direction. "JP King . . . was that a compliment?"

I rolled my eyes and covered my sly smile with a sip of bourbon. "Hardly."

Hazel's eyes narrowed on me. "Are you sure you aren't going to fall in love with me if we move in?"

I shouldn't have liked the way our playful banter made me feel. It was as though the stress of work, my family, *her*— none of it mattered. For a split second, I was just a man sharing an intimate moment on the star-soaked beach with a gorgeous free spirit of a woman.

A woman whose presence I had no right enjoying as

much as I did. But for a moment I could be the kind of man I always hoped to be.

"Please. I make my living assessing risk and reward." I sighed and stretched my legs out in front of me. "Trust me, this is just business."

It amazed me how easily the lie rolled right off my tongue.

TWELVE

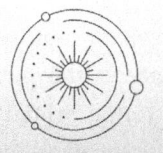

HAZEL

I sat up with a jolt when awareness crept into my peaceful dreaming. Songbirds chirped through the open window, and the sun was much, much higher than it should have been. I took stock of my surroundings, my heart rate leveling when I realized I was still in the spare bedroom of JP's house.

The king-size bed was plush, and sleeping in it had been like floating on a cloud of down and fluffy pillows. *Six*, to be exact. I flopped back down and pulled one over my face. It was poofy and warm and I wanted to drown in it.

I think maybe I've been sleeping in a bus for too long.

I stretched my toes and glanced at the small clock on the table beside the bed. I'd definitely overslept, but I still pouted about not getting another thirty minutes in the world's most comfortable bed.

Resigned to starting my day, I piled my hair on top of my head and slipped on a pair of cutoff jean shorts. The air was cool, so I opted for an oversize sweatshirt with a luna moth and flowers on it.

After brushing my teeth, I went in search of Teddy. My

steps creaked on the hand-scraped, wood-plank flooring. There was so much untapped potential in JP's house. He'd built it with solid bones and expensive features, but it lacked any warmth.

What it needs is a woman's soulful touch.

My hands glided across the picture frame molding in the hallway. The door to the primary suite was on my left, and my heart skipped as I walked past. It was empty, and I was just snoopy enough to take a little peek inside.

Unsurprisingly, JP's bed was made with crisp lines and an unfussy pillow arrangement. The walls were the same boring gray as the rest of the house. Not a painting or picture frame in sight.

Boys.

My eyes settled on the wingback chair and small table, curious about what book he was reading. I looked at the little lamp, remembering how my pulse spiked on the evening when he'd returned my little flicker of light. I hadn't seen him but I could *feel* his gaze on me that night. I'd flicked the light on and off, and sparks danced under my skin when he returned the gesture.

As I descended the stairs, I wondered what it meant. Was it a flicker of hope that there was a gentle human inside him after all? JP was a puzzle written in a cipher without a key.

When I reached the bottom of the stairs, I was hit with the warm, inviting smell of coffee and syrup. My stomach grumbled.

As I rounded the corner, my feet came up short and my eyes went wide. Teddy was standing on a chair in front of the kitchen island, covered in flour. Next to him, JP wasn't much better. A streak of white powder was dusted on his cheek, and his scowl was out in full force.

Teddy held the box of pancake mix up to read. "It says the batter *should* be lumpy."

JP held a spoonful upside down, the thick batter clinging to it. "Lumpy is one thing, but this is hard as a rock. It's practically concrete."

"Maybe we should ask Hazel if she knows?" Teddy asked.

JP shook his head as I clung to the wall, trying to stay out of sight. "No. Let's let her sleep. You can surprise her with breakfast."

"My mom used to make really good pancakes. They did *not* look like this. Hopefully it's the thought that counts."

JP sighed and looked at Teddy. "Do you think it's too late to hire a private chef or something?"

I stifled a giggle as my heart rolled.

Teddy laughed, and I guessed he didn't realize JP was probably serious. "Your mom sounds cool. Anyone who could make good pancakes is all right in my book."

I swallowed past the lump in my throat at the kind and casual mention of my sister.

"Did your mom ever make you pancakes?" Teddy asked.

I leaned in, soaking in every word.

JP was silent for heavy moments. "I'm not really sure, pal. By the time I was your age, she was already gone."

"She died too?" Teddy's innocence was a piercing blow to my heart.

JP cleared his throat, and his eyes were trained on the lumpy disaster in front of him. "Uh . . . yeah, bud. She did. Only I wasn't lucky like you. I didn't have nice pancake memories or a cool aunt to take care of me. My aunt Bug was around, but she's more the no-nonsense type."

The hurt laced in his voice spurred me forward. "What smells so delicious?"

I beamed at them, pretending to not have eavesdropped on the last few minutes of their conversation.

Teddy leaned over the bowl, attempting to cover it with his arms, effectively getting smears of batter on his elbows. "Don't look! It's a surprise!"

"Admit it. It's a disaster, man." JP looked at me and shrugged. "We tried." He gestured toward the coffeepot on the counter. "Coffee's hot."

I poured myself a cup and settled into one of the hightop chairs tucked into the kitchen island. I watched as the two fumbled around each other and did their best to finish breakfast. The pancakes came out as rock-hard little charcoal briquettes. They were dense and dry, and no amount of maple syrup helped to choke them down.

"Mmm." I dabbed at the corners of my mouth.

JP's flat stare nearly launched me into a fit of giggles. "These are terrible."

My mouth popped open and Teddy burst into laughter.

"What?" JP said. "I'm not going to lie to the kid. It's not his fault I can't cook."

I had gone to take another bite when JP slid the plate away from me. "Don't eat that. Last thing I need is you choking on a pancake and me having to give you mouth-to-mouth."

My cheeks flamed as a hot blush crept over my face. I knew *exactly* what his mouth felt like on mine, and I certainly wouldn't have minded it happening again.

Teddy lifted his fork in the air. "The Heimlich."

"Hmm?" I asked, still dazed from JP's offhand comment.

"When you're choking you need the Heimlich, not

mouth-to-mouth resuscitation." He took another syrup-soaked bite.

A sly smirk flickered across JP's features as his gaze lowered to my mouth. I could feel my heartbeat between my legs as every thought dissolved.

"You're right." With a scrape of metal against ceramic, JP dumped the pancakes into the trash. "I vote coffee and doughnuts from the Sugar Bowl."

JP patted Teddy's shoulder. "Go clean up and we can head to town."

With giddy laughter, Teddy leaped off the stool and started toward the stairs.

"Need help?" I asked, turning to watch him run through the house.

Without turning back, Teddy shouted, "Not unless you want to see these buns!"

I sighed and pinched the bridge of my nose with a laugh. "Lovely."

JP smiled into his coffee mug, and I eyed him behind lowered lashes. "So . . . am I also invited to coffee and doughnuts?"

He frowned at me, and my body definitely should not have tingled at the seriousness of his stern brow. "Of course."

Heat and awareness prickled at the base of my skull as I slid off the island stool. "I'll go get dressed then."

Taking my coffee mug with me, I headed toward the stairs at the back of the house. Once I was out of sight, I scampered up the steps with a fresh giddiness coursing through me.

THIRTEEN

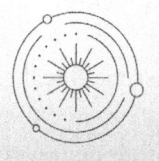

HAZEL

The drive into town was filled with Teddy talking nonstop from the back seat of JP's car. For our trip from Chicago to Michigan, I'd picked up a *Random Facts Every Kid Should Know* book.

I had regrets.

Teddy flipped a page. "Did you know that tarantula spiders can survive two and a half years without food?"

I turned to look at him. "Is that true?"

He gestured with the book and lifted a shoulder. "Apparently."

I shivered. "Yeesh. No thanks."

Teddy read another fact aloud. "The human body has six hundred muscles . . . but that includes your heart, tongue, and the muscles you need to not pee your pants."

A shotgun burst of laughter exploded from my chest.

As we drove, I stared out the passenger-side window and tried not to focus on the veins on the back of JP's hand or the way the corded muscles of his forearms flexed as he gripped the steering wheel.

Or any of his *other* six hundred muscles.

JP looked at Teddy in the rearview mirror. "You think I could borrow that book sometime?"

I glanced over at him. "Doing some light reading?"

A muscle flicked in his cheek. "Nah. It's payback."

My eyebrows raised.

JP continued, "One time Royal got ahold of Duke Sullivan's phone number and began spamming him with random cat facts just to mess with him. It was shockingly effective."

A small laugh bubbled inside me. "But payback?"

His hand gripped the steering wheel. "A long while ago, the Sullivans got me pretty good. They'd hidden these little devices everywhere that emitted a cricket's chirp. That damn chirp followed me around for *weeks*. I thought I was losing my mind until I found one under the seat of my car."

My fingers pressed to my lips. "That's hilarious and actually quite brilliant. Do you know who did it?"

His eyes narrowed, and I hated to admit that seeing a vengeful JP was kind of hot. "Kate planted it but I am fairly positive Lee was behind it. He's due for some payback."

"So, revenge after all this time?" I asked.

He pinned me with his icy stare, and a shiver slid down my spine. "I'm a very patient man when it comes to getting what I want."

My lips pressed together to hide a smile. I settled back into the plush leather seat and soaked in the rolling hills and rambling blueberry fields bursting with dark, ripe blueberries.

From the back seat, Teddy changed topics. "Can we pick blueberries sometime?"

My smile widened. It was nice to see him venturing beyond his typical interests and wanting to try something new.

"I have always wanted to do that! I think it would be fun," I answered.

JP's eyes flicked to meet Teddy's in the rearview mirror. "Sullivan Farms has U-pick hours. I can ask Sylvie if we see her today, and we'll set something up."

Teddy grinned. "Thanks, Dad."

My eyes flicked to JP. His jaw flexed, and he shifted in the same uncomfortable way he always did when Teddy called him Dad—like it physically pained him.

When we made it to town, JP took a side road and parked behind the row of downtown buildings in a parking lot marked for employees only.

I raised an eyebrow as he parked. "Special treatment?"

"Royal owns the tattoo shop, but I own the building." JP shifted the car to park and got out.

Teddy scrambled to unbuckle and I followed suit. As we rounded the car, a woman came out of the back entrance to the tattoo parlor. She had bleached blond hair that was nearly white. Her tank top revealed arms that were covered in intricate floral designs, and her chunky black combat boots thudded on the concrete. When she smiled at JP, diamond studs in her cheeks that matched the ones lining her earlobes glinted in the late-morning sun.

"Hey, JP!" she called with a wave before pulling a pack of cigarettes from her purse.

JP nodded. "Luna."

Luna's eyes moved from JP to me and then down to Teddy. Her smile lifted at the corner. "Family outing?"

JP stuffed his hand into the pocket of his slacks. "Something like that."

"Smoking is bad for you," Teddy announced.

Luna lit her cigarette and raised her chin to blow her smoke away from us. "Don't I know it." She looked at the burning ember at the end of the cigarette. "Been trying to quit for a while now, but this week is kicking my ass."

I shrugged. "Mercury, Pluto, Saturn, *and* Neptune are all in retrograde. Plus, Uranus is on deck. It's a stacked deck right now."

JP blinked at me, but Luna's face lit up as she said, "Will you marry me?"

I laughed. "I'm in no place to marry you right now, but I'm always open to a friend." I stepped forward and extended my hand. "I'm Hazel."

With her cigarette dangling between her lips, she shook my hand. "Luna."

I gestured toward her cigarette. "You can always try St. John's wort tea, but it tastes atrocious. A tincture of lavender oil, lime, black pepper, and angelica has also been known to help with nicotine cravings." I racked my brain for what else might help her. "Oh! Lepidolite in your pocket, if you have it on hand."

Luna pulled her phone from the back pocket of her plaid miniskirt. "What was it again?"

I smiled. "If you want, I can mix a small batch up for you and bring it to the tattoo shop sometime. I think I have everything already . . . though I'm getting a little low on lavender oil. There aren't any spiritual shops in town, are there?"

"Unfortunately not. You have to drive to Kalamazoo for any good metaphysical supplies." She gestured with her phone. "Thanks."

"Anytime." I smiled, feeling like I'd met my first kindred spirit in Outtatowner. "It's nice to share with someone who gets it."

Luna grinned back. "I'm a bit of a spiritual channeler myself, so you're in good company." Her attention landed on JP, and she winked at him before stubbing out her cigarette. "You are in so much trouble."

"Okay, let's go." JP gently herded Teddy's shoulders away from the store toward the alley that would lead us to the Main Street sidewalk.

His phone rang and he pulled it from his pocket. Instead of answering it, he silenced the ringer and dropped it back into the pocket of his pants. It immediately rang again, and he ignored it.

As we walked through the alley with Teddy between us, his phone rang again, but this time he silenced it before returning it to his pocket.

"Trouble in paradise?" I asked.

He shook his head. "Just work."

"But it's a Sunday." Teddy gazed up at him with a frown, and it was uncanny how similar the two looked.

JP sighed and nodded.

I leaned down to Teddy, whispering loud enough for JP to hear my teasing. "When you're a billionaire CEO, every day is a workday, apparently."

"I'm not a billionaire," he grumbled. "The *company* is closing in on the billion-dollar threshold. Not me."

I blinked at him. "And who runs the company?"

JP's face twisted. The pissy look was back, and I stifled a laugh.

"Ha! Exactly." Changing the subject, I inhaled deeply as we exited the alley and stepped onto the sidewalk that ran along Main Street. "*Mmm*. Smell that, Teddy? I think we're close."

Teddy mimicked my inhale, sucking in a deep breath and holding it with round, excited eyes.

JP pointed to the storefront next to Royal's tattoo shop. "It's right next door."

When we reached the Sugar Bowl, JP held open the door for us and I slipped inside, whispering *thank you* as I passed him. His politeness was unnerving. I could handle his bitchy attitude, but when he was considerate and a gentleman, it set me off-kilter.

Inside the Sugar Bowl, patrons were lined up, waiting to order. The bakery was cozy but bright and open with sunshine streaming through the huge picture window in front. Countertop seating with high-top stools lined the window, and nearly all the other tables in the place were filled with people. Chatter folded around us as we stepped forward in line.

My stomach grumbled at the sweet smell of freshly baked pastries and rich, hot coffee.

JP focused his attention on Teddy. "They've got all kinds of pastries—doughnuts, croissants, cinnamon rolls, that kind of thing. I suggest the morning buns. They're a little messy with the cinnamon and sugar, but the best thing on the menu."

Nerves tittered through me as I became acutely aware of curious glances and whispers. I tugged at the hemline of my denim cutoffs. Next to JP in his perfectly tailored slacks and a crisp white dress shirt with rolled sleeves, I looked downright disheveled. Even Teddy was wearing a collared shirt.

I lifted my chin and tried not to feel the stares, but gossipy eyes bounced between Teddy, JP, and me. My palms went slick as I felt more and more uncomfortable the longer we stood in line—a conveyor belt proudly displaying how out of place I was as we moved up the line.

I stood behind Teddy, hoping his small seven-year-old body could shield me from their curious looks.

JP leaned in, and the smell of his rich cologne rolled over me. "What's wrong?" he whispered.

"Nothing," I lied through a forced smile.

He leaned in again and I was given another delicious hit of his masculine scent. "Don't lie to me."

The unexpected command in his voice made sparks ignite under my skin, and my cheeks flamed white-hot.

I swallowed and tried to smile. "They're staring at me."

He was so close and didn't move away. "Who is?"

"Everyone," I said through a gritted half smile.

JP moved a fraction closer to me, and I could feel the heat pumping off his body. He looked around, and a soft chuckle rumbled in his chest.

His breath floated over my ear, and goose bumps erupted along my arms. "They aren't staring at you. They're staring at me."

My eyes flicked up to his. Up close, they weren't the icy, soulless blue I'd initially thought. They were a riot of cerulean and subtle green—a complex and intoxicating hue that drew me in and enchanted me. "Why would they be staring at you?"

His eyes moved over my face, pausing on my mouth for the briefest moment. "It's not every day they see the heartless face of King Equities walking among them."

I chuckled at his self-deprecating assessment. "Too busy striking fear into the hearts of the peons to leave your tower?"

"Something like that." He sighed and tucked his hands into his pockets as he rocked back on his heels. "More like putting out fires and doing what I can to clean up the mess my father left me."

I studied JP's face as he stepped away and stared ahead.

I wanted to ask a thousand questions about his father—*Are the rumors true? How much did you know? Are you okay?*

Instead, the words clogged in my throat and I stayed silent. The line moved forward, and I smiled at Sylvie behind the counter.

She was taking orders at the register, and when we made it to the front of the line, her smile grew. "Good morning!"

"Hey, Aunt Sylvie," Teddy said as though addressing his newfound family was the simplest thing in the world.

JP exhaled and scrubbed the back of his neck, but her hand flew to her chest as she looked at me. "Oh, that's just the *cutest*." She blinked away tears and smiled at him. "How are you, Teddy?"

"Hungry." He grinned. "Dad and I tried to make pancakes, but he said culinary skills were outside his wheelhouse."

Sylvie chuckled and nodded. "Sadly, it's true." She gestured to the display case bursting with a variety of freshly baked pastries, pies, and doughnuts. "What looks good?"

Teddy and I looked over the glass display case with wide, hungry eyes. Teddy wanted to try a raspberry jam Danish, and I opted for an old-fashioned cake doughnut along with a hazelnut praline latte.

"For you?" she asked her brother.

JP shook his head before reaching into his back pocket. "I'm fine."

Without him asking for it, Sylvie slipped a morning bun for JP into the white paper bag. She gave him a small smile. "On the house."

He slid his wallet out of his pocket and handed over his credit card. "Thanks, Syl."

I wondered if JP knew how lucky he was to be surrounded by siblings. Olive was all I had and she was gone. I hadn't appreciated her nearly enough while she was alive. Now it was too late, and every day her absence made itself known in the tiniest, most heartbreaking ways.

I handed Teddy the bag, and he reached in and took a bite of his Danish. He stood off to the side while we waited for my coffee.

"Are you coming to the Fireside Flannel Festival?" Sylvie asked as the barista handed her the paper cup with my coffee.

"What's that? Will Penny be there?" Teddy asked around another hearty bite. Red jam clung to his lower lip in an unusual show of his actual age.

Sylvie slid a cardboard sleeve onto the to-go cup and handed it to me across the counter. "Penny wouldn't miss it. There are beach bonfires, music, craft vendors, a *carnival*." Her eyebrows waggled at him. "With school starting up after Labor Day, it's like our little kickoff to fall. Are you excited to start school soon?"

Shame jabbed at my gut.

Fuuuuuck.

I had been so focused on having an adventurous, carefree summer with Teddy. Then I found my sister's letter and focused everything on getting us here and finding JP. I hadn't even *remembered* that I was supposed to enroll him in school.

I didn't even know where to begin. Did I just walk him up to the building and send him on his way? Surely he wasn't just supposed to walk in on the first day unannounced. Did he need things like pencils and folders? *When even* was *the first day?*

A thousand questions folded over one another as I was rooted in panic, unsure of even where to begin.

"Mom homeschooled me," Teddy announced, and I blanched.

"Um . . ." I started. Having exactly *zero* teaching experience, any amount of me teaching Teddy *anything* was bound to be an utter disaster.

JP stepped in, and I had never felt such bittersweet relief. "Hazel's getting everything lined up. He'll be all set for second grade."

Sylvie blinked at her brother, surprise flickering over her soft features.

"Oh, that's great." Sylvie's nervous laugh wobbled. "Well, the Bluebirds help plan everything for the Fireside Flannel Festival. We meet on Wednesdays at the bookstore. You should come, Hazel."

I couldn't pinpoint why, but I felt a blossoming kinship with Sylvie. Maybe it was because she was so kind and loving toward Teddy. She'd accepted him—and me—with zero hesitation. Maybe it was because she was a mom who seemed to have her shit together and I could learn a thing or seven from her.

"Okay, yeah. I'll think about it." I raised my coffee cup. "Thanks."

With nowhere to sit, we opted to enjoy our late-morning breakfast down by the marina. As we walked, I indulged in a brief, silent mental breakdown.

I considered Sylvie's invitation along with the implications of Teddy and me staying in Outtatowner long enough for him to start the school year.

Is it terrible parenting to have a kid start school and then leave? What if we wanted to try a new city—what then? Is there some online option he could do? But then what about making friends? Would he be destined to be the weird, antisocial kid if he wasn't in a class with his peers? He is already delightfully quirky. What if the kids don't understand or accept him? Olive would have known exactly what to do . . .

I could feel the panic mounting due to my lack of preparation, but I shoved it down and tried to remain calm.

"So what are the Bluebirds?" I finally asked, wondering what I might have gotten myself into by tentatively accepting Sylvie's invitation.

JP smiled as though walking as a trio was the most natural thing in the world. He ignored the sidelong, curious glances that had followed us out of the Sugar Bowl, but I could still feel their eyes on my back.

As we walked down the sidewalk toward the lakefront, he lifted a shoulder. "They're a not-so-secret society of women in Outtatowner who basically run everything behind the scenes. They plot and scheme and it's all very secretive." His eyes moved toward me. "You'd fit right in."

"Hmm." I smiled at the fact that JP thought I could belong.

What would it be like if we stayed, just for a little while?

I tipped my head toward him. "Is it because I'm a witch?" I teased.

He shook his head and laughed. "It's because you're trouble, Hex."

Enjoying the rare lightheartedness of JP's mood, I decided not to poke the bear. Instead, I accepted his comment as a compliment.

"Thank you." I grinned with a nod.

"Exactly my point—you think trouble is *fun*." He playfully rolled his eyes. "But if you want to go, Teddy and I can find some trouble of our own." JP ruffled Teddy's hair, and my heart clanged against my ribs.

Something was shifting, and I wasn't entirely sure I wasn't in a world of trouble when it came to JP King.

FOURTEEN

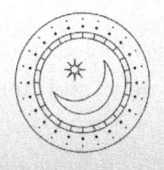

JP

In the doctor's office, Teddy looked at me with worried eyes. "Will it hurt?"

I crouched to level with him. "Not even a little bit. It's a cotton swab—like a really big Q-tip. The nurse will rub it on the inside of your cheek and that's that."

I patted his shoulder and stood next to his chair. The office of the county DNA Diagnostic Center was sterile, and its plain walls and too-bright lighting made my eyeballs ache.

It kind of reminded me of home, and I didn't like it.

I glanced at Hazel, who was fidgeting and picking at her nail polish while we waited to be called back. Lately her eclectic style and love of mood lighting had been taking over the house. At first it was a throw blanket, then something she called a pouf showed up on my living room floor. Yesterday, she had insisted on using only table lamps for indirect lighting instead of the very expensive overhead light fixtures I'd had custom made for the house.

Nothing she added to my house matched, yet everything seemed to tie together in her weird, bohemian style.

I wasn't used to someone else coming into my home and disrupting the order I'd created, but I also wouldn't admit that I didn't *hate* it. The soft lighting was actually kind of nice.

Instead, I mostly grumbled and stayed quiet about it whenever something new and unexpected showed up inside the house.

That's what you get for moving them inside.

"Theodore Adams?" A male nurse entered from the back, glancing up from his clipboard as he looked around the waiting room.

Teddy stood, and Hazel walked with him to the back, where they'd collect his sample and we'd all find out if he was really my kid.

Since we'd seen my sister, Hazel had casually brought up the Bluebird Book Club meeting more than once. It was clear to see that she wanted to go, but we hadn't talked about it since our breakfast a few days prior. I considered what I might do to keep Teddy occupied while she was gone.

My mind came up blank.

"Fuck this," I grumbled and pulled out my phone.

I needed reinforcements.

> I need a favor.

ROYAL
> Uh, oh . . . brothers-only text thread.
> Whose ass is getting beat?

ABEL
> Why are you the way that you are?

WHIP

Childhood trauma is my guess.

> I'm serious.

ABEL

You're always serious.

ROYAL

Look who's talking.

WHIP

While our oldest brothers bicker, what can we do for you, JP?

> Hazel wants to go to book club with the Bluebirds.

ABEL

And?

ROYAL

It's like a rite of passage in this town. Does that mean she's sticking around, Daddy?

> Don't ever call me that again. I have no idea if she's planning to stick around, but if she goes to book club tonight, I'm stuck with the kid. He's a good kid, but I don't have a clue what to do with a seven-year-old.

WHIP

Oh, we got you, Daddy.

> Jesus . . . not you too.

ABEL

Sorry, man. I'm out. Sloane and I have plans but if it happens again, maybe he'd like to hang with Ben and Tillie sometime.

> ROYAL
>
> The women are all at book club together anyway. We can let him stay up late and watch Big Trouble in Little China or some shit.
>
> WHIP
>
> He's seven.
>
> ROYAL
>
> It's classic Kurt Russell. Watching it is practically a passage into manhood.
>
> > Just come over and help me. We'll figure it out.
>
> ROYAL
>
> You got it, Daddy.

I SLIPPED the phone into my pocket and leaned back into the uncomfortable office chair. With my eyes closed and head tipped toward the ceiling, I pressed my thumbs into my eye sockets.

Roping them in is probably a huge mistake.

Stress was compounding, and the pressure in my head was like a kettle that was about to blow. I needed a break. A minute to breathe. A fucking *second* where every decision didn't completely upend a company or ruin a kid's life.

My phone rang, and I stifled a groan before clearing my throat and answering. "What is it?"

Veda's no-nonsense voice was on the other line. "Well, good morning to you too."

I sighed. "Sorry." Veda didn't need apologies, but I still felt like less of a prick if I tried.

"Look, I know you have your paternity appointment today, and I wouldn't bug you if it wasn't important," she said.

My head throbbed. "Go ahead."

Straight to the point, she said, "We lost Data Collective."

I sat up in my seat. "What the fuck." An elderly lady next to me scowled, and I rested my elbows on my knees and lowered my voice. "What happened?"

"They said they aren't comfortable moving forward with the deal. They cited concerns with the contract timeline, but my best guess is—"

"They don't want their company associated with King Equities while my father is on trial for first-degree murder?" I said.

"Bingo."

It was really happening. King Equities was crumbling beneath me, and there wasn't a damn thing I could do to save it.

"All right. I'll figure it out and be in as soon as I'm done here." I ended the call without waiting for her response and set my jaw.

Moments later, the nurse came back with Teddy and Hazel behind him. I stood when he called my name next.

I brushed past Hazel and Teddy as I followed the nurse to the room.

The DNA test was a necessity. Something I could actually check off my to-do list without adding seventeen more items.

It was also the most practical way to get to the bottom of Olive's claim that I was Teddy's father. Despite my deep dive into old emails and text messages, I still came up short whenever I tried to find out more information regarding how—and *when*—I'd met Olive Adams. She had convinced both Hazel and Teddy that I was his father, but I still couldn't find the evidence.

Still, I had to try. It was my job to take charge and get results. My entire life people looked to me for answers and expected me to step up, and I did it.

I simply could not find a plausible connection between Olive and me outside of that photograph. I had always been a realist—that was just how I was built.

Still, I couldn't quite explain the dread that filled my gut as the nurse walked me toward the back.

How do I accept the truth—that I couldn't possibly be Teddy's father—when my feelings for him and the prospect of actually being his dad wouldn't stop growing?

∽

AFTER LEAVING THE TESTING CENTER, I drove Hazel and Teddy back to the house. She informed me they'd be going to the beach and asked if I wanted to come.

There was a tiny spark of yearning—like a reclamation of a childhood I had missed out on.

I shook my head, knowing every minute I was away from the office, more shit was hitting the fan. "No, thanks. You two have fun."

"Back to the office?" she asked.

"I'll be there if you—*he*—needs anything." I cleared my throat, hoping she didn't catch the tiny slip.

Hazel nodded and lowered her lashes. A lock of wavy hair tumbled in front of her face, and my fingers itched to brush it aside. My palm rose, tempted to see what would happen if I gave in.

My fingers curled into a fist and I turned toward Teddy.

"We're doing guys' night in while Hazel goes to her book club. Are you okay with that?"

Teddy shrugged. "What guys?"

I tried to act casual. "Just some of your . . . um, uncles."

I probably shouldn't have referred to them as that, but what else was I supposed to call them?

Teddy's face lit up. "Yeah!" He pushed open the passenger door and bounded toward the house.

When I looked over, Hazel was smiling at me.

"What?" I asked.

"Guys' night?" She asked, and I tried not to stare at how pretty she was when she smiled.

I did what I could to play it cool. "I don't know what to do to keep a kid entertained while you and your coven do whatever it is you do. I figured between all of us we could keep Teddy alive."

Hazel blinked and gave me a flat, unimpressed look. "That's very comforting."

With an impatient sigh, I ignored her jab and leaned toward the glove compartment. I didn't have to, but I let the back of my hand absently drag across her bare knee. She didn't move away, and the jolt of her skin against mine was intoxicating.

I pulled a stack of papers from the glove box and handed them to her.

She accepted the papers with a puzzled look. "What's this?"

I gestured toward the stack. "It's everything needed to enroll Teddy in second grade here. They'll want an address. You can use mine."

She thumbed through a few pages and blinked up at me. "You contacted the school for me?"

With a stern nod, I sat back in the driver's seat. "I took care of it. I know it's going to take a while to get the paternity results back, so he might as well enroll here. Registration is all paid for, but it's not a big deal if you make other plans." I looked out onto the yard so she wouldn't detect the nerves simmering at the edge of my voice.

A tightness seized my chest as I waited for her to confirm they'd be leaving.

"Um . . . thank you." She seemed surprised that someone took the initiative to handle something for her.

"I could tell my sister's questions about the school year freaked you out. Now it's one less thing you have to worry about." I was used to taking care of things. I just wasn't used to how satisfying it felt to take care of things for *her*.

Her hand brushed against the handle of the car door.

I didn't want her to leave. I wanted to stay locked in the cocoon of my BMW and show her what I would rather be doing instead of going to the office. I wanted her to thank me with that lush mouth of hers, only to prove I'd done it because I'd *wanted* to.

The silence in my car grew as we both stared. Her eyes were locked with mine, but in my peripheral vision, I could see the rise and fall of her chest.

"Thank you." Her eyes were soft and unwavering as she looked at me in a way that made me feel twenty feet tall.

The air inside my car was fraught with unanswered questions and lingering tension. I knew better, but the feral part of me didn't care who she was. I lifted my hand and brushed that stray lock of hair from her face, tucking it behind her ear. I should have dropped my hand, but instead I reveled in the way my fingertips could feel the hammering of her pulse behind her ear.

Her mouth opened as if she was going to say something, but stopped when I dropped my hand.

"Goodbye, Hazel." I sat back in my seat and stared out the front window.

Without a word, she pushed open the passenger door and left, taking my breath with her.

FIFTEEN

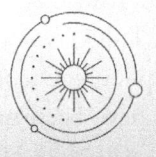

HAZEL

On the door of Bluebird Books, a small sign read *Closed for the Bluebirds*.

A huge grin pinched my cheeks. There were few things I loved more than a secret society of strong, powerful women. With my shoulders back and a confident smile, I pulled open the glass door and stepped inside. I was greeted with the warm scent of old books. Against the window there was a plush bench, perfect for reading on a rainy day. A few small tables with chairs were dotted around, inviting book lovers to enjoy the comfort and camaraderie of a quaint little bookshop.

Once inside, wooden displays revealed rows and rows of new and used books. I could hear the faint murmurs of conversation coming from the back and followed the glowing lamplight. Near the cash register, a wall of framed photos caught my eye. Some were black-and-white, while others were more modern. All were of women, and I recognized Sylvie and Lark among them. One older photograph drew my attention. The woman in it could have been Sylvie's twin sister, had the picture not clearly been taken several years ago. The woman wore red lipstick and a sly smile. Her light-brown eyes were soft and kind, and she had the most gorgeous blond hair.

It had to be Maryann King.

Surrounded by six kids, I wondered which was JP. I leaned in, studying the picture. On one knee, she balanced a little girl who couldn't have been more than two or three. On the other was a boy with dark hair, seafoam eyes, and a serious expression. My fingertip reached to brush across his sweet, serious brow.

JP.

Sadness rolled over me for the little boy he had been.

"Hazel. I'm glad you could make it!" I turned at Sylvie's voice and smiled. "She was ethereal, right?"

I hummed in agreement. "So are you—you're identical."

Sylvie tucked a strand of blond hair behind her ear. "Thank you." She gestured toward herself. "Come on. I'll introduce you to everyone."

I followed Sylvie and found the source of the chatter I'd heard earlier. At the back of the store, mismatched chairs, settees, and benches were placed in cozy arrangements. Women of varying ages were engaged in conversations, many with wine or other drinks in their hands.

Quiet laughter and conversation flowed into each other as I followed Sylvie into the gentle fray. Across the room, I saw Bug and waved. She returned my greeting with a nod and polite smile.

When we reached a semicircle of women, I stopped at Sylvie's side. Most I had already met at the barbecue, and I was greeted with friendly waves and smiles.

"Ladies, most of you have already met Hazel. For those that haven't, she's JP's, well . . ." She looked at me, seemingly unsure of what to say next. "She's Teddy's aunt and guardian."

I moved my hand in a rainbow. "Hi."

Annie, whom I'd briefly met at the barbecue, scooted to the side and patted the bench next to her. "Welcome!"

Kate walked over with two plastic champagne flutes. She moved one toward me. "Bubbles?"

I accepted the cup. "Are we celebrating?"

Lark laughed and propped her feet on an ottoman. "We're *always* celebrating at the Bluebirds."

JP's little sister MJ took a sip of her own drink. "We've had heavy times lately. Tonight we're all glad there's no drama and we can just relax with friends."

A woman across from her snorted. "No drama? Whip's been in a tailspin since *someone* hemmed his work pants three inches shorter." She gestured toward Annie with her cup. "Every. Single. Pair."

Annie laughed and covered her mouth. "I cannot get over how much our men act like *children*. First they hate each other, then they become *bros* or something, and now they're back to pinching each other's butts or whatever it is they do."

"They're children. All of them," Kate chimed in with a chuckle.

"It took Lee *weeks* of teaching himself how to sew." Her brow furrowed as she imitated Lee's voice. "If you're going to do it, better do it right."

Lark sighed and gestured toward me. "At least you don't have to worry about JP getting caught up in all of it. Somehow, even though it's the men being ridiculous, sometimes we get tangled in it too."

"Yeah, no shit." Veda, Royal's girlfriend, popped a grape

into her mouth and crossed her long legs. "My first day I got a face full of milk and eggs, thank you very much."

The women laughed and continued chatting as I thought about JP and him asking about Teddy's random facts book. He might not be at the forefront of the pranks, but he wasn't above pulling some strings behind the scenes.

I smiled to myself and let the conversation roll over me, participating when I could, but mostly sitting back and observing the happy camaraderie of the women of Outtatowner. Young or old, they all laughed and shared stories, and the night went on.

He may have called it a coven to tease me, but he wasn't wrong.

The Bluebirds were a sisterhood. A group of women bonded by love and friendship.

Unexpected emotion stung the bridge of my nose, and I poked at a tear that had formed at the corner of my eye.

Sylvie's hand rested on my back. "You okay?"

"Yeah." I swallowed hard. "Just missing my sister a little bit." I gave her a sad, watery smile and was comforted by her kind expression.

"Could you tell me about her?" she asked.

I shifted, scooting so my knees could face her. "Sure. She was older than me. Liked to boss me around . . . typical big-sister stuff, I guess. Olive was funny—always the life of the party. She had this knack for getting people out of their shells. *Everyone* loved her."

Sylvie sighed. "Oh, sometimes I envy people like that—people who just have this glow about them, and light up a room in the best ways."

I nodded. "Exactly. There was a spark, you know?" When my voice wobbled, I cleared my throat. "When she found out she was pregnant, she wasn't scared. She just knew it would all be okay. Even after she told him and he—"

I chewed the inside of my lip, willing the swell of emotions not to overtake me in a room full of new friends.

"Oh, honey." Sylvie folded over me as I clamped my mouth shut.

I'd almost said it out loud and told her what he'd done—what he still wouldn't admit actually *happened* between the two of them.

Guilt, slick and slimy, crept in at the edges of my awareness. I had been fighting my attraction to JP since I met him.

What kind of person did that make me?
What kind of sister?

I exhaled and sat back, swiping underneath my eyes and hoping my mascara wasn't running all over the place.

"That's it," Annie said as she began texting something on her phone. "This calls for more alcohol."

"Oh." I laughed a watery chuckle. "I really can't. I borrowed JP's car and drove here."

Annie waggled her phone with a grin. "Already taken care of. While the King men are busy having guys' night with Teddy, the Sullivans just became our designated drivers."

"In that case . . ." Veda held a fresh bottle of champagne and expertly popped the cork with a laugh.

Playful whoops and hollers rang out as Veda poured the champagne into our plastic cups.

Sylvie held up her drink and winked at me. "To the Bluebirds, new and old."

Together we toasted and sipped, the champagne tickling my nose as I sent up a silent toast of my own.

To the Bluebirds . . . Olive sure would have loved you.

SIXTEEN

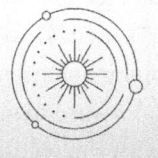

HAZEL

It was late by the time Beckett Miller's black SUV rolled down JP's driveway. Kate, Emily, Veda, and I were giggling in the background as the grumpy builder smiled and shook his head from the front seat.

"All right." He parked and turned toward the back. "It was nice to meet you, Hazel."

"You too," I answered as I crawled out of the back seat with Emily right behind me.

Kate was already making her way across the center console and nearly sitting in her husband's lap as she giggled. Her butt was in his face as she awkwardly made her way into the front passenger seat. He slapped her ass and laughed as she plopped down.

"Veda, are you ditching me?" Kate asked as Veda climbed out of the back of the SUV behind me and Emily.

She smiled and adjusted her skirt. Veda pointed toward JP's house. "My man is in there. He's coming home with me."

Kate waved. "Sounds good. Have fun you three."

We waved as Beckett and Kate backed out of the driveway and disappeared into the darkness. Veda tossed her arms across Emily's back and mine.

"You good?" she asked me.

I squeezed her arm. "Great. Only slightly tipsy."

Veda laughed, dropping her arms. "Well, that's a shame. I am very much looking forward to giving Royal a *very* tipsy striptease." She toyed with the gold chain around her neck, and my cheeks heated.

"Woman." A voice boomed from the darkened porch, followed quickly by Royal's hearty laugh. "What are you waiting for? Get your ass up here and kiss me."

Veda covered her giggle with her fingertips and sauntered up the porch steps. Her arms wrapped around Royal's neck as his thick, tattooed arms wound around her waist, lifting her heels off the ground as he kissed her.

I blushed and looked away when he growled and their kiss deepened.

"Get a room." Whip playfully pushed past Royal and took the porch steps in one leap before pulling Emily in for her own greeting. After a quick peck, he bent to toss Emily over his shoulder. She squealed and patted his butt.

"Good night," I called to them as Whip headed straight to his truck.

Royal sauntered down the steps with Veda tucked into his side. "The kid's cute, I'll give him that."

"No Abel?" Veda asked.

"He went with Sloane to do some back-to-school shopping for the twins, I guess. Next time." He looked at Veda. "Ready, Precious?"

She grinned, and as we said goodbye, my heart pinched. I was surrounded by happy couples and people doing back-to-school shopping. My hands gripped the banister as I climbed the porch steps and tried not to think about how different my life had become in such a short amount of time.

I silently opened the front door, and the house was eerily quiet. A newly opened board game was scattered on the coffee table in the living room, and there were popcorn bowls and kernels littering the floor. A cartoon movie had been paused on the television.

When I didn't see Teddy or JP, I climbed the stairs and headed toward the bedrooms. I quietly padded across the wooden floor. When I reached Teddy's room, my heart stopped. JP was holding a limp Teddy in his arms and gently swaying. Teddy was fast asleep, and JP was attempting to pull back his bedsheets with one hand.

I watched from the door as JP lowered Teddy to the bed and scooted his legs under the covers. "There you go, buddy." JP paused and looked down at Teddy.

For a moment, he just stared.

I wondered what he was thinking. Did he see how alike they were? Did he finally accept that Teddy was his child? Did he regret how things had crumbled between Olive and him?

My heart caught when JP leaned down and brushed a soft kiss on the top of Teddy's head, then squeezed his shoulder.

"Good night, kid," he whispered.

Before he could catch me, I turned and rushed down the hallway. I crept down the steps and scurried toward the living room, hoping he wouldn't realize I'd been watching him tuck Teddy into bed.

When the stairs creaked, my heart jumped. I stacked

the bowls of leftover popcorn and pretended like I hadn't heard a thing.

"I can get that." JP's voice was thick and low.

I smiled at him. "It's okay. I got it. Did you have fun tonight?"

JP raked a hand through his hair and exhaled. "I didn't realize seven-year-olds were so exhausting."

I laughed and nodded. "Yeah, I learned pretty quickly that even the good ones have the attention span of a gnat." I looked around the disheveled living room. "Looks like you did okay, though."

JP scooped pieces of the board game into the box. "I had reinforcements. I think Teddy likes the fact that Whip plays by the rules, but Royal cheats." He chuckled, and the low rumble made goose bumps erupt across my skin.

"What about you?" I asked after dumping the leftover popcorn in the trash and depositing the bowls in the sink. "Are you a cheater?"

Only the dim lighting of a lamp on the countertop illuminated the room. We were folded in soft lighting, and I admired how the golden light cut across his sharp cheekbones.

In the faded light, his eyes were softer.

Kinder.

He moved toward me, crowding me as my back pressed against the countertop. JP leaned into my space as he placed a cup in the sink behind me.

His face was inches from mine. "I'm not the villain you think that I am, Hazel."

My mind raced as my throat went hot and thick. I swallowed past the uncertainty and tried to find the words to tell him that I suspected he might be right about that.

His gravelly voice tickled the back of my neck, and my thighs pressed together. "I'm also not a cheater, but I do play to win."

My breath was shaky, but I smiled. "Let me guess. Ruthless?"

A wolf's grin spread across his face and my pulse danced. "Every time."

Over his shoulder I could see the scattered game pieces still covering the coffee table. I swallowed. "You know . . ." I licked my lips and his cool eyes tracked the movement, sending a bolt of lightning straight to my clit. "I'm pretty good at that game. Do you want to play a round?"

JP glanced over his shoulder to the living room. His lips twitched. "I'm a little bored with that one." He shrugged. "I deal with properties and finance every day in my real job."

"Ahh," I teased. My palms gripped the marble countertop at my back. "You prefer the thrill of a real acquisition."

JP's hip brushed mine, and I wanted to ignite. "I like taking what someone says I can't have."

I slinked past him, needing space before I did something stupid like grab him by his T-shirt and press my mouth to his.

Again.

I cleared my throat and faked a smile, hoping he couldn't see the way my nipples were actively broadcasting how keyed up I was. "How about . . . you try something new?"

JP took my spot against the counter, moving one ankle over the other and crossing his arms. "Like?"

"Let me do a tarot reading with you." Excitement built as I considered the prospect of getting some insight into the elusive JP King.

His brow furrowed. "Like fortune-telling?"

I rolled my eyes and laughed. "Tarot isn't fortune-telling. It simply gives you insight. It's a powerful way of revealing the truth about your life."

He gave me a flat look. "So . . . it's bullshit."

I scoffed. "Fine. Be a stick-in-the-mud."

I turned to leave the kitchen when his quiet voice stopped me. "Okay."

I eased back around to find him staring at me. Energy crackled under my skin. "Okay?"

He sighed and dropped his hands to his sides. "Let's get this over with."

The tiny quirk at the side of his mouth was endearing. He tried so hard to be an asshole that it was easy to forget there was a man I'd yet to fully understand hiding just beneath the surface.

I scampered out of the living room and dashed up the stairs to my bedroom. My tarot deck was wrapped in cloth. I also grabbed a smudge stick, matches, and a small piece of selenite crystal.

When I walked back downstairs, I paused to notice a few candles had been lit. I smiled at JP's back.

He was focusing on something in the kitchen, and when he turned, he was holding two glasses of wine.

I raised an eyebrow. "Setting the mood?"

His jaw flexed and my stomach bunched. I couldn't help the fact he was so easy to annoy, and that stern look just *did* something to my insides.

Giving him a break, I motioned with my head to the kitchen table. "Come on."

He followed and I sat at the head of the table, unfolding the mat and placing the selenite crystal beside it. If he was freaked out, he didn't show it. JP simply took a drink of his wine and slid the other glass closer to me.

I placed my hand over the white sage smudge stick. "This is for purifying and cleansing negative energy. Is it okay if I do that?"

He nodded once.

With a smile, I lit a match and ignited the sage. Once it was lit, I blew it out, allowing the embers to gently smoke. I wafted the fragrant smoke around us. "It's okay if you don't believe in it."

JP shrugged. "It's fine. Luna practically bathes me in smoke every time I see her at the tattoo shop. I'm used to it."

I snorted gently and set down the bundle. "I knew I liked her."

JP exhaled and leaned in. "Between you and me? Sometimes I think it actually works."

I smiled at him before I closed my eyes. I tipped my head back and rolled my head. I moaned, trying not to giggle. I could feel his wary gaze on my skin. "What? What's that?" I whispered. I put my fingers against my temple. "Who is it? Who's there? Molly?" My eyes flew open. "Molly, you're in danger, girl!"

JP looked around in panic as though he might see a spirit standing in his kitchen. "What? Who the hell is Molly?"

I couldn't hold in my laughter. JP's features went stern and I laughed even harder. "Okay. Okay, I'm sorry. I'm just teasing. Haven't you ever seen the movie *Ghost*?"

JP huffed, but smiled. "You're ridiculous."

I grinned. "Thank you. Now, come on, scoot over here." I tamped down the giddy smile that played on my lips and exhaled. "I can do a three-card reading. If there's anything you are searching for or want guidance from the universe about, you can hold on to those thoughts while I shuffle."

He eyed me skeptically, but with a shake of his head, closed his eyes. Closing his eyes was unnecessary, but I took the moment to soak in how truly handsome he was. His dark features softened, and I wondered if he looked that peaceful when he slept.

My hands trembled as I cut the deck and began to shuffle.

After I was satisfied the deck was mixed, I flipped over the first card.

"Okay," I said with a gentle smile. "This is a good start. The Ten of Cups. This card represents harmony." I pointed at the ornate illustration. "See how the couple is lovingly embracing? Their children are playing nearby and all ten cups are full."

JP studied the card with a frown. "Seems nice."

I smiled at him, relieved that there wasn't a hint of mockery in his tone. "It *is* nice. It's meant to represent emotional fulfillment and lasting happiness."

He took a deep breath as I shuffled again. The scent of white sage clung to the air and wrapped around us.

I flipped the next card. "Oh, okay. This is the Four of Wands. See how the pair is dancing? They're celebrating. It's a card that represents homecoming—that could be an *actual* homecoming or an emotional one, like finding the lost parts of yourself. It usually represents a safe and secure home environment."

He looked around the dim living room and kitchen bathed in flickering candlelight. "I like that." He shifted, resting his chin in his hand. "What's next?"

I gently released my breath and shuffled again. My fingers twitched and two cards fell from the deck, face down. "Oh, you have some jumpers." I set the deck aside. "Jumpers are when a card—or in this case, two—jumps out. It means it's a message the universe wants you to have."

I waggled my eyebrows at him, then flipped the cards over one by one and stared.

Oh, shit.

His eyes bounced from the cards to me. "What?" He chuckled. "Is it bad?"

I slid one toward him, using my hand to cover the illustration. "No. There are no *bad* cards. It's all about interpretation and intention. Um . . ." My brow furrowed as I scrambled to think how to approach explaining the cards that jumped.

"This is the Tower." I slid it closer and removed my hand so JP could see it.

"Jesus. Is that guy jumping off the building?" His eyebrows tilted inward as he inched closer.

I swallowed past the lump that had expanded in my throat. "He's falling. Receiving the Tower typically means a moment of great upheaval. Your entire worldview crumbles in the face of tragedy."

"Well, who is he?"

I blinked at him. "The King."

The irony wasn't lost on him. JP scoffed and sat back. "Well, that shit tracks." JP dragged a hand down the corners of his mouth.

I moved the second card next to the Tower. "It's paired with this one—the Two of Swords. You have a difficult decision ahead of you. An impasse. Do you see how the man here has his head down? He is looking inward rather than outward. It may mean there is going to be a decision and only *you* can make the choice."

He stared at the cards for a tiny flicker of a moment

before looking at me. "That's fine. I make difficult decisions every day."

Tension stretched between us. My hand paused over the deck, ready to pack it up and consider the reading—and the moment—over.

When I slid the deck toward me, JP's hand landed on top of mine. "I have one more, right? You said a three-card pull."

I glanced up at him and faked a smile. "Of course."

With a quick shuffle, I pulled the last card.

"Oh." My eyes fixed on the card and the breath was stolen from my lungs.

JP's attention was pinned to the last card.

The Lovers.

I blinked and closed my mouth. With a gentle throat clearing, I sat higher in my seat. "The Lovers card indicates a strong soulful connection between two people." As I spoke, I could feel my cheeks heat.

Candlelight flickered in his blue eyes as they moved from the card to my face.

"Um . . . it doesn't necessarily mean, like, *lovers* lovers. It can be a familial connection or a deep, loving friendship. Regardless, it's a connection of the souls." I tapped my fingers against my breastbone.

His eyes fixed to where my heart thumped beneath my chest. "But it can, though, right? Mean actual lovers?"

JP's stare was igniting my insides, setting my skin on fire. All I could imagine was letting the world fall away and riding him until nothing but that moment mattered.

I raked a hand across my flushed neck. "It could."

The corner of his lip tilted up. With one hand, he gripped the underside of my chair and slid it around the corner of the table to pull me close to him. He shifted to face me.

My heart hammered against my ribs. I had no right being in Olive's place, but my body's reaction to him was instinctual. JP slid my chair between his spread legs. My clit hummed at the sheer masculinity and ease of his movements.

My knees were trapped as he leaned in. "It could."

SEVENTEEN

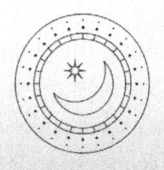

JP

In the smoky candlelight, Hazel was irresistible. The fact that I was in the middle of a paternity case with her nephew didn't matter, because I simply did not give a fuck.

I couldn't make sense of Hazel Adams, but I was utterly enchanted.

My eyes were pinned to her chest as it went red, and I could just make out the outline of her nipple piercings through her white T-shirt.

My jaw shifted.

I dragged my eyes up to her face. Certain my expression was akin to a glare, I tried to soften the scowl that felt permanently etched on my face.

My blood warmed as Hazel tilted her chin in a defiant way that made my blood hum. Her eyes were ablaze, like she got off on the way I had been staring at her tits.

She isn't afraid of you.

My fingers curled around the edge of her chair and my grip tightened. My cock hardened and pressed against the zipper of my jeans, begging for release.

I wanted nothing more than for her to crawl on my lap and ride my dick until we were both exhausted.

"Hazel." My voice was an unrecognizable growl as her soft brown eyes lifted to mine. Struggling to hold myself back, I tried like hell to keep things appropriate. "I think we should call it a night."

Her cheek twitched with a smile and she leaned in. Her cinnamon and citrus scent snapped through me as her breath floated over my ear. "What if I'm not tired?"

I knew she was baiting me. The tether on my control was fraying, about to snap.

I knew better than to get involved with a woman like Hazel Adams. She was too wild, too alluring, too fucking perfect.

The walls I'd built over the years were meant to protect me. Protect everyone. It was safer to have them securely in place, but something about Hazel made the reasons for those protections seem irrelevant.

My knuckles trailed up the outside of her arm, taking my time and savoring the softness of her skin. I glided across her collarbone and along the column of her neck. My hand slid into her hair, combing through her strawberry blond strands.

Hazel tilted her head, allowing me access to caress and luxuriate in her softness. She was trapped between my knees, but it was me who was unable to move.

"What are we doing?" she asked, closing her eyes and reveling in my touch.

I have no fucking clue, honestly, but I don't want to stop.

I leaned in, letting my nose brush against her jawline. "I'm seeing if those cards are full of shit or not."

I was crossing lines left and right. The moment I yanked her chair forward and crowded her space, everything shifted. I paused to look into her eyes as they fluttered open.

They were dancing with delight. With certainty.

I could feel myself falling. A smile stretched, unused and uncomfortable, across my face as I leaned in. I pressed my mouth to hers and was met with warm, willing lips. Hazel opened for me, tilting her head to accept the kiss.

My hand cupped the side of her face and I shifted, deepening the kiss. Her gentle whimper fueled a deep and wanting hunger. I couldn't remember a time when something as simple as a kiss had been so intoxicating. From a single kiss my chest felt cracked open and exposed.

Raw.

Hazel's fingertips smoothed over my shoulders, pulling our bodies closer. They slid up the back of my neck and across the short crop of hair at the base of my skull.

I had fantasized about the moment we would kiss again, and it wouldn't be an impulsive, emotion-fueled mistake. My pathetic, late-night fantasies didn't even come close to the real thing. No—she was so much more.

She was everything.

Her short, flowy skirt was riding high on her knees. I gripped the flesh at her hips and in one move dragged her onto my lap.

Hazel yelped, and I swallowed her sweet little gasp with another kiss. Her ass ground into my hard cock as she shifted her hips. Her tits pressed against me, and I moved one hand up to cup her breast, moving my thumb to graze over her hard nipple. Her bra was thin, and I gently toyed with her piercing. She sucked her breath in a hiss.

I held back, easing away when she pressed her hips into me. "No," she breathed. "Don't stop."

My dick twitched against my pants, hating the fabric

that kept me from being able to plunge into her. My hands slid up her thighs, moving under her skirt to grip her ass as she rocked her pussy over my cock.

I eased back from the kiss to look up at her. Hazel's hair was wild and falling in a soft red curtain around her face. Her pupils were wide with desire, and for the moment she was *mine*.

"More," she demanded.

I teased the silky hem of her thong. "More what?"

She lowered her head for another kiss. "More you. More everything. Just . . . more."

I groaned and let my fingertips drag over the seam where her panties just covered her pussy. My tongue slid over hers as I moved one finger beneath her underwear.

She was wet and hot as I dragged my finger across her bare pussy. "You're desperate," I teased and nipped her neck.

Her hips rocked, trying to place my finger exactly where she wanted it. "Yes," she whispered.

I smiled as I looked up at her. She hummed against my lips as I stroked her pussy, but didn't enter her.

Hazel braced her hands on my shoulders as she pulled back to look at me. "What do you want me to do? Beg?"

An eyebrow shot up my forehead. I licked my lower lip and grinned. "Yes. I want to know you're so desperate that you'd beg me to finger-fuck you."

One hand gripped my face, holding me in place as she looked down on me. "You're an asshole."

My eyes blazed, knowing her words were hollow and she was primed and aching for me.

I slid one finger to tease her opening and she hissed. "Beg," I demanded. "Beg for it so I can finally take care of you."

She hummed, gripping the back of my T-shirt. Her forehead lowered to mine. "Please," she whispered.

The word was barely out before I plunged my finger into her tight, hot cunt. She gasped and pulsed around me. "That's my good fucking girl."

We both moaned as I added a second finger, then worked in a third. She stretched around me as I moved in and out of her.

She rocked her hips and I matched the rhythm she craved. Her nipples were sharp points and I captured one in my mouth, sucking and teasing her through the fabric of her bra and tee.

I wanted more. I wanted everything.

Her pussy clenched around my fingers as she rode my hand. My mouth moved to her neck, sucking on the pulse point as her heart beat faster. I pressed my thumb into her clit, and she nearly came unraveled.

I needed her to feel as good and free as she made me feel. I didn't understand what she was doing to me, but I knew it was magical. I didn't have the words to explain it, but I could show her.

Her breaths came out in heavy pants and my cock wanted to explode. As desperate as I was for her, the moment wasn't about me. It was about giving her everything she needed and taking nothing for myself.

Her pussy fluttered around my fingers and I kept my pace steady. A hot surge of wetness coated my hand and she unraveled. Hazel clung to my shoulders as I let her ride out her orgasm.

Time dragged on, our breaths the only sound filling the air. Hazel gulped and leaned back, bracing herself on the edge of the chair but not getting off my lap. Her nipple piercings were straining against the thin fabric of her white

T-shirt, and my mouth watered. I couldn't wait to get her stripped bare and ready so I could explore every inch of her skin.

I stared at the way her pulse throbbed, and my cock twitched. She ground her ass against my erection and I nearly came, like some inexperienced teenager. I tightened my grip on her hips and groaned.

Hazel sat up. Her soft brown eyes were alight and playful. She looked at me, brushed a strand of hair away from my face, and sighed.

I wanted to lean forward. To wrap my arms around her and carry her to my bedroom so we could finish what I had started.

When she climbed off my lap, my heart sank.

Standing, Hazel smoothed the rumpled edges of her skirt and turned to leave. I stared as she paused and looked over her shoulder.

"You know," she said with a laugh. "You may not be the villain, but a hero doesn't fuck like *that*."

Tension dissipated as a hearty laugh rang from my chest. I stood and slapped her ass before leaning close to her ear.

"That wasn't fucking, Hex. And while I might not be the villain, I'm not a hero either."

I palmed her ass and squeezed as I moved around her to blow out the candles.

She turned, crossing her arms and putting those irresistible tits on display. "So what are you then?"

I glanced down at the table. Her tarot cards were still spread from her reading. I picked the Tower card up before dropping it on the top of the pile. "I guess I'm just the king, trying not to fall out of his damn tower."

In the darkness, I was struck by how angelic she was. Her features were soft and ethereal.

She smiled softly at me. "Sometimes the king needs to fall in order to remember what it's like to live in his kingdom."

I scoffed to myself.

If only...

Hazel raised an eyebrow and gently gestured toward the stairs with her head. It was an invitation. One I had no right accepting.

I stuffed down my feelings and shoved my hands in my pockets. "Good night, Hazel."

Even in the darkness, I could see the hurt flash across her soft brown eyes. Her lashes fluttered down, and the flush was back in her cheeks. "Good night, JP."

My lips pressed together as she made her way to the stairs and climbed, looking back at me with a soft, sad smile.

I wanted to follow.

I wanted to take my time with her and fuck her hard until she rattled the trees as she screamed my name.

I wanted to show her that if the universe wanted me to hurl myself off the tower, I just might do it for her.

Instead, I did what I was best at—kept her at arm's length and pretended like it wasn't fucking killing me.

∽

IF LIFE HAD TAUGHT me anything, it was that happiness came at a price. When I was twelve, I had begged my father for a dog. He was rarely home, and Aunt Bug had agreed to help take care of it as long as my father gave the okay. It took weeks for me to gain the courage to even *ask* him if we could adopt a puppy. I was shocked when, after I presented all the reasons it would be beneficial to the family, he agreed.

Nothing had meant more to me at the time than that dog. It was a mixed breed with a dingy, wiry coat and paws that were too big for his body. I had spent every dime I'd earned mowing lawns to pay for a dog bed and food. Aunt Bug and I picked him up from the animal shelter and brought him home. MJ was ten and enamored with him. Even my older siblings couldn't believe I'd managed to get Dad to agree to having a dog.

I was flying on a cloud as we drove home with him in my lap.

It wasn't the first time my father had taught me that happiness comes at a price, but it was the hardest.

It took many years to realize that my father was *jealous*. He couldn't stand the loving attention with which his children showered the dog.

Within a week, the dog was gone.

Sylvie, MJ, and Whip all cried. Abel and Royal exchanged a look I couldn't decipher. I simply stared at the empty lead in the yard that our beloved dog had been tied to.

"But I just let him out." I couldn't stop staring and trying to make sense of it all.

Dad had shrugged and looked at his watch like he had somewhere better to be. "I guess he got off the chain . . . If you cared, you would have kept a better eye on him."

That was my father's only explanation. The dog had been let outside for mere moments, and it was gone. There was nothing we could do.

My happiness came at a price, but I refused to cry about it. I wanted to show my father I was tough like him—that I could handle myself. I wanted so badly for him to approve, and instead he got into his Porsche and drove away while we all stood in the backyard.

At the time I thought that was the hardest lesson.

Until today.

I couldn't dodge the incessant feeling that just as things were going well with Hazel, something else in my life was waiting to go to utter hell.

Teddy laughed as Hazel made goofy faces at him over breakfast. She'd intentionally shoved bits of bacon into her teeth, but pretended like she didn't know they were there. Teddy was doubled over, his arms clutching his belly as he tried desperately to tell her she had something in her teeth. Every time, she moved her finger, avoiding the bacon, and asked, "Did I get it?"

My cheeks ached from smiling.

When my eyes caught Hazel's, a zip of energy coursed through my veins. There was something about her that was effortlessly shifting my entire world.

Ever since she'd ridden into my life, driving that ridiculous skoolie, everything was different.

And different was a real problem.

I pressed the heel of my hand into the center of my chest and paused—discovering it was that unfamiliar ache of happiness.

I dropped my fork. "What do you two think about a beach day?"

Teddy's soft eyes lifted, and a huge grin spread on his face. Hazel's caramel browns narrowed slightly as she sucked the bacon from her tooth.

"What about work?" she asked.

"It's supposed to be one of our last warm days." I

frowned and shrugged. "Work can wait. I haven't been to the beach in years."

A peal of laughter erupted from Teddy. "Years? But you *live* here."

Hazel finished the last scoop of scrambled eggs and stood, clearing her plate. "I think it might be fun. What do you think, Teddy? Do you want to walk down to the beach for a little bit?"

Teddy was emphatically agreeing when I stopped her. "I was thinking about going to North Beach."

She raised a skeptical brow. She'd gotten to know me well enough to realize that a day off work was unusual, but a day off work paired with the very crowded, very public beach was downright unheard of.

"I'll get the sunscreen!" Teddy was gone before Hazel could ask him to clear his breakfast plate.

I stood and shooed her away. "I'll take care of it. Go."

Hazel planted a hand on her hip. "I hate when you're so bossy."

A flash of desire crossed my face as I recalled just how much she *hadn't* minded my bossiness last night. I looked down at her pretty features. "Are you sure about that?"

She sucked her lower lip into her mouth and tried not to smile. She bumped me with her hip. "I'll go change."

I nodded. "Good. Make sure you're well covered up, though. The late-summer sun can be surprisingly harsh."

"Mm-hmm." She nodded, definitely not believing my bullshit. Hazel tossed the towel onto the table and disappeared up the stairs while I finished cleaning up.

Within minutes, Teddy was dressed in swim trunks, a rash guard, and goggles perched on the top of his head. I laughed and patted his shoulder. "You know, for someone who thought the beach was too sandy, you're awfully excited."

He grinned. "Some things can grow on you."

I looked at him and my heart rolled. "I know what you mean, kid."

EIGHTEEN

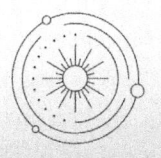

HAZEL

I STARED at JP from behind the safety of my mirrored sunglasses. While he may have thought I was soaking up the sun and watching the waves, I was studying his every move.

Best twelve-dollar sunglasses I've ever purchased.

I was still reeling after we'd crossed *several* lines in his kitchen. I'd nearly clawed his clothes off and begged for his cock. Oh, yes . . . I'd looked at that line and tap-danced right over it.

What the hell is wrong with me? That's my sister's ex . . . whatever they were.

Shame coursed through me, but I couldn't stop the tiny, incessant thoughts that kept poking at my brain. His dick felt big—like *big*, big. In the candlelit room, he was still as powerful and commanding as he was in everyday life, but there was an attentiveness to him that surprised me. A softness. It was tempting to peel back the layers and see the man he worked so hard to keep hidden.

I looked around at the people who were laughing and playing at the beach. I wondered whether anyone really knew him. All around us, nosy people still whispered and pointed, but I came to realize JP was right—they were staring and whispering at *him*.

Summer was dwindling. You could feel it in the way it took longer for the air to warm in the mornings and how the breeze was just a tiny bit cooler than it had been the day before. I stretched my legs across the beach blanket and burrowed my toes into the warm sand. In front of me, Teddy and JP were in a debate about the merits of a castle with turrets versus isolated towers as a defense strategy.

"What about a moat?" I offered.

They turned and the twin stares of annoyed confusion were enough to make me giggle.

"It was just a suggestion." I shrugged.

Teddy drew an invisible line around their half-built castle. "That's a stage three build. We're still developing stage two."

"Oh . . . my bad." I chuckled and leaned back on my elbows to continue watching them.

JP was bare chested. His pecs stood out against his flat stomach. I could make out the individual muscles of his abs as he reached for another sand shovel.

He was fit in a way that said he cared about his physique but didn't spend every waking hour at the gym. He wasn't bulky, but lean and cut with corded muscles that bunched and flexed with every casual movement. He carried himself with the calm confidence that made it clear he knew how good he looked.

Jerk.

My life would be infinitely easier if he'd been unattractive and schlubby instead of . . . *that.*

He leaned in toward Teddy. "The moat's not a half-bad idea, though."

Teddy smiled a devilish grin. "Filled with lava and sharks."

JP's eyebrows bounced playfully. "Definitely."

They got back to construction, and their dark hair ruffled in the breeze. I guessed they decided to compromise because it looked like turrets *and* towers were taking shape.

"Teddy!" A young voice called out, and we all looked up to see Penny running toward us, barreling past blankets and coolers. A very pregnant Lark was slowly waddling behind her.

Teddy shot to his feet and ran toward his friend, kicking up sand in JP's direction.

He brushed off his thighs and sat back on his hands. "Well, I guess I've been replaced by someone cooler."

My lips twisted to hide a smile. "Sorry, champ. Penny is pretty cool."

Next to us, Lark started to set up a blanket, and JP popped to his feet to help her. She paused as though she was surprised by his helpfulness but didn't comment about it. He took her small cooler and set it aside before unrolling the beach blanket and helping her get settled.

"Thanks," she groaned as she lowered herself to the blanket.

"How's he doing in there?" I asked over the rim of my sunglasses with a smile.

"Still cooking." Lark laughed and tipped her face to the late-morning sun. She peeked open one eye to look at JP. "Playing hooky? That's gotta be a first."

JP smiled and looked out onto the vast waters of Lake Michigan, his hands on his trim hips. "Veda is a workaholic. She can hold down the fort for a few hours."

While he looked away, Lark shot me a surprised yet

pleased look, and my skin tingled. "Is Teddy excited about second grade?"

I grinned. "He can't wait. I don't know if it's the routine or the learning itself, but he really likes school. Summer is fun and all, but I have the feeling he was bored and needed someone more mentally stimulating than me."

It wasn't a big deal to admit that I didn't know anything about raising a kid. To me, I was doing my best, and that was good enough.

Lark smiled. "Teddy should try the library camps for kids. Emily puts them on and they are *fabulous*. Penny is always raving about how much fun they have."

Library camps?

For whatever reason, the thought of things like enrichment camps felt a lot like putting down roots. I didn't know where I was going to be next month, let alone next *year*. A pressed smile and stilted nod were all I could manage.

JP walked over to the waterline where Penny and Teddy were kicking at the waves. I tracked him with my eyes, soaking in the long lines of his back as the muscles bunched. His swim trunks were snug, and I smirked at how he'd been hiding such a great ass beneath those tailored suits.

"He's changed," Lark said.

My eyes didn't leave JP's back. "You think so?"

Lark scoffed. "I *know* so. Sure, he's still bristly and kind of a snob, but he's softer somehow." She nodded toward them. "Being a dad looks good on him."

I exhaled and pushed away the sharp pinch under my ribs. "We're still waiting for the paternity results."

Lark hummed. "Maybe so . . . but, I mean . . . *look* at them. The dark hair, the eyes, the grumpy scowls? And don't even get me started on the neckties."

I chuckled. "I see it too." I squinted against the sun and sipped my water to quell the tiny wave of nausea that rolled through me. "Plus, I believe my sister."

Lark pushed her sunglasses onto her head. "He really didn't know?"

I crossed my legs and picked at the blanket. "It's something that still doesn't make sense. Olive wrote me a letter. In it, she was very clear that JP was Teddy's dad. She did say that their romance was brief, but she was certain. She listed him on the birth certificate application. She even came to Outtatowner once."

"No!" Lark's eyes were saucers as she hung on my every word.

I shrugged. "It did not go well, apparently. She didn't reach out again. Olive always said it was his loss and that he knew where to find her if he ever changed his mind. I guess toward the end she had second thoughts, and that's why she finally asked me to find him."

Lark's hand covered mine as my voice went thick. "I'm sorry you lost her."

"It's okay," I lied. I looked at Teddy's sweet, smiling face. "To be honest, it's Teddy I'm worried about. He doesn't really talk about Olive, and now he's got stars in his eyes for JP. I just don't want him to get hurt."

A tear slipped from my eye and I brushed it away.

"Maybe he should talk with someone—process what's happened and have a support system once everything gets worked out."

Lark was right. Teddy *should* talk to someone about losing his mother and all the changes he's experienced.

She was a good mother.

Unlike me, who didn't even remember things like school registration or who thought it was a good idea to just show up and confront the man who was supposed to be his father.

The kind of woman who was okay with fooling around with her sister's ex was not prime mother material, but maybe I could learn to be better.

Beside me, Lark groaned and pressed a hand into her round belly.

Thankful for the distraction, I asked, "How are you feeling?"

She laughed and gestured toward the water. "Like if you rolled me out there, people would think I was an actual whale."

I smiled at her. "Aww, I think you're glowing."

"I think that's sweat, mostly." Lark wiggled her toes. "I have forgotten what my ankles look like. Wyatt joked that he thought cankles were sexy." Together we laughed. "At first I laughed, then I cried and I made him sleep on the couch, until I got mad at him in the middle of the night for not being in bed. All he did was hold me, and I cried all over again. These hormones are *wild*."

I wondered what it would be like to be pregnant—to have a life growing inside you and a partner that could laugh and cry with you through it all.

My sister had endured it alone, and I didn't know if it was something I would ever experience for myself—or if I even wanted to, for that matter.

Lark exhaled as we watched the other people on the beach. "You know . . . Wyatt's not here today because they're dredging the lake."

"Oh . . ." My gut churned. "I didn't realize that was today."

Her lips pressed together in a sad twist. "The DNR showed up yesterday and closed public access to all of the trails. I just didn't want Penny around there today . . . just in case they find anything."

Like JP's mother.

Wyatt and Lark lived at Highfield House, and I had learned that Wabash Lake was set in the forest between Sullivan Farms and their property, connected by hiking trails and walking paths.

She motioned toward JP. "How's he been handling it?"

"Fine, I guess." My brow furrowed. "He doesn't talk about it. Ever." I shrugged. "At least not to me."

Come to think of it, he doesn't really talk about *anything*. I had no idea when they'd scheduled the lake to be dragged, let alone for today. I had no right to feel the tiny pang of hurt, so I shoved it down.

Lark shook her head. "I hope he's okay. Russell King sure did a number on all those kids. It's so heartbreaking. I could never imagine treating your own children like commodities the way he did."

I swallowed hard as I watched JP laugh at something Penny said. "Yeah," I squeaked. "Me too."

JP sauntered toward us, water glistening off his pecs as it sparkled in the sunshine.

"Hey," he said, breathless. "They're begging for an ice-cream cone." He looked at Lark. "Are you okay if I get Penny something at the Snack Shack?"

"Of course. Just as long as you get me something too." Lark smiled as she reached for her bag, but JP stopped her.

"I got it." He bent down to fish out his wallet, but before he stood back up, he winked at me.

My body immediately responded, and an electric shiver worked its way down my back.

"You need anything?" he asked me with a sexy grin.

Oh, I need something all right.

JP knew exactly what he was doing with his devastating smirk and the sensual knowing glittering in his blue eyes.

"Surprise me." I blushed and called out to Teddy, who was running up to us: "Please stay close to JP and Penny."

Teddy nodded and slipped his hand into JP's as my heart rolled. I watched Penny flounce in front of them while JP and Teddy walked hand in hand toward the Snack Shack.

Two little lost boys without a mother.

NINETEEN

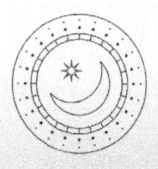

JP

I couldn't recall the last time I had enjoyed a midday, leisurely stroll through downtown.

Probably never.

After Teddy got restless at the beach, we'd packed up, and Hazel said she planned to find them another adventure so I could finally head to work. We parted ways, but it surprised me how I couldn't stop thinking about what they were up to.

Do seven-year-olds nap?

Did they check out the library?

Maybe I could call Sylvie and see about blueberry picking.

There's a new go-kart place that just opened up. Would he like that?

Early-morning beach day with Hazel and Teddy was messing with my head . . . and my routine. Typically my workday started at 5:00 a.m. with sorting emails while I ran three miles on the treadmill. By seven I was sequestered in my office, hunched over proposals, projections, and paperwork.

I released a breath and took in my surroundings. Somehow I had forgotten how quaint and folksy my hometown was. By now summer was waning and the vacation crowds were dwindling. We were in that precious lull where tourism shifted from the peak of summer on the beach and transitioned to a cozier fall with apple picking and hayrides.

Even the air smelled different.

I hadn't missed the way the slight chill of the lake breeze made Hazel's nipple rings press against the flimsy fabric of her lavender bathing suit top. She didn't seem to care at all that she was driving me mad by simply existing.

Despite the mirrored lenses of her sunglasses, I could feel her eyes on me all morning. Whether she was assessing my interactions with Teddy or recalling the way my teeth had nipped at her neck as she rode my hand, I didn't care. I liked how her appreciative gaze heated my skin and puffed my chest.

I shook her from my thoughts.

Walking in my direction, Ms. Tiny was bustling down the street, staring at me with a strange expression. The elderly woman's face looked like a worn leather couch that was pissed off you'd ruined the finish. When I realized I had been whistling, I cleared my throat and stuffed my hand into the pocket of my slacks.

"Ma'am." I tipped my head in her direction.

"Mr. King." Her thin lips pressed into a demure smile.

Mr. King.

I had noticed that, around town, more and more people had stopped calling me JP. It was an unofficial recognition that I was now the head of King Equities. My stomach roiled and bile scorched the back of my throat.

"Please. Call me JP." I attempted a smile, but it felt more like a grimace.

Her lip curled. "I'll call you whatever I like."

She brushed past me and I stifled a snort. At least one thing hadn't changed, Ms. Tiny was still mean as a snake. "Tough old bird," I muttered at her back.

As I waited at the corner for the light to change, I sat back on my heels and looked up at my corner office building. The building itself was one of the original structures constructed when the town was established, and it was starting to look its age.

Veda and I were cramped in the tiny upstairs office. When I'd set up the temporary office space, I was tempted by the circular bay window that provided a panoramic view of Outtatowner—from the lighthouse at the end of the pier to the stretch of Main Street that welcomed tourists downtown.

Once it was fixed up, it could make a stellar office with high ceilings and functional meeting spaces. Veda had made comments about how perfect the afternoon lighting was, and she didn't know it yet, but I'd just purchased the entire thing and planned to renovate it. If we really were going to take over the world, she could have the corner office to enjoy the view she loved so much.

It felt like the least I could do for her role in helping put my father behind bars.

The crosswalk light turned, but my phone rang, so I stepped to the side. Abel's name flashed across the screen and my heart sank.

Tourists flowed around me as I pressed a finger into my ear. "Hello?"

"Hey." Abel's voice was grim—more than usual, and that was saying something. "You need to come out here."

I could feel the blood drain from my face. All day I'd tried to ignore the fact that a crew was dredging Wabash Lake and divers were looking for evidence to use against our father.

I steeled my voice. "They found something?"

He blew out a sad stream of breath. "Not just something." The hairs prickled on the back of my neck as his pause stretched over the line. "They found Mom."

~

Leave it to Dad to finally unite the King siblings in the most horrible way possible.

He did this. It was his fault.

The six of us were standing in a line along the far side of Lake Wabash's south shore. Abel looked as though he was about to plow his fist into something. Whip's arms were crossed as he slowly shook his head. Royal's jaw flexed as he fought back emotion. He slung an arm across Sylvie's shoulder. She and MJ locked arms and silently wiped away tears as quickly as they fell.

The Sullivans were off to the side, offering their silent support. It seemed they understood we needed this moment.

I watched in restrained horror as the coroner confirmed that the remains they found were, in fact, human.

It struck me as funny how quickly I could recall being five years old. We had woken up one morning and Mom was just gone. No note. No tearful goodbye. No promises of coming back to get us.

Nothing.

It was the exact same confusion and emptiness I felt when we all realized what the divers had found. For the twenty-seven years she'd been gone, I did everything I could to not miss her. I set my emotions aside in a little box and refused to open it—I had to in order to survive. Even as a child, it was drilled into me that the only thing I should do was step up and fix whatever problems arose in her absence.

This was no different.

Only now it wasn't anger and betrayal I felt at her absence. It was the unshed grief of a five-year-old boy.

"She was here the whole time," MJ whispered, her voice wobbling at the edges and giving voice to what we'd all been thinking. "She was so close."

Sylvie swallowed and rubbed MJ's arm. "She got to see a lot of life here. Kids laughing. Picnics. Surrounded by nature. There are worse places, I guess."

I didn't want to cry. I didn't want to feel the bone-deep loss of the mother I had loved more than anyone.

He did this.

My bones were rattling with rage as we watched from a distance. Beyond the police tape, the medical examiner took great care of the remains while divers continued to search for and collect additional evidence.

"What are we going to do?" Royal turned to me. Despite being the younger brother, my siblings were always looking to me for answers. Once again, it was my responsibility to step up and fix the problem.

"We don't know for sure it's her," Whip added, though the lack of hope in his voice was telling.

We all knew.

It would only be a matter of time until it was confirmed that Maryann King's remains had been intentionally hidden. It was why Dad had dragged Veda here to threaten and scare her. It was why he fought so long and so hard against June Sullivan when she turned the lake and its surrounding land over to the Department of Natural Resources. Our father's odd affection for June Sullivan had soured when she stood against him and facilitated the development of the hiking trail. It was, in part, her way of shining a spotlight on what she'd suspected he had done to his wife.

For nearly thirty years, he had done everything in his power to successfully keep his secret hidden.

"Nothing changes." My face hardened. "This is good news."

Sylvie's gaze sliced toward me, tears simmering in her eyes. "How could you say that?"

My jaw flexed. "We knew she wasn't coming back. Now we know why. Dad can't buy his way out of this one."

MJ surged forward, squeezing me in her embrace. Her face was buried against my suit jacket, muffling her words. "It's okay to feel it. It's okay to be sad."

My nose burned.

I *did* feel sad. An aching emptiness. A final *knowing* that my mother wasn't off having some exotic adventure without us. She hadn't willingly abandoned us.

She'd never even left town.

My arms wrapped around my little sister as emotion won out. I buried my nose in her hair and struggled to keep my sob in check. Behind me, Royal caught us in a bear hug and squeezed the air from my lungs. Soon Sylvie, Whip, and Abel joined in and we stood in a clump, holding on to one another and trying to make sense of it all.

For a moment, wrapped in a cocoon of sorrow with my siblings, I allowed that little five-year-old boy to feel the sadness of losing his mother. We cried and held on to one another as we each let the pain of the truth sink in.

When we finally separated, Lee stepped forward with glassy eyes to hand us some tissues before pulling Whip in for a hug. I thanked Lee with a nod and wiped under my nose, then cleared my throat and reined in my scattered emotions. Duke grabbed Sylvie and offered comfort to his grieving wife.

"Why don't we meet up at the brewery. Lunch and a few beers on me," Abel said.

He was met with gratitude and acknowledgment, but I simply shook my head. "I'm going to head into the office. I've got work to do."

My father's reach was long and wide. I didn't trust the investigators to not be tempted by whatever strings Dad thought he could pull from behind bars. Outtatowner's crime rate was astonishingly low, so reports of human remains being found at Wabash Lake would be all over the news within hours.

We needed to get ahead of it.

I needed to show the world that there was a new ruler at King Equities, and nothing—not even this—would shake us.

~

THE PORCH LIGHT was on as I slowed down the driveway. Hazel's skoolie was still parked haphazardly in the drive, and I cruised past it to park. After turning the car off, I sat in silence and sighed.

What a fucking day.

I was tired—bone-deep weary and worn thin.

As I'd suspected, news reporters called nonstop asking for a comment. Colleagues voiced their "concern" while poking and prodding, trying to get information on the future of King Equities.

We lost another huge account. *Go figure.*

I pressed my thumbs into my eye sockets and tried to remember how to breathe.

A sharp knock on the glass beside my head jolted me. "Holy fuck!"

"Sorry!" Hazel's voice was muffled by the window. I looked over to see both of her hands up and a strained grimace on her face.

I opened the car door with a huff.

"Hey . . ." she started. "I'm so sorry. I heard you pull in and then you were out here for a while . . ." Nerves rolled off her small frame. She took two steps back. "You know what? I should go, I'm sorry. You look like you need a minute. I shouldn't have—"

"Stop." I stepped from my car and shut the door behind me. I leaned against the car, and my arms hung at my sides in defeat.

Hazel stood, frozen in the darkness as she stared up at me. In the moonlight, the strands of her strawberry blond hair were silver wisps.

I reached forward to clasp her wrist. I closed my eyes with a heavy sigh and pulled her closer.

I didn't know what I was doing. It was very likely a mistake, but I needed something.

I needed *her*.

"Come here." I wrapped my arms around her and Hazel sagged into me. Her arms wound around my waist and she squeezed. My head fell on top of hers and I breathed in her warm, citrusy scent, filling my lungs and holding it inside. If I could focus on her, I wouldn't have to think about anything else.

My bones were so tired it amazed me I was still upright. All five foot six of her was holding me up, and she didn't even realize it.

My eyes burned and my throat was thick as I released her. "Ah . . ." I cleared my throat. "Thanks."

Hazel was looking up at me, waiting for me to make sense of my actions. My hand found her face. "Thank you," I said again, this time with more intention as I gazed at her pretty face.

Her smile was soft and sweet. "You keep thanking me, but I'm not sure what for."

My eyes bounced between hers. A wry chuckle bubbled in my chest. "Honestly, I don't even know either. Being here? Stepping up and being a good mom for Teddy? Hell if I know." I looked down at her and my fingertip brushed away a rogue strand of hair. "All I know is it was nice to not come home to a cold and empty house tonight."

Her brown eyes were shaded in the moonlight. "Even if I am a squatter?" she teased.

A smile twitched the corner of my mouth. Sparring with her was exactly the levity I needed. "And a witch," I added.

The musical notes of her laughter soothed my soul. She playfully rolled her eyes. "Obviously a witch. Always."

She stepped away, but my hand grazed the thin skin on the inside of her arm. I needed that connection, to feel her warmth, even if I didn't know what that meant.

Her warm eyes looked up at me as I watched the tears shimmering along her lash line. "I'm so sorry about your mother."

My thumb grazed the outside corner of her eye, brushing the tear away. "You don't have to cry for me."

Her wet lashes closed, and she squeezed her eyes tight as she whispered, "But if I don't, who else will?"

Her words were a dagger to my heart. My hand moved to her face, tipping it backward and urging her to look at me.

My thumb brushed her cheek as I studied her features. "I don't want to make anyone cry—least of all you."

My eyes dropped to her mouth as her lips parted on an inhale. My thumb dragged across her lower lip.

She was too young.

Our situation was far too complicated.

She deserved a man who wasn't me.

I lowered my head and placed a whisper of a kiss at the corner of her mouth. Her quick inhale was nearly my breaking point, but I pulled back.

"Good night, Hex."

TWENTY

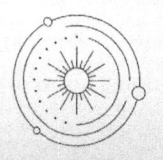

HAZEL

Why won't he just do it already?

Yes, I am fully aware that simple thought made me a *terrible* person. The man just found out his mother was actually dead, and all I could think about were the many, many ways he could seek comfort in *me*.

When JP's kiss landed at the corner of my mouth, my knees wobbled. I stood in dazed confusion as he pulled back, and a devastating and sad smile hinted at his lips. He turned and walked into the house as I stared at his back, too stunned to move.

Grief still lingered around his heavy shoulders.

My fingers itched to do a tarot reading or burn some white sage or something.

How could the universe be so cruel?

I needed something—anything—to help me understand.

Olive would know exactly what to say.

From my back pocket, my phone rang, and when I looked at it, MJ's name flashed on the screen.

My chest pinched. "Hey," I answered. "I am so sorry for what happened today."

MJ's voice was thick, and I could tell by her stuffy nose she had been crying. "Thanks. I'm sorry to call so late. I just wanted to check in on JP. How's he holding up?"

I leaned against JP's car and looked at the darkened house. I blew out a breath. "I don't know. He's okay, maybe? Honestly, I feel like I don't know him at all. Everything is just so . . . awkward."

MJ's wry laugh hummed through the line. "I'm not going to lie, no one was more shocked than me when he said you two were moving in. He's always been so closed off. That's why I'm worried about him. He could really use a break . . . time off from working so hard."

"You're a good sister," I said, my wheels already turning.

MJ sniffled again, but her voice sounded stronger. "He's different around you and Teddy, you know."

I fumbled for the right words. "Oh, I don't know about that. I—"

"It's true," she interrupted. "He's always been so driven. Determined to succeed. I think it was his way of surviving Dad. With you and Teddy he's a little softer somehow. Like he can't make heads or tails of you, and instead of taking charge, it's like he's along for the ride."

I chuckled quietly at her assessment. JP had thrown me for a loop too. When I'd come to Outtatowner to find him, I had expected him to be as flippant and dismissive as he'd been to Olive. I never expected our snippy banter to be so much fun, and I certainly didn't expect the way his eyes softened or how tender he could be.

"Just . . . don't give up on him, okay?" MJ's voice was watery again.

"Um . . . okay." It was all I could do to not cry alongside her. "Hey, MJ?"

She hummed.

I picked at my nail polish and gathered the courage to continue. "Look, I know things between your brother and me are kind of weird and your whole family is going through a lot right now . . . but if you could use another friend, I'd love to be her."

I could hear her smile through the phone. "I'd like that too."

I exhaled a sigh of relief. *Why was making friends as an adult always so freaking awkward?*

"Thanks again for checking on him for me," she said.

"You bet." My eyes glanced up to see the soft light glowing from his bedroom.

We ended the call, and I wrapped my arms around my middle as I stared up at the second-floor window.

JP was controlling, demanding, and stubborn, but there was also a fiercely protective side that I was just getting to know. He was surrounded by people who loved him, even if he sometimes forgot to see it.

Just don't give up on him.

But what could I possibly do?

Resigned, I pushed off his car and started to walk toward the house. My eyes had landed on my skoolie when the ridiculous, reckless, *perfect* idea popped into my head.

∽

I CUPPED my hands and peered into the darkened interior of King Tattoo. The shop door was locked, but a soft light glowed from the very back of the parlor.

"What if he's not here?" Teddy asked as he also tried to peer through the glass.

"Veda said he comes in early." I looked down at Teddy's sweet, hopeful face. "This might work."

When Luna rounded a corner from the back to walk up the main hallway, I knocked on the window, then jumped up and down and waved to her as Teddy grinned.

She waved back, a friendly grin spreading across her face. She pointed toward the door, and I met her there as she unlocked it.

Luna was dressed in black leggings, combat boots, and a cropped Pantera T-shirt riddled with holes. Her black eyeliner was fiercely winged, and her bold red lip was what dreams were made of.

"Morning, you two!" She chirped as she held the door open for me.

Luna's attention landed on Teddy. "Is it time for your first tattoo? You know, we don't open for a few more hours." Luna smiled at me and winked.

"No tattoos today, but it *is* kind of an emergency—a fun one!" I wrung my hands, excitement and energy buzzing through me. "Is Royal around? I texted Veda and she mentioned he should be here."

"Hey, boss," Luna called over her shoulder toward the back. "You've got a few visitors. Couple of cute ones." Luna turned toward me. "Thank you for the tincture. I've been smoke-free ever since. You have a gift!"

I grinned. "Happy to help."

"Your aura is lemony yellow today." Luna pointed, and her finger was stacked with silver jewelry as it circled in the air. "You're up to something."

Teddy stifled a knowing giggle and my eyebrows waggled. "We are!"

Royal King walked out of the first booth and closed the door behind him. He was tall and commanding. Tattoos covered his neck and trailed down his arms and across his knuckles. If it weren't for his affable grin, he'd be downright intimidating.

"Morning, Hazel." He nodded in greeting. "My lady mentioned you might be swinging by." He crossed his thick arms and smiled. "What can I do for you?"

I straightened and hoped I didn't sound certifiably insane. "Well, I've been thinking. JP's always so focused on work. Teddy is still trying to get to know him, so . . . so we want to do something to help him loosen up a little. Maybe have some fun." My arms spread wide. "Kind of like a last hurrah before Teddy starts school."

His eyes glowed with excitement as his eyebrows crept up his forehead. "Like a prank?"

My brow furrowed. "Um . . . not a prank, no." I looked at Royal and hoped he didn't think I was losing my mind. "More like a . . . kidnapping?"

Royal's hearty laughter burst from his chest, and he pulled me into a tight hug. His shoulders shook as I struggled to breathe around his bulky frame. He released me, holding me at arm's length. "I love you."

I blushed and returned his grin. "So you'll help us?"

He turned toward the desk where Luna was typing on the computer. "Luna, I'll be back in time for my one o'clock."

She shot him a bland look, followed by an eye roll and a nod before returning her attention to the computer screen.

He nodded in her direction, unfazed by her bratty dismissal. "Perfect." He turned toward Teddy and gently tugged on his bow tie. "Let's go mess with your dad."

Later that day, as I stood outside my skoolie in a forest clearing near a bluff, nerves simmered beneath my skin.

This might not have been my best idea.

My toe tapped as I impatiently waited for Royal to show up with JP. Teddy was inside the bus, reading his book while I checked my watch and my phone for the eleventh time.

Royal was later than we'd agreed upon, and I worried that JP had refused to come along. My chest pinched thinking about how I could break the bad news to Teddy that JP had chosen work over us.

The crunch of dirt and rocks under tires whipped my attention to the trailhead, and Royal's huge truck rolled into view. I'd sent him a location pin so he could find us and was relieved when he pulled to a stop in front of me. Royal hopped out of the truck, but his mischievous grin gave me pause.

I frowned. "Where's—"

He held up a finger and rounded the truck before pulling open the back seat. To my horror, JP's suit was rumpled, and there was a black mesh bag over his head.

"Cut the shit, Royal. What the hell is going on?" JP was angry.

Very, very angry.

Royal only laughed and leaned in, dragging his little brother from the car. His hands were loosely bound with a thin black cord.

"Oh my god!" I surged forward, untying the bindings. My eyes narrowed at Royal. "I didn't mean an *actual* kidnapping!"

Royal laughed. "Oh, come on. It was fun."

When his hands were free, JP whipped the black bag

from his head and threw it at Royal. "Would it have killed you to wash the bag? It smells like your sweaty nutsack."

Royal caught the bag and sniffed it. "Ugh. Sorry, man." He pointed at me. "This was her idea."

Royal shot me a look before he rounded his truck and climbed behind the wheel. It roared to life, and he pulled a U-turn in the clearing, waving and grinning like a fool as he drove away, leaving JP stranded with us.

JP's eyes whipped to me and narrowed. "What the hell is going on?"

With my back to the skoolie, I spread my arms. "Surprise?"

JP pinched the bridge of his nose. "I have work to do, Hazel."

"Veda and I discussed everything. One day and one night away won't actually kill you. She's handling everything while you take some much-needed time off." He tried to interrupt, but I raised a finger. "MJ *also* thought you looked like you needed a break from work."

My arms were still spread in a *ta-da* position, but my bubble of excitement was slowly leaking air.

JP looked around the remote campsite. "Time off?"

"We're camping!" I hoped my smile didn't waver. "Well . . . we have the skoolie, so it's more like *glamping*, but you get the idea."

I was fairly certain he was about to call the whole thing off when Teddy realized he'd arrived.

"Dad!" He bounded down the skoolie's steps and launched himself at JP.

JP's arm wrapped around Teddy's back and he softened. "Hey, kid."

"You made it! Are you surprised? We packed you a bag

and everything!" His excited words tumbled over one another.

One eyebrow lifted as he looked at me. "Packed a bag?"

Teddy nodded. "Yep! Hazel had to touch your underwear!"

My cheeks heated as JP looked down at him and chuckled. "Well, that's very helpful."

I smiled and fought back a laugh. "Teddy was curious why your boxers looked so tight."

For the first time, I could barely make out tiny red splotches forming from beneath the collar of his rumpled dress shirt.

I lifted his duffel bag from the ground and tossed it to him. "Go on, get changed. First thing we have planned is a hike."

JP frowned at Teddy, but there was humor dancing at the edge of his mouth. His eyes narrowed playfully at Teddy. "I'm not getting out of this, am I?"

Teddy grinned. "Nope!"

JP sighed and climbed into the skoolie. "If you say so, but only if there are s'mores later."

I opened my arms, beckoning Teddy to me. He hugged my middle and I squeezed him back, relieved that my haphazard plan hadn't completely blown up in my face.

Yet.

TWENTY-ONE

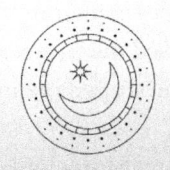

JP

"Are you mad?" Beside me, Hazel's soft, tentative voice whispered in my ear as we hiked.

We were walking side by side along a dirt path that wound us higher and higher toward a peak. Teddy was zigzagging his way across the path, tossing rocks and picking up random sticks. I was pretending that the way Hazel's breath was huffing in and out of her lungs didn't make me want to pin her against a tree and hear it up close.

Her legs were smooth and bare. The muscles bunched with each step, and I appreciated how her tight shorts hugged every curve. Her calves tapered to white socks that peeked out over her hiking boots.

"No," I answered honestly. "I'm not mad."

Annoyed? Yes.

Inconvenienced? Definitely.

Charmed? Possibly.

Her exaggerated exhale made me smile. "Oh, thank god. When I recruited Royal, I swear I had *no idea* it was going to go down like that."

I kicked a small rock out of our path so she wouldn't

trip. "That's the thing about Royal. No matter what it is, he's always going to take it a step too far."

I glanced at her, appreciating the way the afternoon sun highlighted the strands of copper in her hair. "He called me out of my office and asked me to meet him in the back alley. I was ambushed, and he stuffed me in the back of his truck, you know."

She grimaced and my heart clunked. "Sorry. In my head this was a cute and whimsical escape from all the craziness that was happening around you."

Truth be told, a few days away was probably exactly what I needed. Not that I'd ever done it to know for sure. In fact, her brand of crazy was surprisingly endearing.

I exhaled and looked up to admire how the light filtered through the canopy and the coastal breeze ruffled the leaves.

"Are you sure you're okay?" she asked.

I had no idea how to even begin to answer that question.

Yes? Maybe? Not really? I didn't really know what *okay* actually felt like.

"I guess, on one hand everything feels like too much—Dad, the business, my mom—" I gestured toward Teddy without having to say his name. "But on the other hand, I don't mind the chaos. I'm good at solving problems. We finally have answers about my mother, and there's a little bit of peace in that. Plus, he's a cool kid." I shrugged and hoped she could follow my erratic stream of consciousness.

Hazel stretched her arms in front of her and wrapped them around herself in a tight hug. "I don't know how you do it. It's like you're a master at chess and I'm just out here playing hopscotch."

Her self-deprecating laugh floated on the breeze.

I shook my head. "You take time for this, though. You're living your life, showing Teddy how to exist in the moment." I shrugged. "Kids probably need that." I gestured toward the nature that sprawled ahead of us. "Showing your adoring fans what a gem Michigan is."

She swallowed and looked at the trees. "I think I'm on a bit of a hiatus." She huffed a breath. "I don't know. It makes me feel a little like a fraud, but I've been sharing less content about traveling, for obvious reasons, and more content about my experience raising a kid when you have no idea what you're doing."

I watched as uncertainty and nerves bounced through her.

"I'm sure they tune in for you, not just travel content." *Hell, I know I would.*

Hazel blushed and smiled, then playfully bumped my shoulder. "Look at us . . . getting along and balancing unexpected parenthood."

I narrowed my eyes but was enjoying the playful banter. "You did have me kidnapped this afternoon—let's not forget that."

She blew a raspberry between her full lips. "Tiny detail."

When Hazel's foot slipped on a rock and she stumbled, my arms wrapped around her waist to catch her.

"Careful." My voice was gruff and angrier than I'd intended.

My hand splayed across her ribs as she scrambled to remain upright. My fingertips landed under the hemline of her crop top, nestling into the grooves of her rib cage. Her skin was soft and warm as I pulled her closer.

Her body was flush with mine. "Be careful," I repeated, softer this time. "Please."

Her tongue darted out to wet her lips, and I stared at her mouth. It would be so easy to be lost in the moment with her. All it would take was the tiniest movement and my mouth could be on hers again.

The perfect distraction.

She cleared her throat and the moment dissipated. I stepped away from her, wiping my hand against my thigh and trying to forget how right she felt in my arms.

"I'm tired." Teddy's whine made the last word stretch on as he trudged toward us, effectively snapping me back to reality.

I crouched in front of him. "Legs are beat?" He nodded, so I gestured with my head. "All right, hop on."

Teddy's not-very-tired-looking eyes lit up. "Really?" He scrambled onto my back before I could answer.

I stood and hiked him higher to make sure he was secure. "Better?"

Teddy grinned and nodded. My attention landed on Hazel, who was staring up at me with a strange look on her face.

I frowned, taking in her reddened cheeks. "Are you tired too? Your face is all flushed."

She swallowed and shook her head.

I tapped Teddy's leg, needing an excuse to create some space between her and me. "Let's go see what we can find over that way."

~

THE CAMPFIRE CRACKLED as I stared into the flames. Crickets chirped and owls hooted as nighttime fell in a blanket of stars around us. I had been pathetically helpless when it came to building a campfire. I knew the basics, but Hazel called the shots. Teddy and I gathered the supplies—larger sticks and fallen branches—as she worked. She then taught Teddy how to build a log cabin structure with sticks, starting with tinder, then kindling.

Hazel poked the roaring campfire with a stick to shift a log and smiled proudly. Across the fire, I watched as Teddy leaned into Hazel, and a smear of dirt-caked marshmallow streaked across his cheek. He looked more like a seven-year-old kid than he ever had.

I was busy explaining the key differences between mergers and acquisitions, like he'd asked. His eyes were drooping, and I let my speech quietly trail off as he fought sleep.

It was sad to admit that I'd never been camping, especially given the beautiful landscape that surrounded my hometown. When I was growing up, Dad had zero interest in actually parenting, and Aunt Bug had done the best she could to raise six kids from a distance. Even if she had offered to take us camping or on a vacation, there wasn't a world in which my father would have let us have that moment with her.

Teddy wouldn't have to experience that—at least not with me around. Sure, I didn't know anything about nature or camping, but that was what Hazel was for. Between the two of us, Teddy could have experiences all kids should have.

That is, if you are his dad.

My heart thumped. Somewhere along the line, I had started to forget the very real possibility that Teddy wasn't my kid. I swallowed hard and ignored the coil in my stomach.

Hazel hummed as she looked at the fire and poked at it. Light flickered across her features, creating sharp contrasts where her cheekbones stood out.

My mind buzzed, and despite the peaceful nature

around us, I couldn't wind down. I wiped my palms across my jeans and looked across the fire at Hazel as Teddy snoozed on her shoulder.

I frowned. "So you just . . . sit here?"

Hazel grinned. "Yeah . . . I sit here and breathe." She tipped her face to the moon and inhaled deeply. "Isn't it great?"

I harrumphed. It was too quiet. Too easy to let my mind wander to what-ifs.

What if everything falls apart and Dad gets away with it?

What if Teddy is my kid?

What if he isn't?

What if I'd met Hazel first?

What if that didn't actually matter after all?

I didn't like how the quiet allowed the what-ifs to creep in.

When leaves rustled in the tree line, I jumped. From across the fire, Hazel covered a giggle.

My expression sharpened. "It's not funny."

She bit her lower lip and looked up at me from beneath her lashes. "It's a *little* funny."

I gestured to the forest at her back. "You want to get eaten by bears?" I hissed.

It was a bit out of my depth, but I figured a large rock or fallen branch would do, should anything come barreling out of the woods. Fighting off a bear with my bare hands wasn't ideal, but I wouldn't go down without a fight.

Hazel's eyebrows shot up. "The ferocious and deadly bears of southwest Michigan?"

I rolled my eyes and stood. "Whatever."

Hazel laughed and I looked down at her. Mischief danced with firelight in her eyes. She was ridiculous and infuriating. Her sunshine radiated, even under the cloak of darkness.

She was impossible to hate.

Teddy shifted against her shoulder and drew my attention. "He's out cold."

Hazel tossed her stick into the fire, watching the flames consume it. "I'll take him in."

I stepped forward, crowding her space and bending to scoop him up. "I got him."

Teddy's weight sagged in my arms and I moved toward the skoolie with Hazel at my heels. She opened the bus door and I climbed inside.

Hazel pointed around me. "His bed is over there, on the right."

It still amazed me how much space was inside the old school bus and how much work it must have taken to transform it. Once inside, I walked between the small couch and dinette set. On the left, her small kitchen still had graham cracker crumbs and marshmallows scattered on the white countertop.

She popped a marshmallow into her mouth as she walked behind me.

Across from the kitchen stove was a small bed. Above it were more cabinets for storage. One was slightly open and caught my eye.

Was that ... an urn?

Hazel slinked around me and closed it with a snap. "That's nothing."

Letting it go for now, I ducked and gently set Teddy on top of the space-themed comforter.

Hazel moved around me with a wet wipe, and she did what she could to wipe the sticky marshmallow from his face.

"He'll need a proper shower tomorrow, but this is good enough," she whispered. When he didn't wake, she chuckled. "He's really tired."

I slipped his sneakers off his little feet and neatly placed them beside the bed. It suddenly struck me how domestic and routine it felt to be tucking Teddy into bed after a long day—Hazel and I working together to get him in bed, that fraction of a second I looked down at him and watched him sleep.

It all felt oddly *normal.*

He was a good kid. He deserved to be taken care of like this.

I watched his eyelids flutter as he rolled.

I'll do right by you, kid. I promise.

I backed away, allowing Hazel to adjust a blanket on top of Teddy. She leaned in and kissed him before gently closing the curtain to his sleeping area.

Hazel stood and pressed the back of her hand to her mouth and stifled a big yawn.

She stretched her arms. "I'm beat too."

I pressed my lips together and nodded. The small space of the skoolie closed in on me. The air was filled with her citrus-and-spice scent mingling with the lingering smoky aroma of the campfire. "I'll put out the fire."

Hazel nodded, and I escaped the confined quarters to pull in deep lungfuls of fresh, coastal air.

I needed to clear her from my head.

After dousing the fire, I returned to the skoolie. I could hear movement from the back of the bus, and I had assumed Hazel was settling into the living quarters in the back. I opened a cabinet above the couch and was relieved to find an extra blanket.

I stared at the tiny couch and grumbled.

When Hazel emerged from the room at the back, she was holding a pillow and blanket. I reached for them. "Thanks."

Hazel shifted, pulling the pile away. "These are for me. I'll take the couch." She gestured toward the queen-size bed at her back. "You can take the bed."

I flattened my stare. "Don't be ridiculous."

"I'm not the one being ridiculous. You're never going to fit on that couch. *I* barely fit on it."

I scowled. "I am not taking your bed, Hex."

Hazel plopped the blanket and the pillow onto the floor and crossed her arms. "And I'm not letting you sleep out here."

I mirrored her stance with my arms crossed and stared down at her. With her chin raised and a glint in her eyes, she was feisty and not backing down.

I fought the urge to get lost in the comfort of her soft brown eyes.

"Rock, paper, scissors?" she asked.

"What?"

"If I win, we share the bed and both get a good night's rest. If you win, you can be a glutton for punishment and sleep out here, and I don't have to feel bad about your shitty choices."

My jaw clenched as I fought a smile. "You are impossible."

Hazel grinned and thumped her fist on an open hand. "Thank you. Ready? On *shoot*."

I rolled my eyes but readied my fist.

Rock. Paper. Scissors. Shoot.

Shit.

Her rock beat my scissors.

I blew out an annoyed breath. "Fuck me."

Hazel tsked and grinned. "On the first date? What kind of girl do you think I am?"

My face heated as I watched her turn and head toward the back of the bus.

"Come on." She smiled again. "Let's get cozy."

For a beat I stared at the couch. I *could* be a pouty bitch and sleep out there . . . I watched the curve of her ass as she retreated to the back of the bus—and temptation eventually won out.

TWENTY-TWO

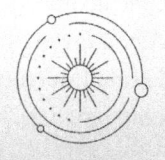

HAZEL

Rock *always* won. Everyone knew that.

With a triumphant smirk, I walked back to the room at the far end of the skoolie, my eyes flicking to the cabinet above the sink. I was relieved it was still closed. Somehow the latch to the cabinet where I kept my sister's ashes had popped open, and I made a mental note to fix that tomorrow.

He really doesn't need to know you're carting around your sister's remains because you don't know what to do with them.

I peeked up at him as I started to close the sliding barn-style door. "Give me two seconds to change and I'll be ready."

JP stared at me like he hadn't already been more than acquainted with my body, and my cheeks flushed at the memory.

I slid the door closed the rest of the way and hurried to disrobe and slip on a night shirt. I piled my hair on top of my head with a scrunchie and tossed my dirty clothes into a hamper. When I slid the bedroom door back open, JP was bare chested and in nothing but his black boxer briefs.

My eyes flicked from his crotch to his face and back again. A warm buzz hummed beneath my skin as I appreciated the cut lines of his trim waist. When my eyes moved back up, he was looking me over, too, and a small, nervous laugh escaped me.

"You forgot to pack me pajamas." His voice was low and thick.

I blinked. "It's fine." The strangled squeak of my voice betrayed me.

I rounded the bed and rearranged a pillow before resting on top of the covers. Lying on my back, I stared at the ceiling while JP closed the door and climbed into bed beside me.

Heat from his body rolled off him, and I squeezed my thighs together. He smelled rich and spicy and a little like camp smoke. Side by side we stared at the ceiling. The side of his calf tickled my leg and I jerked.

"Sorry," he mumbled.

A giggle built inside my chest and I pressed my lips together. My shoulders shook.

"What?" he asked.

I rolled to face him, tucking my hands under my head. "I can't believe Royal actually put a bag over your face."

JP mirrored my position and he smirked. "Royal is an overgrown child."

I grinned as I studied his handsome features. "He got you here, though."

His eyes moved over my face. "Yeah . . . I guess he did."

I licked my lip, summoning every ounce of courage I could find. "So . . . are we just not going to talk about what happened? The other night?"

JP's knee grazed mine, and I was all too aware of the tiny points of contact between us.

"It was . . ." he started.

"A mistake?" I finished for him despite the tightness in my chest.

JP's signature scowl flashed across his face. "I was going to say 'a good time.'"

My world spun. "Oh . . ."

He smirked and a soft rumble sounded from his chest. "Did you think it was a mistake?"

I swallowed hard. "No. Not really."

On top of the blanket, his fingertip grazed the top of my thigh, moving from my knee to my hip.

"What are you doing?" I whispered.

His wicked grin widened. "Getting cozy."

My playful words from earlier taunted me. His touch was searing, igniting a path as it slowly dragged to my hip and up my torso. My eyes flicked to the closed door, and he understood my concern.

"You'll have to be quiet so we're not interrupted. Can you do that?" His mouth twisted into a devilish smile as my world went fuzzy at the edges.

His touch was sensual, soft, and deliciously sinful.

"Maybe?" I whispered, fully confident I would *not* be able to remain calm if he kept touching me like that.

Instead of going any further, he stroked his fingertips down my arm, capturing my wrist. He gently pulled my hand forward.

My pulse skipped. Every cell in my body ignited when he moved my hand over his hip. I let my hand slide down slowly until it was in his lap.

His hard cock pulsed under my touch and I squeezed.

JP sucked in a breath. "I want you to feel what you do to me. How fucking insane you make me on a daily basis."

I shifted my hips forward and wrapped my hand around his rock-hard dick. With another gentle squeeze, I hummed and let my body take over.

My throat was tight.

JP's gaze on me was like fire. Awareness sparked to life and my blood warmed. My legs shifted, desperate for any kind of friction. He shifted, rising over me and gripping the back of one knee to straddle his hips.

He settled back on his heels and, with a tight grip on my hips, pulled me closer. My hand slid away from him, and I pressed my palms to his stomach and enjoyed the way his abs flexed and bunched with every movement.

I stifled a squeal as his hand grazed down my thigh, starting at my knee and working his way closer.

One hand gripped my hip, and I became suddenly aware that his other hand was busy stroking his cock over his boxer briefs. He stared at me as though he was memorizing every feature in the dark.

A soft grunt escaped his lips and my clit pulsed. My mouth watered.

I wanted him more than I'd ever wanted another human being, and my body didn't care how wrong that was.

For a moment the only sound was the two of us panting in the darkness.

My hand covered his, and he let his slip away. Under my palm, his cock was hard and warm and so fucking thick.

"Take it out," I whispered.

JP's face loomed over mine. Moonlight shone through the curtains in my bedroom, highlighting the sharp planes of his face.

His hand slid down my arm and captured my wrist. He guided my hand to the hemline of my shirt. His fingers laced with mine as together we stroked the outside of my cotton underwear.

My breath hitched.

His deep voice rumbled in my ear. "Can I take these off?"

I would have given anything to keep JP looking at me the way he was—like his control was seconds away from snapping and unleashing all his pent-up frustrations on me.

I gulped and nodded. His fingertips hooked into the top of my underwear, and I shimmied to work them down my thighs.

Sitting on his heels, JP stopped moving as he stared at the hemline of the T-shirt, which did nothing to cover my pussy. "Touch yourself, Hex. *Please.*"

His voice was strained. Desperate.

My fingers trembled as I gained the confidence to slowly slide my fingers over my stomach and between my legs. I stroked the top of my mound and JP groaned.

His hands slid into his boxer briefs, pushing them down and freeing his cock. His abs rippled as he fisted it. I could barely blink as his hand stroked up and down its length, running his thumb over the tip with a soft groan.

"I like that," I whispered, slipping my fingers between my thighs as I stared. "Keep touching yourself and think of me."

His dark chuckle sent goose bumps erupting on my skin. "You're all I think about. That's the fucking problem."

The temperature inside the bus skyrocketed and my cheeks flushed. I licked my lips as I watched his hand move up and down.

"Doesn't that feel better when it's wet?" I asked.

His eyes flew to mine, and his furrowed brows darkened his eyes.

A coy grin spread on my face as I sat up and leaned forward.

"Hazel," he growled, already leaning back.

My name on his lips in that dark, commanding way was like a drug. My eyes flicked to his. "I'm only helping. Just for a second."

His hand stopped at the base of his cock as my tongue teased the head. We both groaned as my mouth slipped over him. JP stopped moving altogether.

My confidence built as I moved my mouth lower, using my saliva to wet his dick. My tongue swirled over the veiny underside, and I went deeper.

I hummed, shifting my weight as my pussy went slick. He stifled another groan as I bobbed on his cock.

When he groaned again, I released him from my mouth and licked my lips.

His eyes were wild, darker, and he stroked up and down his slick cock. I lay back down in front of him, legs propped on either side of his hips.

I was soaked, and my fingers slipped inside my pussy. My hips bucked, and I whimpered as I moved my fingers in and out, recalling how hard and thick he was.

JP inched closer, propping one hand beside my head for leverage. His breath was hot on my neck as we both drove ourselves closer and closer to the edge. The pressure of my fingers increased and my pleasure doubled.

Behind my eyelids I relived the moment in the kitchen when he'd made me come, how only moments before, his cock had filled my mouth and nearly gagged me, how desperately I wished we were alone so I could ride his dick and scream his name.

I desperately wanted to be reckless. To let him slip inside me and fuck me long and hard. But I didn't have any condoms, and I was too fervent to stop whatever was happening between us.

He worked himself in smooth strokes, his breathing becoming more ragged the closer he got to release. JP's mouth fell open, but his eyes never left me.

"Hazel," he gritted through his teeth, and it was nearly my undoing. My body buzzed as I chased my orgasm.

He could ruin me. Ruin everything, really, but I couldn't find it in me to care. We were lost in the moment, in each other.

My nipples strained against the fabric of my T-shirt, and my free hand reached up to tug on one piercing. I was barreling toward release as I watched him grunt and his hips twitch as he stroked himself.

I added another finger and saw stars at the back of my eyelids.

"Open your eyes," he demanded. "I want you to look at me when you come."

My eyes fluttered open, and the intensity of his stare was intimidating. His strokes were rough and sensual. I was consumed with him, drowning in his intense blue eyes when my orgasm crashed over me.

My free hand flew to my mouth as I stifled a cry and rolled my head to the side. Waves of pleasure broke over my body as my mouth found his wrist. My teeth dragged across his skin as my body shuddered.

"Let me taste you," he demanded. "I want to lick your cum from your fingers."

Without hesitation, I pulled my fingers from my pussy

and raised them. A moan vibrated through him as his mouth closed around my two fingers. His tongue slipped between them, sucking and tasting my orgasm.

When he finished, JP sat on his heels and chased his own release. He sucked his lower lip, savoring my flavor as he stroked. My pussy clenched in anticipation. With a grin, I hiked up my top, pulling the T-shirt up to expose my chest.

My free hand gripped his thigh as he pumped and finally allowed himself release. His eyes never left me as he finished on my chest. Thick ropes of cum hit my breasts and dripped down.

He reached up, brushing his thumb over my nipple piercing and painting me with his cum. His confident smirk was intensely erotic.

I'd never felt sexier.

The tiny bedroom was quiet, except for our breaths and the choir of cicadas outside the window.

JP sighed and sat back on his heels. He flopped down beside me, putting his hand beneath his head as he stared at the ceiling. He smiled, and the tension was gone from his jaw. He looked younger. At ease.

I smiled to myself and carefully rolled, pulling tissues from the small bedside table, and handed some to him as I wiped between my boobs.

He stopped my hand. "Let me."

Our eyes locked, and the room spun as JP shifted and started cleaning me up.

I knew how to handle JP when he was unbearable. I knew how to handle him when he was being a grumpy little bitch. It was when he looked at me with softness that threw me off-kilter. When he showed the bits of himself that were tender and sensitive, I lost my footing.

It poked something tender inside my heart and I had to look away. "Thank you."

When he was finished, JP quietly exhaled and wiped at his stomach before he crawled off the bed. "I'm going to clean up . . . make sure the fire is out and the bus is locked up."

I rifled around the bed for my underwear as my cheeks heated. "Okay. Thanks. I'm going to clean up and turn in."

JP nodded and slid open the door. He paused, his hand gripping the entryway like maybe he wanted to say something, but didn't.

I waited, listening for him to finish in the bathroom and walk down the steps of the skoolie. Once he was gone, I sneaked into the bathroom, cleaned myself up, and got out a fresh pair of pajamas. In the bedroom, I gently pulled back the covers and slipped beneath them.

A few minutes later, I heard JP's footsteps returning. I clamped my eyes closed and tried to level my breathing, pretending to sleep.

My heart thumped, and I was sure he could hear it. JP could have changed his mind and slept on the couch, but he came back. As he slid into bed beside me, I tried not to move.

Facing him, I kept my eyes closed and my breath steady. JP leaned in close and paused. Heat from his body was only inches away as he hovered over me.

"Thank you for the perfect day." His lips whispered over my hair before a kiss brushed across my temple. My heart clenched, and I struggled to breathe.

JP shifted next to me and inhaled. "Sweet dreams, Hex." He rolled over, and I listened to his heavy breathing even out until he fell asleep.

Tears pricked beneath my lashes.

Why, out of the four billion men in the world, did I have to develop a soft spot for the one man who was completely off-limits? Olive would never understand, and she wasn't even there so I could explain myself. I clamped my hand over my mouth and nose to hide a silent sob.

What have I gotten myself into this time?

TWENTY-THREE

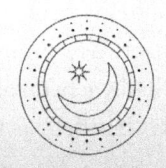

JP

If she could pretend to be asleep when I'd crawled into bed last night, then I could pretend I was unintentionally spooning her and wishing the sunrise would wait. Beside her, sated and warm, I slept better than I had in years.

My first thought upon waking wasn't the laundry list of bullshit I had to deal with; it was her. Hazel's rose gold hair was fanned across her shoulder, and my legs were hiked up behind her. My hand flexed on her hip as I breathed in the bright citrus of her scent.

She shifted and I clamped my eyes tighter, fighting the reality that our night was over. In my arms, she tensed as she started to wake. I kept my eyes closed as Hazel quietly slipped from beneath my hand.

I stifled a laugh when she bumped the bed and whisper-shouted, "Son of a *biscuit*!"

Through lowered lashes I watched as Hazel pulled on a pair of shorts. She whipped off her sleep shirt, and I enjoyed her perky little tits bouncing as she pulled a clean tank top over her head.

My cock surged to life, and I rolled to hide the fact that her mere presence had caught his attention.

When she slipped out of the bedroom and closed the door behind her, I rolled to my back with a groan. I was rock hard and tented the sheet. My brain was looping on how things could have gone had we been alone, or at my place, or in any other situation besides a thirty-five foot diesel school bus.

I could hear Hazel talking quietly with Teddy, so I sat up and scrubbed a hand over my face.

I wonder what her tarot would have to say about last night.

I smirked and pulled a fresh shirt from the duffel bag on the floor before going in search of Teddy and Hazel.

Through the window, I spotted them outside, walking around the campsite and straightening up. I walked down the steps and squinted in the early-morning sunshine. "Morning."

"Morning, Dad," Teddy called over his shoulder with a yawn.

Some unknown emotion flashed across Hazel's face as her attention moved from Teddy to me. She didn't say good morning, and despite the urge to walk over to her and greet her with a kiss, I stuffed my hands into my pockets.

Something was on her mind. I could tell in the way she avoided eye contact and focused every ounce of her attention on Teddy as he bounced around the campsite.

We had definitely crossed a line last night.

Again.

Still, I couldn't find it within me to regret it.

"Can we swim in the lake this morning?" Teddy asked. "Please?"

Hazel's mouth opened and shut as she looked at me. "Uh..."

"Sorry, man." I could be the bad guy if she needed me to be. "I have to get back to work. Vacation is over for me."

His face fell and I felt like a total asshole. "Oh, okay." Glumly he kicked a rock and walked past me toward the skoolie, his shoulders sagging with disappointment.

"Don't take it personally," Hazel said, but she still wouldn't look at me. "I think he's testing out *guilt trips* as a new manipulation tactic."

I leaned back on my heels. "Got it. I won't." I studied her as she folded up a camping chair and stuffed it in the storage locker under the bus. "I'm kind of taking the cold shoulder from you personally, though."

Her attention moved to me and her features softened. Her delicate hands covered her face. "I'm sorry." She gestured between us. "I'm just . . . last night was . . . you're just so . . ."

I raised an eyebrow. "I hope I'm going to like the way those sentences are supposed to end."

She laughed and exhaled. "It's very confusing. I am supposed to *hate* you."

My lips flattened and my gut twisted, imagining any reality where Hazel Adams actually hated me. "I see."

She let out a frustrated growl. "See? That." Her hand flipped in my direction. "How am I supposed to stay mad at you when you're just so . . . *you?*"

I mulled over her words and nodded. "Why don't you let me in on *why* you're supposed to hate me and we can go from there."

Hazel toyed with her lip. She paused, blinking as indecision buzzed through her. Finally, she sighed and slapped her thigh. "Fine. Stay here."

Hazel breezed by me, and I sneaked a tiny hit of her perfume as she passed, breathing it in deep and holding it in my lungs.

When she came back, she stood in front of me and held out a letter. "Here."

I took it from her and slipped the rumpled note from its envelope. It was handwritten in loopy feminine handwriting.

"It's from Olive," she explained. "There's a lot in there, but read here . . ." She flipped the paper over and pointed to the middle of the page. Her finger stabbed into the paper. "She tried to tell you. She came here to tell you about her pregnancy, and you wouldn't even *speak* to her. You sent a crying, pregnant woman away in the rain. She said your father was the only person who cared enough to listen."

My eyes scanned the page. "My father?" I scoffed. "That's impossible." I grabbed the paper and tried to focus on reading the words as my mind spun.

. . . he was there and refused to see me. He couldn't even look me in the eyes and tell me to go away. Instead, he had some old guy wearing Moon Boots ask me to leave and practically tossed me out in the rain.

Later that day, I was crying my eyes out at a diner when his father came to see me. We sought comfort in each other. The things he said about his son were horrible, but that wasn't the man I met at Cask & Keg and spent one amazing night with. The JP I knew was self-deprecating and sensitive and a gentleman. I came to realize Russell wasn't the man I thought he was either.

But I am out of time and out of choices.

One day you'll see that I'm doing this for Teddy. So he has a chance to have a father who has the capacity to love him. Without JP, Teddy may never have that.

My blood cooled. It made no sense that Olive had the impression she'd come to Outtatowner, that I *knew* and refused to see her.

The Cask & Keg.

The trees around me spun as blood left my face. Cask & Keg was a tiny dive bar the interns frequented. It had cheap drinks and shitty karaoke on Thursday nights. A fuzzy memory began to take shape. A Halloween party with too many shots and a cute blonde with a wild streak and a great laugh.

Oh, fuck.

I pinched the bridge of my nose. "Hazel, it was a misunderstanding."

Her soft brown eyes hardened and narrowed. "So you *do* remember her."

"I—I'm not—" I huffed, frustrated at myself that I was stammering and unable to parse out the truth. "I think it's possible that I knew her, yes."

She swallowed hard. "I told you. I knew it." Hurt soaked her words, and I felt like the smallest man to ever live. "I *knew* it and I still let you in." She fought tears and my chest ached.

I raised both hands, the unfamiliar rush of panic threatening to overtake me. "I can explain . . . I think."

"You didn't even remember her *name*. I don't need an explanation." She ripped the letter from my hands, tearing the corner. "I think I need to get away from you."

My chest tugged into a knot. *I was just starting to feel whole—for the aching emptiness to go away.*

"Hazel, please—" My hand twitched and pathetically reached for her before falling.

She spun on her heels, pinning me with an icy glare.

I searched for the right words but came up flat. A solemn nod was all I could muster.

She was right, after all. I hadn't recalled the one night I'd spent with Olive, until now. It was an alcohol-fueled good time that hadn't meant much at the moment. I would have sworn on anything holy that I had always used protection, but it was so long ago, I couldn't be sure.

I had no recollection of Olive coming to Outtatowner—I knew that for certain. She claimed I had dismissed her, sent her away only for my father to swoop in and comfort her.

The entire situation reeked of his manipulation.

On the way back to town, I focused my attention on Teddy and not the gnawing sense that I had already lost whatever footing I'd gained in Hazel's favor. Her knuckles were white as she wound down the forest roads, back to reality. She had pegged me as a heartless asshole from the start, and recent revelations only proved her point.

As soon as she dropped me off at the office, my phone was in my hand, dialing Dad's attorney. He answered on the second ring.

I didn't bother with a greeting. "I need you to set up a visitation with the Department of Corrections. I'm going to see him."

∼

Russell King had sat in the small, stark cell of the Remington County Jail, his once-imposing figure slightly diminished by the ill-fitting orange jumpsuit that clung awkwardly to his broad shoulders. His salt-and-pepper hair, which he had always kept meticulously groomed, had begun to lose its sharp edges, curling unruly at the nape of his neck—a subtle betrayal of the weeks that had passed.

His piercing eyes, with the same intensity I had inherited, still gleamed with that familiar mix of arrogance and defiance, the look of a man accustomed to commanding rooms, not languishing in them. Even in that miserable place, behind those dull, unyielding bars, he had held himself with an air of superiority, convinced that his influence—his money, his connections—would soon have him walking free.

I watched him through the window as I was cleared to enter. His jaw remained stubbornly set, and despite the sallow hue creeping into his once-vibrant skin, he exuded a haughty confidence, as though the entire ordeal of being accused of murdering my mother was merely a temporary inconvenience—a minor blip on his path back to power.

As he sat, waiting for me, the other inmates gave him space, not out of respect, but because of that unsettling aura he projected—one that said he was untouchable, even there.

I hated him for it, but more than that, I hated how clearly I recognized it. I could see the same tension in his posture that sometimes crept into mine, the slight tremor in his hands when he thought no one was looking. It was the fear that maybe—just perhaps—he had underestimated the system he had always believed he could bend to his will.

I loathed that I understood it all too well.

He was instructed by a guard to meet me in the visitors' section.

I sat across from my father in the cold, sterile visitors' room of the county jail. The air was thick with the smell of bleach and something far less clean—like the stench of fear or regret.

A glass partition separated us, but it could have been an ocean, a chasm carved out by years of lies, manipulation, and whatever twisted games he had played under the guise of fatherhood. His piercing eyes locked onto mine with the same smug superiority that had defined him for as long as I could remember.

It didn't matter.

After his conviction, he'd be transferred to a state correctional facility where he'd be stripped of every shred of freedom, along with that shit-eating grin.

He grabbed the telephone we needed to communicate and leaned back in his chair. The orange jumpsuit stretched and accentuated his paunch, but somehow he still managed to look like he was the one in control—like this was all just another business meeting, and he was about to close the deal. The flickering fluorescent lights buzzed overhead, casting sharp shadows that made his face look even more hollowed out than it already was.

"So," he drawled, that irritating smirk playing at the corners of his mouth. "Finally found the time in your precious day to see how I am holding up?" He leaned forward. "Or have you been too busy running my business into the ground to step away?"

I clenched my fist under the table, willing myself to stay calm. But the anger was there, simmering just beneath the surface, and I wasn't sure how long I could keep it in check.

"I didn't come here to play games, Dad." The words tasted bitter on my tongue. I hated that I still called him *Dad*—he didn't deserve that title. "I came to ask you something, and I want a straight answer for once in your life."

He raised an eyebrow, clearly amused. "I've always been honest with you."

I ignored the outright lie and swallowed around the pebble in my throat. "Did a woman ever come to you . . . tell you she was pregnant? With my child?"

For the briefest moment, something flickered in his eyes

—recognition, maybe. It was gone just as quickly as it had appeared, replaced by an old, familiar smugness.

He leaned forward, his voice low and dripping with condescension. "You were careless with that woman, JP," he said, shaking his head as if I were some errant schoolboy. "But there's not a chance that child is yours. Don't worry, it was taken care of."

The words hit me like a punch to the gut, and suddenly it was all I could do to keep myself from slamming my fist against the glass between us.

"Taken care of?" My voice rose despite myself. "What the hell did you do?"

He smiled, a slow, cruel grimace that made my blood run cold. "You don't have to concern yourself with it anymore. The woman was handled. Just like I always do."

The room seemed to close in on me, the gray walls pressing in, the air growing thinner by the second.

I stood up, my chair scraping loudly against the floor, but I didn't care. "You're a monster." My voice shook with barely controlled rage. "I stood by and watched you manipulate good people for *years*, but I kept my mouth shut. This is different—it was my *life* and I had a right to know. You should have told me."

He scoffed, unfazed by my uncharacteristic outburst. "She was a whore looking for a paycheck. Didn't even look pregnant, if you ask me."

I shook my head. There was absolutely no getting through to him, even now. "I'm glad you're rotting in here. I'm going to celebrate the fact that you get to spend the rest of your miserable life locked away for everything you've done."

He didn't flinch. Instead, his smile widened, as if he was reveling in my anger. "Rotting in here? Oh, JP," he said, his tone almost pitying. "You really think this is the end for me?"

I glared at him, my breath coming in sharp, angry bursts. "What are you talking about?"

He settled against the back of his chair, the picture of calm, his eyes glittering with something dark. "I've been offered a plea deal. And I intend to take it."

The words hung in the air between us, thick and suffocating. My grip tightened on the telephone. For a moment I couldn't breathe, couldn't think. "A plea deal," I repeated, the disbelief clear in my voice. "For the murder of my mother, which you admitted to . . . you're just going to walk away from this?"

He shrugged, as if it was the most natural thing in the world. "I was coerced. There's no proof. Bootsy and Bowlegs were blackmailing me. All those years I lived in fear for what they did to my beloved wife." His teeth glittered as his smile widened. "It's all just a game, JP. And I always win."

I stared at him, at this man who had once held so much power, so much influence, and I felt something break inside me. Not just anger, not just hatred—something deeper, a final severing of whatever thin, frayed thread had still connected us.

His lips were dry and cracked as he spoke. "I know you want excuses—you want to blame me for what you've become, but I can't give you that. You'll come to see that every move you've ever made was born of selfishness and self-pity."

Fury bubbled inside me. "Selfish?" I leaned forward and lowered my voice. "I have done everything you've ever asked of me. I ran the company when you couldn't. All I ever wanted was a shred of acknowledgment. Of love." I clenched my jaw and refused to let my voice crack despite the emotions thickening my throat.

He scoffed. "Love? Is that what you wanted?" The chair creaked as he shifted. "You know, I learned early on that Abel was too stubborn to fall in line. Royal, too reckless. Whip loved your mother too much to ever listen to me, but you . . ." He wagged a finger at me. "You were my insurance policy."

Lead filled my veins.

"You were moldable." He thumped his chest with one stubby finger as he continued, "I made you. Everything you are is because of me. I deserve a *thank-you* for the life I've given you, not this blatant disrespect. You're better than that."

Tension in my neck wound tighter, like a screw twisted into soft wood and ready to snap.

I stood and smoothed a hand down my dress shirt, calming my nerves before I broke through the glass and wrapped my hands around his neck.

The conversation was over.

"You might think you've won," I said quietly, my voice steadier and angrier now. I had heard all I needed to hear. "But this isn't over. Not by a fucking long shot."

His smirk faded slightly, a hint of uncertainty creeping into his eyes. I didn't wait for a response. I hung up the phone, turned, and walked away, the sound of my footsteps echoing in the hollow, empty space between us.

TWENTY-FOUR

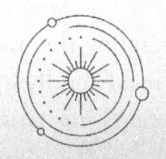

HAZEL

"You're not fooling anyone behind those mirrored lenses. I can see you're still staring."

"Staring at what?" I lied, dragging my attention to Veda and trying my best to look innocent.

She hiked an eyebrow and stared at me over her own sunglasses. "More like *who*."

Veda's emerald-green eyes had flecks of gold like a cat, and it was unnerving the way she was always analyzing. "You're staring at JP. Unless you're actually staring at Royal, which I would totally understand." She pushed the glasses up her nose and leaned back in the Adirondack chair with a soft exhale. "I'd still have to claw your eyes out, though."

"I'm just keeping an eye on Teddy. He gets upset if his clothes get too dirty." It wasn't *technically* a lie. Though Teddy, Ben, and Tillie were currently chasing a three-legged dog and a duck around the barn, with Gus toddling behind them.

They were all dusty and giggling, so what the hell did I know?

"Mm-hmm," Veda answered, clearly not believing my bullshit.

Sylvie had invited Teddy and me over to the farm for some late-season blueberry picking and a barbecue. Across the yard, Duke was operating the massive grill while Royal and JP appeared to be in a friendly but heated debate. Abel was on the outskirts, matching Duke's grumpy energy as they pointed at the grill.

I shifted under Veda's quiet assessment. She was sharp and seemed to have a built-in bullshit detector. It was pretty freaking obvious I was sneaking glances at her boss every other second.

Ever since he came on my tits, then I yelled at him, things had been weird.

Imagine that.

Not weird because I discovered there was a filthy mouth hidden beneath that buttoned-up suit, but because he was attentive.

Tender, even.

JP looked genuinely stricken when I confronted him about Olive's letter, and I didn't slow down for a second to hear him out. He'd been avoiding me for the past few days, and I couldn't stand it. A large part of me wanted to give him another chance—to allow him to explain his side of the story, but after I told him I needed space, he gave it to me.

Sometimes it's really freaking annoying to get what you asked for.

Instead of talking about it, I'd been wrestling with guilt over how intimate we'd been . . . *so* many lines had already been crossed. I knew better.

Olive had JP first, and I had no right to feel the way I did about him. Only, another part of me didn't care and wanted more.

I wished I could crack open his skull and look around inside. *Was he as torn up about it as I was? Did he think of me and wish it were different?*

I shifted and looked at Veda. Maybe I couldn't peek inside JP's head, but she spent a lot of time with the man. Maybe she had some insight into what made him tick.

"Truth?" I glanced around, making sure no curious ears were around to overhear me. I leaned toward Veda. "Things have gotten . . . complicated with JP."

Her jaw set with a tiny nod, but she didn't look my way. "Aren't they always with this family?"

I inhaled, gathering my courage. "We've fooled around . . . more than once."

Her dark eyebrows popped up as her head turned. "I see." She was quiet for a moment, then shrugged. "Teddy's enamored with him. You are two consenting adults. What's the problem?"

My jaw dropped. "The problem," I hissed, desperately trying to keep my voice low, "is that *he* was involved with my sister—my *dead* sister—and is very likely Teddy's biological father."

"But that was only once, right? It's not like they had some long-standing relationship. Sure, it might seem a little odd to some, but it was a long time ago."

I didn't like how logical she was thinking. I toyed with my lower lip. She couldn't possibly understand the hours of self-shaming I'd been putting myself through. My entire life I'd been the emotional, reckless, impulsive sister that made rash decisions and simply hoped for the best.

Now I was expected to be the *responsible* one, and I was royally fucking it up.

Veda looked at me again. "You know, in business, when something is no longer working, you cut your losses. So whatever mental gymnastics you're putting yourself through, ask yourself if it's working. Sometimes it's best to analyze the situation from a different angle and see if it's worth continuing."

I stared at the woman beside me. She was so self-assured. So confident.

She was also absolutely correct. I was having a hard time even understanding my own feelings, let alone trying to figure out what was rolling around in JP's head and what it all might mean.

I needed some clarity—to step back and breathe for a minute.

"What do you suggest?" I asked.

Her painted lips spread into a grin. "Well, that depends. When it comes to sex, sometimes men need a little incentive to get their feelings on board." Her finger tapped her lower lip. "Are we talking about a little prodding or a heartless scourge of misery?"

I blinked in her direction. "Um . . . maybe the first one?"

Her lips twisted. "Pity. From what I can tell JP walks an unbothered, rigid line. He might benefit from a little bothering." She waggled her eyebrows and shifted in her seat. "There's always the option of untangling your feelings while getting tangled up in someone else."

"Oh." I sputtered an uncomfortable laugh. "I don't know about that."

"Here's the thing." She leaned in and I mirrored her movement. "I don't really know you or the situation well, but I do know him. My opinion is that you need to harness your feminine energy. Stop waiting around for clarity. Live your life. Certainly don't wait around for him to wake up and see what's right in front of him."

Veda leaned back, stretching her long legs in front of

her, and tipped her face toward the slanted light of the afternoon sun. A sharp catcall whistle drew our attention, and she raised her sunglasses to see Royal smirking in her direction. When their eyes met, he grinned and lifted his chin.

"Trust me." She smiled and placed the dark glasses back on her face. "The worst thing you can be for a man is convenient."

I smiled and looked out across the yard as the men milled around. Duke had his son propped on his hip with the dog and duck at his heels. JP was jostling a giggling Teddy upside down while Royal and Abel drank their beers and watched Ben and Tillie weave between nearby blueberry bushes.

"Live my life." I repeated her words like a mantra.

I'd never had a problem marching to my own drum and living my life out loud, but it was oddly comforting to have the reassurance from someone who had her shit so completely together.

Behind us, Sloane and Sylvie walked down the stairs with a pitcher of lemonade and cups. MJ followed with a tray of fresh fruit. We smiled and shared a greeting, and I accepted the tall glass of lemonade that Sylvie handed me.

She smiled. "There's blueberry infused vodka in that one."

My eyes widened and I raised it in cheers. "In that case, I'll have a double." I took a healthy sip while Sloane cackled and sat in the chair beside me.

Together, we made a semicircle that looked out onto the expanse of Sullivan Farms. Past the barn, the fields of blueberry bushes rolled out as far as I could see. Trees lined the property in the distance, but I had learned that just beyond it sat Wabash Lake.

My heart squeezed. "How's everyone holding up? You know . . . *after*."

Sylvie's features went soft. "We're getting by. The forensic divers collected all of the evidence they could. The DNR is allowing us to do some kind of memorial for her—maybe a bench or an etched boulder or something nice." She shrugged.

I reached for her hand and squeezed.

Sylvie was strong. Resilient, even through repeated heartbreak.

She smiled at me and sipped her lemonade. "There's a small family cemetery on the property where she can be laid to rest. We're going to do a celebration-of-life ceremony here. You should come."

"Oh, I—" The women all looked at me like it was the simplest thing in the world for me to be included. "Um, thanks."

"How are things going with JP and Teddy?" Sloane asked, and Veda gave me a sly, knowing look.

"It's been okay," I admitted. "He works a ton, so Teddy and I have been spending our days at the beach or shopping for new school clothes. He's convinced he'll single-handedly bring bow ties back into fashion. Sometimes JP's home for dinner, but even then he mostly talks to Teddy. He avoids looking at me until he grumbles *good night* and almost always wants to tuck Teddy into bed, so I let him."

Sylvie and Sloane clucked and exhaled twin *awwww*s.

It was cathartic to get everything off my chest. I missed having girlfriends to talk to. I exhaled and continued, "He doesn't let me pay for anything . . . he just leaves stacks of bills everywhere with notes like *School supplies are expensive* or *Get something nice for the both of you*. It's . . . really odd."

"That's kind of sweet and thoughtful." MJ chuckled and shrugged. "In his own kind of JP way, at least."

I scrunched my nose. "Is it?" I was having a hard enough time wrapping my head around the hot-and-cold routine to know for sure.

"I would greatly accept male affection in the form of cash." MJ raised her palms and closed her eyes like she was waiting for her mystery man to descend from the sky.

"You know what we need? We need to go out, no kids," Sylvie announced. "Duke's been a bear lately too. Maybe something ridiculous and fun—a way to celebrate the summer coming to an end." She winked at MJ. "Find that millionaire mystery man of yours."

Veda raised her cup. "I already have my man. No kids, but I'm in."

Sylvie's eyes lit up. "I have the perfect idea! I saw this thing on social media where you get a group together and shop at a thrift store or charity shop for your date-night outfits. Everyone has to pick clothes for someone else. There's a set budget, and you *have* to wear whatever someone chooses for you."

It was utterly ridiculous and I was *immediately* excited.

Sylvie had her phone out to check her calendar. "Saturday?"

Sloane laughed. "I can tell you right now that Abel would rather cover himself in fire ants. Plus, I have a weird thing about musty clothes." She shook in an exaggerated shiver. "How about I have the kids over for the night? A last hurrah before they start school."

I glanced at Teddy, who was holding hands with Gus and helping him reach blueberries. "Are you sure you can handle all of them overnight?"

Sloane waved a hand in the air. "Piece of cake."

I looked at MJ. "Want to be my date?"

Her eyebrows bounced playfully. "Only if you put out."

We all laughed and my gaze shifted to JP. He was such a stick-in-the-mud. I couldn't even imagine a world in which he'd agree to something fun like a thrift store date. It was a good thing the rest of his family knew how to have a good time.

Planning wasn't my strong suit, but the rest of the women had that down pat. I could just go with the flow, like I'd always done. Being the flighty one meant never having to let someone down when you didn't meet their expectations.

My eyes found JP.

It was impossible to let someone down when they never expected much from you in the first place.

I finished my vodka lemonade in one last gulp and swallowed down my complicated feelings along with it.

TWENTY-FIVE

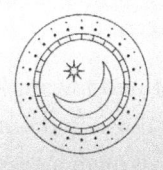

JP

I couldn't stop staring at her.

It really was starting to become a fucking problem. Hazel was sitting in a semicircle with the women of my family, laughing and smiling. I tried to focus on whatever Royal was saying, but the way her laugh floated on the early-autumn air was downright distracting.

When Hazel had made an offhand comment that she and Teddy were going up to the farm for a barbecue, I'd offered to drive.

Hell, I hadn't even been invited.

It was my own fault, I knew that. My entire life I'd been living in my father's shadow, groomed to take over the business, and I was expected to operate as an extension of him. Trouble was, that role had felt more and more like a cheap suit I couldn't wait to shed.

The distance between my siblings and me was the direct result of my choices. They should hate me for it, but instead they greeted me with smiles and handshakes when I'd shown up with Hazel and Teddy in tow.

Conversations with my siblings were still stilted and awkward, but I was trying.

"She's not going anywhere." Royal chuckled beside me.

I tried to hide my frown by taking a sip of my beer. "What?"

"Your girl." He gestured toward her, and I immediately wanted to pull his arm down and scold him for not playing it cool. "You can stop stalking her every move."

I ground my molars together. "She's not my girl."

The words were sour on my tongue, and I washed them away with another quick sip of beer.

She may not be my girl, but sometimes it sure as hell felt like she was—times when she looked at me, without saying a word, and gave me that soft smile, the one that tugged at the center of my chest.

I need to get away from you.

I'd been hearing versions of that sentiment my entire life. I was too cold, too focused on my career, too willing to do whatever it took to keep the family business afloat. It stung when Hazel had said it, but I understood.

It was why I had kept my distance for the past few days. I still needed to figure out a way to help her understand my perspective—fine. I didn't *exactly* remember Olive, and that was shitty. I couldn't change that. What I could change was how I showed up for Teddy. For her. A plan was forming, and step one of that plan was giving her a few days to cool off so we might have a conversation and work it all out.

See? It's logical, and she is definitely not my girl.

Royal let out a hearty laugh. "Okay. Sure."

I diverted my attention to Teddy, who had joined Ben and Tillie in the blueberry fields. Their legs were caked by dust clinging to their sweaty skin. Their pockets were bulging, and their fingertips were already stained purple.

"I slept with her sister, man. Come on." I shook my head.

Royal shifted his weight. "So you remember it, huh? Was it when you were interning in Chicago?"

I nodded. "That time frame lines up." I scrubbed my hand on the back of my neck. "I don't *really* remember it, if you know what I mean." I peeked up at him, feeling the shame of my one-night stand and its consequences wash over me.

He shrugged. "We've all been there." He gestured toward Teddy with his bottle. "You got a cool kid out of the deal, though. So there's that."

I didn't bother hiding my smile at the mention of Teddy. "Yeah. Who would have guessed?"

"That is, if the paternity comes back a match," he added.

My gut churned as I swallowed. "Right. Of course."

"But the sister . . ." He waggled his eyebrows. "Make your move yet?"

Jesus.

I was absolutely not discussing her—or the fact I knew what her tits looked like covered with my cum—with my older brother.

"Grow up," I shot back, pushing his solid frame and knocking him off-kilter.

He grinned. "Never."

In a quick move, Royal tossed his arm around my neck and put me in a headlock. My beer bottle went spinning in the grass.

I pushed at his arm and tried to get free, but he held on to me.

"Say it," he demanded as we wrestled. "Say it . . ."

"You're a fuckhead." I tried to free myself and almost

got him off balance when he shifted and tightened his grip around my neck.

"Come on, John Pierce . . . say you love me." His laugh rolled through me, and I grinned alongside him.

I looped my leg around his and shifted my weight. I might not be as bulky as he was, but I was quicker. Tossing my hips, I was able to knock him off balance and we both tumbled into the grass and dirt.

My laugh rang out as I rolled away from him.

"Fine." I stared down at a laughing Royal and held out my hand. "I love you."

He gripped my hand and I pulled him to his feet. "See? Doesn't that feel good?" He slapped a hand on my back. "I love you too."

Abel gestured toward us while talking to Duke. "You see what I have to deal with?"

Royal pursed his lips and made kissing noises toward Abel. With a laugh, he handed me a fresh beer and folded me into the conversation with ease.

I sneaked one last glance at Hazel and let myself pretend that it could always be like this.

∽

MUCH OF OUR WORK, between placating our current business partners and seeking new opportunities, was tedious. It largely consisted of researching businesses and analyzing their data and performance. It made buying the struggling companies much simpler when you understood and could exploit their weak spots.

On the side, we were digitizing decades of paperwork and account ledgers. Untangling my father's web of deceit was practically a full-time job.

I looked at my computer screen. "Where are we at with the offshore account balances?"

From behind me, Veda answered. "Looks like we're nearly up to date, so that's something. What are you looking for?"

I pressed my lips together. "I'm not exactly sure yet."

I clacked the keyboard, shoving down the tiny pang of guilt for lying to my partner. I knew *exactly* what I was looking for.

Opening the drive that housed the digital business records, I opened the search bar.

Olive Adams.

My pulse raced when not one, but *several*, results popped up. My eyes swept over my shoulder before opening the first one.

A check for $50,000. The image of the cashed check had a feminine signature scrawled across the back in large, loopy handwriting.

I clicked back to the other results. Ten thousand every year, and she'd cashed them every time.

The *help* Olive claimed my father gave was money. He had paid her off to keep her silence. She had been under the impression I was cold and callous, with no desire to help a struggling single mother. With that narrative, my father was able to give her money, keep her quiet, and keep my reputation intact.

The only cost was a child thinking his father wanted nothing to do with him.

Teddy's innocent face flashed in my mind, and my fist clenched.

I wasn't angry at Olive. In fact, I was angry *for* her. She was unaware of how manipulative my father could be in order to get his way. He saw her as nothing more than an obstacle.

A pathetic inconvenience to placate and keep out of the way.

I scanned the other entries. Most were aligned with scheduled payments to Olive, but one record snagged my attention. It was a ledger for an investment account, one of many, but this one had to be in some way associated with Olive as it came up in the document search. I clicked it and scanned the file.

My eyes landed on two words: *sole beneficiary.*

Well, that didn't make any sense. Why would Dad name Olive as the beneficiary to a very healthy investment account if he was solely keeping her quiet?

I leaned back in the chair and groaned.

Veda's eyes slid toward me, unamused. "Do I even want to know?"

I sighed and shook my head. "Probably not. Do you have any good news for me? I could use it."

Veda swiveled in her chair to face me and crossed one leg over the other. "Well . . . your brother's Pulse account is being featured on *Wake Up, Chicago*. That's exciting."

My face twisted and I fought back a smile. My siblings and I had recently learned that Pulse was an adults-only website where Royal made content. "You can't be serious."

"What can I say? The people love him." She shrugged. "There's good money in what he does. Plus, he loves it and that's all that matters to me."

I groaned at the ceiling, closing my eyes and willing the throb in my skull to go away. "Why? Why is my life so unhinged?"

Veda's hand landed on my shoulder. "Probably because

you always focus on the wrong things and haven't learned how to loosen the reins yet."

Ouch.

I watched my brother's girlfriend swivel back and focus on work like her flippant comment didn't just rock me to my core.

Focus on the wrong things? Please. I focus on what needs to be done.

Loosen the reins? If I do, everything goes to shit.

Spurred by determination and stubbornness, I dove into my day.

Four meetings later, I was officially back on my game. Three multimillion-dollar deals were closed, and one holdout was playing hard to get. I wasn't worried. He'd call by Monday, and his fledgling company would be purchased. He'd get that vacation home in Aruba, and King Equities would maintain that JP King was the man who got it done.

It dawned on me that maybe Veda was right when it came to solving my problem with Hazel.

I'd been focused on the past and forgotten to look at our situation like everything else. A business transaction. The only thing left for me to determine was whether it was a merger or an acquisition.

A merger meant Hazel and I had to come together to provide for Teddy. An acquisition required one of us to gain control and the acquired company no longer existed.

I rubbed the sudden, sharp stab that poked my rib.

Well, that couldn't happen.

Hazel made it too easy to forget that if I looked at the facts, they were simple. Because of Teddy, we were stuck together.

Any feelings that had started to develop for her needed

to be tucked away before they became a problem I couldn't handle.

You can't build a future on the ruins of the past. Everyone knew that.

At the very least, I hoped that for Teddy's sake, we could manage to be friends. I didn't have many of those outside the business world, and those were surface-level, at best. My life was unfolding in ways I had no control over, but I refused to be an outsider while everyone happily moved on without me. If that meant focusing on a friendly merger with Hazel, then so be it.

I had to make this right with her.

With a new goal of winning Hazel's friendship, I pulled down my driveway with a renewed sense of energy. It was late and the house was dark, but there was a comfort in knowing the brick and glass had been transformed.

Within a matter of weeks, the two of them had turned it into a home.

A dim light shone through the back window of Hazel's skoolie. The curtains were drawn, but I could make out her figure as she rustled around on the inside. I waited for her, leaning against my car with my arms folded.

After an eternity, she bounded down the steps of the skoolie. Her steps halted when she saw me and startled.

"Shit!" she screamed, her hand pressed against her chest.

I raised my hands. "Sorry. Just me."

She smirked. "Good. For a minute there I thought it was a big, scary *bear*." The plain, mocking look she shot my way rippled through me.

I didn't mind that she teased me. That was what friends did ... right?

"Look . . ." I kicked a blade of grass with the toe of my

shoe and tried to find the words. "I know things have been ... different."

When I sneaked a glance, her arms were crossed and one eyebrow was lifted. "You mean since you've been avoiding me?"

I chuckled. "Fair enough, but you asked for space, and I tried to give it to you." I sighed. "Look, I don't know what I'm doing here. Teddy, you ... these are uncharted waters. I know it's complicated with your sister and we still haven't gotten the paternity results." She moved to interrupt, but I stopped her. "Regardless ... I don't like lurking around my own house." I shoved a hand in my pocket and stepped forward. "And I'd be lying if I didn't admit that dinners with Teddy are always entertaining."

Her chin raised and I fought the urge to get lost in the chocolate-and-caramel hues in her eyes.

"He misses you too."

The idea of being just friends with Hazel nearly dissolved in the heady, coastal air. I had stared at her for a beat when curiosity won out. "Is he the only one?"

A small snort pushed out of her nose. "The absence of your scowls has not gone unnoticed."

My fingers itched to feel the smooth skin of her cheekbones. "Be my friend, Hazel Adams."

Her long lashes swooped. "Don't you have enough friends?"

My cock instantly twitched at how her voice went husky and low. I stepped forward, pressing my chest against hers. "A guy could use one more."

She shouldn't have licked her lips. I immediately had very *unfriendly* thoughts but reeled them in. Hazel stepped back and shoved a hand between us. I clocked how the cool night air pressed against the fabric of her dress, revealing the outline of her nipple piercings.

In a strictly platonic, friendly observational kind of way.

I groaned internally.

Who the fuck was I kidding?

"Friends." She held out her hand and waited.

I slipped my hand into hers, my thumb moving across her skin as I memorized its softness.

"Something like that." I finally let a grin overtake me.

When Hazel stepped back, I observed her outfit and I huffed a laugh. My hand moved over my mouth to wipe away the smile.

"What?" she asked, the tiny lines furrowing between her brows.

She was dressed in a gold lamé dress that looked like it was made in the seventies but cupped every curve like it was made specifically for *her*. On top was a clashing oversize knit cardigan with a sewing theme—crocheted thread and yarn balls, even a sewing machine knitted on one side.

"Oh." I scrambled to find the right words. "Uh, you look . . ."

Hazel laughed, realizing why I was at a loss for words. "Amazing?" She twirled once, and the short gold skirt floated dangerously high on her thighs. "This is for my thrift store date. I was just trying it on. Do you like it?"

I didn't bother answering her question. Instead, I frowned at her. "Date?"

Her lips pressed together. "Yeah. The girls asked me to go on a double date with them this weekend, but it's a thrift store date."

I crossed my arms. "Am I supposed to know what that means?"

Her shoulders bounced. "I don't know. I thought maybe

it was a thing around here. Sylvie said she saw it online somewhere—you go on a date, but beforehand you pick out each other's clothes from the thrift store. The rule is you can only spend twenty dollars and you *have* to wear whatever someone purchases for you."

My expression flattened. "That's the dumbest thing I've ever heard."

Hazel twirled again. "I thought it sounded fun. Veda and Royal are going, too, so they invited me along."

I breathed a sigh of relief. There was no reason I should get wound up when Hazel was going to be the fifth wheel on some ridiculous date with Duke and Royal in tow.

"I can watch Teddy if you need me to," I offered.

See? Friendly. I'm nailing this shit.

"No need," she said. "Sloane is having him for a sleepover with Ben and Tillie. We're all meeting at Abel's Brewery. MJ bailed—something came up at work. I guess there's a new elderly resident, but his grandson is a real jerk, apparently." She shrugged. "I guess they found some dude to take pity on me so I wasn't just some sad fifth wheel."

Some dude?

No way in fuck was she having a sleepover date with *some dude*.

I lurked behind her like a goddamn stalker as she walked toward the house.

I cooled my tone, attempting to hide the fact I was having a complete internal meltdown over it. "What's his name? Maybe I know him."

She glanced at me but kept her attention forward. "Charles something. He's a big wine guy, I guess."

"Charles?" My molars ground together. "Attwater?" He was an out-of-town transplant weasel who was always sniffing around the single women at the Grudge.

She lifted a shoulder as she climbed the porch steps. "Yeah, that sounds right."

A low grunted *hmm* was all the acknowledgment I could muster. I didn't enjoy the very unfriendly thoughts I was having. Frustrated, I stepped inside and headed toward the stairs.

Hazel smiled, and mischief danced in her soft brown eyes. "Good night, *friend*."

I offered a sad salute. "Bestie."

Hazel's nose scrunched as she grinned. She scurried down the hallway toward her room. From the doorway of my room, I watched her as she waved good night one last time and closed the door behind her.

I shook my head. Something about Charles Attwater screamed *I've got a fancy car and a big dick to match*.

Yeah, well, he wasn't the only one, and I already didn't fucking like him.

TWENTY-SIX

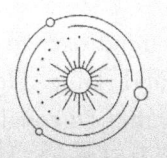

HAZEL

The somber clouds surrounding Outtatowner had just barely started to lift. Whispers about Maryann King had only intensified after it was confirmed that she had finally been found. After I read an exposé on her and saw the photograph of her smiling, I would catch myself thinking about JP's sweet little face and feel a sad tug of emotions.

He often carried that same sullen expression on nights he came home from work and I would find him staring off into space.

Maybe the guy really did need a friend.

Sadly, I did not want to be his friend. I wanted something . . . different. I just didn't know exactly what that was yet.

I exhaled, shaking my fingers and bouncing on my toes to bring more-positive life to my body. Stagnant energy wasn't serving anyone, and it was on me to find a bit of happiness every day. Getting out of JP's house and breaking my routine of stressing about Teddy was exactly what I needed.

I turned from behind the steering wheel of the skoolie to look at my nephew. "Ready to roll?"

Teddy bounced in his seat, clutching his overnight bag. "You bet!"

He was out-of-his-mind excited for his first sleepover with "big kids" Ben and Tillie. He'd even picked out a tuxedo T-shirt to wear after I'd convinced him an *actual* tie was a little formal for a sleepover.

The tires of the skoolie groaned as I pulled an awkward, eighty-seven-point U-turn in the driveway. "I don't know, kid. Maybe I need a daily driver if we're going to be here for a while," I joked as the bus struggled to make the wide turn, trampling some of JP's manicured lawn in the process.

"Yeah," Teddy agreed. "Gas mileage on the bus is terrible too."

I barked out a laugh. "You're a pretty weird kid, you know that?"

We shared a cheesy grin as I pulled out onto the road and headed toward town.

"Only a few more days before school starts. Excited?" I asked over the bouncing rhythm of the radio.

"Yes." Teddy tapped his fingers against his knees. "Dad said he also had Mr. Fromidge as a teacher, and even though he smells like cheese, he's really smart and nice."

Dad.

My chest still pinched every time Teddy called JP that. I worried my lip between my teeth. "You know, until we find out for sure . . . um . . ." I glanced at him again and Teddy's brows were pitched down. A nervous laugh tittered out of me. "You know what? Never mind. So the guy smells like cheese, huh?" I pinched my nose. "Pee-yew."

"Dad said they called him Mr. *Fromage*—it's a fancy

type of cheese." Teddy's eyes went wide with glee, and we both dissolved into a fit of giggles.

"Aww." I tried to breathe between bouts of laughter. "That's really mean. Poor Mr. Fromage!"

"You mean Mr. Velveeta!" Teddy squealed.

The joke was silly, but he was seven, and I had the sense of humor of a child, so we laughed again.

My mood was so much lighter by the time we pulled into the parking lot of Abel's Brewery. I positioned the bus out of the way on the far end of the parking lot, put it into park, and turned toward Teddy.

"Come here, kid." I gestured with my hand before pulling him into a tight hug on my lap. "You're pretty great. You know that?"

He nodded and squeezed back. "You too."

I gave him my most serious expression. "Now, I want you to have fun tonight. Stay up late. Eat too many sweets. Get into trouble." I *booped* him on the nose. "Just not too much trouble. Nothing super illegal."

"I'll try." The seriousness in his voice almost sent me over the edge again, and we giggled.

"Fair enough." I squeezed him one last time and pulled the lever to open the school bus door. "You're a good kid."

"Thanks." Teddy walked down two steps before turning back. "You're a good mom."

I stared. My eyes instantly watered, emotions overtaking me.

Mom.

A title I didn't ever know I wanted. A title I wasn't entirely sure I deserved or was ready for. It was ridiculous how a child could so flippantly say one little thing and you felt like you'd been struck by a Mack truck.

I continued to stare, full of love and awe, as Teddy hiked

his little red duffel bag onto his shoulder and carefully crossed the parking lot.

When he realized I wasn't behind him, Teddy turned to look at me and slapped an impatient hand on the outside of his thigh. "Are you coming?"

I laughed, wiping the tears from my eyes, and climbed out of the skoolie. I smoothed the gold fabric of my dress and pulled the atrocious sweater across my chest. "Let's do it!"

I gasped softly as I really took in the brewery for the first time. It was nestled into a large sand dune at the edge of Lake Michigan. The dune overlooked the lake, and huge garage-style doors opened to allow a breeze to float through the brewery. The building was masculine and upscale with its large wooden beams and iron accents. The soft beach grass swayed in the wind, beckoning me to enter.

We walked inside and it was even more stunning. There were double-sided fireplaces, high-top tables, and patrons flowing in and out between the indoor and outdoor spaces. On the exterior, there was ample cushy seating nestled around cozy firepits.

Beyond the patio, Ben and Tillie were playing tag and squealing in the sand. Teddy tugged at my sweater. "Can I go?"

I nodded, patted his shoulder, and watched him take off like a bolt. "Remember," I called, "nothing super illegal!"

I laughed to myself and sighed, looking around for a familiar face.

"Just not *super* illegal, huh?" JP's voice startled me, and my laugh lodged in my throat. My fingertips grazed my lips as I turned toward him.

A laugh sputtered between my lips, and my eyes went wide.

JP was dressed in an ill-fitting polyester tracksuit. The black sweatpants clung to his narrow hips, and a white stripe ran down the outside of each leg. His feet were tucked into a pair of white sneakers. On top, his hooded sweatshirt had the words *Big Bad Wolf* scrawled across it.

My eyes went wide. "Is that . . ." I coughed through a laugh. "A gold chain?"

JP's arms went wide to show off the cheaply made gold chain and the gigantic crucifix dangling from it. "It's a part of the 'fit. But you didn't even see the best part."

With his hands tucked in the front pockets, JP turned. Sprawled across his back was a lone wolf, howling at the full moon.

"Oh, wow." I choked on my laugh.

JP smirked and my insides went mushy. "You should talk, Grandma Hazel."

We grinned at each other and my smile pinched my cheeks. This was a new side of JP—a silly, carefree side that I hadn't known existed.

"What are you even doing here?" I asked with a playful smile.

JP's face scrunched. "It's *my* family, interloper."

I crossed my arms. "Well, *I* was invited. Were you?"

JP pressed a hand to his chest. "Words hurt, Hazel."

A laugh burst out of me, and the corners of his eyes scrunched as he laughed along with me.

"Nah, you're actually right." JP's smile was striking and my breath hitched. "I was a last-minute addition."

I swallowed down the hit of desire that creeped up, and I looked around for Veda, Sloane, *anybody*. "So . . . where's the group?"

He lifted a brow. "You mean Mr. Attwater?"

My eyes went wide and my voice was nowhere to be found. *Was he . . . jealous?*

The muscles near JP's jaw flexed, and I could have sworn he was biting back a wicked smile. "He couldn't make it." JP shrugged. "I subbed in."

I narrowed my eyes at him—there was more to that story—but a heady rush of relief flooded my system. To be honest, I'd been dreading the idea of having to endure a night with Charles. Everyone swore it wasn't a date, but with the rest of the group paired up, it was hard to not feel like it wasn't, at least in part, a setup.

"Huh, that's too bad," I teased, discreetly eyeing him again and chuckling at how the universe is always a tricky minx.

After everything, I still ended up paired with JP. Go figure.

Royal's cheerful laugh boomed behind us. Together we turned and collectively lost our composure.

He was dressed in a pair of floral swim trunks that were several sizes too small. His tattooed thighs stretched the leg openings, and they were so tight that he was walking funny. On top, his shirt was a ratty fisherman's vest with nothing underneath but muscled, inked skin. He even wore a bedazzled pink, child's-size cowboy hat.

Behind my fingers, I whispered to JP: "Did you pick that out?"

He shrugged and grinned. "It's not my fault there wasn't anything that would fit him. Plus, he deserved a little payback."

Royal pulled us both into a hug. Veda walked up behind him. She was stunning, of course, even in a Christmas-themed sweater vest on top of what looked like a prom dress from the nineties.

Sylvie's laughter quickly followed them. Duke looked sufficiently grumpy in a snug, baby-pink T-shirt and a pair of too-short, pink plaid pajama pants. With a giggle, Sylvie grabbed his broad shoulders to turn him around. We all laughed when we read *Heartbreaker* in pink glitter letters across his backside.

Sylvie was in the outfit I had picked out for her—a floral muumuu with matching shower cap and fuzzy slippers.

"Oh my god, I have to get this." A flash caught our attention as Sloane laughed and took another picture. She motioned with her hands. "Go on, stand together."

Royal stepped forward, stretching out his arms, and when he spread his legs to lower himself into the front row, he ripped the seat of the swim trunks. We doubled over in a fit of laughter as Sloane captured the moment. The gaping hole in his swim trunks revealed neon-green boxer briefs underneath.

"Do you need to change?" I asked through a giggle.

"Nah." Veda slapped his ass. "Can't be any worse than it already is."

He growled in her ear, pulling her close. She giggled, and whatever he whispered to her made Veda blush.

I could feel my cheeks heat, so I turned to Sloane. "You're sure you're okay with Teddy staying the whole night?"

She grinned. "Perfectly. The twins are so excited."

I exhaled. "Okay. You have my number if you need anything."

"Go on," she said. "Have fun. Besides, Abel had to practically keep JP from putting his fist through Charles's face, so . . . you might as well enjoy it."

I blinked at her and glanced at JP, who was chatting with Duke and Royal. I moved closer to whisper. "Wait, what? I thought he only stepped in because Charles couldn't make it?"

Sloane's eyebrows rose as she pretended to lock a key over her lips. "Have fun," she singsonged and turned toward the kids. Stunned, I stared at her back as she walked away.

I turned to find JP staring directly at me like his next meal and swallowed hard.

Friends.
Friends.
Friends.

TWENTY-SEVEN

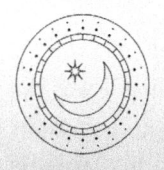

JP

"So what's the plan?" I asked, clapping my hands together and attempting to get this show on the road.

"The plan"—Sylvie rolled her eyes at me—"is to have fun." She grabbed my shoulders and tugged. "Come on. Show me who's excited to be here."

"Thrilled." I deepened my scowl before making a subtle, silly face at her. When hers lit up with a smile, the tension in my shoulders lifted.

Maybe it wasn't so hard to be a decent human after all.

I peeked at Hazel, only to catch her eyeing my forearms while she chatted with Veda. I hiked my sleeves a little higher since a sick part of me seemed to get off on the fact that she appreciated the way I looked.

I was acutely aware of Teddy's presence at the brewery and knew I should probably stop eye-fucking his aunt, but I couldn't help it. The tension between us was palpable.

Probably because you came all over her tits and that dress does nothing to hide the fact that she's braless.

I smiled at myself. If it weren't for me stepping in, Charles would be the one to appreciate how the gold fabric hugged her rib cage and flared out at her hips. When I had stopped into his wine shop to deliver the news that he was uninvited to the outing, he had had the audacity to scoff and try to dismiss me.

Fucking dick weasel.

Joke's on him, because I was not above a mild threat to buy the entire building and open my own wine shop for the sole purpose of sinking his business. One tiny, unfounded threat to his precious business and he caved.

He didn't deserve her.

I tried to focus on whatever story my ridiculous older brother Royal was weaving, but my gaze—and my thoughts—kept wandering to Hazel.

I had tried so hard to dislike her. Disliking her was so much simpler, but after spending weeks together, watching her effortlessly enjoy life and how patient and loving she was with Teddy . . . I was starting to worry that I might actually *care* for her.

Caring for someone was dangerous. It gave *them* the power. I could confidently say I'd never allowed myself to truly love a woman.

I'd never wanted to.

But somehow, with Hazel, it no longer felt like a choice. My sad attempt to be her friend was already failing miserably.

Our bodies circled each other as our group mixed and mingled, slowly orbiting until I found myself side by side with her. I made no bones about tilting my head toward her and pulling her signature fragrance into my lungs. She was bright, rich, and sensual.

All I could think about was whether she'd taste the same with my face buried between her thighs. I wanted that ridiculous date to end, but Hazel was laughing in a way that told me I'd be a complete prick if I hauled her over my shoulder like a caveman and took her home with me.

My dick twitched at the thought.

Instead, I reined myself in and tried to relax. Sloane and Abel brought Teddy around to say goodbye when they left the brewery and headed back to their place for the sleepover. He was so excited that I'd barely gotten a second glance. I shook Abel's hand with a pinched smile, and a jerky head nod was my way of offering him thanks.

Royal walked over with Veda tucked beneath his arm. "Now that Abel's gone, it won't hurt his feelings if we head up to the Grudge. You in?"

"We'll go!" Sylvie slid her hand into Duke's. He looked down at his wife and smiled. That man was so gone for my sister he would willingly suffer through another bar just to make her happy.

Hazel deserved something like that. Not someone itching to get out of a cheap polyester tracksuit and find comfort in the solitude of his quiet home.

My eyes flicked to Hazel as excitement danced through her, and my chest pinched. She was young. Dancing at bars was still probably her thing.

"It's karaoke night up there, right?" I asked my brother.

Royal grinned. "Sure is."

I bit back an annoyed groan and discreetly flagged down a server. After I paid the bill for our group, we made our way outside. Curious glances and whispers were expected given the fact we looked absolutely ridiculous. The walk from Abel's to the Grudge was only a few minutes up the main road. The sidewalks were narrow, and I found myself shoulder to shoulder with Hazel.

Ahead of us, Veda was still tucked into Royal's side, and Duke carried a laughing Sylvie piggyback style up the hill.

"So," Hazel asked as we walked, "how is it?" When I didn't answer, but just looked confused, she continued with a wry smile. "Relaxing. Having *fun*."

My brows furrowed as I teased her. "Oh, this isn't fun. This is a pity date. I'm only here because the girls didn't want you to be a fifth wheel."

She sputtered a laugh. "Oh, this *definitely* isn't a date. Pity or otherwise."

I looked down at her and tried not to smile. "No?"

Her eyes flashed up and back down again, and maybe it was wishful thinking, but I could swear her cheeks flushed.

She cleared her throat. "I don't know. Maybe we're friends."

I stopped and turned toward her. The rest of the group kept walking, blissfully unaware that Hazel and I had dropped behind. "Do you think that we're friends?"

My eyes raked down her neck, and her pulse beat a quick rhythm. I dragged my attention back up, mentally reliving all we'd done together.

Her eyes were wide as she swallowed. Her lips were begging to be kissed. "Aren't we?" she whispered.

My fingertip dragged down the outside of her arm and slid down the length of her pinkie. "I don't know what we are, but I'm not sure *friends* is going to cut it."

∼

THREE HOURS, two nonverbal threats for random guys to *back the fuck up*, and one group rendition of "Sweet Caroline" later, I was fried. All night I had to bite my tongue as I watched loser after loser try to shoot his shot with Hazel. She politely declined each time, but I was still annoyed they even considered themselves in her realm of possibilities.

As a collective, we had laughed all night. Royal had even goaded me enough that I did a pretty decent rendition of "Don't Stop Me Now" by Queen.

Hazel's grin was worth the humiliation of belting Freddie Mercury in front of the entire town.

When I finished, I was out of breath but coursing with adrenaline.

Hazel cupped her mouth and shouted. "Encore!"

With a deep bow, I waved to the cheering crowd and hopped off the small stage.

Veda's eyes were huge.

"What?" I asked, breathless.

She laughed. "I am very rarely surprised, but you shocked the hell out of me tonight."

I shrugged. "I guess that makes two of us."

Hazel's eyes were bright, and she was still grinning. I shot her a wink and smiled at her.

With an exaggerated sigh, I held out my hand to Royal. "Well, there's no topping that. I'm going to call it a night."

He gripped my hand. "You sure, man? That was incredible!"

I shook my head. "Always gotta go out on a high note."

He pulled me into a hug and thumped his hand on my back twice.

After saying good night to Veda, Sylvie, and Duke, I turned my attention to Hazel, dipping my chin and holding out my hand for her. "Good night."

Her brown eyes widened as her palm slipped into mine. I could feel the eyes of my family as they waited for her response. Red splotches bloomed on her neck under my attention.

After gently releasing her hand, I had turned and was

striding toward the exit when she called out, "Hey! JP, wait up!"

My back stiffened, and I slowly turned around, stifling a smile.

Her hands were clasped in front of her. "I'm beat, too, and these shoes are pinching my toes. Care to give me a ride back?"

I eyed her. She didn't look tired. In fact, she looked bright-eyed and ready to take on the world. "Tired, huh?" I asked.

Hazel faked a yawn and grinned up at me. "Exhausted. Probably even too tired to drive myself. I'll just catch a ride with you."

My jaw flexed. Over her shoulder I could feel the gaping stares of my family. I dipped low so only she could hear me. "You really are trouble. Let's go."

Hazel's little squeal was all it took to spur me forward. I gently gripped her upper arm and protected her from getting bumped as we wove through the crowd and out into the night.

Electricity crackled in the air as we walked down the sidewalk, past the marina, and into the dim parking lot of Abel's Brewery. The fresh air did nothing to calm the nerves that ratcheted higher with each step closer to the parking lot.

When we reached my car, Hazel was grinning. "*Ooooh*, he's a gentleman."

I wrenched open the door with an eye roll. "Get in."

Hazel laughed. Even she knew I was acting ridiculous, but I couldn't help it. It would be pure torture to spend the next several hours alone in my house with her—knowing the right thing to do was to leave her alone.

Knowing the last thing I wanted was to do the right thing.

In the passenger seat, Hazel's shimmery gold dress rode high on her thighs. Her soft skin taunted me, begging me to reach over and slide my hand across her bare legs. Every cell in my body hummed for her.

As the world whizzed by, Hazel let out a dramatic sigh. "Well, my date was a bust. How was yours?"

I glanced over. "I thought it wasn't a date."

She nodded in agreement. "You're right. I was *supposed* to have a date tonight, and instead some weird guy showed up."

I scoffed. "Weird how?"

She smirked and shifted in her seat, causing that damn skirt to shift higher. "Well, I keep getting mixed signals. He's disgustingly handsome, but it turns out he really isn't interested. He wants to be *friends*. He practically ignored me the entire time except for when he'd stare at me like a creep from across the room."

I played along. "He sounds like an idiot."

She laughed. "Oh, I agree. Total dumbass. He can sing the hell out of Queen, though."

I laughed. She had no idea the litany of lurid thoughts I'd had about her while I was *staring at her like a creep*. She wasn't wrong. Maybe I was a creep.

I harrumphed and tightened my grip on the steering wheel.

"What about you?" she asked. "How was your night?"

I licked my lower lip, trying not to smile. "It was all right, I guess. There was a girl there—real pretty—but I don't think it'll work out. I tried staring at her to get her to read my mind, but she couldn't." I shrugged. "Kind of a deal-breaker, because I tend to like them a little witchy."

A barking laugh rolled out of her and filled my car. "Witchy? Is that so?"

I tried to play it off. "It's a new thing I'm into, apparently."

Hazel's legs shifted when she pulled her hair to one side, and my cock began to thicken. If she kept squirming like that, these track pants were going to do fuck all to hide the erection trying to make an appearance.

Heat and tension filled the car. I grumbled and shifted in my seat.

From the corner of my eye, I could see Hazel's fingertips drag across her collarbone. Her voice was husky and quiet. "Something bothering you, JP?"

I swallowed past the ache in my throat. "No."

Hazel stripped off her old-lady sweater and tossed it into the back seat. Her tits stretched the fabric of her too-small dress, and I could clearly make out the outline of her nipple piercings.

"I'm curious," she continued, "what would have happened if this really had been a date?" Her knees separated and I nearly drove off the road.

I wanted her.

Desperately.

My pulse was racing and my mind struggled to stay focused on getting her home without tearing her clothes off.

"How would *you* have liked to end the date?" I knew countering her question was the coward's way out, but I was struggling to maintain some semblance of control.

Every part of me wanted to pull over onto the side of the road, bend her over the hood of my car, and fuck her until she forgot her own name.

"Hmm," she hummed, pretending to think as she tapped her lower lip. "Well, if it was a *great* date, I might have shown him my appreciation for such a nice time with an enthusiastic blow job."

The car swerved as I jerked to the left. "Damn it," I muttered as I adjusted my grip on the steering wheel.

Hazel chuckled, and it was enough to drive me wild. My foot hammered the gas, and the car hugged the curves of the road as I made my way toward home.

When I pulled into the driveway, the darkened house called to me. I needed distance from her before I did something utterly stupid.

I put the car in park and didn't risk looking at her as I got out. "Good night, Hazel."

"That's it?" Her door slammed behind me and she sounded pissed, maybe even a little hurt.

Damn it.

I turned toward her and took in the fire that blazed in her eyes. Her chin was high and her cheeks were flushed. "I get a shitty nondate where you ignore me and then just . . . *good night?*"

I blinked. She didn't want to know what I really wanted. The way I obsessed over wanting *her*.

"What do you want from me?" I hated how cold and calculated my voice sounded.

Hazel scoffed, unafraid of the callous mask I'd unintentionally slipped on.

"Not this." She gestured toward me. "I want that guy."

Hazel pointed at the car. "I want the guy who can make a joke. The guy who wears a disgusting tracksuit because it's funny. Who sings like Freddie Mercury and shakes his ass in front of the entire town. The one who couldn't stop looking at me like I was the only woman in the room."

Frustration gripped me. She was too damn young. It was far too complicated.

"You *were*," I ground out. When her brow creased, I continued. "You were the only woman in the room . . . to me." I raked a hand through my hair, giving up on fighting it. "Do you really want the truth? The truth is, I can't *stop* staring at you. You consume my thoughts. I want to know what you ate. What made you laugh today. What you'd think about every tiny decision I make and whether or not you think I'm a good person."

I stepped closer, closing the space between us and letting my gaze fall on her face. "I think about how I would live with the fact that I'm a bad man if you even saw a shred of good in there somewhere."

Her chest rose and fell with labored breathing. Heat flared in her eyes. "But that's just it! You *don't* let me in! No one gets past the walls you've put up, least of all *me*."

She doesn't understand.

My nostrils flared as I evened my breathing. "It's my responsibility to hold it together. It always has been."

"I am not your responsibility!" Her voice rose.

I stared at her, unwilling to back down, unable to move forward at the risk of sacrificing everything.

"Don't just stare at me. Say something!" The crack in her voice was what tipped me over the edge.

I took another step toward her. "What do you want me to say? That I've never felt whole until you and Teddy showed up?" My fingers jabbed at my breastbone. "That I prayed for this aching loneliness to go away, and like some sick joke from the universe, the one woman to take it away is the one I can't have? Is that what you want from me?"

Hazel shook her head, unafraid of the emotional vitriol I had just spewed in her direction.

"I may not know exactly what I want"—her eyes searched mine—"but what I do know is that I don't want this calculating, cruel version of you that you pretend to be. It's not real. I've seen the man you hide behind the mask. I want the real you. I want to *watch* you fall apart. To give in. To finally take something just for yourself."

I barely recognized my own voice as I stepped closer and crowded the last inches of her space. "You don't know what you're asking."

"I know exactly what I'm asking, you're just too chickenshit to show up and let me in." Hazel spun, her rose gold hair whipping me in the chest as she turned.

Her and that fucking irresistible mouth.

My hand shot out and grabbed her arm, stopping her from pulling away. Hazel's chest slammed into mine as I turned her.

She arched into me and the last thread snapped. My hands cupped both sides of her face as I looked down at her. Our breaths sawed in and out, filling the night air.

She held my glare as a war of emotions waged in my brain. I was standing on a cliff, wind in my face and unsure if I'd survive the fall.

"Fuck it."

My mouth crashed to hers as I swallowed her moan. I poured every ounce of yearning into that kiss. Her soft lips opened for me and my tongue swept over hers. My teeth tugged on her lower lip before diving back in to taste her again.

I stepped forward, banding my arm around her back and pressing every inch of her against me. Her hand slid up my back, and her nails scraped against my scalp. I moaned into her, driving my hips forward.

Hazel murmured and heat crawled up my spine. Since our first accidental kiss, I'd wanted to taste her mouth again. Every inch of exposed skin was soft and warm. My hands explored while my lips burned a path across her jawline and down the column of her neck.

We hadn't even made it into the house, and all I could think about was sliding into her and letting the world dissolve. For a man who'd spent his entire life treading water, all I wanted to do was drown in her.

My mouth found hers, and I bent to grip the back of her thighs. Her arms wound around my neck as I wrapped her legs around my waist and stomped toward the house. Hazel arched and continued kissing me as I dug the keys from my pocket and thrust open the door. It slammed against the wall, and she had the audacity to giggle.

I kicked it closed with my foot and shot her a wicked grin. "You think that's funny? I'll destroy this entire house as long as you don't stop making those sexy little noises."

My hand slipped up her flirty little skirt to toy with her panty line. Against my fingers, her pussy was hot, and I knew the bedroom was too fucking far.

I set her onto her feet. Desire flushed her skin the prettiest shade of pink, and I couldn't wait to see if my teeth would make the same marks. She cocked her head at me in question.

I looked over her shoulder toward the stairs and grinned. "Run."

TWENTY-EIGHT

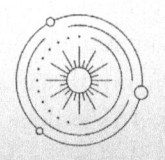

HAZEL

Run.

Panic and desire coursed through me as I turned and bolted toward the stairs. It was a sick, primal thrill, knowing he was steps behind me as I sprinted toward his bedroom. I wanted him to chase me.

To catch me.

Behind me, his heavy footfalls echoed on the hardwood floors.

My heartbeat ratcheted higher as he closed in on me. He scooped me up in his arms, just as I made it to the threshold of his bedroom. His heady laughter rumbled through me, and I braced myself against him as he carried me toward his bed. He released his grasp, and I fell onto the mattress.

JP stepped back to look at me. His shoulders were tense, and his blue-green eyes were dark in the dim bedroom. "You like to push me, woman."

My teeth sank into my lower lip. "Maybe."

He moved between my knees. "Why?"

I smirked, despite the nerves simmering beneath my

skin. "Because you like it."

"You have no idea how pissed off and turned on and utterly helpless I feel in your presence." He exhaled as he dragged a hand through his dark hair, unraveling the uptight man in a single movement. "It's a spell, isn't it?"

A giggle formed in my throat at how surprising and sweet he could be. I lifted a shoulder. "A hex is more like it."

He loomed over me, darkening the room and consuming me with his presence. "I knew it." His dark whisper floated over me. My nipples puckered, and my stomach bunched, my knees lifting.

"Can I tell you a secret?" He dropped a soft kiss on my bare shoulder. I looked up at him and nodded. "I do like it."

His teeth sank into my skin and I hissed. A soft moan floated out of me as my head pressed into the comforter.

"That's my good girl. There's no one here but us." His hands were soft and warm as they moved across my arms.

A shiver ran through me. JP was stern and commanding, yet his tender words melted my insides. His hand slid over my neck and up into my hair. His mouth lowered to mine, tipping my head to deepen the kiss. A deep rumble rolled out of him as my body wrapped around his.

I was pliant.

Eager.

Desperate.

My hips jutted forward, silently begging for more. The cold metal of his ridiculous gold chain cooled my skin. He lifted, staring down at me. I slipped the chain from around his neck, and it clanged against the wood floor as it fell.

He shifted, removing the top of his tracksuit and peppering me with fervent kisses as he undressed. When he stripped off his T-shirt, I sucked in a breath. Up close, his chest and abs bunched and flexed. I ran my hands over the planes of his stomach and trailed a finger down the soft line of hair that disappeared into the waistband of his pants.

His hips surged forward, rewarding me with the hard outline of his cock. Anticipation caused goose bumps to erupt across my skin. JP's intense blue eyes roamed over the flimsy gold fabric clinging to my body.

His hands moved over my chest, across my breasts, and paused on the neckline of the dress that came to a V. "Do you like this dress?"

I bit back a smirk as I squirmed. "Hell no."

With one jerk, JP tore the dress open. My boobs bounced from the movement, and he immediately captured one nipple in his mouth. A surge of wetness coated my thigh, and I moaned.

His desperate hands shoved the skirt of my dress up, and his palms rested on my hip bones.

He paused, his breath ragged as he looked down at me. "Is this okay?"

"Yes." I shifted. "Please don't stop."

His hands moved up my belly, taking the skirt with it. I arched back, lifting my arms so he could remove the tattered dress and toss it on the floor.

For a beat he stared down at my body, clothed only in a black thong.

"You are so fucking gorgeous." His voice was thick and full of awe. He meant it. I wasn't ashamed of my nakedness or being utterly exposed in front of him.

I reveled in it.

I'd never felt more beautiful than under his appreciative gaze.

JP paused, his mood shifting as he looked down at me. His hands circled my waist and his eyes dropped. "I don't want to ruin this."

When his eyes lifted, they were full of concern, and I understood. In my short time here, I'd grown to understand how tightly JP held the reins. He had lived his whole life proud to shoulder the burden of his family. On the outside, he may have appeared unemotional, but that simply wasn't true.

My palm found the side of his face. "You won't."

His eyes didn't meet mine, and instead he buried his face in my palm. I hooked my leg around his hips, pulling his weight onto me. I needed to show him how desperately I wanted him. How unafraid I was of whatever lay beyond tonight.

His hand landed on my throat, and the tension in my body ratcheted higher. My fingers dug at his hips, pushing down the waistband of his pants.

"I think I might ruin you after all, Hex." JP's chuckle hummed through me as the tip of his nose ran up the side of my neck. "I'll ruin you for any man who thinks he can look at what's mine."

"JP," I whispered in the dark—a quiet plea for more.

For everything.

"Hazel." He stopped to thumb over my swollen lower lip. "I need you to know something."

I swallowed and nodded.

His eyes were nearly black with desire. "After tonight, you're mine, and what's mine, I keep."

A strange surge of relief washed over me—like my lost, wandering soul had finally found the tether it had been searching for.

His hand slid up my thigh, and he pushed a finger inside me. I clenched in surprise. He shifted his weight, spreading me open. He ran soft wet kisses down my inner thigh. His teeth dragged against the thin skin just before he reached my aching core.

Heat coursed through me as he dragged one slow lick through my pussy. I squirmed against his tongue in a silent plea for more.

"Tell me," he demanded, slipping his finger back inside me. "Tell me who you belong to."

My back arched and my eyes slammed closed. "You," I whispered. My body moved under him. "Only you."

His wide palm splayed across my stomach, and he buried his face between my thighs. He devoured me, and he didn't start off slow. Instead, he feasted.

I writhed against him, my hands finding the back of his head and riding his face. My arousal built. I squirmed, desperately trying to apply pressure to my clit as he tasted and teased.

Two fingers slipped inside me, along with his tongue, and I moaned. My pussy fluttered against him as my pleasure built and stacked in neat little bricks, ready to be pushed over the edge. When his teeth scraped against my clit, I hissed and nearly came off the bed. His other hand planted me firmly into the mattress as he pumped his fingers into me.

I was close. *So fucking close.*

I used every ounce of restraint to not come as I lifted myself onto my elbows. He glanced up at me, his stern look sending new sparks straight to my core. His hair was a mess, tousled from my desperate hands.

His lips glistened and arched into a grin. "I'll give you whatever you want . . . as long as you ask for it."

I rolled my lips and gathered my courage. "I want to come on your cock."

Without missing a beat, he was all over me. His weight

was heavy as my legs spread for him. He shoved his pants and underwear to the ground, and the heat of his cock was pressed against my pussy. The tiniest shift would be all it took for him to slide inside me bare.

My eyes flashed to his. "Condom?"

His jaw flexed as though stopping for protection was the last thing on his mind. He reached into the bedside table, tearing open the package and rolling the condom over his thick, hard cock.

His hands were rough as he gripped my thighs and pulled me forward. I fell to my back and draped my legs around his waist. JP gripped the base of his cock as he slid the head through my lips. I bucked, begging for more, my pussy stretched around him.

"You're desperate for it. I like the way you squirm." The gravel in his voice sent a shiver up my back.

The head of his cock slipped inside me. I gasped and clenched around him, breathless and desperate with the need to be filled.

"More," I pleaded as my back arched.

His dark chuckle rolled over me as he teased me with shallow thrusts. "Your greedy little cunt is already so wet for me."

His hips pushed forward, thrusting into me, and I gasped as he stretched me open. JP moaned, and it was the single most erotic sound I'd ever heard.

He pumped into me.

My nails raked across his back as I moved in rhythm with him. One hand slipped under my ass, and when he changed the angle, I nearly came apart.

The base of his cock dragged across my clit, and I could feel the pressure of an earth-shattering orgasm begin to build.

"Tell me," he said. "Tell me what you want."

My mind spun, unable to fully articulate my needs.

Everything. Something. More.

He pulled out, teasing me with a wicked grin.

"Kiss me," I demanded. My legs shook as he slid himself in and out of me. His face lowered, and he kissed me hard.

His hands moved over my breasts as his hips shoved forward, going deeper and harder. The pressure was intense, and he worked himself in and out.

"Oh," I whined.

JP shifted back, looking down at me and taking stock of the desperate mess he'd created. "Is it too much?" he asked.

Yes. No. Maybe?

I shook my head and gently raked my nails down his chest.

His head dropped beside mine, nipping at my earlobe. "That's right. My girl can take it."

My girl.

Heat unfurled in my belly as he fucked me. He was clearly in control as his hands moved over my body. Every movement was measured, with purpose, focused on my pleasure. I reveled in his attention.

"You're so fucking tight. So goddamned perfect." His murmur was low, his words only for me.

His cock pulsed inside me as every inch of him stretched me. He gave me everything I had asked for, and all the while he watched me carefully. Assessed every need and delivered.

Desperate for release, I gripped his veiny forearms. His brow was pinched, his gaze intense.

He's holding back.

I knew exactly what he needed to tumble over the edge

with me. A spark of determination ignited as I looked into his eyes. "I'm yours. Show me I'm only yours."

With a grunt, JP slowed to a long, deep thrust as his fingers slipped between us and found my clit. My legs quivered, and he stilled just as my orgasm hit its peak.

In slow, aching thrusts, JP rode the waves of our pleasure. He jerked and spilled himself inside me as I wrapped myself around him and whispered, "I'm yours."

TWENTY-NINE

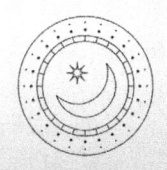

JP

My throat was raw when I dropped back down over her soft, pliant body. My lips found her skin, peppering slow, messy kisses over her neck and shoulder. My lungs weren't working, and all I could see were the strands of her hair as my face buried into her.

Considering I'd fantasized about Hazel for weeks, I was rocked to my core.

Nothing—and I mean, absolutely *nothing*—compared to the real thing.

Hazel hummed as her nails scratched through my hair. "You really did it."

I grunted something akin to acknowledgment or maybe a question, but I didn't make any effort to remove my weight from her.

She was too fucking perfect.

"You've officially ruined me for any other man." Her voice was heavy and satiated, and it relaxed the pinch in my shoulders.

I braced my weight with one arm and glared at her.

"There won't be any other men. If there was, he's a fucking dead man."

Delight flashed in her eyes. "Oh, I like this feral side of you." She grinned and kissed my neck. Her tongue slid across my skin, and I hummed.

She thinks I'm joking.

I shifted, lying on my back and taking her with me so that she was tucked into my side and draped over me. I loved feeling connected to her—like there was nowhere else in the world we needed to be but wrapped around one another.

Her eyes were dreamy and heavy. I kissed the tip of her nose as I slipped out from under her and stood. The sheets were tangled, and I traced the perfect shape of her ass with my palm. She wiggled and I smacked. Hazel yelped, and I enjoyed the jiggle of her ass as I rubbed it afterward.

Her lips quirked up, and I was struck by just how gorgeous she really was.

Gorgeous, and all mine.

I walked to the bathroom to take care of the condom. After I slipped it off and wrapped it in tissue, I stared at it in the garbage. It had been Hazel who'd stopped me from fucking her raw.

I stifled a groan at how fucking good it would have been to take her bare. How much I had *wanted* it.

She made me reckless. I'd already had one possible child, and I hadn't given protection a second thought when she was exposed and begging in front of me.

I raked a hand over my face, stuffing down the fact that I wanted nothing more than to fill her with my cum. I wanted to pull out and watch it seep down her leg, only to use my fingers to shove it back inside while she clenched around my fingers.

Somehow Hazel had unlocked some unhinged part of me that wanted to claim her in every fucking way possible.

"You get lost in there?" Hazel's playful voice shook me from my dizzying thoughts.

I walked out of the bathroom to find her tangled in my sheets with a grin. She shimmied to one side and pulled the covers back for me. I had never really been a post-sex cuddler, but with her, I wanted nothing more than to be wrapped up in her until morning.

Maybe forever.

I lay beside her on my back, slipping one arm around her and gently yanking her body against mine. Her leg draped across me, and I kissed the top of her head.

I exhaled a deep, contented sigh and looked up at the ceiling.

"Amen, mister," she said, snuggling into me. I chuckled and buried my nose in her hair.

"Safe to say your date ended on a high note?" I teased.

She giggled and curled into me. "Five stars. No notes."

Pride swelled in my chest. "That's what I thought."

She swatted at me and laughed. "You're such an arrogant prick."

I frowned and tried to look at her. "Ouch. That's hurtful. I like to think of it as a healthy confidence."

She hummed and her fingers traced the hills and valleys of my bare chest. "Why did you come tonight?"

"To the date?"

She nodded. "Yes. You're not really the type willing to get uncomfortable, so I was just curious . . . why even come?"

I mulled over her question, partly annoyed that I hadn't made it clear that I had gone out of my way to ruin

Charles's evening for the sole purpose of having Hazel to myself.

After a slow stretch of silence, I landed on the truth. "I was willing to be uncomfortable for you."

I could feel her grin grow against my side. "Thank you."

I pulled her into a hug and enjoyed the quiet afterglow of amazing sex with an incredible woman.

For the first time, I had the indescribable urge to crack myself open to her. I didn't want anything between us. No more secrets.

I had to tell her what I had discovered about her sister's meeting with my father.

I cleared my throat to break the ice. "I want to tell you something, and it's important."

I shifted so I could look her in the eyes, and she gazed up at me. Hope and uncertainty warred in her warm caramel gaze.

"JP..."

"I discovered something about your sister." I continued on despite the nerves. "After she came here, my father paid her off. A large lump sum at first but then every year after that, he paid for her silence and she accepted it."

"Olive?" Hazel frowned as she gently shook her head. "No... she couldn't. She wouldn't."

"She did. And, look, I'm not mad." Sure, I was fucking furious at my father, but I understood how someone in need might be tempted by the kind of money he was willing to throw around.

My lips pressed together. "He always looks out for his own interest, but in this case, I'm sure it actually helped her ... at least, in a way that I couldn't. But I promise you, Hazel, I didn't know about her or Teddy."

Her eyes bounced between mine. "How much?"

My molars clenched. "Does it matter?"

Her lips twisted. "I guess not."

My fingertips ran over the bumps along her spine. "It was substantial, but also . . . not enough?" My free hand dragged through my hair. "I don't know. I just hate that I wasn't even given the chance to talk with her about it." I blew out a breath. "Though to be honest, I doubt I would have made things any better. I don't know if I would have even believed her."

She held her hand above my chest where my heart hammered. "You don't give yourself enough credit. I didn't know you then, but I like to believe that you would have found the good man that lives in here."

I harrumphed. "And I think there's a chance he may only exist because of you."

Hazel snuggled closer to me, like my opening up to her made her happy.

My pulse quickened just at the thought of being close to her. The way her lush hair fanned across my pillow, the soft curve of her exposed shoulder—every detail drew me in, making it hard to think about anything but the urge to pull her into my arms and let the rest of the world fall away.

Her soft sniffle drew my attention. I slipped two fingers under her chin and lifted. "Hey . . ." My fingers swiped away a rogue tear. "What's going on?"

She sniffed again and wiped at her face. "I'm mad at her. I wish she would have talked to me about Teddy, you. All of it. It's like there's a whole part of her I didn't know. So I'm mad at her, but I miss her so much."

My arms wrapped around Hazel and I squeezed. I didn't have words of comfort to offer her. I simply made space and stayed quiet.

"Does it ever go away?" she whispered.

"Does what go away?"

Hazel pressed the heel of her hand into her chest. "This feeling. The ache."

My throat was thick and I swallowed. The last thing I wanted to do was tell her the truth—that no, it pretty much always hurt. My thoughts tumbled over one another when I settled on what to say. "I'd read once that grief is a lot like a stone in your pocket. It's there. It's something you always notice. You feel it there all the time." My palm rubbed down her arm. "The pain never really goes away. But over time, you get stronger, and it seems to get a little lighter, but no . . . it never truly goes away."

"That's good." She exhaled and I looked at her in surprise. "I don't want to forget. I don't want Teddy to forget his mom either."

My lips pressed into a firm line. "That won't happen. We'll be there to make sure he remembers her and knows how much she loved him."

Hazel let out a watery laugh. "See . . . I knew you were a big softy."

I could have made a joke about how, whenever I was near her, there were parts of me that were definitely never soft, but I let it slide.

My voice cut through the darkness. "Can I ask you a question?"

She hummed in response.

"Do you have an urn in the skoolie?"

Even in the dim lighting, I could make out the pink splotches that moved up her cheeks. "I do. Temporarily." Silence stretched between us. "Do you think that's weird?"

I thought for a moment. She'd lost her sister and was practically a nomad. It made sense that she hadn't committed to a final resting place.

I shrugged. "A little . . . but not *weird* so much as . . . strangely understandable."

I listened to the rhythm of her breathing until it felt like we were inhaling and exhaling in tandem.

"Thank you," she whispered. "I like when you're honest with me."

I hadn't told anyone else about the meeting with my father, and I found I *liked* being honest with her. "He's taking a deal." My bitter voice cut through the darkness.

Hazel rolled toward me. "Who? Your dad?"

I nodded, reining in the seething hatred his presence produced. "I went to confront him, and he practically laughed in my face." I let loose a pathetic sigh. "He's pinning it on Bootsy and Bowlegs and taking a plea deal. I have to face the fact that he's won."

"Isn't there anything you can do?" she whispered.

A dark chuckle rumbled through me. "Besides hiring someone to kill him and make all of my problems go away? Unlikely."

Hazel went stiff beside me. "You wouldn't . . . I mean— you're joking right?"

I was, wasn't I? Sure as hell didn't feel like it.

"I don't know. Honestly, I don't want to think about him right now." I curled into her, pushing away my problems and bathing in her warmth.

Her hands found the sides of my face. "Promise me, JP. Promise me you won't do anything that you'll regret later."

I looked into her caramel-colored eyes and told her the only truth I knew. "I won't lie to you, and I will never promise you anything I can't deliver."

She swallowed hard and nodded.

I knew I hadn't done a very good job reassuring her, but I meant it when I said I wouldn't lie to her. I still hadn't figured out exactly what I was going to do about my father and his impending plea deal. He sure as fuck wasn't about to go free and think he could come back here to find things the way they once were.

I'd worked too long and too hard.

My hands stroked across her soft skin until her breathing was deep and steady.

"Hey, I have an idea." I said it into the darkness, unsure whether Hazel was even awake.

"Mmm?" Her hum indicated she was on the cusp of dreaming, but I kissed her head and continued anyway.

"We did the camping thing and the thrift shop date thing . . . but now I want to show you what a real date with me is like." I was already grinning like a fool as one idea leaped over another.

"That sounds good." Her hand reached up, and she clamped a drowsy hand over my face. "Now shut up and go to sleep."

I chuckled, pulling her into me and settling into sleep.

She's got no idea what's coming for her.

THIRTY

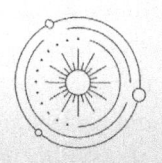

HAZEL

"You DID WHAT?" Surely he wasn't serious.

JP glanced at me as he filled his mug with strong black coffee. His face twisted in that pissy way that always made me want to smile. "What? I made a few calls so Teddy has viable options."

I blinked at him. "So you're telling me that you're giving a seven-year-old the option between sleepovers and Lego camp or *Italy*?"

He took a sip and shrugged. "Essentially. But ultimately, I'll leave the decision up to you."

My brain couldn't keep up and the room started to spin. "Italy."

"That's the plan." He walked past and dropped a kiss on my head like he hadn't just told me that we could be leaving for Italy in two days. "But first we'll go to the Fireside Flannel Festival. I didn't want to miss showing Teddy the carnival."

He looked at me as a sheepish smile crossed his face. "It's kitschy, but fun."

My heart stuttered as I paced in the kitchen. "JP, I can't

just pack up and go to Italy." My scowl deepened as I chewed the inside of my lip. "I don't know how I feel about leaving town when Teddy is just starting school in a new place. I have Teddy to think about, a social media account that I have sorely neglected as of late, and a skoolie that is the center of the whole thing!"

JP's eyes were soft and understanding. "I thought about that, too. I can call the whole thing off, but the reality of the situation is he's excited for school, surrounded by family, and it would only be a few days for an amazing trip." JP's smile widened and I could see the excited little boy beneath his typically stoic demeanor.

"Teddy is more than welcome to come if he wants to. School doesn't start until after Labor Day and missing a few days of second grade isn't going to kill anyone. Your social media account is already dedicated to travel." He spread his arms wide. "And you'll be traveling again." His shoulder lifted. "Sadly, the skoolie has to stay here, but I doubt your followers are going to mind. The Amalfi Coast is beautiful this time of year."

My eyes narrowed at him. "It's really annoying when you're cocky *and* logical."

He nodded once and popped a kiss on my mouth as he rounded the kitchen island. "Noted."

I stared at the wood flooring and tried to wrap my head around what was happening. "Italy. Italy? Holy shit."

"Unless you'd rather go to Paris?" He paused, and a crease deepened on his forehead.

A cackling laugh burst from me. "You're ridiculous."

The corner of his mouth lifted. "No. I'm rich."

I preened and blinked innocently in his direction. "And so modest," I teased.

He scoffed. "Fuck modesty. I can afford to take my girl

on a long weekend trip to one of my favorite places in the world." He stuffed his hands into the pockets of his slacks. "Give me one good reason we shouldn't go and I'll cancel the whole thing."

I crossed my arms to pout. "Because I'm not a gold digger."

Unfazed, he simply looked at me. "Never thought you were. Tell you what, you can buy me a sticker at the airport if it makes you feel better."

I rolled my eyes. "Please. You aren't a sticker person."

He grinned. "You don't know that. Maybe I have a whole collection you don't know about yet."

My eyes narrowed to slits. "Do you?"

"No." He chuckled and moved toward me, setting his mug on the island and placing his hands on my shoulders. "Look . . . I *want* to do this for you. For us. I need a break from this town and everything going on with my father too. All you have to do is pack your bags, sit back, and let me take care of you. You are not taking advantage of me. If anything . . . when I get my way, I'll be the one taking advantage of *you*." He dipped low to nip at the skin of my neck and I yelped. "So we agree?"

I couldn't concentrate on anything with the way his mouth was leaving a trail of hot, wet kisses up my neck. "Okay," I breathed as I leaned into his kiss.

"That's my good girl." He captured my chin between his fingers as my insides went liquid. "Now, let's go get our kid and see if he feels up for a trip."

I stared at his face, wondering how I could have ever thought he was a callous bastard.

∼

"So how long is the flight?" Teddy held JP's hand and stared up at him as they wove through the crowd at the Fireside Flannel Festival.

They wore coordinating outfits—JP in denim and a T-shirt that showed off his physique with a blue buffalo check flannel on top. Teddy was also in jeans, but he wore a crisp white shirt, buttoned up to the top. JP had found a bow tie that matched his flannel exactly, and Teddy was thrilled. Together they made the cutest little duo.

I had been told, more than once, that at the Fireside Flannel Festival, a flannel shirt wasn't optional . . . it was a dress code. I'd dug one out from the back of JP's closet, and while I wished it could have been blue to match them, it smelled like JP, and that was even better.

"It's about ten hours, give or take. We'd have a layover along the way." I loved that JP always spoke to Teddy like he was a little adult.

"Would I have to miss school?" he asked.

"A couple of days, yes."

Teddy nodded as he considered his options and continued walking hand in hand with JP. "I'll think about it and let you know."

"Fair enough." JP chuckled and looked out into the crowd.

A sea of plaid flowed out before us as we made our way through town and toward the beach. Storefronts offered discounts, hung plaid banners, and set up small tables on the sidewalks to catch passersby on their walk toward the festival. Chalkboard signs pointing people toward the waterfront were strewn throughout the town, and far in the distance I could see tents and general commotion as the festival got underway.

We moved through the crowd until we reached the edge of the beach, and Teddy's excitement grew with each step. To the right, more tents with snacks, crafters, food, and beer and wine tastings dotted the small parking lot.

I spotted Charles Attwater. His table was lined up with women clamoring to taste his wine and soak up his attention. He seemed to be doing just fine. As we passed, his gaze lifted and stopped on us. JP's eyes narrowed, and I watched as Charles visibly gulped, diverting his attention back to the blonde in front of him.

Up ahead, the pier jutted into Lake Michigan, with the lighthouse at the end. To the left, along the stretch of sandy beach, were stacks of wood, dotted along the shoreline.

Royal was already claiming a circle of logs and organizing them into a seating arrangement. When JP caught his eye, he grinned and jogged over to us. "Hey, fam."

My heart rolled at the casual way he greeted us.

JP shook his hand and laughed. "What the fuck are you wearing?"

Royal looked down as though he was surprised at what he had on. His flannel shirt appeared homemade and was a patchwork of various gaudy mismatched plaids that were haphazardly sewn together. His shirtsleeves were rolled, putting his extensive ink on display.

"What?" he asked.

JP laughed and shook his head. "Nothing, man."

Royal looked down at Teddy. "Nice bow tie, kid. I wish I would have thought of that."

Teddy beamed and stood taller as JP asked, "Is Veda here?"

Royal grinned. "Of course. She's meeting up with the hens for a drink while I set up for the fire." He looked back down at Teddy. "Hey, Big Dog. Come by after you check out the rides. I'll save a s'more for you and tell you about the time your dad puked on the Tilt-A-Whirl."

Teddy buzzed with excitement. "Thanks, Uncle Royal!"

"I did not puke." JP looked at me with a serious face. "I didn't."

My lips pressed together to hide my laugh. "Okay."

After saying goodbye to Royal, we started heading toward the carnival. Crafters and exhibitors were selling everything from Sullivan Farms jam to handmade quilts. One man had an ornate display of antiques for sale.

I stepped up to run my fingers along a brass candlestick. A trill of excited mischief danced through me. "Excuse me, sir?"

The man turned and smiled.

"Do you by chance have any haunted amulets?" I turned toward a stunned and confused JP. "Don't worry. I'm getting the spell reversed."

A wicked grin lifted the corner of his mouth as he wrapped an arm around my shoulder and playfully tugged me away from the table. "You're such a brat," he whispered in my ear and tingles danced along my spine.

Messing with JP brought out a playful side of him that I craved. With his arm still around my shoulder, we walked through the crowd, stopping at any booths that looked interesting. JP bought a few jars of jam from Duke and we'd gotten a beer from the tent set up for Abel's Brewery.

Teddy tried a hot apple cider and an apple doughnut. His cheeks were coated with cinnamon sugar. I had bent down to help wipe his face when I spotted JP's aunt Bug making a beeline toward us.

"Oh, thank goodness. I'm glad you're finally here." She smiled and winked at Teddy and then looked directly at me. "We desperately need your help."

Confused, I looked around and pressed a hand to my chest. "Me? Okay..."

Bug swatted the air between us. "Oh, well, it's always something. Mabel was supposed to hire a fortune teller for the fair, but now Ms. Tiny has her granny panties in a bunch because she swears she recognized the woman as—and I quote—the charlatan from Chicago who scammed her out of talking to her late husband Slingshot. Madame Claire overheard, and the two got into a tizzy about the fact Tiny's *first* husband had come through the reading, and that was not her fault. Ms. Tiny ran her mouth, and now Madame Claire is refusing to *tap into the other side.*"

My eyes went wide. "That's... a lot."

Bug released a frustrated exhale. "You have no idea. Can you sit at the booth for a little bit while I try to calm Madame Claire down? You can use some of those magic cards of yours and entertain the locals. An hour, tops."

I glanced at JP. "I mean, I do have my tarot deck in my bag... I guess I could help."

JP grinned and shrugged. "Sounds like your special talents are needed."

"Perfect." Bug put her arm around my shoulder and tried to guide me toward the row of white tents on the north side of the beach. "This way. Let's go. The fools are waiting."

I looked back at JP for help and he only laughed. "I got this." JP scooped up Teddy and hoisted him onto his shoulders.

Cue ovary explosion.

He leaned down and kissed my forehead. "Have fun. We'll see you in an hour."

Teddy giggled as they wound through the crowd, and I was left staring at their backs and wondering how we'd gotten so lucky.

THIRTY-ONE

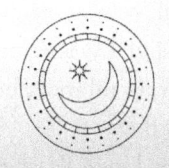

JP

The sun was fading, but carnival lights bounced off each other and illuminated our path. Teddy was riding a sugar high from his dinner of deep-fried Oreos and a cotton candy the size of his head. He'd gotten shy when a few kids his age came up to him to say hello. The parents made introductions, and I informed them that Teddy would also be starting second grade soon. After a few minutes, the boys asked him to go on a ride together. He looked at me, and his shy smile was a dagger to my heart.

"I'll be waiting right here," I assured him. "Go have fun."

Teddy grinned, and I kept an eye on him as he stood in line with his newfound friends, waiting for the Tilt-A-Whirl.

"You're not going to go on?" Abel's voice from behind had me turning with a smile.

I steeled my gaze and buried a laugh. "Fuck off."

His laughter bellowed out into the night air. "Come on. It was years ago. Surely almost everyone has forgotten how you vomited all over Shelly Winters's shoes."

I shook my head. "First of all, it was Marlene Christmas, and I didn't puke. I just gagged a little."

Abel's hand clamped down on my shoulder. "Whatever you need to tell yourself."

He laughed again, but I wasn't mad. Camaraderie with my siblings was still in its infancy, but it was feeling more and more natural every day.

"Sloane off with the kids?" I asked as I kept one eye on Teddy and his friends.

"Yeah," he answered. "They're riding the Ferris wheel, and then Sloane wants to get a reading from Hazel. I promised the twins they could get a funnel cake and ice cream." He rocked back on his heels and I took him in. It wasn't all that long ago that my oldest brother was an outsider—shunned by what my father had done to him and living on the fringes of our small town. Now he was a family man, and I'd never seen him happier or more at ease.

"I'm happy for you, Abel."

My oldest brother looked at me. "Thanks. I'm happy too. Broke—because I swear these carnival rides are a total rip-off—but happy."

I smiled at him. "You should consider what I told you. Abel's Brewery could expand distribution. Bars are driving up demand for high-quality, small-batch breweries. You're leaving money on the table by being stubborn."

"Maybe." He shrugged, then laughed. "Probably." Abel turned his attention to me. "What about you? King Equities seems to be clawing its way out of the shithole Dad created, thanks to you."

My jaw clenched and I crossed my arms. The tinny cadence of the carnival music was starting to grate on my nerves. The last thing I wanted to do was talk about our father, but Abel needed to know.

I kicked a patch of dirt. "Not sure how much longer I'll be the man in charge. Apparently he's getting out."

Abel angled toward me, stunned. "What the fuck?"

I shook my head. "I went to see him, and according to him, he's been offered a plea deal. I believe him."

"Motherfucker," Abel muttered under his breath. "When?"

"I'm not sure. I'm looking into it and doing what I can to stop it, but if a plea really has been offered by the prosecutors, it's done."

Everyone around us was laughing and having fun at the festival. Even locked away behind bars, my father had a knack for ruining our good time. "Sorry to be the bearer of bad news."

Abel's jaw clenched, but he surprised me when he pulled me into a hug. "And I'm sorry you've had to carry the weight of it." Abel looked into the laughing crowd. His features darkened in a way that reminded me of the hard time he'd done behind bars. "We'll figure it out . . . no matter what happens."

I thumped my hand on his back and swallowed down the lump of emotions in my throat. Sharing the burden still felt unnatural. I was so used to bearing the brunt of my father's decisions and having to be the only one to make the tough calls.

When I released Abel, a streak of red zipped past me, and I watched as the group of boys that had been with Teddy ran by and disappeared into the crowd. I looked at the exit for the ride, but didn't see Teddy. I waited for him to appear, and when he didn't, my heart thudded against my ribs.

"Teddy?" I called out and looked around again. "Ted?"

Leaving Abel behind, I moved through the crowd in search of him. "Teddy?"

"I'll go this way," Abel called out, but I ignored him as my panic grew.

You knew he tended to wander.

How the fuck could you have lost him?

Hazel would never forgive me—hell, I would never forgive myself—if something happened to the kid.

I shouted through the crowd as I pushed past rowdy teens and families enjoying the carnival. My throat was raw when I called out to him again. "Teddy!"

I was drawing curious glances as murmurs grew around me. Beside me, the rides spun at dizzying speeds and my stomach churned.

I was going to be sick.

I moved forward, but a couple blocked my path. A teenage boy with long, greasy hair was leaning in toward a young girl when he said, "Want me to show you over there?"

My face twisted. Annoyed and impatient, I looked right at the girl. "Don't do it. A real man wouldn't sneak you off into the dark. He'd be proud to show you off."

The girl smiled and stood taller as the kid looked at me in disbelief. "Dude . . ."

"Get out of my way." I pushed past the kid and kept searching for Teddy.

As I moved toward another clump of people, I called out to Teddy again. They turned and the crowd parted, and I could just barely make out his crisp white shirt.

My stomach plummeted.

Teddy was standing in line for the Ferris wheel, chatting with Sloane and her twins.

I called his name and immediately scooped him up. "Jesus, you scared me!"

My voice was angrier than I'd intended, and when I set him down, worry flooded Teddy's features.

I crouched in front of him, rubbing my hands down his arms, reminding myself that he was okay. "I'm sorry. I didn't mean to yell. I'm not mad at you."

His chin wobbled.

I shook my head. "Actually, I am a little mad. You can't run off like that. But I was mostly scared." I rubbed his arms again and pulled him into a hug. "Come here."

I released him and he looked at me. "I saw Ben and I wanted to talk to them about the sleepover."

Sloane held up her phone. "I texted you and Hazel as soon as I saw he was by himself."

My hand slipped into my pocket and, sure enough, there was a text from Sloane telling us she was with Teddy near the Ferris wheel. In my panic, I hadn't even heard the message come through and hadn't thought to check my phone.

Relief flooded my system. "Thank you."

Sloane smiled. "No worries. It takes a village and *sometimes*"—she waggled her eyebrows at Teddy—"they like to wander without telling their parents where they're going."

Teddy blushed and I pulled him into my side. He glanced up at me. "You're sure you're not *mad* mad?"

I squeezed his shoulders. "I'm sure." I checked my watch. "We should get back to Hazel." I glanced at Sloane. "Thanks again."

Holding tightly to his hand, I led Teddy back through the carnival toward the booths. My heart still thunked against my ribs.

An endless succession of dark thoughts played on a loop in my mind.

He could have been gone.

Something could have happened to him and it would have been my fault.

I can't lose him.

I swallowed down the bile and worry and stress. As we walked, it struck me that the concern and helpless feeling might just be a part of the territory.

Having Teddy around was a surreal feeling, mostly because it had taken only an instant. Just like that, I finally felt like I'd become a real dad.

THIRTY-TWO

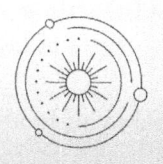

HAZEL

"Here are the keys to the skoolie if you need anything. It's got a full tank of gas. Teddy has all of his stuff, but you never know." I wrung my hands in front of me.

I still couldn't believe Teddy had chosen to stay with Abel and Sloane instead of flying with JP and me to Italy.

I guess that's kids for you.

JP handed Abel an envelope. "There's a few thousand in there for incidentals. It should cover anything that comes up."

Abel tried to refuse the money. "Get the fuck out of here."

"Take it." He tipped his head toward me. "She'll feel better knowing it's all taken care of, and so will I."

Abel begrudgingly accepted the cash. In the background the kids were already screaming and giggling as they tore through Abel and Sloane's house.

Something clattered to the ground, and I grimaced at the noise. "Are you sure you're okay with this?"

Sloane beamed. "More than sure." She bumped her shoulder into Abel. "Besides, we've been talking about adding a few more, so this will be a little test run to see how we do when we're outnumbered."

Abel grinned down at Sloane, and my heart fluttered at how obviously in love with her he was. If she wasn't careful, she'd likely get a whole gaggle of kids that looked just like Abel.

JP stuck out his hand to his brother. "We'll be back in a few days. Thanks again."

Abel nodded and shook his hand as I pulled Sloane into a hug.

"Just have fun," she whispered.

I called over her shoulder. "Okay, Teddy, we're leaving!"

His laughter drew closer as he squeezed past Sloane and slammed into my legs with a hug. I bent down to squeeze him back. "Be good. Have fun. Nothing—"

"Nothing *super* illegal. I remember," he answered with a giggle.

I cupped his face and squished it. "I love you, kid. See you soon."

"Love you too." He grinned at me and then turned toward JP. "Love you too, Dad."

My eyes whipped to JP's as his brow furrowed. He curled himself over Teddy to return the hug, and my heart wanted to explode. "Love you too."

His voice was thick, and Sloane's quick intake of breath was nearly my undoing.

Before he could realize what a moment he'd created, Teddy was gone—off chasing Tillie in another round of tag.

We quickly said our goodbyes and turned toward JP's car. He reached for my hand and gripped it. JP lifted my knuckles to his lips before opening the passenger-side door. "Get in. You're all mine now."

∼

"You do realize this is *not* how normal people travel, right?" I raised an eyebrow at JP and smirked.

He wiped the corner of his mouth with the cloth napkin and placed it beside his plate. "I never promised you normal."

I grinned back at him. It was only an hour into the flight and we'd been served an appetizer—goat cheese with a fig reduction that was to die for—and an entrée that looked more expensive than the ones at most restaurants I'd visited.

"The last time I flew on a plane this small, there was a crate of chickens in the back. It was terrifying." I smiled, recalling the rickety flight I'd once booked while traveling in Belize. It had been so shaky from turbulence that I'm still shocked the pilot had been able to land it with both wheels intact.

"A private plane is more efficient. Plus, it's much more comfortable." The ease at which JP carried himself was reassuring, and I sighed into the plush leather chair.

"A girl could get used to this," I warned as I stretched my legs, rubbing my calf against the outside of his leg.

"That's the plan." A wicked grin spread across his face, and a tingle raced up my back.

The buttery leather chair was smooth under my palms. The wood paneling gleamed, and the ceiling was tall enough that neither of us had to awkwardly duck to move around. There was even a king-size bed near the back, already made up with the fluffiest white duvet I'd ever seen.

I glanced at the bed over JP's shoulder as highly inappropriate thoughts about the mile-high club danced through my brain. Across from me, JP sat in silence. As though he could read my every thought, his knowing eyes moved across my body.

"Ready for dessert?" he asked.

I wasn't sure whether he was talking about actual food or himself, so I simply nodded.

I'll take both, thank you very much.

He pressed a call button near the armrest of his chair and immediately a flight attendant appeared.

"Yes, Mr. King. How may I be of service?" The woman who had introduced herself as Joan was an experienced attendant with dark-brown hair pulled tightly into a slick bun.

"I think we're all done here. We'd like dessert in the back and then to be left in private. About an hour before we land, we'll take breakfast and coffee. Otherwise I'll ring if anything is needed."

The attendant nodded and began clearing our plates.

I leaned forward to whisper, "Does everyone always do what you tell them to?" One eyebrow lifted to my hairline.

JP reached under the table between us and slid his hand up my thigh. "Usually."

"And if they don't?" I lifted my chin, my stomach bunching in anticipation.

He moved forward, leaning across the small table that separated us. "Then there are consequences."

My blood tingled and pressure built between my thighs. "I'll have to keep that in mind."

The attendant finished clearing our dinner and moved down the hallway with a bottle of champagne and a plate covered with a metal cloche. She set the plate beside the bed and uncorked the champagne before setting it into a chilling bucket with ice. She didn't speak another word before enclosing herself inside her own private quarters.

JP stood, holding out his hand for me. "We have a long flight, but it's overnight. We can get some rest and arrive in Italy in the morning, local time. Less jet lag that way."

I slipped my hand into his as we made our way toward the back of the luxury aircraft. With every step, my body hummed. I stared at the bed as JP closed the door behind us. When the lock clicked, I leaned back against him. JP's hand fisted at the nape of my neck, tugging gently so my head lay back and he could capture my open mouth.

I shifted, turning into him as his hand tangled deeper in my hair and the other gripped my ass. "*Fuck.* I can't get enough of you."

I moaned against him as I palmed his cock through the fabric of his slacks. He was already hard, and excitement danced through me.

His hand moved across my collarbone, gliding over my breasts and down my belly. He stopped between my legs, teasing my clit from the outside of my clothes.

The entire day had felt unreal—the date, the plane, his attention. It was like I was living another life.

JP's voice was silk rippling over gravel. "You'll do as I say."

The air escaped my lungs, but my defiant streak had come out to play. "Or there will be consequences. I remember."

His jaw flexed. "That's right. On your knees."

Without breaking eye contact, I lowered myself to the plush carpeting. Beside me, the world was dark beyond the window, cocooning us in our own world. JP may be the kind of man who was used to being in charge, but I had a secret.

On my knees, the power was mine.

With a wicked grin, I undid his belt and lowered the

zipper to his slacks. JP hissed as I freed him and ran my tongue along his shaft from the base to the tip.

He was under my spell and I reveled in it—a goddess bathing in the moonlight of her own sensuality. My nails dug into his hips as I slowly pulled him to the back of my throat. With every moan, I went deeper until I could feel my gag reflex start to kick in. My pussy clenched, knowing it was only a matter of time until he'd fill me.

I hummed in anticipation when his hands gripped my shoulders. I looked up at him, lips stretched around his cock, eyes watering.

His finger stroked down my face. "You are so fucking beautiful."

To my surprise, he gently pulled himself from me and swiveled toward the bed, taking me with him. His hands slid up my thighs, pulling my dress off and dropping it in a pile on the floor. A finger hooked into my underwear as he dragged them down my thighs. I stepped from them as he sat on the bed to take in my naked body.

His hand slid between my legs. "You're soaked."

My nipples pinched into hard points. His rough words during sex never ceased to ratchet my desire even higher.

He moved farther up the bed. "Sit on my face."

My eyes went wide. "I'll smother you."

His grin widened. "God willing."

THIRTY-THREE

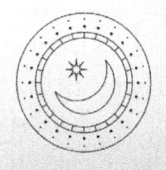

JP

Hazel was standing in front of me, unsure of what to do next. I hooked an arm around her waist and pulled her toward me, inhaling her heady perfume.

Holding her, I leaned back, making us both tumble to the bed. Hazel yelped, and I pulled her up my body and settled her right over my face. I kissed her inner thigh, making my way up. My palms gripped her ass and urged her down over me so I could lick and suck and *finally* taste her again.

"Oh my god," she moaned, bracing herself against the headboard. Her hips moved back and forth over my face as I sucked her clit. I pushed my fingers inside her, stretching her and reveling in the way she contracted around my fingers.

"That's it, Hex," I urged, her nickname rolling off my tongue. "Come on my face."

With both hands, I pulled her down and devoured her while her orgasm took over. She ground against my face, and I lapped up every delicious drop.

Her breathing was hard and fast, but I wasn't done with her. When she finished, I moved out from under her, keeping her on all fours. My hand moved over her ass. "Stay there."

I made quick work of undressing and rolling a condom on. Behind her, I teased her with the tip of my cock.

"Yes."

One breathless syllable and I nearly came apart. I inched the head just inside her and stopped. "That's it. Beg for it."

Her back arched as her hips pushed backward, begging for more. "Please."

My hand moved up her spine. "Say it."

"I want—" Hazel looked over her shoulder and licked her lips. "I want you to fuck me."

I grinned, giving her more inches and feeling her stretch around me. "Good girl."

She was so fucking wet that I slid in and we groaned in unison. Slowly I dragged in and out of her, enjoying how snug and wet she was. Her pussy tightened around me with every thrust. I could feel my spine tingle, ready to pump her full of my cum.

I fucking hated that I couldn't fuck her raw—nothing to stop my cum from seeping out of her and painting her inner thighs as *mine*.

"Jesus, you feel good." My hands roamed over her ass as I chased my release. "I want to fill you with my cum."

Her strawberry blond hair whipped over her back as she looked over her shoulder at me. "Do it." She lowered her tits to the bed, deepening the angle. "You can have me bare. I'm on birth control."

My mind was at war with my body. I wanted nothing

more than to feel her with nothing between us, but my controlling nature was screaming at me that it wasn't a good idea.

But this was Hazel.

She was mine.

She was *everything*.

In one move, I slid out from her and pulled the condom off my cock before lining up at her entrance again. Without a barrier between us, she was slick and hot.

I pushed into her and she tightened around me.

"Fuck," I groaned. "You feel unreal. You have no idea what you're doing to me."

Nothing and no one had ever been so perfect.

So made for me.

I pumped into her, feeling her coil and ready to be set free. I wrapped my hand around her hip and slid between her legs, thrumming her clit as I moved in and out. She clenched around me and I hissed at how tight she was.

"You were fucking made for me. Do you know that?" I was so close to finally letting her past every wall I'd put up to keep me safe. So close to telling her that I was in over my head with her, drowning in her.

"Say it," I demanded, my hand running up her spine and tangling into her hair. "Tell me you need this as much as I do."

"Yes. Yes, I need you, JP." I pumped into her as my chest tightened.

Hazel's face buried into the pillow as she cried out and I finally gave in, sending me over the edge with her.

I folded over her to press a kiss on her spine as I gripped her hips. Achingly slowly, I pulled out of her, watching my cum spill out of her and coat her thigh, exactly like I knew it would. My fingers stroked up the soft skin on her inner thigh, pushing my cum back inside her.

Hazel collapsed on the bed with a satisfied laugh, and I lowered myself beside her.

She shook her head and stifled a giggle into the pillow.

"What?" I asked. "What is it?"

Her hand covered her face as she laughed. "Nothing."

I stared at her and she giggled again.

"This. You. Us?" Her finger swirled in the air. "A private jet to Italy."

I moved a strand of hair that stuck to her face and hooked it behind her ear. "The jet and the trip don't mean anything." I reached down her arm to capture her hand. "I learned a long time ago that it's just money. It makes life comfortable and it's necessary, but it doesn't bring you happiness." I raised the back of her hand to my lips. "But you, on the other hand . . ."

Her shy smile grew. "I make you happy?"

I wouldn't have been able to stop my smile if I had tried. "You're impulsive and undisciplined and sincere." I focused my attention on tracing my fingers over hers so I wouldn't lose the nerve to finally open up to her. "With you I feel whole for the first time in my life." My eyes flicked to hers. "You make the emptiness go away."

Her fingers linked with mine as she snuggled closer. "I warned you. When I did your tarot reading, I warned you that something was going to upend your entire life." I chuckled at the irony. "I just didn't realize it was *me*."

I pulled her closer, burying my face into her hair. Our limbs were a tangled mess. "I knew. It scared the shit out of me, but deep down I knew it was you."

Hazel had consumed me from our first meeting. Every

minute of every goddamned day she'd consumed my every thought.

I wrapped my arms around her and kissed her hair.

"You make me happy too," she whispered.

I tightened my embrace, emotion burning the bridge of my nose.

Hazel sighed and closed her eyes as she melted into me. I could tell she was drifting off.

I wanted to tell her. Tell her that I loved her so completely that nothing would ever be the same. I had plans for the three of us.

I almost woke her to tell her.

Instead, I let her sleep, closing my eyes and drifting off next to her, dreaming of a world where all my plans wouldn't clip the wings of her free and adventurous spirit.

A world in which, for once, something worked out for me.

∼

The Amalfi Coast was a gorgeous seaside town with its salmon-hued cliff sides and the cheerful pastel houses that dotted the coastline. In my experience, early autumn was the best time to visit. The weather was sunny and clear without being stifling. The impending harvest season also meant an avalanche of chestnuts and other local delicacies on the local menus.

A driver had taken us from the airport and dropped us in the heart of the village. I planned lunch for us before the next leg of our adventure.

"It's like a postcard!" Hazel's grin spread wide as she looked up at the pastel-colored buildings perched on cliffs overlooking the glistening turquoise waters. She snapped a few pictures with her phone and flipped it around to take a selfie.

I stepped forward with my hand out. "Let me."

She blushed and handed me the phone. Instead of taking a picture of her in front of the gorgeous landscape, I tucked her into my side and held out my arm to take a selfie. As I took the picture, I dropped a kiss onto her hair.

"There." I handed her the phone.

She looked at the picture of us and smiled. "It's perfect." Hazel looked down at her phone. "What's the time difference again?"

I checked my watch. "He should be getting out of school soon."

Hazel grinned. "I still don't know if I should be proud or hurt that he couldn't have cared less if we were there for the first day of school."

I lifted a shoulder. "Kids are resilient. From the sound of it, he's having a ball without us."

In truth, I was eager to check in with Teddy too. I knew Sloane and Abel would make sure he was well taken care of, and he'd have a great time with the twins, but I still worried.

"We can call him before lunch or wait until we're on the yacht." I slipped on my sunglasses.

"Yacht?" Hazel nearly choked on the word.

"It's private, of course. There's a satellite phone there and plenty of quiet places to talk."

Hazel snorted. "Oh, hello . . ." She was putting on a fake snooty accent, clearly impersonating me in the most ridiculous way. "Yes, my name is JP King." Her arm swung wide. "That's my jet. Here's my private yacht."

I stared at her and tried not to laugh at her rather spot on, if not totally annoying, impression of me. "To be fair, I don't own it."

Her hand moved to her chest. "Oh . . . how embarrassing."

I wrapped my arm around her neck and pulled her into me, rubbing my knuckles on her head as she squirmed. "You're such a little shit," I teased.

Hazel giggled and pushed herself free, her coppery blond hair wild from the mess I'd made of it.

"This feels like too much." Hazel sighed and spun in a circle, her sundress floating on the coastal breeze. "But I love it. Thank you."

"You deserve it." I stepped forward and kissed her nose. "Come on, I want to show you something." I held out my arm for her. "This village, Conca dei Marini, has a long and lurid history with witches."

Delight flashed in her eyes. I smiled and continued as we walked down the cobblestone road toward the village near the water. "Local legend is that long ago, witches populated this small fishing village. They would meet at night to practice magical rites and prepare love potions and hex remedies. They were believed to be witches at night and pretty women during the day. They were said to lure tourists and fishermen as victims."

Hazel grinned as I wove the tale of the Janare. She smiled and nodded at passersby and leaned into my biceps as we walked.

"How do you know so much about this?" she asked.

I grinned. "I did my research."

Her eyes narrowed at me, and I sighed. "A weekend getaway to Italy is impressive, but Italy with witches?" I shrugged. "Come on."

A light laugh escaped from behind her fingertips.

"Are you impressed?" I asked.

"Very." She laughed and my chest swelled with pride.

"Good." I enjoyed how perfectly Hazel fit into my side as we walked. "I like taking care of you."

She sighed and I hoped it was a happy one. "Did you ever think this would be your life?" she asked.

I smiled and looked at her. "Did I think a wild, cheerful woman and a cute, quirky kid would fall into my life and make me realize just how stuck I had been?" I shook my head, laughing. "No. I can't say that I saw that one coming."

"He is pretty cute." She bumped into my arm. "Kind of looks like his dad."

My chest pinched. We hadn't gotten the paternity results back, but it was hard to deny the fact that Teddy was like a mirror image of me.

It struck me that I hadn't grown the balls to tell her just how deeply I'd fallen for her. I hadn't even alluded to the fact that I was just as enamored with Teddy too. I turned in the middle of that cobblestone road to face her.

Hazel gazed up at me as I dragged my thumb across her eyebrow and cupped her face. "I'm glad you brought him into my life. I'm better with him . . . and with you." I pressed a gentle kiss to her lips. "Thank you."

When I looked at her again, fresh tears were shimmering against her lashes. She swiped them away. "I don't know why I'm crying. I had this plan where I was going to show up and face the jerk who'd broken my sister's heart. I was going to demand you sign over your rights. Then we'd leave and I would never look back." She laughed and shook her head. "Now look at me . . . I'm running away on a holiday to the Amalfi Coast with the guy."

I smirked, knowing full well how I had also done a complete one-eighty in regard to her when she'd shown up in town. "Now here we are."

Her hands slipped into mine. "Here we are."

I looked over her shoulder, spotting the apothecary boutique I'd found for her. I leaned in to whisper in her ear. "How about you spend some more of my money." I flicked my chin in the direction of the store.

Hazel looked over her shoulder and grinned. "I could put a spell on you, you know."

With a swift kiss, I sauntered ahead of her. "Already have, Hex."

THIRTY-FOUR

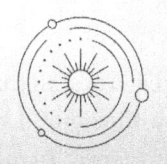

HAZEL

JP

I'd like a status report on Teddy.

MJ

You're such a robot sometimes. Just say you miss your kid.

ABEL

He's good, but damn it gets loud with three in the house.

SLOANE

Get used to it, big guy. And yes, Teddy's great! Such a little gentleman.

JP

Thank you for taking him for a few days.

MJ

Say it . . . say you miss him.

JP

Shouldn't you be working?

And yes . . . I miss him. Happy?

If you ever find a man who's a little prickly, secretly tender, and also obscenely wealthy? Even if the dude has got some baggage, go for it.

Highly recommend it. You can thank me later.

With warm, happy thoughts, I stretched and yawned against the plush comforter as I snuggled deeper into the bedding. The private yacht JP had procured was completely over the top. A butler, private chef, and housekeeper were all available to us at any time. We spent two days sailing the west coast of Italy, stopping at hidden alcoves and private beaches that felt made for only us. I had loads of content to post on my social media but focused my attention on the man lying beside me.

I was in love.

There was absolutely no denying it.

JP was stretched out on his back, totally naked, and still peacefully dreaming. I took a tiny peek under the sheet and giggled. The night before we had finally collapsed in bed, exhausted and satiated in the wee morning hours.

As magical and romantic as the whirlwind trip had been, I missed Teddy. I missed Michigan and the weird little coastal town we'd wound up in. I missed the skoolie and couldn't wait to decorate her with a few quirky knickknacks JP had bought me.

I looked at him again, and the butterflies in my tummy sprang to life.

Maybe JP still frowned when he slept, but he looked peaceful doing it.

I couldn't help but feel the giddiness in knowing that maybe I'd had a hand in creating that peace.

It was our last day in Italy and JP had something up his sleeve. Last night he'd spoken to the staff in whispers and sidelong glances. I was nosy enough to try to listen in, but I couldn't hear enough details to know anything other than he had *something* planned for us tonight.

A tiny ball of excited energy bounced around my belly.

Would it be insane if he proposed?

The rogue thought stopped me in my tracks. What the fuck was that about?

I wasn't even supposed to *like* JP, let alone begin fantasizing about what life would be like with him long-term.

I pressed my fingers into my eyes and tried to shake the thought. "God, what would Olive think?" I whispered to myself as I searched for a shirt.

"I think she'd be grateful for how much you love Teddy." JP's thick voice startled me, and I let out a nervous laugh as his hand ran over the tense spot where my shoulder met my neck.

I leaned back into him, closing my eyes with a sigh. His chest was hard and warm, and I buried the guilt of knowing I had fallen for my sister's ex . . . whatever he was.

I swallowed hard, put on a brave face, and turned with a smile. "Morning."

JP's dark brows pitched down. "Hey." His eyes roamed over my face. "What's wrong?"

I hated that he could read me so well. I could have lied. I could have told him nothing was wrong or that I was homesick.

Instead, JP's expression reflected trust back to me, and I couldn't do it. He deserved my honesty.

I looked up at him, praying he would understand. "I'm feeling . . . guilty, maybe?" I swallowed down the lump in my throat. A whisper was all I could manage. "Like maybe it should have been Olive here instead of me."

A deep noise rumbled in his chest. His arms wrapped around me, and I melted into him. "You're wrong." He cupped my face. "Look, I understand why you would say that, but you're wrong. Sure, guilt has come up for me too—not because I have any latent feelings there, but because of Teddy. He lost his mom and I know how deeply that changes someone. I don't remember much about my own mother, and it kills me that Teddy might not remember how much his mom loved him . . . but I wouldn't be here with anyone other than you."

Hot tears sprang to my eyes. "I just don't want him to forget about her."

"Shh," he soothed as he held me close. "He won't. We won't let him."

We.

One word and I felt my heart completely unravel.

"It's only been a few months, but he doesn't cry. He doesn't even *talk* about her. That's not normal." I was lost and couldn't help but feel like I was completely failing my nephew.

The cabin of the yacht shrank around us as JP opened up to me. "In a strange way, I know what he's going through. It wasn't exactly the same for me—I thought my mother left us—but she was still gone suddenly. I couldn't speak her name for a long, long time."

My chest ached for the lost little boy he had been. "What helped you?"

A wry laugh escaped him. "I didn't get help." He eased back to look at me. "But we'll do better by him. Do whatever it takes to help Teddy. I promise. But please . . . don't ever think you're someone else's placeholder, because you're not."

My eyes clamped shut and I buried my face into his chest. "Thank you."

JP's attention bore into me as though he was assessing my every need. I'd never felt so cherished.

So taken care of.

"We have one more day, but if you want to go home, we can leave right now," he said.

Part of me wanted to say yes—to head back and hug Teddy so tightly that he would always know how loved he was.

I shook my head and offered a watery smile. "I'm good. I promise. Just a little tired, I think. I'd like to stay."

JP looked at me and gave a firm nod.

What I failed to communicate was that I didn't really mean I wanted only to stay in Italy.

My heart wanted to stay with him indefinitely.

~

"SCUSA, MISS." Tommaso, our private butler, handed me a tall stemmed glass. "Prosecco for the lady."

I accepted the slender glass of golden bubbles as I walked from the cabin out onto the bridge deck. Tommaso held out his hand so I wouldn't trip on my dress. "Thank you."

JP had spoiled me with a shopping trip in an obscenely expensive boutique. I got to live out my girlish fantasy of trying on expensive dresses just for the hell of it. When I'd stepped out in a slinky, floor-length gown that pooled at my feet and cut in a low V in front, his jaw had visibly dropped.

I had protested at the price, but JP insisted and we'd walked out of the store with the dress to be delivered to the yacht.

I had never felt more elegant.

With my hand in the nook of Tommaso's arm, he guided me toward the small table at the end of the deck. "The wine is light bodied with aromas of pear and honey. Mr. King requested your approval."

I took a small sip and enjoyed the rich flavors as they washed over my tongue. The bubbles tickled my nose. I smiled. "It's delicious."

Tommaso nodded. "Very good, *signora*."

On the bridge deck, a small table had been arranged for our dinner. Warm candlelight flickered, and the aroma of freshly cut flowers mixed with the sea air. JP was standing at the back of the yacht in a dark suit, his back to us.

As we approached, we caught his attention and he turned. A smile lifted his features, and I was struck by how devastatingly handsome he was. With one hand in his pocket and his other holding his own glass of Prosecco, he looked as though he was born to enjoy a life with a yacht.

He certainly fit in more there than when we'd been camping with the skoolie. The thought caused a small giggle to titter out of me.

JP's hand brushed down his suit jacket. "Something funny?"

I nodded a thank-you at Tommaso as he guided me toward JP and slipped away into the darkness. I took another step toward JP. "Just thinking about how this yacht suits you a whole lot more than the skoolie, that's all."

His arm snaked around my waist and pulled my body flush to his. "I think you suit me."

I inhaled sharply as his mouth found my jawline and moved its way down my neck. Warmth hummed in its wake, and heat curled down my back. When his lips reached my collarbone, he stopped, his entire body stiffening.

I stepped back with a small laugh, hoping I'd remembered deodorant. "What?"

His eyes were pinned to my chest, his face in a hard mask.

I placed my hand over the necklace I'd chosen to wear. "What is it?"

"Where did you get that?" His voice was as hard and tense as his expression.

I toyed with the small diamond cluster that hung from a silver chain. "This?" I asked. "It was Olive's." I was confused and concerned with the sudden shift in his mood. "Why?"

JP straightened and his expression was unreadable. Nerves rippled through me. He sighed and his jaw flexed. "Where did she get it?"

My face twisted as I tried to keep up. "I don't underst—why are you asking me this?"

JP sighed again. He didn't look mad or annoyed, but utterly exhausted. Wrung out. "Where did your sister get that necklace, Hazel?"

My throat burned and I took a sip of wine, but it did nothing to ease the ache. "I don't know. It was mixed in with the items she left when she died. I don't usually have a reason to wear it but figured Italy might be the time, so I packed it. Why are you being weird about this?"

His face was stern, as though he was performing mental gymnastics to try to figure out what was happening.

I knew exactly how he felt.

Then a thought bloomed. "Did you—did *you* give this to

her?" It didn't make sense, but it was clear that he recognized the piece in some way.

His head twitched. "No, of course not." He sighed and dragged a hand through his perfectly styled hair, mussing it up in the process. "But I do recognize it."

I waited, breathless.

"It was my mother's."

THIRTY-FIVE

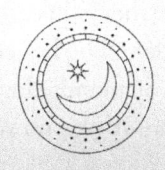

JP

Thousands of miles away and he was still fucking things up for me.

I had planned for the sunset dinner to be special for Hazel. I was prepared to lay my heart on the line and my cards on the table.

I wanted her and Teddy in my life, forever.

When I saw her wearing my mother's necklace, the blood drained from my face.

What were the chances he'd given two women identical necklaces?

The entire concept irked me, but given the fact we had already discovered he had an *entire family* we didn't know about, I couldn't put it out of the realm of possibilities.

Even if my father *had* given Olive an identical piece of jewelry... why?

Hazel's amber eyes were wide and worried. I took a step back, reeling from being confronted with another painful memory from my past. I was used to stuffing those feelings in a box and leaving it at that, but with Hazel, I was continually bombarded with old wounds. It wasn't her fault, but the reality was that her sister and my family appeared to be more connected than I'd assumed.

I leaned back against the rail of the deck and exhaled. Hazel was stunning in her slinky black dress. It was as though it had been made to hug her curves and show off her feminine shape. The diamond cluster necklace was the perfect, elegant addition. It was no wonder she'd chosen to wear it.

With champagne still in her hand, Hazel twisted her fingers nervously, and I reached out for her. "Hey, come here."

She stepped forward, and I placed both of our glasses on the table before wrapping her in a hug.

"Why do things have to be so complicated?" she whispered.

Her pained words were a knife to my heart. I looked down at her, tucking a wisp of hair behind her ear. "Nothing is so complicated that it changes anything between us. It's just . . . odd."

Hazel toyed with the necklace, looking down at it with a frown. "Are you sure it's hers?"

I gestured vaguely at the sparkling necklace. "The cluster of six diamonds. Six diamonds for six kids. It's in almost every picture we have of her before she was gone."

She swallowed hard and emotion was thick in her voice. "Oh my god."

The muscles in my back were tense, but I tried to keep my touch tender. "Giving your sister money to keep her pregnancy quiet was one thing, but a diamond necklace? Why would he give her that?"

Hazel shook her head and scowled. "And why would she keep it?"

We were both at a loss, holding each other and trying to make sense of it all. Nothing seemed to fit.

The sun was slowly sinking behind the mountains and casting the deck in delicate shadow. Hazel stepped back, reaching behind her neck and unclasping the chain.

With it balled in one hand, she held it out. "Please." When I didn't move to take the necklace, she closed her eyes and stepped forward. Slowly, she reached for my hand and opened my palm, gently placing my mother's necklace in the center. "Please take it. It was your mother's. You should have it back."

I stared at the necklace, wrapping my hand around it to feel its delicate weight. I carefully opened my palm and removed the necklace. "It was your sister's." I leaned forward and clasped the necklace around her neck before adjusting it so it lay correctly against her perfect, creamy skin. "It's a piece of herself that she left for you, and I won't ever take that away from you."

Her hand rested across the necklace. When she gathered the courage to look up at me, her face was creased with worry. "Are you mad?"

I could breathe for the first time in what felt like forever. "Of course I'm mad, but not at you." I cupped her face. "Not even a little bit. I will figure this out."

I did what I could to salvage our last night in Italy. Hazel was a little quieter than usual, but as we watched the sun sink into the ocean, I held her close. Together we lost ourselves in quiet moans and heavy sighs. We used each other to forget the heaviness that had blanketed our evening.

On the plane ride home, I used the hours to attempt work. My mind kept wandering—to Hazel, to Teddy and the impending paternity results, to Mom. An ache in my chest had formed overnight and was still dogging me.

I rubbed it absently with the heel of my hand, hoping I wasn't having a heart attack or a pulmonary embolism or something equally inconvenient.

All the while I sat at the table and stared at Hazel. She was curled up in the bed at the back of the plane. After we ate, I urged her to get some rest, and after very little protest, she'd fallen asleep quickly. Her strawberry blond hair fanned out behind her, and her hands were tucked under her chin. Her body was curled into a delicate ball, and every cell in my body wanted to wrap myself behind her and let the world slip away.

Instead, I sighed and refocused on the laptop in front of me. Veda had done a beautiful job of handling most of our affairs, but my unread emails were still hovering in the thousands. I rubbed my eyes and picked up my phone. It was late—or maybe early?—but I texted Veda anyway and smiled when she responded almost immediately.

> Any fires I need to know about?

VEDA
> Depends. Do you want me to ruin your day?

I glanced at Hazel and sighed.

> Might as well.

VEDA
> Word of your father's impending plea bargain has spread. Envoratu pulled the plug on the latest deal and are actively searching for something else.

. . .

That was it.

The final nail in the coffin of King Equities. Envoratu was a multi-national alcohol distribution company. Landing them as a client had been my biggest success to date.

Envoratu had used King Equities to buy failing distilleries and breweries to become the force they were today. When they first came on, the company had owned a number of brands, businesses, and assets that were not in the core alcoholic drinks category. My idea was to streamline—become laser-focused on one category and dominate. The company gradually disposed of unnecessary assets to focus on beverages as its core business.

They'd made billions because of me, but it was all for nothing. The more companies that exited as clients, the faster the rest would leave.

As painful as it was to admit, soon there would be nothing left to salvage.

> We'll tie up the loose ends when I get back.

I didn't wait for Veda to respond and instead turned my phone to *Do not disturb* and closed my laptop. I glanced at Hazel and the few feet between us felt like too many. With a few quick steps, I strode over to my girl and nestled in behind her. Dreaming, she barely shifted, but her body melted against mine.

I looked down at her for long enough that anyone would

consider it creepy, but I didn't care. I placed a kiss on her bare shoulder and rested on the pillow beside her. Outside of the airplane window, life was barreling forward, but for the next few hours, I wouldn't allow anything but her to matter.

THIRTY-SIX

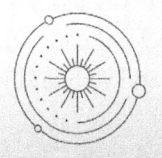

HAZEL

The titter of Bluebirds was a soothing soundtrack to my Wednesday evening. Sure it was a far cry from the lull of crashing waves against a yacht on the Amalfi Coast, but it was perfect.

It had been almost a week since our trip to Italy and my head was still in the clouds. I'd be lying if I didn't say that I missed Tommaso's cappuccino.

I kept catching my thoughts wandering back to why Olive would have Maryann King's necklace. The stunned look on JP's face told me there was no mistaking it was hers, and it seemed like it was no coincidence.

He had been so tender and selfless in letting me keep something of his mother's that had also belonged to my sister, but it only added to the mounting questions I had about Olive.

What other secrets was she hiding?

Listening to the conversations around me, I sighed and settled into the plush velvet of my wingback chair.

"You okay?" Emily's kind face was creased with concern.

"I am." I gave her a soft smile. "I thought I would miss Italy, but it feels really good to be home."

Her eyebrow pitched up. "Home, huh?"

I could feel my cheeks heat, and I tried to hide it with a sip of whatever rum cocktail concoction Annie had brought with her. It was fruity and rich and just the perfect amount of sour.

I raised the glass to Emily. "Home is where the skoolie is."

Her lips twisted in playful disbelief. "Mm-hmm."

A sharp laugh lurched out of me. "Oh, and thanks again for Lego camp."

If she was dizzy from my sudden change of topic, Emily didn't let it show. Instead, she smiled widely in the way she always did when she spoke about the children's programs she ran at the local library. "Did Teddy enjoy it? I think we had a lot of fun!"

I grinned. "He did. Loved it, actually. He's still talking about it and how we need to scour a few stores to find the *really good stuff*. He wants to build another set to go with the next book he's picked out to read."

Emily sat back in her chair with a contented sigh. "That makes me so happy. I knew I could snag a few curious minds if I mixed books with kids' love of building. The feedback is really helpful."

I took another sip. "I'm sure he'll be wanting to sign up for the next activity. I'll keep you posted."

Emily's hand rested on my forearm. "I'm happy you found your way here to us. Both of you."

A tightness in my chest bloomed and unexpected tears sprung to my eyes. Everything about this quirky coastal town was unexpected, yet drew me in.

The people.

The quaintness of the small town.

Him.

Emily took a drink, quietly eyeing me as if she could see my thoughts hopping in my head. "Have you heard anything yet?"

I swallowed down the emotion and shook my head. I knew she was talking about the paternity results. In reality, the impending results only increased my anxiety, so I had buried it deep down and focused on the *now*. I hated anytime the doubts and insecurities cropped up.

What if JP wasn't Teddy's dad?

What if he was?

What if this thing between us develops into something more?

Would I be Teddy's aunt and *his mom?*

My throat was thick as I swallowed and tried to focus on Emily before I spiraled into oblivion.

"Nothing yet. I'm literally checking the mail every day." I looked down at the pink, fruity cocktail in my hand and dug for a sliver of courage.

"Honestly, I'm not really sure it matters anymore," I whispered.

Emily's brows tipped down. "What do you mean?"

My fingers tingled and my head was swimming. "Well, I only came here because Olive wanted me to. I had every intention of having JP sign away his parental rights. The judge insisted that he could only do that with the paternity results." Nerves tittered through me as I quietly gave voice to the fears. "But what if I don't want him to sign his rights away anymore?"

Emily's smile was soft and understanding as she touched my arm. "Does JP know you're feeling this way?"

I shook my head. We hadn't discussed the specifics yet.

I was fairly sure that both of us were actively pretending like it wasn't happening and were simply attempting to enjoy the present.

But what if he was still planning to sign his rights over to me? Teddy would be crushed.

My impending mental spiral, along with our conversation, was interrupted when muffled shouting turned louder as the bell to the bookshop clanged against the glass door.

Our heads collectively whipped around as we all watched MJ stomp into the bookstore. Her cheeks were flushed and her typically sweet and good-natured demeanor had all but evaporated.

"How *dare* you follow me!" MJ's chin was high and her fists were clenched, like she was ready for a fight.

The air in the bookstore was thick. Every woman around me tensed, like they were all ready to spring into action to protect one of their own.

Behind MJ, an enormous man sauntered in, seemingly unaffected by her outburst. He was handsome, with dark hair that looked like it needed a trim. He had a mustache that stood out a little thicker than his scruff and had muscles for days. But not just regular muscles—his thighs were thick and his arms crossed over his broad chest as he grinned at MJ.

"Relax, Thunder." The man was smiling, but there was an edge of teasing in his tone. "You might hurt yourself if you keep stomping around like that."

"Thunder?" she shouted, stepping forward. He was so much taller that her chin lifted higher, but she didn't back down.

I stayed perched behind the high back of the chair, peeking out and soaking up their interaction. My eyes bounced between them.

He scoffed. "Yeah. You've got this whole storm cloud vibe happening. It's cute."

He licked his lip, and I noted the quiet, yet audible, gasp of the women around me.

"*Cute?*" Fire danced in MJ's eyes. "You are absolutely unreal. Do you know that? First you skulk around an assisted-living facility—*after hours*, let me remind you—then you have the balls to insinuate that I'm a—a—a lady of the night!"

A *what now?* I was totally lost but enthralled by whatever drama was unfolding in front of me.

"You been thinking about my balls, Thunder?" The man was clearly trying not to laugh as he shifted his stance.

Beside me, Emily stifled a giggle as MJ threw her hands in the air with a frustrated growl.

A whisper came between Emily and me. "You know that's Logan Brown, right?"

Emily's head whipped around. "The rugby player?"

Lark's eyes glittered with delight. "The *Olympic* rugby player. Apparently football and rugby are like sports cousins or something. Wyatt is always analyzing sports strategy, so the Olympic Games were constantly on. He's actually from Michigan, and trust me . . . I would *not* forget those thighs."

The women giggled as my eyes shifted back to the drama unfolding in a very public way. "Yeah, but how does MJ know him?"

"And why is he *here?*" Emily added.

"I came to apologize." Logan's voice was thick, but sincere. It was enough to stop MJ mid-rant. Her mouth hung open for a second before she snapped it shut.

"I had just gotten into town and wanted to say hello to my grandfather. The girl at the front desk said a quick visit wouldn't be a problem." He stepped forward into her space, and I could feel everyone's collective inhale. "Safe to say I was surprised to see a woman who looks like you having a candlelit dinner with my eighty-six-year-old grandfather."

MJ's fists were still clenched, but the fire in her eyes had dimmed to a smolder.

"You said your piece then." Bug stepped beside MJ, placing a supportive hand between her shoulder blades. "You've disrupted our evening enough. Good night."

Logan looked around, noticing the sea of wide eyeballs staring at him. His grin widened.

He raised his hand, his huge palm spread wide. "Hi." He chuckled and shook his head. "Bye."

A few of us waved back, stunned into a stupor.

Before he walked out the front door of the bookstore, Logan stopped and looked back at MJ. "Maybe I'll see you around, Thunder."

MJ rolled her eyes with a huff and turned her back to him, walking straight toward us. "I need a drink."

We were absolutely *salivating*.

Lark was the first brave soul to speak up. "That was . . ." She blinked twice. "Interesting."

MJ's typically sweet face twisted into a scowl. "That man is certifiable. He followed me all the way from Haven Pines."

"You went to work like that?" Lark gestured at MJ's slinky dress. It was a far cry from her usual navy scrubs.

MJ pinched the bridge of her nose. "It's a long story. Can we please talk about something else?"

Kate said *sure* at the same time as Emily's *no* and we folded on ourselves with pent-up laughter.

My fears, the stress I had been carrying, all of it seemed to evaporate as the Bluebird Book Club lifted my spirits.

For so long it had only been Olive and me, and after a while my travels meant I'd flown solo for a really long time. *Too long.*

Maybe Emily was right.

Looking around at my new friends, who felt more like family every day, I couldn't help but feel like maybe the paternity test didn't really matter as much as I'd made it seem after all.

I had no idea that the very next day I would find out how much it really did matter.

THIRTY-SEVEN

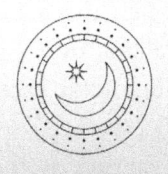

JP

I HAD BEEN STARING at the envelope for eleven minutes.

Its crisp white edges and the Remington County DNA Diagnostic Center stamp stared back at me.

Whatever was inside that envelope would change everything.

Or maybe it changed nothing?

Fuck, I don't know.

My hand scraped against my jaw as my stomach bunched. My palms were sweaty and my neck was hot.

"They're here!" Teddy's elated shouts rang through the house as he dashed toward the front door.

Hazel's hands had been shaking when she had gotten the mail and showed me the letter. Quietly, we'd both agreed that opening it in front of Teddy was a bad idea. She'd called Sloane, explained the situation, and asked if the twins would be up for an ice-cream cone. Thankfully, Sloane was more than happy to entertain Teddy for a little while so we could open the letter and read the results.

Teddy was still in his school clothes—a gingham shirt

with a navy bow tie and jeans. In the mirror by the door, he straightened his tie and gave himself an approving nod.

My chest squeezed.

When he pulled open the door, the noise expanded with Ben and Tillie talking over each other to say hi to Teddy. Without so much as a backward glance, he was gone.

I hung back, still staring at the envelope, as Hazel thanked Sloane. My sister-in-law leaned in to give Hazel a quick hug and offered me a tiny wave before she left.

Hazel walked back toward me, her eyes trained on the envelope in front of me.

We stood, shoulder to shoulder, and she sighed. "Are you ready?"

It didn't matter if I was ready or not. Whatever truth that lay within that envelope wouldn't change. It didn't care about my feelings.

Without a second thought, I ripped open the envelope and unfolded the papers.

My eyes scanned, searching for the words I was looking for.

Beside me, Hazel sucked in a breath and whispered, "I don't understand."

My eyes fell to the words she had read.

Probability of Paternity: 0%

I stared at the zero like a black hole sucking me in.

"What does that—but . . . *how?*" Hazel's voice cracked and my heart cracked alongside it.

I read the paper aloud. "The alleged father, John Pierce King, is excluded as the biological father of the tested child, Theodore Adams. Although paternity is excluded, there is a significant number of shared alleles between John King and Theodore Adams across multiple loci. This suggests a close biological relationship, but is not consistent with a father-child relationship. Probability of paternity: 0%."

Hazel shook her head. "I don't understand all of the science words." She snatched the paper from my hands. "What is it even saying?"

Despite the panic rising in her voice, mine was painfully cold. "Keep reading."

Hazel's worried eyes flicked back to the paper as she continued reading, "Probability of paternity: 0%. However, the relatively high number of shared alleles may indicate that John King is a close relative, such as a half sibling (sharing one biological parent), to Theodore Adams."

The pit in my stomach expanded with every word she read aloud.

"JP?" She was on the brink of tears. "What does this mean?"

Frustration got the better of me. My head snapped up, and sharp words were on my tongue. "It means I'm not his father. I'm his . . ." I could barely say it. "I'm his fucking brother."

I watched in horror as I witnessed the ghost of another life in her eyes.

Another life where the letter confirmed I was Teddy's father and we laughed. Where I scooped her up and hugged her as we excitedly planned how to tell Teddy the incredible news.

But that life was gone.

He had taken that from me.

My spine was steel and my steps wooden and I reached for the envelope. It crumpled in my fist as I strode to the door.

"Wait. JP!" Hazel called after me, but I didn't stop. "Wait, where are you going?"

With the door in my hand, I glanced back at her. My tone was cold and hard. "My father has some explaining to do."

∽

My foot stomped the accelerator as I wove through highway traffic toward the prison where my father was still being held.

"I don't give a shit if it's after visiting hours. You're his attorney. Get me in a room with him. *Now.*" The venom in my voice dared Dad's attorney to have the audacity to not line up and follow my orders.

I hung up the phone without waiting for an answer.

My hands gripped the steering wheel as blind rage drove me toward the county jail. By the time I got there, Dad's attorney was already waiting for me.

His dress shirt was rumpled and his expression was well past annoyed.

"This is highly unusual," he said.

Still, he led the way toward the visitors' center, presenting his credentials and assuring the receptionist and guard that he was requesting an emergency attorney-client meeting. A few smooth words and placating smiles later, I was led to a room where we waited for my father.

The attorney's attention was focused on his phone when it rang. "I need to take this. Don't speak with him until my return."

I nodded, fully intending to say whatever I needed to, whether or not my father's attorney was present.

Fuck that guy.

The air in the room was stifling, and the cool metal table in the center of the room suited my grim mood.

When the door opened and my father sauntered in, it took everything inside me to not come unglued.

"JP." He smiled. "I wasn't expecting to see you here."

"Sit down." My voice was ice, and even the guard's eyebrow pitched up. He stayed silent as he uncuffed my father and allowed him to sit.

When he moved toward the corner of the room, my eyes sliced in his direction. "Get out."

My father crossed one leg over another. "Now . . . that's no way to speak to this gentleman." He gave the officer a kind smile. "Please excuse his appalling behavior. I think we just need a moment to speak in private."

The officer nodded with a smile and removed himself.

I scoffed. "You say jump and people fall over themselves to ask *how high*."

He spread his hands before clasping them in his lap. "It's a gift."

This was fucking ridiculous. I wanted to cut the shit and get at the heart of the matter. "I came to you and asked you about Olive Adams."

Dad rolled his eyes and let out a mocking laugh. "I thought we already dealt with that?" He laughed again and my blood ran hot. "You're losing your touch, kiddo."

His patronizing tone grated on my nerves. "The child that Olive had. It's not mine. We had a test to confirm it."

He picked at an invisible piece of lint on his pant leg. "I could have told you that. In fact, I'm pretty sure I already did."

I just stared at him.

Realization dawned on him and he *laughed*. "It's not . . . mine, is it?"

He laughed again and I was struck mute by blind hatred.

He exhaled with a laugh and wiped a tear from the corner of his eye. "It didn't take much comfort before that whore spread her legs for me, but *damn*."

His hand moved over his mouth as he tried to wipe the grin from his face, but it clung to the edge of his lips. "I did not see that one coming."

Red rings of fury seeped into my vision as my voice rose. "How dare you. How dare you call Teddy's mother a whore. She was a young woman who'd come to you for help. For comfort."

Unmoved, my father shook his head. "You really are that fucking stupid, aren't you? She didn't come to Michigan looking for comfort. She wasn't even pregnant. She came looking for a payout."

"A payout?" The pieces were rapidly clicking into place, and I was too stunned to believe it.

My father rolled his eyes as he continued: "She went to the office, looking for you. She had plans to tell you she was pregnant in order for you to give her money for an abortion."

He scoffed and laughed again to himself. "When I found her at the café, she broke down and admitted everything. She was going to use your reputation against us. Turns out she left with what she came for. Well . . . maybe a little more than she bargained for, but it all worked out in the end."

I felt sick.

"For years you kept paying her. Did you know about Teddy?"

He gave a halfhearted shrug as though the entire conversation was boring him. "I knew she had a kid, but I didn't care enough to ask if it was mine. She warmed my bed on occasion, and I paid her handsomely for it." He rolled his eyes and leaned back until the chair groaned against his weight. "That's what whores are for."

Fury seeped from my pores, and I vibrated with hate. "And Mom's necklace?"

"Your mother didn't need it where she was." A sick grin slinked across his face. "Maybe with this kid, I can get it right this time . . . mold him in the way I could never quite do with you."

I snapped and dove across the table.

My fists gripped his shirt, and I slammed him forward. Rewarded with his pained grunt, I reveled in the shock that crossed his face before it hit the metal surface.

Blood spurted from a fresh cut above his eyebrow and seeped down his face. He wasn't laughing anymore, but I was. My fist landed in a sickening thud as it connected with his face.

My father fell back and onto the floor, the metal chair scraping as it tumbled with him. The commotion drew attention, and the door flew open. Dad's attorney stepped in with an officer on his heels.

"What the hell?" He surged toward my father, but I pushed past him. "That's assault, Mr. King!"

My father was enraged, wiping blood from his eyes and drawing ragged breaths as he struggled to stand. "I will press charges!"

I kept moving, leaving him and any shred of loyalty I had to him behind. "I hope you do."

THIRTY-EIGHT

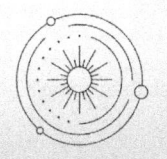

HAZEL

I PACED across the living room floor. JP had been gone for nearly two hours, and panic was setting in. After their ice cream, Teddy was buzzing from the sugar, and it took a hot bath and two bedtime stories to get him relaxed enough to close his eyes.

Alone in the kitchen, I whittled my nail polish down to nothing while reading the paternity results again.

And again.

And again.

Shock had morphed into utter, aching sadness.

Every time I had smiled when Teddy did something that reminded me of JP—every frown, their uptight nature, all the quirks that silently reassured me JP was his dad—meant nothing. The two were similar because they were related.

Brothers.

The thought of Olive sharing a bed with Russell King sickened me. If only there was a way I could talk to her—one last time—and ask the dozens of questions I still had.

An idea sparked to life, and I pulled out my phone.

. . .

> How much do you know about performing a séance?

LUNA

More than most, less than some?

> I can make that work.

Got someone you need to talk to?

> My sister.

Send me the address. I'm on my way, but we'll need reinforcements to amplify the signal.

THINKING ON MY FEET, I created a group chat with some of the women from the Bluebirds. Hopefully they wouldn't think I was completely losing it and at least a few of them would be open to helping. I toyed with my lip and thought of the best way to explain what I needed but opted for a direct, lighthearted approach.

> Hi! It's Hazel. I'm hoping the Bluebirds can come through for me tonight. It's a big ask, but I need anyone open and willing to come to a séance? I wouldn't ask if it wasn't important.

ANNIE

When and where?

> JP's house. Immediately?

> VEDA
>
> He's going to hate that. I am definitely in.
>
> MJ
>
> Let's do this!
>
> SLOANE
>
> I can be there in five.
>
> SYLVIE
>
> Sloane, pick me up.
>
> LARK
>
> I want to come!
>
> KATE
>
> Me too!
>
> EMILY
>
> Well I'm not missing it either. Carpool!

ONE BY ONE, my phone chimed with enthusiastic support. I grinned even when a ripple of nerves ran down my back. I needed to get moving to create the perfect space for my sister's spirit to come through.

Sure, I'd never *actually* successfully conjured a spirit, but there's a first time for everything, right?

Drawing in a cleansing breath, I centered myself before gathering our supplies. I laid a blanket across the kitchen island. Rummaging through the kitchen drawers, I found a few emergency candles that would have to do. I tossed them in the middle of the island and pulled open the spice cabinet. Thanks to JP's meticulous nature, they were alphabetized and I grabbed out a few sprigs of rosemary. I hurried as I found my tarot cards, white sage, and the picture I had of JP and my sister.

I stared down at her grinning face and my heart ached. JP looked so young and free. Olive was fierce and having the time of her life.

I placed the picture down on the makeshift altar and unlocked the front door. Moments later, headlights turned into the driveway, and I waved.

One by one the women piled out of the SUV. Luna wasn't far behind them.

On the porch, I lowered my voice. "Teddy is asleep so we'll have to be quiet. Thanks for showing up."

MJ peered around my shoulder. "Where's my brother? Is he in on this?"

I swallowed. "He's . . . out right now."

I moved toward the door when Luna stepped forward. "For this to work, we need to clear our energy. Any skeptics or those not open to the *possibility* of connecting to the other side will only ruin the experience. Now is the time to excuse yourself."

Our eyes floated across one another as we were cloaked in darkness.

In a silent agreement, tiny nods rippled through the semicircle of women.

"Okay then." Luna nodded. "Let's go."

We arranged ourselves in a circle around the kitchen island. Luna took a small dish from the cupboard and filled it with water as I arranged the altar. Curious eyes stared in wonder, but the women stayed silent.

I held out my hands at each side. "Please hold hands."

The women joined hands, completing the circle.

I closed my eyes and let the quiet surround me. In a shaky whisper, I set our intentions. "Thank you for being here. I am lost and need answers. Thank you for being sisters in support." My hands were both squeezed in a show of sisterhood, and I smiled. There was no judgment, only soft, supportive smiles.

I looked to Luna and nodded.

She lit the candles in the center of the makeshift altar, and a gleam sparked in her eye. Her eyebrows bounced. "Let's find some ghosts, shall we?"

Nerves tickled my belly as the soft smoke from the white sage floated toward the ceiling. Luna breathed in and out, her head drifting back until her face tilted toward the ceiling.

"This is so cool," MJ whispered.

Beside her, Kate bumped MJ's arm. "Focus. We're supposed to be . . . channeling or whatever."

Small giggles rippled through the circle.

Luna grinned. "The energy feels good. You've chosen the right amplifiers."

I smiled at the women who'd shown up for me.

"Close your eyes," Luna instructed. "Tonight we seek answers from Olive Adams. We welcome only spirits with good intentions to join our circle. Make your presence known."

I silently repeated Luna's incantation, peeking one eye open. Everyone was holding hands and kept their eyes closed.

Luna repeated her words, then added, "If you are with us, make your presence known."

A light gasp forced my eyes open. Kate was staring at the candles in the center. "One went out."

A chill ran up my back.

"Keep the circle intact. Hold hands," Luna gently instructed. "Olive Adams, if you are with us, your sister Hazel seeks your knowledge and comfort. Make your presence known."

When the second candle flickered and sputtered out, my stomach dropped so quickly it nearly fell out of my butt. My heartbeat ticked higher.

Luna grinned. "Go on," she whispered to me. "Ask her."

I looked around the circle. I wasn't prepared to drop the news that Teddy wasn't JP's child, so I chose my words carefully. "Olive, it's me." Tears burned in my nose. "I miss you." My friends squeezed my hands, and I took a breath. "I know the truth . . . at least some of it. I need your help figuring the rest out." I looked around.

The air was eerily still, but nothing happened. "Please," I pleaded.

One hot tear burned a path down my cheek. "Please, Olive. I don't know what to do."

We all gasped when a loud thud broke the silence behind us.

My head whipped around to see my purse had tumbled off the table and its contents spilled on the ground, her folded letter spinning to a stop near my foot.

"Holy fuck," someone whispered.

"Any more questions?" Luna asked me.

I was rooted to the spot. I had about twelve billion questions, but all I could do was stare at my purse and shake my head.

"Thank you for joining us," Luna said. "We thank you for your guidance and love. You may go in peace." She let her hands drop and clapped her hands together.

We all jumped as Luna laughed. "Woo! That was fucking *wild*!"

I pressed my fingertips to my cheeks, breaking the circle and exhaling.

Murmurs rippled through the women. We were all in

various stages of shock and disbelief over what we'd just experienced.

"Are we a coven now?" Annie asked.

Luna threw her arm around her shoulders. "If you want to be, babe."

Sloane grinned. "Well, this beats a rerun of shitty reality TV."

"No kidding," Veda agreed.

Sylvie turned to Luna. "Are you for hire?"

I eyed my overturned bag as MJ stood next to me. "What do you think is in there?"

I shook my head and crouched to gather the spilled contents. "I guess I'll find out."

I scooped the contents back into my bag, leaving my sister's letter. It was heavy in my hand.

Luna leaned into me and whispered, "Maybe the answers you need are already there?"

I shook my head. "I've read it a thousand times."

Luna patted my back. "Fresh eyes see new opportunities."

I looked at the creased pages. "Maybe."

Sylvie came up behind me. "Do you want us to stay?"

My throat was tight. "No," I whispered. "I think I need to sit with this for a minute."

Her soft, reassuring smile brought me comfort. In her maternal and loving way, she rounded up the women.

My friends.

I couldn't have done it without them. Once they'd left, I stared at Olive's words. Tilting my face to the ceiling, I whispered to her, "Help me see what you need me to see."

I looked again.

We sought comfort in each other.

The words from Olive's letter brought on a new

meaning now that we knew the truth. After she sought out JP, Russell had met with her. Somehow they'd ended up sleeping together, and that was when she got pregnant.

But why had she come in the first place? Could it be that she was actually trying to get money out of JP by saying she was pregnant when she wasn't? Why pretend JP was Teddy's dad at all? Unless she had discovered for herself what a monster Russell really was . . .

Tears blurred my vision as I sifted through her words.

I came to realize Russell wasn't the man I thought he was either.

But I am out of time and out of choices.

One day you'll see that I'm doing this for Teddy. So he has a chance to have a father who has the capacity to love him. Without JP, Teddy may never have that.

I read, and reread, her scribbled words.

A father, not *his* father. Over time, she had seen Russell's true colors. Maybe in her desperate mind, she thought the best option would be to fool everyone, including Teddy, into thinking JP had been the man to get her pregnant.

I read over the rambling words again, landing on anything that could give me a clue as to how she could be capable of something so deceitful.

I've done things I'm not proud of. I've been hurt and angered by men who thought I would stay quiet and fade into the background. I know who I am, but please let Teddy believe his mother was a good person.

I sank to the floor.

The truth had been in her rambling, emotion-fueled letter all along, and I didn't need a séance to prove it.

She wanted Teddy to believe that his mother was good. She was so desperate that she was willing to lie.

I hated to think such thoughts about my own sister, but given the recent revelations, it was entirely possible. Olive had done things she wasn't proud of . . . like having a one-night stand with JP—a rich, handsome man—and lying about an accidental pregnancy to get some money out of him.

My stomach rolled and I swallowed back the nausea.

Trouble was, Olive hadn't counted on JP's dad. Russell King was a master manipulator. I could easily understand how a man like him would prey on a young, vulnerable woman and use her to his sick advantage.

Russell had conned her into bed and gotten her pregnant. She continued to see him in secret and accept his money. How Olive truly felt about being his mistress was a secret she had taken with her.

He'd given her money, jewelry, and promises.

My sister had lied to me—that much was clear. Olive had molded the narrative so that everyone would believe it was JP who had gotten her pregnant.

She was a dying mother who was searching for a way to paint herself in the best light possible.

I didn't agree with her choices, but a tiny part of me could understand them.

My chest ached and my mind was racing with how I was ever going to explain this to a seven-year-old.

THIRTY-NINE

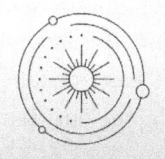

HAZEL

The sound of JP's car turning down the driveway drew my attention. I wiped my palms down the front of my pants and waited for him. When he opened the door, a defeated man stood in front of me.

I rushed to him, putting my hands on his arms. "Are you okay? What happened?"

His jaw flexed but his eyes were tired. "I had a conversation with my father. It didn't go well."

I swallowed hard, not sure what that meant, as I searched for the words to explain what I had uncovered in his absence.

"Is . . ." He gently sniffed the air. "Is something burning?"

I shook my head and waved my hand. I did not have time to explain that I'd just invited his sisters and the Sullivan women to a séance to contact my dead sister. "It's sage."

He shrugged, and my heart melted a little with how he'd come to simply accept I did weird shit while he was gone.

I had opened my mouth to speak when he pulled me

into an embrace. "Did you tell him?" JP's voice was hollow and near breaking.

I looked up at him. "No. Of course not—not without you. JP, look at me." My hand moved to his face, forcing him to look at me. "We'll figure this out, okay?"

His blue-green eyes were distant and somber. "I'm not sure what there is to figure out. It's all right there in the results."

I stammered, unsure how to respond. Surely he didn't intend for *Russell* to have any involvement with Teddy. The man was a liar, a cheat, and a murderer.

I went to voice my concerns when JP cut in. "I should have seen the signs. Olive was even listed as a beneficiary to an investment account. I didn't think much of it, but given the information we have now . . . it's clear they were more involved with each other than we thought. In a way, he cared or felt guilty enough to take care of her financially." JP's shoulders lifted in a weak shrug. "It seems that was the only way he knew how to show he wasn't completely heartless."

I nodded. "I think I figured it out."

A chill caused goose bumps to pinch my arms and I stepped back to rub them. I didn't want JP to hate Olive, but he deserved to know the truth. "I think . . ."

Fuck, why was this so hard?

I cleared my throat. "I think after you slept with Olive, she came here and lied about being pregnant. Thinking back, she was going through one of her wild streaks around that time, and money was always tight. She'd have a job for a few weeks and then just decide to stop showing up. I think she met you and—" My voice cracked. "I think maybe she met you and saw an easy paycheck."

He was rigid and cold, but nodded. "My father intervened. Sent her away just so he could be a source of comfort for her."

My voice wobbled. "After that, I think she knew Russell was Teddy's father. She kept it a secret from everyone, but when she realized he would never choose her or maybe when she saw his true colors . . . then she got sick and I don't know—I think she thought the better option was to lead you to believe you'd gotten her pregnant."

His face was hard and angry as the pieces started fitting together in a sad, manipulative puzzle. JP had been my sister's pawn, and she'd used her son to her advantage. It was horrible, even if she thought it was the best thing for her child.

"I'm so sorry, JP. I swear, I had no idea." I melted into him and his strong arms pulled me closer.

"I know," he soothed.

Concern flashed over his gorgeous features before his logical demeanor took over. "My father is getting out of prison, which means he will be back. He isn't one to let go of any influence he has over any situation. He manipulated your sister, and he'll try to manipulate you. When he gets out, he will be in control of the narrative."

Fear seeped into my awareness and gripped my chest. *In control of the narrative? What does that even mean?*

I searched his eyes for answers. "Will he try to hurt us? What should I do?" Panic was rising, and all I wanted to do was bury my head into JP's chest so he could tell me everything would be all right.

JP stood, hard and unmoving, in front of me. "There's no telling what he will do. My best guess is that he'll assess the situation—see if he can manipulate you the same way he did Olive. He'll see Teddy as a pawn, something to stroke his ego. He will seek custody, Hazel."

My heart pounded as I shook my head. "That's impossible. No judge would give him custody over me with his record, would they?"

JP's lips flattened into a grim line. "He could make things happen."

I sucked in a shocked breath, taking a step backward. "No. Why would he even want custody?"

JP stared at me. "It's what I would do."

I was sickened at the thought. "You're nothing like him."

A sad, disbelieving grunt was all he gave me.

Tears filled my eyes. "What should I do? JP, what do I do? Do I leave—take Teddy and run? I—"

A sob broke free and I crumpled.

JP's hands pulled my shoulders. "I will not let him near you or Teddy. I will keep you safe, even if it kills me."

His hands stroked my face, and my eyes lifted to meet his. "There is nothing I wouldn't do for you."

His lips lowered to mine. In the dark kitchen, I pinched my eyes closed, willing every worried thought to float away.

"You think I don't see the candles and the tarot cards and whatever else is burning on my kitchen island? I know what I've gotten myself into."

A smile tugged at the corner of my mouth. "A hex?"

He smiled back. "*My* Hex."

I let his mouth warm my skin as his lips touched my neck. I hummed, luxuriating in the way his touch let every worry float away and pop like tiny bubbles.

With him, we were safe.

We could figure anything out.

We were loved.

My mind was exhausted, and I wanted nothing more

than to get lost in the man I had fallen in love with. I leaned into his kiss, pressing my body against his.

His palms smoothed up my arms and over my shoulders, slipping beneath my cardigan and pushing it back down my arms.

We were both on edge—scared and needing some kind of reassurance it would all be okay.

"Make me forget," I whispered. His blue eyes caught mine. "Make me forget everything but you."

Without a word, JP scooped me into his arms. My legs wrapped around his waist, and his arms supported my weight. Our kiss was deep and sensual as he walked me to the bedroom.

Frazzled and drained from the day, a frenzy started between my legs and spread up my back. I didn't want to think. I wanted to *feel*. His strong arms held me as one hand kneaded my hip.

He placed me on the bed, standing between my legs. His index finger stroked down my nose, catching my lip before trailing down my neck and between my breasts. He gathered the fabric of my shirt, peeling the layers over my head and exposing my bra. My nipples pressed against the fabric, yearning to be touched.

Tasted.

He toyed with the barbell that poked against the thin fabric, and I hissed a breath.

"I want you." His thumb strummed my nipples as his other hand stroked down his cock. "I want all of you."

I arched my back. "I'm yours."

On a growl, he prowled over me, lifting my body higher onto the bed. We tore at each other's clothing, hating anything that separated us.

His hand dipped between my legs. "So fucking wet for me."

I gasped as his finger glistened in the dark room, then disappeared into his mouth. He rumbled an appreciative moan and my thighs clenched around him.

His hard cock stood between us as I stared up at him. A defiant glint sparked in my eye. "I like it wet."

One dark eyebrow shot up. He eyed me, then spit on my already slick pussy.

"Jesus." I couldn't believe how filthy and in command he was.

"Better?" he asked with a haughty edge to his voice.

My core was on fire as he slipped one finger, then two, inside me. I gasped, clenching around his fingers.

"Yes," I cried, unable to form a coherent sentence.

He pumped in and out of me as my legs trembled. He slid another finger inside of me.

"Fuck," he hummed. "I like feeling you work to fit me in."

His fingers curled inside me, stroking the spot that had my legs shaking. "Please," I pleaded.

"Please what?"

JP was so hard and all I wanted was to feel him slip inside me. "More," I begged.

He adjusted his position so he was settled between my legs. The head of his cock notched at my entrance, but instead of thrusting inside, he eased his way in.

Inch by glorious inch, we watched his cock disappear inside me. I stretched around him, struggling and adjusting to being wholly and completely filled by him. It was a cruel and delicious torture.

My heart thudded against my ribs as he finally sank

deeper and his hips met my body. We exhaled as one and goose bumps broke out along my arms.

With an aching deliberation, JP pumped in and out of me until the world faded away.

Every worry—every doubt—faded into oblivion until nothing remained but the two of us. "You are so fucking tight," he ground out. "So fucking pretty taking my cock."

He pinched my nipples, rolling my piercings between the pad of his fingers, and a hot surge of warmth spread between my legs.

I gasped as my pussy pulsed and my orgasm rolled through me. Bracing himself over me, JP pumped harder and faster as I rode the wave of my orgasm. My tits bounced as he thrust deeper.

JP's hand gripped my face. "Look at me."

I wrenched my eyes open to find his intense stare focused on only me. "You're mine."

"Yes." The word was nothing more than a pathetic little noise, but I was already completely unraveled.

"I'm going to fill you with my cum so you know who you belong to."

Jesus. The mouth on that man had my feminism flying out the window as I whimpered, unable to hold off any longer. A second orgasm slammed into me as we both toppled over the edge.

JP cursed as his back tightened and we rode the wave together. He collapsed beside me, running his rough palm over my slick skin. I preened and stretched, feeling his warm cum slowly coat my inner thigh.

You're mine.

Our fingers intertwined, neither of us concerned about the mess we just made or the weight of the evening we just had. I rolled toward him as he mirrored my position.

A painful, unspoken truth floated between us.

I was too afraid to give my fear a voice—too afraid not to. Emotion sprang to life as my eyes welled with tears.

Had I never sought out JP, we never would have known that Russell King was his biological father. Teddy would never have been in danger and the two of us would be driving down some winding highway with the windows down and the music up.

"Hey," he whispered and stroked my cheek. "What is it? Did I hurt you?"

I shook my head.

"I never should have come here," I whispered, a tear slipping free. "But I'm glad I did. I'm happy that he met you ... that he got to experience a father's love. I don't care what that paper says, you've been more of a dad to him than anyone."

He eased forward and his forehead dropped to mine.

"Don't run." His voice was laced with desperation. "Whatever you do, don't run."

How did he know?

Every cell in my body was screaming to run. I wanted to scoop Teddy up and bundle him in my arms. We could pile into the skoolie and head west and never look back. I didn't need Michigan if it meant Teddy would be safe from a terrible man.

But my body refused to move. Cocooned in his arms, I melted into JP with a sob. "I'm so afraid."

In my life, I had learned to do hard things, but nothing seemed more impossible than having to tell Teddy the truth about JP.

THE NEXT MORNING Teddy was his usual quirky self. I painted on a happy smile as he got ready for school.

"What are you doing today?" he asked.

Oh, nothing. Just figuring out how to break your heart and also keep you safe from your biological father, who happens to be a psychotic narcissist.

"Editing some pictures. I really need to be better about posting . . . the fans are restless." I sighed and shrugged. I hoped my smile and cheery tone sounded genuine.

Teddy frowned, and it was an arrow to my heart. He looked *so much* like JP that I still struggled to believe they were half brothers. "Do you still love it?"

I frowned. "Love what?"

Teddy hiked his backpack on one shoulder, then the other. "Traveling. Posting about the skoolie. Being super famous."

I chuckled. "I've told you . . . I'm not super famous. I do enjoy the freedom of my job. But now that you mention it, I haven't missed the traveling part as much. I liked building the skoolie and posting the progress but . . ." My shoulders lifted. "Now I'm not so sure."

"If it's not fun, then do something else." His serious face was so sweet.

I grinned. "That's solid advice. I'll think about it."

I fluffed his dark hair. "Ready to go?"

Teddy stopped. "Where's Dad?"

A lump expanded in my throat. "Oh, uh . . . JP had to head into the office early. I'm sure we'll see him later."

His face twisted at the odd use of JP's name but, thankfully, he let it go. As we walked to the bus stop, I let Teddy carry the conversation. By the time he waved at me from his seat and the bus turned a corner and disappeared, I was emotionally wrung out.

I started to send a quick message to JP, letting him know that Teddy was off to school, like I'd always done.

After last night, I was sure he needed, as badly as I did, a way to reconnect and get reassurance that everything was going to be okay.

Instead, I steeled my nerves and slipped my phone back into my pocket.

FORTY

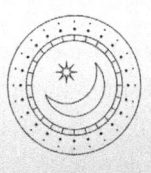

JP

I frowned down at my phone.

Normally, if I left early for work, Hazel would tell me how the morning had gone and what she planned to be up to while he was at school.

I tried texting her, but it went unanswered.

The past few days had been fraught with tension and the uncertainty of how to broach the subject of Teddy's paternity.

The last thing I wanted to do was fuck the poor kid up for life.

I leaned back in my chair and exhaled, hating that we even had to tell him at all.

How gloriously simple would it be to pretend like the paternity results were different and Hazel and I were still playing house and living a life where we both took care of Teddy?

I needed to quell the riot of uncomfortable emotions I was fighting.

Hazel's notable withdrawal was surprisingly painful,

even if it was unintentional. She wouldn't be the first woman in my life to leave me, but damn did it leave behind an uncomfortable ache in my chest.

This was different.

She was different, and I meant what I'd said—she was mine and there was no surviving if she ran away and took Teddy with her.

That's not going to happen.

I shook my head and looked around. My pathetic attempt at self-reassurance wasn't doing a damn thing.

Work was the only solution.

King Equities was hanging on by a thread. But with the prospect of my father's return imminent, I simply couldn't find it in me to care.

Still, Veda and the other employees were counting on me.

Sure, I could burn the company to the ground, but my father would find a way to survive. He was like those cockroaches that survived the extinction of the dinosaurs.

The only people who would suffer were those stupid enough to follow me into that battle. I was stretched thin and on the verge of breaking.

"Boss." I jerked at Veda's voice and exhaled. She held her hands up. "Whoa, sorry." Veda gestured vaguely at her laptop. "I need to know how you want to play this."

I sighed. "Veda, you deserve to hear it from me." I swiveled in my chair and rested my elbows on my knees. "I'm done."

Her dark eyebrows pinched down. "Done?"

I swallowed hard. She'd taken a risk in coming to work for King Equities, and I'd failed her. I'd failed everyone. "There is no saving King Equities. We've lost too many investors, and those that are left can't afford to take any more losses. They'll go down with the company if they stay. When my father comes back, he won't care about that. He'll leverage what's left to salvage whatever he can, and it will be at their expense."

Her face was hard as stone, but she didn't waver. Her arms crossed and her chin lifted. "So what's the move?"

I dragged a hand through my hair. "We close up shop. Bit by bit we let our remaining investors out of their contracts so they can recoup as much as possible before the ship actually sinks."

A soft smile graced her lips. "That's the honorable thing to do, but giving away a billion-dollar company will make some serious waves. Your father will come back to nothing but the corpse of the business he built."

Good.

"He has enough money personally invested to be fine . . . unfortunately." The words tasted bitter. "But I don't want to give him the opportunity to rebuild on the backs of the companies and people that trusted him—trusted us."

With a slow nod, Veda turned back to her desk. "I'll start drawing it up."

"I'm sorry," I said softly. "I know you trusted me to salvage this, but . . . I just couldn't."

"Give yourself a break." She looked over her shoulder and smirked. "I'm not that worried about it. We'll figure it out with the next one."

The next one.

Veda had a willingness to follow me in whatever business venture was next and had the kind of blind faith I envied. I had no idea what was next for me, but I knew that she wouldn't be my employee.

Veda would be an equal partner.

Hours later, final offers were sent to King Equities' remaining investors. Each was legally sound, but only a fool would pass up such generous and lucrative terms. By the end of the month, King Equities would be nothing more than a sad story of corruption and greed inked in the glossy pages of some business magazine no one reads.

My neck was sore and my shoulders were tight by the time I looked up from my computer screen. Outside the windows, night had fallen and not a single text message from Hazel.

I sank lower. I knew she was scared and looking to me for answers on how to approach the subject of Teddy's paternity with him. Still, I couldn't bring myself to say the words.

Not out loud, and certainly not to him.

He would be crushed and my soul would be breaking right alongside him.

The drive back to my house was dark and lonesome. I'd rolled the windows all the way down, letting the cold September wind slap my face. I'd hoped it would jolt me out of the funk I was in, but I had no such luck.

Without having Hazel's sunshine to warm my day, my mood was surly and sour as I pulled into the driveway. I rolled past Hazel's skoolie, and my chest ached.

How had so much changed in such a short amount of time?

Light glowed from the inside of the bus, and I was curious as I parked my car. When I stepped out, Hazel was on the front porch.

"Hey," I called, trying to shake my mood.

"Hey, yourself." She didn't sound right—a little too distant for my liking.

I cleared my throat. "How was your day? Mine was a

mess. King Equities is being dismantled . . . bit by bit. That bastard won't know what to do once he's back at the helm, and I won't be there to fix it for him."

Her lips were pressed in a flat line and she shrugged. "I had a crummy day too." Hazel crossed her arms, and I couldn't help but feel an unspoken chasm open between us.

I studied her face as she spoke. "I spent the day going over every word of Olive's letter—*again*—and every memory I have of her, trying to understand why she would lie to me. Then I spent the majority of the afternoon trying not to cry because Teddy was over the moon excited to tell you about Bring Your Dude to School Day."

I frowned and stuffed my hands into my pockets. "Bring your dude to school?"

Hazel shrugged. "Apparently it used to be Bring Your Dad to School, but they've gotten a tiny bit more inclusive, so I guess that's something."

Her lip quivered. "He wants to bring you. He went on and on and on about how amazing it was going to be to show off his dad."

"Hey . . ." I stepped forward, climbing the steps and wrapping Hazel in my arms. "I'd be happy to be his dude."

That earned a watery chuckle and her whisper wobbled. "We have to tell him."

My gut churned. I shook my head, despite knowing she was right. "I know."

She stepped back to swipe at her splotchy, tear-soaked face and groaned. "Ugh . . . my emotions are all over the place."

My hands rubbed down her arms. "I feel it too. I'm sorry if I don't always show you."

She chuckled softly. "You showed them by dismantling the company your father built. Vengeance at all costs."

I shrugged. "Maybe it was vengeance . . . though it didn't feel quite as good as I'd expected."

Hazel nodded and gestured toward the bus. "Teddy's in the skoolie. He was playing around after dinner while I edited some content, and he fell asleep in the big bed." Her eyes stayed focused on the big white bus.

"I can bring him in," I offered.

She shook her head. "It's okay. We can let him sleep there tonight. I'm pretty drained, too, and I think I'll cuddle up with him for the night."

Hazel reached up on her tiptoes and dropped a soft kiss on my lips before turning and walking toward the skoolie.

I frowned as she walked away, feeling the chasm yawn and stretch wider.

It was *me* I wanted her cuddled up with, but I had no right to take that from Teddy. Instead, I entered my too-quiet house and slowly made my way to the primary bedroom that overlooked the driveway.

I watched as her shadow moved across the windows of the skoolie. Reaching beside me, I flicked the small lamp on and off and waited. I tried again—on and off.

Come on. Do it back. Show me you're still with me.

My back ached by the time I gave up the fight and crawled into bed. I stared at the ceiling and imagined life without Hazel and Teddy. Hours ticked by as I ran through every possible scenario, and they all came to the same, horrifying conclusion—if Hazel left, she'd be taking the last shred of goodness inside me with her.

She couldn't leave. There had to be another way, and it was up to me to find it.

I was no longer afraid of Russell King. His influence was nothing more than a misplaced sense of superiority, and he no longer held any claim over me.

Hazel and Teddy were mine.

If he wanted a fight, I'd bring that fight right to his fucking doorstep.

FORTY-ONE

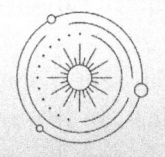

HAZEL

The soft creak of the bus's wooden floors beneath my feet was the only sound as I paced back and forth, running my fingers through my hair, tangled from another restless night.

I caught my reflection in the little mirror by the kitchen sink—my eyes were hollowed, staring back at me. Usually they were wide and bright, filled with hope and curiosity.

Now they looked haunted and lost.

The interior of the skoolie was dimly lit by the string lights hung along the ceiling, casting soft shadows. It was intended to be cozy, like a cocoon, but tonight it felt too small, too tight. I could feel the walls closing in on me, wrapping around my chest like a vine threatening to choke me.

Teddy was asleep in the big bed, his gentle breaths steady and innocent, completely unaware of the chaos in my heart. In such a short time, that quirky little guy had become my world—my reason for being.

And now, because of one twist of fate and my sister's unfathomable choices, I might lose him.

I wrapped my arms around myself, trying to hold it together.

How had everything unraveled so quickly?

JP wasn't Teddy's father. Russell was.

Russell King.

The thought of him sent a shiver down my spine. I could still see the coldness in JP's eyes whenever the topic of his dad came up. The way his name filled every room, demanding attention, control. He was a man who always got what he wanted. And now he knew about Teddy.

How long before he showed up, lawyers in tow, ready to rip my world apart?

I dropped down into the worn leather seat by the window, pulling my knees up to my chest.

It was all my fault.

I never planned for this, for any of it. I never planned, period. I lived in the moment, let my emotions steer the ship. I was impulsive, untethered. I had read Olive's letter, and though I was doing exactly what she wanted for her son, I just jumped in without thinking it through.

And now there I was. Alone. Scared.

I looked out the window toward his bedroom. It was dark inside, but I flicked the lamp beside me on, then off.

I waited and waited, but his room was still dark.

I let out a shaky breath at the thought of the man I had fallen in love with. He made me feel safe, grounded, like all my wild ideas and messy emotions weren't something to run from, but to embrace.

With him, I wasn't just a free spirit floating through the universe—I had an anchor.

But how could I keep holding on to him, knowing that Teddy wasn't really his? Knowing that, in the end, I might lose everything?

My heart ached at the thought of pulling away from him, but what choice did I have? JP didn't deserve to get caught up in this mess, and I didn't know if I could take him down with me. Maybe it was better to let him go now, before things got even more complicated.

A small noise broke through the fog of my thoughts, and I turned to see Teddy standing there, rubbing his eyes. His dark, messy hair stuck up in every direction, and he looked at me with that sleepy, innocent gaze that made my heart both swell and break at the same time.

"Hazel?" His voice was soft, still thick with sleep. "Why are we not in the house?"

"You fell asleep. It's okay."

He frowned at me and my heart rolled. "Why are you sad?"

I tried to muster a smile, but it didn't reach my eyes. "I'm not sad, buddy. Just . . . thinking."

He padded over to me, his bare feet making little thumps on the floor, and climbed up onto the seat beside me. He wrapped his small arms around my waist, leaning his head on my shoulder.

"You don't have to think so much, you know," he said, his voice wise beyond his years. "The universe already knows what's supposed to happen."

I blinked back tears, the lump in my throat growing tighter.

Of course he would say that. Of course.

"I don't know if it's that simple, Teddy," I whispered, brushing a hand through his hair. "Sometimes it feels like everything's too messy for the universe to figure out."

He looked up at me, his blue-green eyes serious. "But the universe is really big. You said it can fix anything."

God, he was too pure for this world. Too good for the mess I'd brought him into.

I kissed the top of his head, holding him close. "You're right, buddy. The universe is big."

But no matter how big the universe was, I wasn't sure if it could fix this. I wasn't sure if anything could stop Russell from sweeping in and claiming Teddy as his own. And I wasn't sure if I could survive losing the only family I had.

Teddy shifted beside me, pulling back just enough to look at me, his face full of childlike sincerity. "You're happy when you're with Dad, right?"

I froze, not expecting the question. Teddy was staring up at me, waiting for an answer.

Slowly, I nodded. "Yeah. JP makes me happy."

"Do you love him?" His big blue eyes stared at me.

I swallowed hard. "I do."

He grinned. "Me too, and that's all that matters." He shrugged like it was the simplest thing in the world. "If Dad makes you happy, and I make you happy, then everything will be okay."

I swallowed hard again, tears pricking the back of my eyes. "You really think so?"

Teddy nodded, his sleepy smile returning. "Yup. The universe will figure out the rest."

I watched him curl up against me, his breathing slowing as he drifted back to sleep.

How was it that this seven-year-old could see things so clearly when I couldn't?

He was right, in a way. I was overcomplicating everything, letting fear take over. JP made me happy. Teddy made me happy. The love we shared wasn't meaningless, no matter how much the world tried to tell me otherwise.

Maybe it wasn't about planning or having everything

figured out. Maybe it was about trusting—trusting the universe, trusting myself, and trusting that somehow, some way, we'd find a way through this.

Together.

I looked out the window, the stars twinkling in the vast night sky over Lake Michigan, and for the first time in what felt like forever, I let out a deep breath.

I squeezed my eyes shut and sent up a prayer to my sister and anyone else who would listen.

Please let Teddy be right.

FORTY-TWO

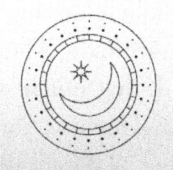

JP

My phone rang before 5:00 a.m.

I groaned and cursed whoever was on the line. My eyes ached from lack of sleep, and the muscles in my neck were screaming at me.

When Abel's name flashed across the screen, I sat up, wiping the sleep from my eyes.

"Hey." I grunted to clear the fatigue from my throat.

"It's Dad." His voice was stone.

"He's already out?" My blood was cold and my brain was running through dozens of scenarios.

"Not exactly. I'll explain on the way." Abel hung up before I could ask any follow-up questions.

Annoyed by my brother's cryptic statement, I took a quick cold shower and got dressed. I scribbled a note for Hazel and tucked it under the windshield wiper of the skoolie just as Abel's truck turned down my driveway.

He lowered his window. "Let's go."

I climbed in as he passed me a to-go cup of hot black coffee. "Thanks."

"You're gonna need it." Abel reversed down the driveway and started on the highway out of town.

"Where to? To be honest, I am not in the mood to see Dad, so if that's what you're planning—"

"Fuck no," Abel scoffed. There was no love lost between Abel and Dad, that much was clear. "But we are headed to the correctional facility. Something happened last night." He glanced at me. "I got a call early this morning. It was big."

On the quiet drive, my fingers drummed an erratic rhythm on my thigh. It was before visiting hours and the guard eyed us warily.

Abel leaned out the window. "We have a summons from this attorney." He handed the guard a business card. "He said it was an emergency."

The guard spoke into the radio on his chest and, after a moment, let us pass. We entered the building and walked into the lobby.

I leaned toward my brother. "What the fuck is going on?"

Abel looked around, knowing there was an infinite number of eyes and ears. "Remember Oliver Pendergrass?"

My eyes narrowed. "The guy you shared a cell with? I thought he got out."

Abel grunted. "He found himself in some trouble. I got a call from his lawyer this morning, and he specifically requested we *both* show up."

Confused but intrigued, I waited until we were called back. In an eerily similar room to the one I'd assaulted my father in, we walked toward Pendergrass's lawyer.

Abel shook his hand. "I'm Abel King." He gestured toward me. "This is my brother JP."

"Gentlemen." The attorney shook our hands and let

loose a deep sigh. "My client has requested to speak with you before his placement into solitary confinement. He is being considered a danger to himself and others. Would you like an armed guard present?"

I looked at my brother, who only shook his head.

The attorney appeared tired and annoyed. "Fine. I'll send him in."

When he disappeared behind the door, I leaned toward my brother. "What the hell is happening?"

Abel was hard as stone. "I have no idea."

Moments later, Oliver was led in, shackled at the wrists and ankles. A wide grin spread across his face.

"Ollie." Abel stepped forward.

Oliver gestured toward the table. "Please. Sit."

The guard added a shackle, bolting him to the table.

He laughed and rolled his eyes. "Such drama queens around here. I'm not going to hurt my friends."

The guard didn't comment, but his eyes flicked up to us. Moments later, we were alone in a room with Oliver.

Abel spoke first. "What's going on, man?"

Oliver nodded and pressed his lips together. He stomped his foot and tried to pound on the table to get someone's attention. "Hey!" he called out. "Can I get my suit and tie back in here?"

He was making enough of a racket that the door pulled open and his lawyer stepped inside the room. "Did you bring it?"

The attorney stifled an eye roll and returned with a single plastic cup with two fingers of what smelled like bourbon.

Oliver scoffed at his lawyer. "Kind of stingy on the pour, but I guess thanks is in order."

His attorney's eyes flicked toward the camera in the

corner of the room. "Don't forget who's watching. Keep your mouth shut until the red light goes out."

"Ah," he scoffed. "Too late for secrets, bud. Now leave me with my friends."

When we were alone again, Oliver sighed and looked us over. The three of us waited in silence until the little red dot on the camera blinked off.

Oliver exhaled and looked at Abel. "You deserve to hear it from me. I did it. I took care of him for you."

My eyes narrowed as Abel's voice remained frighteningly calm. "Took care of how?"

Oliver's hand jerked up twice, the chains rattling and restricting his movements. "Shiv to the kidneys. One to the lung so he couldn't cry out." He sat back in his chair with a satisfied grin. "It was masterful. Artwork."

"You attacked our father?" My attention intensified as the words settled over me. "How did you get a weapon past the guards?"

"Made it." Oliver's eyes glittered with delight. "Plastic toothbrush rubbed against the concrete to file it to a point. Saw that in a movie once... surprisingly effective."

Abel stared at his friend.

"Is he dead?" I asked. Unclear emotions coursed through me.

Oliver's shoulders bounced. "That was kind of the point. Oh!" His eyes brightened and he sat straighter. "What about the other two? The old men. Want me to—" He clicked his tongue and made a slicing gesture toward his throat.

"Jesus, Ollie," Abel groaned. "No. You've done enough."

This is unbelievable.

I eyed Oliver, trying to figure him out. I gestured toward

the cup as my stomach bunched. "If you're so pleased with yourself, then what's with the alcohol?"

Oliver's attention was drawn to the plastic cup in front of him. He leaned down, gripping it with his teeth and shooting it backward. Once the booze was gone, he opened his mouth with an audible *ahh* and the cup tumbled to the ground. "I'm disinfecting from the inside out—emotional disinfectant." He chuckled at his own joke. "Just because I'm a killer doesn't mean I don't feel a little bad about it. I have a conscience . . . kind of."

Unamused, Abel's head hung low, his shoulders rolled in a defeated slump. "You were almost out, Ollie."

Oliver shrugged, but his mouth was turned down. "The world is changing and I don't care for that. Here, I've got three meals, a bed, work. I know who my friends are. The only skill I've learned here is how to survive *here*." He gestured toward the window. "I can't use that out there. Out there, I'm an unemployable felon. I can't get housing. A job. In here I'm somebody. I matter. It's where I belong."

Abel's voice wavered as he looked at his friend. "I told you that I'd have your back when you got out."

"You're a good man, Abel. You've always been a good friend to me. You protected me in prison when meatheads tried to run me through. But we're even now." He tried to hold out his hand, but it was restricted by the shackles. "We're even, brother."

Abel stared at his hand and finally filled it with his own.

I lifted my chin. "We won't press charges." The two looked at me. "If he is dead, we're next of kin. We will not be pursuing charges."

Abel jerked his head in my direction, and he gave Oliver a sad smile. "I told you he wasn't all bad."

Still, the realist in me knew this battle wasn't over for

Oliver. "The state's attorney is another issue. They could go after you even if, as the family, we don't."

"What about his *other family*?" Abel ground out the bitter words.

My jaw clenched. They were an entity I had altogether tried to forget about. We had only recently discovered my father had a family in Chicago—a wife who appeared comfortable looking the other way so long as the money kept rolling in and adult children we knew nothing about. His lies and deceit seemed endless.

I shook my head. "That will be for them to decide. They can worry about his messes for once."

Oliver shrugged, seemingly unaffected by how bad this all was for him. "Even if they do come after me, Abel made enough friends here to ensure they keep their mouths shut. Depending on what was caught on security cameras, I'll get some years added, but like I said . . . staying was kind of the point."

Abel stood and clamped a hand on his friend's shoulder. "You take care of yourself."

"You too," he replied. "Kiss the wife and kids for me."

Abel shook his head and I followed him to the exit. Abel's fist knocked on the door, and it was opened for us.

Oliver's attorney looked up from his phone with a solemn expression. "We just received word from the hospital. Your father has succumbed to his injuries."

FORTY-THREE

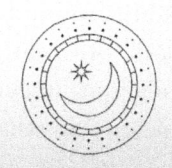

JP

Russell King was dead.

Dead dead.

As in *gone forever*.

The words tumbled around in my head as I tried to quantify the emotions that rolled through me. It was the end of a frightening era for the Kings. The man who'd ruled with an iron fist was officially out of our lives.

The man whose approval I had sought for so long was never coming back.

My eyes stayed locked on the road as Abel's truck barreled toward home. So much had changed. Dad's death would send ripples through our family and community, but in the end, nothing would ever truly be the same.

My thoughts wandered to Teddy, then to Hazel.

A sick part of me was elated that Dad would never have the chance to manipulate her and use Teddy for his own twisted advantages.

With Dad gone, I could keep them safe.

My throat was tight, but the truth was burning a hole inside me. "Teddy isn't my kid," I blurted.

Abel glanced in my direction but kept his focus on the road. "No shit?" He shook his head. "Damn."

The truth was worse, and he deserved to know all of it. "Turns out we, uh, have another brother."

Abel's gaze was hard. "Are you serious? Dad and the mom?" He muttered something under his breath, but whatever it was, it didn't matter. "So what are you going to do about that?"

My eyes were burning and I dragged my fingers across them. "I'm not sure what there is to do."

He sent a withering glance my way. "You and I both know that's a crock of shit. You know *exactly* what to do."

I rummaged around the pit in my stomach, but every scenario that didn't end with the three of us together felt wrong.

"You need to talk to her," he continued. "Dad fucked us all up—probably you more than most because he groomed you to be just like him. Now . . . we can all step up and care for that little boy as our own, but you've been more of a dad to him these last several weeks than he's ever had. Now if you don't want—"

"I do," I bit out. "I want both of them." I exhaled, trying not to let my emotions run away from me. "You have no idea how badly I wanted those results to confirm what I was already feeling."

The corner of Abel's mouth lifted. "And what was that?"

"I'm his dad."

I'm his dad.

Words I hadn't let myself think or feel opened the floodgate of emotions. I focused on breathing and clenched my jaw to keep the hot tears at bay.

I'm his dad.

Abel put his truck into park, and I realized we were already back at my place. "Then you need to step up and own it. Be that guy." Abel sighed. "No one is going to care what some paternity test says. When it comes to taking care of each other, does any of it really matter?"

I shook my head.

"Good." Abel gestured toward my house. "Now get the hell out of here."

I offered my hand to Abel. He glanced down at it and placed his palm in mine before pulling me into an awkward, but fierce, side hug.

He thumped two hard pats on my shoulder.

"Make things right with your woman and the kid." Abel was quiet in his serious kind of way. "I'll let everyone else know what's going on. Then you need to decide—are you ready to finally take over? Because it will be you who needs to step up if we've got a chance of surviving this."

"Me?" I frowned in his direction.

"It was always you, kid." Abel smiled. "You might not be the oldest, but we've always looked to you. That much isn't going to change."

I swallowed hard and started to get out.

Abel's voice stopped me. "You know, you're nothing like him. Don't go convincing yourself otherwise," he said.

I pulled Abel in for another hug, finally letting go.

When we separated, Abel swiped under his nose and cleared his throat. "Now get out of my truck."

I chuckled and climbed out, waving to him as he left.

The sun was climbing above the horizon, but the air was calm. Songbirds chirped a happy tune, and I looked around my property.

We could make this a happy home.

I'd never once considered making changes to my place for the sake of a family, but she'd changed everything.

They both had.

I couldn't wait another second to talk to her. Using my fingers, I pried open the skoolie door. I climbed the steps and startled Hazel, who was making herself a cup of coffee from the machine on the counter.

Coffee splashed over the rim and she clutched her chest. "Jesus!"

I pointed at the door. "I told you to lock that."

She shot me an annoyed look. "It *was* locked. I couldn't sleep so I went for an early walk." She lifted a piece of paper between her fingers. "Got your note. You okay?"

I rushed forward, then took her coffee from her and placed it on the counter. I scooped her into my arms, breathing her in to settle my nerves. "No. Not really. He's gone—dead."

She clung to me, offering support even when she had no idea what I needed.

But all I needed was her.

I grunted to clear my throat. "I don't like you sleeping out here."

Hazel pulled back and rolled her eyes at me.

"I'm serious," I said. "I don't like sleeping away from you, and I don't want to do it again. So, if you feel like *glamping* or whatever this is, let me know and I'll sleep out here too."

"You're ridiculous," she shot back, but there was humor dancing at her lips.

"I know." I pressed my forehead to hers.

Hazel sighed. "I don't have the answers, JP. I know I can be wild and reckless, and half the time I don't even know what the hell I'm doing, but I—"

I shut her up with a fierce kiss. I poured every ounce of myself into it as I moved my tongue over hers.

Hazel moaned as I deepened it before leaning back. "Hazel?"

"Mmm?"

"Stop talking." She smiled and held on to me. "I know exactly who you are, and I love you for it."

Her gaze shot to mine, questions written all over her pretty face.

"Yeah." I nodded and laughed. "Fucking nuts over you. It's a real problem for a man like me."

Her eyes bounced between mine as her lips rolled in.

I stroked the strawberry blond hair away from her face. "I love you, Hazel Adams. I love Teddy too. I know that things are complicated and are going to take a bit of time to figure out, but I know we can do it. I want him." I brushed my thumb across her cheekbone. "You too. Forever."

"It's not complicated!" Teddy's voice burst from the back of the skoolie as he came barreling out of his bed and threw himself into us.

Hazel laughed and my arm reached around to include him in our embrace.

"Hey, kid." I lowered to one knee. "You weren't supposed to hear all that."

He raised his chin and his eyes sparkled. "Then you shouldn't have talked so loud. I did hear it. You love her and you love me and we love you back."

I glanced up at Hazel, who was crying. She lifted a shoulder and nodded with a smile. "We talked about it. We love you *a lot*."

Emotion tightened my throat. I brushed my hand down Teddy's arm. "Can I take you somewhere? There's something I'd like to talk with you about."

∼

WE PULLED up to Sullivan Farms, and Teddy grinned as Three-Legged Ed ran circles around my car.

"Don't hit him!" Hazel shouted.

"I won't." I put the car in park. "That dog has about twelve lives, but I'm not trying to take one from him."

My sister Sylvie walked down the porch with little Gus gripping her shoulder. Her hand shielded the sun from her eyes. "Morning! This is a surprise."

Hazel and Teddy walked with me as I went to her. "Sorry for the intrusion. I was hoping to talk with Teddy up that way." I gestured toward the small family cemetery where Mom had been laid to rest on their land.

Sylvie offered a soft, understanding smile. "Of course."

"Did you talk to Abel?" I asked.

Her lips pressed together. "Just a few minutes ago."

My hand found her free shoulder and I squeezed. "I'm sorry, Sylvie."

She sighed. "That's kind of you to say. I'm just wrestling with the guilty feelings of *not* feeling all that bad about it, you know?"

I swallowed hard. "I know what you mean, but we'll be okay."

She smiled and looked down at Teddy, who was letting Ed lick his fingers. "Yeah. We will, won't we?" She turned her attention to Hazel. "Can I get you a cup of coffee? Tea? I was just making an English muffin with some of Duke's homemade blueberry jam, if you'd like to sit for a while."

Hazel looked at me and smiled. "I'd love that."

I nodded as my sister and Hazel walked up to the porch. "Come on, Teddy. There's someone I'd like you to meet."

A frown dusted across his face, and I wrapped my arm

around his shoulder. Together we walked past the large barns and the blueberry fields. Most had been picked over, and the farm itself was in the throes of preparation for winter. We climbed a small hill and wove through trees until a clearing came into view. Headstones dotted the small meadow, some very old and one very new. New grass had grown over her plot and someone—Sylvie, I'm sure—had placed a small bouquet of wildflowers at the base.

Concern laced his sweet face, but he slipped a trusting hand into mine.

We walked to the new headstone.

"Maryann King," Teddy read aloud. "Who is that?"

I crouched to pick a few weeds around the headstone. "This is my mother."

Teddy's eyes went wide.

"She died when I was about your age, but she was missing for a very long time. Now she gets to be here among the trees and the flowers." I pushed through the ache in my chest. "That way, if any of us ever needs to talk to her, we know where to find her."

Tears glistened at the corner of his eyes, and his voice was small. "Do you talk to her?"

My lips twisted. "No, I haven't been very good about that. Sometimes it hurts a lot to talk about her or think about her too much."

He nodded, because he understood it all too well.

"But I'd like to get better at that and I think coming here is a good start."

Teddy's hand gripped mine and gave me the bravery to continue. "I thought maybe if you think she'd like it here, we could lay your mom's ashes to rest here too. That way you can always come talk with her."

Tears streamed down his face, and it took everything in me to not fall apart.

"Does that mean I get to stay?" He sobbed and I pulled him into me. I hadn't realized how much Teddy was holding inside. All he wanted was to be loved and accepted.

He didn't realize that loving him was the easy part.

"Of course. Yes. You are always welcome here. You belong with us." I rubbed his back and knew I needed every ounce of strength to get through the next part.

I cleared my throat. "But there's something else." He looked at me with such hope and love that it nearly killed me. "We got the results back." My chin wobbled. "Turns out . . . I'm not actually your dad, but your half brother."

Teddy's intensity grew as he let my words fall over him.

"We have the same dad, which I guess is why we are so alike sometimes. But . . . if it's okay with you, I would still like to take care of you. I want you and Hazel to live with me and for you to live here in Michigan. What do you think about that?"

Teddy wiped away a tear, leaving behind a streak of dirt. "Can I still call you Dad?"

My heart fractured as I pulled him into my chest again. "You can call me whatever you want to."

"Then okay." He looked around the meadow. "I do think Mom would like it here too."

I stood and held out my hand to him. "Me too. I love you, kid."

"I love you too, Dad."

"Okay." I squeezed his hand and sucked in a lungful of cool September air. "Let's go find Hazel and tell her the good news."

FORTY-FOUR

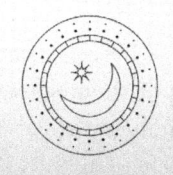

JP

The room felt too quiet, too still, considering everything that had happened.

Aunt Bug's house, the place that had once been loud with the sounds of our messy, chaotic childhood, now held a strange stillness. The kind that comes when the air is thick with unspoken words. My siblings and I sat around the dining room table, staring at the urn in the middle like it might get up and start yelling at us the way Dad used to.

He was dead. We all knew that, but the weight of it hadn't settled yet.

"I can reach out to his other family," MJ said softly, her voice almost drowned out by the ticking of the old grandfather clock in the hallway. "Maybe they'll want the ashes . . . his wife, or . . . someone."

Her words hung in the air, and I could see the sympathy in her eyes, like she still wanted to do the right thing despite everything.

MJ, always the good one, always trying to fix what was broken.

Royal leaned back in his chair, giving her a long look. "You're a good person," he said quietly.

I felt the familiar pang of guilt shoot through me.

I wasn't.

I had scooped a bit of his ashes earlier, when no one was looking. I planned to put them somewhere in town, somewhere he would absolutely hate.

The old community garden.

A place he despised. The man had hated anything that thrived on its own without his control, and the garden was like a little act of rebellion against him. That was exactly where I'd put him. That way he would always see how well we were doing without him.

I wanted that knowledge to torture him forever.

Was it petty and a little unhinged? Probably. But I couldn't find it within myself to care.

Aunt Bug sighed from the end of the table, her hands nervously twisting the edge of a kitchen towel. "I always tried to keep you safe, you know," she said, her voice cracking with the years of weight she'd carried. "Even though I didn't want to believe he took your mother . . . I tried my best."

We stared as the strongest woman we knew nearly crumbled.

"But you've always been our mom," Sylvie said, her voice firm, cutting through the heavy silence.

There was no hesitation in her words, no doubt. The rest of us nodded, and a chorus of agreement filled the room.

"Bug, you were more of a mother to us than anyone else ever could've been," Abel added, and for once, his usual gruffness softened.

Whip leaned in, nudging me with his elbow, his grin appearing despite the tension. "Yeah, you definitely fed us more sugar than was good for us. If that's not love, I don't know what is."

We all chuckled, the mood lightening, and Bug's eyes misted over as she looked at each of us, her makeshift children.

"Damn straight I did," she replied with a proud sniff. "And I'd do it again."

In that moment, as the laughter and warmth spread through the room, the weight of Russell's death didn't feel so suffocating.

It didn't matter what happened to his ashes.

What mattered was here, in this room.

Us.

∽

THE EVENING BREEZE ruffled Hazel's hair as we strolled through the quiet streets, the fading light painting everything in soft pastels. Teddy ran ahead, his laughter ringing out as he hopped from stone to stone on the sidewalk, chasing the last of the fireflies.

Watching him, my chest tightened with a warmth I couldn't fully explain. He had no idea how much he'd changed my life.

"You know, I've always loved this time of day," Hazel said, her voice carrying a soft, thoughtful note. "Everything feels perfect, like the universe finally stopped spinning so fast, and I can just breathe."

I glanced over at her, the sight of her pretty face in the dusky light nearly stealing my own breath.

She was right. Everything about that moment felt right. But it wasn't just the quiet town or the fading sun.

It was her. And it was Teddy.

Hazel's hand slipped into mine, and I squeezed gently, feeling that familiar spark of connection. She was always talking about the universe and its signs, but tonight, for once, I could see she wasn't looking up at the stars for answers.

She was looking at me.

"JP," she started, her voice hesitant, "I was thinking—maybe it's time we make this official."

I stopped walking, turning to face her fully. "Make what official?"

She rolled her eyes, but there was a playful glint in them. "You know what I mean. This . . . us. Maybe Teddy and I should officially move in. I mean, it's not like we're going anywhere. And let's be real, my skoolie doesn't exactly scream 'long-term family planning.'"

I grinned, feeling the familiar warmth bloom in my chest. I caught the way her eyes softened as she looked up at me. There was something different about her now, something more certain, and that made my heart pound even harder.

"And that's what you want, Hex?" I asked, searching her face, needing to hear her say it.

Her lips curved into a soft, knowing smile. "It is. I want this. I want you. I want Teddy to have the life he deserves. I want us to be a family."

My heart swelled at her words, but I knew this was my moment. "I love you," I murmured against her lips, sealing the words with a kiss.

She giggled. "I love you too."

"I meant it." I stepped closer, cupping her face in my

hands, feeling her lean into my touch. "I need you to know something. I've spent my whole life wondering if I could be the kind of man who deserved a family like this. But when I met you, everything changed. You and Teddy . . . you make me want to be better. You've shown me what it means to love someone with everything I have."

Her eyes glistened, her breath catching slightly. She wasn't used to hearing these kinds of words from me, but I'd spend the rest of my life changing that.

She had been so focused on protecting Teddy, on keeping her own heart safe, that she hadn't let herself imagine this kind of love.

"Teddy's my son in every way that matters," I continued, my voice thick with emotion. "He's part of me, just like you are. I want you both in my life, Hazel. I want us to be a family, officially. Stay with me. Let's stop pretending like this is temporary."

I kissed her, slow and tender, pouring everything I couldn't say into that moment. She kissed me back, her fingers curling into my shirt, like she was holding on to the anchor I had become for her.

When we pulled back, Teddy had returned, tugging on the hem of Hazel's dress with a sleepy smile. "Can we go home now?" he asked, his eyes half closed as he leaned against her leg.

Home.

The word settled over me like a warm blanket. I scooped Teddy up into my arms, carrying him as he rested his head on my shoulder. His hands curled into my shirt, and I felt that familiar surge of love I had for him.

He was mine—whether anyone else had anything to do with him or not.

Hazel watched us with a soft smile, her eyes reflecting

something deep and sure. This was our family. No more looking for signs. No more waiting for the universe to tell us what to do. We had everything we needed right here.

"Yeah, bud," I said, my voice full of warmth as I glanced at Hazel, who walked beside me, her hand slipping back into mine. "Let's go home."

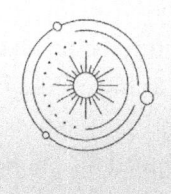

EPILOGUE

Hazel

The beach was dark as waves crashed ashore. The sky was a riot of navy and indigo as pinpoints of starlight scattered as far as the eye could see. My wild and restless spirit loved how insignificant the expanse of Lake Michigan could make me feel.

A small fire crackled beside me as I shuffled my tarot deck. The breeze had a biting chill in it, and I pulled my sweater tighter across my chest.

Footsteps drew my attention and I smiled as JP, with his pants cuffed and feet bare, walked toward me.

"Hey, handsome." I grinned at him as he drew closer.

"Gorgeous."

My skin heated, not from the fire, but from how special he always made me feel. "He's out cold up there, but did request a good night kiss when you're done."

I smiled and nodded. Having a partner was gloriously unexpected, and JP carried the weight of caretaking seriously. Tuck-ins had become a very big deal in the King–Adams household.

I exhaled a contented sigh and continued shuffling, trying to focus my attention on the deck.

The sound of a picture being taken had me looking up. Shyness crept over me as my cheeks heated. "What are you doing?"

JP shrugged and slipped his phone into the pocket of his pants. "Remembering this moment."

I looked around. We spent every evening together, some at the house and others, like tonight, at the beach, savoring it before it got too cold to enjoy.

"Why?" I teased.

He paused, considering, before offering a simple shrug. "I don't know. I guess thirty years from now I want to look back and think, *God, we were so young.* I want to watch your hair go from copper to silver. I want to watch your laugh lines deepen, knowing I put a few of them there. I want to capture every second, and when you look back at the pictures, I want you to recognize that the love I had for you then is the same unrelenting love I have for you right now."

I struggled to find any words—to even breathe.

JP sat behind me, plopping a kiss into my hair and wrapping his arms around me. "You okay?" he asked.

I nodded, fighting tears. "Just really happy, that's all."

"Good." He kissed my neck. "So what question are we asking the universe tonight?"

I laughed lightly as my hands split and rearranged the deck. I sighed, "I don't know. It's always the same—who am I? What do I need to learn?"

He hummed. "You don't need those cards to tell you who you are."

I smirked. "And who am I?"

His arms squeezed as his rough voice tickled my neck. "You're just a romantic, slightly witchy optimist who always believes people can be better. What you may not realize is that people are better because of *you*. That's really what your gift is."

His chin rested on my shoulder as his words warmed me. "We're just lucky enough to be in your glow."

JP eased back on the bench and gripped my hips, moving me so I could turn and face him. I draped my legs over his and scooted forward, wrapping my arms around his neck.

His stormy eyes were dark and intense in the dim lighting. My skin hummed at every point of contact.

"Did your cards see this coming?" JP smirked before fishing something out of his pocket and holding it up.

My breath caught. Between his fingers, JP held a slim gold band. Perched on top was an obscenely large hexagon-shaped stone. The center stone was a deep and moody peacock blue, and each side had a cluster of three diamonds.

"JP," I whispered in utter shock.

His jaw flexed as he reined in his emotions. "Hazel Adams, be my wife."

"That's not a question." I laughed through the tears that tightened my throat.

JP smirked as he grabbed my left hand. "That's because I'm not asking." He slipped the ring onto my finger—a perfect fit. "Be my wife." His forehead dropped to mine. "Walk this life by my side. Make me earn your love and respect every day. I promise you, I will. Let me show you how much I love you and Teddy with every breath. Be my wife. I'm not asking, I'm begging."

My arms clung to him as a sob broke free. "Yes. Yes!" I

giggled as shock and emotion took over. "You said you don't make promises if you can't deliver, right?"

He grinned. "That's right. But I promise you right now, you will never regret becoming my wife."

I leaned back, pressing a hand to my mouth and finally looking at the ring. JP was grinning as he took my hand and looked at the engagement ring himself. "It's alexandrite—symbolizing fortune, luck, and embracing change. It's considered a mystical stone because under incandescent light, it completely transforms. So it's like me, when I'm near you. The king who fell from the tower, only to realize *you* were the exact change I needed."

"It couldn't be more perfect." I peppered his face with kisses as he laughed and stood, taking me with him. He spun, kicking up sand as we twirled and laughed like love-struck teenagers. He set me on my feet and an uptick of giddiness zipped through me.

One black eyebrow on his forehead arched higher as a mischievous grin eased across my lips.

He knew exactly what I was up to.

Suppressing a smile, he lowered his voice. "Run."

∽

With a contented smile, I had dug my sister's ashes out of the cabinet in the skoolie. Together we laid her to rest on the beautiful hillside at Sullivan Farms, where Teddy could always visit her. Duke and Sylvie were kind enough to allow Teddy to choose the location, and he'd opted for a sunny area close to a soaring oak tree.

Both Kings and Sullivans were present. When I asked JP about it, he shrugged and said, "I guess we're all family now."

I knew he still thought it was odd, but I loved that my little family had expanded from only Teddy and me to JP, his siblings, and all the Sullivans. They were a large, rowdy group, but no one could say they didn't show up when people they loved needed it.

I'd never seen JP hugged so many times, and it made me laugh to think about how much he probably hated it.

I found it all to be very endearing.

Many tears were shed, and after I'd given a heartfelt, though rambling, eulogy, Teddy had asked to talk with his mom alone.

Choked with emotion, I nodded and gave him space.

His cheeks were splotchy when he walked down from the hill, but in a way, his shoulders seemed lighter—a little less burdened somehow.

JP and I had decided that finding a child and family therapist would help us all navigate our grief, and we were looking forward to our first family session next week.

Sylvie had used the opportunity to open her home for an extended family dinner. Their simple farmhouse was bursting at the seams, but the fire made it cozy, and I listened as conversations folded over one another.

When JP walked up to Duke Sullivan, curiosity got the best of me and I scooted closer to eavesdrop on their conversation.

JP crossed his arms. "I've been thinking a lot about the blueberry farming industry."

Duke's skeptical eyebrows shot up. "Thinking of trading in that suit for some dirty jeans?"

"Fuck no." JP scoffed but immediately looked around to see if any of the kids had heard him. He shook his head. "I'm thinking about a producer-owned, berry-growing-and-marketing cooperative."

Duke's head tilted. "A co-op?"

"Of sorts." JP grinned. "I've been watching the numbers, and the local growers are cannibalizing sales. You're all fighting for the same consumers, but it doesn't have to be that way. Michigan is unlike anywhere else in the world. You have what people need."

Duke's lips formed a stern line, and I smiled at how good JP was at his job.

"I'm listening," Duke said.

"So here's what I'm thinking," JP continued. "A producer-owned company, under a unified brand. Marketing is streamlined, profits are consolidated. A bad crop for one family is no longer as devastating because another farm is picking up the slack. I'm talking diversity in varieties, a plant-breeding program, expansion into the frozen-food market. With enough leverage, this could be a massive win for the farmers of Western Michigan."

Duke nodded along, and an excited shiver danced through me. JP and Veda had worked tirelessly on the pitch. They were equally confident that the new business venture would not only be wildly successful, but truly beneficial to the dying art of family farming.

I was so proud of him. He was a good man, trying to do incredible things for people he cared about.

I walked around, making small talk and observing the loud, blended family before me. For so long I had wandered —searching for something I couldn't quite name. I felt at ease, knowing my wandering days were behind me. I had even had a little pitch of my own up my sleeve.

I had learned that the little shop downtown that had once held Annie's pottery studio was still empty. JP didn't know it yet, but our visit to Conca dei Marini and learning about the Janare witches had gotten my wheels turning.

Luna was right—there was a need in Outtatowner for a little witchy magic, and the idea of my own apothecary boutique had already taken root.

I smiled as I watched Teddy wrap his arms around JP, and they mirrored each other with stern nods and animated frowns as they spoke.

My heart squeezed.

After Teddy dropped into my life, I was more determined than ever to get things right.

Then JP came along, and just like that, we were home.

∽

WANT MORE HAZEL AND JP? Get an exclusive bonus scene here: https://www.lenahendrix.com/get-hazel-and-jps-bonus-scene/

SNEAK PEEK OF JUST SAY YES

Getting tangled up with an Olympic rugby player seemed like the perfect way to forget about how my life was falling apart. Until I realize that he's my ***ex-boyfriend's best friend.***

Logan Brown walked into my small town with a charming grin and mischief in his eyes. He's a world-class flirt and his confident masculinity is almost as distracting as those rugby thighs.

Given my inexperienced history, I'm no match for our undeniable chemistry. I vow to keep him at arm's length. But with Logan, every lingering stare—every forbidden touch—awakens something inside of me I thought I had buried for good.

We both know we shouldn't cross that line, but I have spent my entire life being a good girl, and suddenly, I'm tempted to be very, very bad.

Especially when Logan tells me to *just say yes*.

Order *Just Say Yes* here!

HENDRIX HEARTTHROBS

Want to connect? Come hang out with the Hendrix Heartthrobs on Facebook to laugh & chat with Lena! Special sneak peeks, announcements, exclusive content, & general shenanigans all happen there.

Come join us!

ACKNOWLEDGMENTS

As always, words cannot express my appreciation and gratitude for the unwavering support, friendship, and wisdom. Without these people, this book (and to be honest, what's left of my sanity) would not have come together.

Paula Dawn at Lilypad Lit, James Gallagher at Castle-Walls Editing, Julia Griffis at The Romance Bibliophile, One Night Stand Studios, Elsie Silver, Kandi Steiner, Corinne Michaels, Catherine Cowles, Ashley Estep, Echo Grayce, Sarah Hansen, Anna Winnicki, Trinity McIntosh, Megan Macy, my content creator team, the Hendrix Heartthrobs, and my incredible readers!

Last on the list, but first in my heart, to my family, who has zero respect for a closed door, but who I love anyway. Thank you for understanding when my fictional small towns bleed into our everyday lives. You're the number one reason I sit down at the computer every day. I love you more than you'll ever know.

ABOUT THE AUTHOR

Lena Hendrix is an Amazon Top 5 bestselling contemporary romance author living in the Midwest. Her love for romance stared with sneaking racy Harlequin paperbacks and now she writes her own hot-as-sin small town romance novels. Lena has a soft spot for strong alphas with marshmallow insides, heroines who clap back, and sizzling tension. Her novels pack in small town heart with a whole lotta heat.

When she's not writing or devouring new novels, you can find her hiking, camping, fishing, and sipping a spicy margarita!

Want to hang out? Find Lena on Tiktok or IG!

ALSO BY LENA HENDRIX

Chikalu Falls

Finding You

Keeping You

Protecting You

Choosing You (origin novella)

Redemption Ranch

The Badge

The Alias

The Rebel

The Target

The Sullivans

One Look

One Touch

One Chance

One Night

One Taste (prequel novella)

The Kings

Just This Once

Just My Luck

Just Between Us

Just Like That

Just Say Yes

Printed in Great Britain
by Amazon